BY SCOTT SIGLER

THE GENERATIONS TRILOGY
Alive

NOVELS
Infected (Infected Trilogy Book I)
Contagious (Infected Trilogy Book II)
Ancestor
Nocturnal
Pandemic (Infected Trilogy Book III)

GALACTIC FOOTBALL LEAGUE SERIES
The Rookie
The Starter
The All-Pro
The MVP
The Champion

GFL NOVELLAS
The Reporter
The Detective
Title Fight

SHORT STORY COLLECTIONS
Blood Is Red
Bones Are White

ALIVE

ALIVE

BOOK ONE OF THE GENERATIONS TRILOGY

SCOTT SIGLER

DEL REY

NEW YORK

Copyright © 2015 by Scott Sigler

Published in the United States by Del Rey, an imprint of Random House, a division of Penguin Random House LLC, New York.

DEL REY and the HOUSE colophon are registered trademarks of Penguin Random House LLC.

Library of Congress Cataloging-in-Publication Data
Sigler, Scott.
Alive / Scott Sigler.
pages ; cm.—(Generations trilogy ; Book One)
ISBN 978-0-553-39310-1
eBook ISBN 978-0-553-39311-8
I. Title.
PS3619.I4725A79 2015
813'.6—dc23   2015012213

Printed in the United States of America on acid-free paper

www.delreybooks.com

2 4 6 8 9 7 5 3

Book design by Caroline Cunningham

For my mother, who loves and leads by example

PART I

DARKNESS
AND LIGHT

ONE

A stabbing pain jolts me awake.

It hits quick but deep, a here-then-gone stinging where my neck meets my shoulder.

Did something bite me?

No . . . just a dream. A nightmare, maybe.

That's not how I should wake up on my birthday. I'm twelve. I can hardly believe it—I'm *twelve,* I'm not a little kid anymore. I should get to sleep in, I should get to sleep all day. There should be cake, and my friends, and I shouldn't have to go to school.

School.

The thought of that place chases away my excitement. I'm so tired. Feels like I've never slept at all. If I missed my alarm, I'll be late for classes again. Mom will kill me. I don't want to go. At school, the tooth-girls and the circle-stars always make fun of me. And I shouldn't be teased on my birthday. I hate school, I hate them, I . . .

A tingling coolness on my neck, right where I felt that sting. Tickling, spreading . . .

. . . am I *bleeding*?

I open my eyes to darkness. *Total* darkness. I hear my own breathing, but nothing else. And . . . and I *can't move*. Curved bars, cool and rough, hold my wrists by my sides. I roll my hands, trying to slip free, but the bars are so tight they scrape against my skin.

"Mom?"

The word sounds too loud, almost a scream. Something is wrong. My voice sounds odd . . . kind of muffled.

Mom doesn't answer.

"Dad?"

Nothing.

I pull harder, but it's not only my wrists that can't move— something holds my ankles, and my hips are pinned so tight I can't even turn.

This isn't my bedroom. This isn't my house. My parents aren't here.

My chest seems to squeeze in, as if it is clamping down on my hammering heart. My body tingles, every ounce of me scream-ing *Get up! Getupgetupgetup!*

"Is anyone there?"

Nothing.

"Someone help me. This is . . ."

My breath catches.

I don't know my own name.

I thrash and pull, yank desperately at the unforgiving bars holding me down.

"Someone, *help me!*"

No one answers.

I scream so hard it tears at my throat. Someone *had* to hear that. Someone *has* to come get me, come help me.

I wait.

Still nothing.

I lift my head—my forehead clonks against something solid and unmoving. That's why my voice sounded funny: there is a board right in front of my face.

No, not a board . . . a *lid*.

Padding beneath me and at my sides.

I am in . . .

. . . oh no, oh no . . .

. . . am I in a *coffin*?

"Help! Somebody get me out of here!"

The pain that woke me plunges into my neck again, a sting so deep it locks me up, all tight-eyed and rigid and frozen.

I am trapped in the dark and something is biting me.

(If you run, your enemy will hunt you. Kill your enemy, and you are forever free.)

That thought seems familiar, a memory that stuck. Rage blossoms, gives me the focus to move despite my agony, gives me the strength to try harder. I pull and push, lift and twist. I focus all my strength on my right hand—*pull*, dammit—the skin of my wrist tears against the rough material, but I *have* to get out. . . .

Pull, push, twist, yank, harder and harder until my coffin rattles.

I feel the bar crack. I can move my right hand more. Only a little, but *I can move it more*.

The sting slides deeper into my neck, and I cry out.

No one came before, no one will come now.

Will it hit a lung? Pierce my heart?

Will I die?

I jerk so hard the bones in my wrists grind against the bars holding them down. I hear another small crack, then another—my right hand flies free.

I slide my fingers up my body to my neck, blindly grab at the thing slicing into me. My hand locks down on wetness, slickness, a cold snake that moves and wiggles. It's trying to slither away, but I have it and I won't let go. I yank it to my mouth and bite down, taste something horrid, crush my teeth together so hard my jaw hurts. I thrash my head, I bite harder—something inside of it crunches.

It falls limp in my hand and mouth. I fling it aside, then spit, trying to get that vile taste off my tongue.

Right hand to left wrist. I grab the restraint. Its surface crumbles at my touch, powder falling away to reveal pitted hardness beneath. Right hand yanking, left fist lifting, the cracking sound comes quickly and my left hand is free.

Both hands grab the bar that curves across my waist. I attack it, *push-pull-push-pull-push-pull,* making the whole coffin shake around me. The bar breaks.

Now for my feet.

The lid is so close to my face and chest that my hands can reach down only to my thighs. I'm wearing some kind of short skirt? I must reach farther, must keep trying. I have to get out, whatever it takes. I twist to my right hip, use the ankle restraints as resistance to wiggle my body lower, reach down with my left hand. My shoulder and face drag against the coffin's smooth lid, pulling at my cheek and nose and closed eye, but even then my fingers barely touch my knees.

I must pull harder, *harder,* I must keep fighting, *must* get out of the darkness. If I can't reach my feet, I will die here alone and screaming and—

—my fingertip brushes the rough bars pinning my ankles. So close, just a little farther. Contorted muscles and twisted bones vibrate with pain as I wedge in even tighter, but finally my left hand grips a bar. Grab and shake and yank, must get loose . . .

Crack, crack—both feet come free.

I slide up the coffin until I am again flat on my back. I press my palms against the lid.

I push: it doesn't budge. I'm not strong enough.

Think. THINK. *You have to get out.* . . .

I need to use my arms and my legs, use *all* of me. . . .

I twist and turn until I'm lying on my stomach. There isn't enough room to get all the way to my hands and knees, but I push down as hard as I can while I arch my back against the lid. Sweat drips into my eyes. Sweat and maybe blood. I press until my back screams . . .

. . . something in the lid snaps.

A sliver of blinding light hits the bed of my coffin, so bright it burns to look at it. I close my eyes and push even harder. I feel the lid lift, just a little, enough for me to slide my knees all the way beneath me.

(Attack, attack, when in doubt, always attack, never let your enemy recover.)

I take a breath, focus, and shove upward with everything I have left.

The shuddering complaint of something bending and tearing. At the end of the fight, the strong lid breaks like a brittle shell— I am *up* and *out* and *standing* . . .

. . . and *falling*.

I land hard, kicking up a thick cloud of something powdery. My heaving lungs suck it in. The floor spins and whirls beneath me, and there is light *everywhere*, so bright it stings even through clenched eyes.

Lying on my side, I blink, trying to see. I cough, trying to breathe. I wait for my eyes to adjust, hoping they do before whoever locked me in the coffin comes to put me back inside once again.

TWO

The light blinds me, makes my eyes water. Grainy dust on my tongue, coating my raw throat, so deep in my lungs it makes me cough again and again. The noise might bring the people who did this to me, but I can't stop. I can't see, I'm too weak to move.

I am helpless.

The coughing fit eases. My body relaxes enough for me to sit up. I pull my knees to my chest, wrap my arms tight around my legs. I rub my wrists; the rough bars ripped my skin raw.

My coffin was warm. I broke it open, hatched from it, and now I'm in this cold room. I'm shivering. I'm out, yes, but alone, exhausted and terrified.

Where are my mom and dad? Why aren't they here? Where is *here*, anyway?

I smell things I don't fully recognize. Dry odors, stale scents. This place smells . . . dead.

The light still stings, but not as much. I can finally see a little.

Gray. The dust is gray. It blankets everything, hangs in the air, floating specks that spin with my every breath.

My neck throbs where that thing bit me. I reach for the spot. A shirt. I'm wearing a shirt, and a tie. I slide my hand inside the collar, feel the wound . . . my fingers come away with a pasty mix of dust and blood.

I look at what I'm wearing: white button-down shirt, the short skirt—which is red and black plaid—black socks that end a bit below my knee, no shoes. My shirt feels tight. The sleeves end halfway between my elbow and wrist. The tie is red, embroidered with a yellow and black circle of tiny images. White thread in the middle of that circle spells a word: *MICTLAN*.

I have no idea what that means. And these clothes . . . are they mine?

My vision is blurry; I can't see anything but my coffin. Sitting on the dusty floor, I'm too low to look inside it. The lid split evenly down the middle, from top to bottom. The half closest to me slid neatly against the side. The far half sticks straight up. Maybe I broke that half, bent something so it can't move like it's supposed to.

Parts of the lid gleam under the lights—bloody finger streaks, I realize, from where I grabbed it, wiping away the thin layer of dust that clings to the surface.

Why won't someone come and help me?

The thing that bit my neck . . . what if it's still alive? What if it's in the coffin, coiling, getting ready to slither out and attack me again? I don't want to look inside, but no one else is here and I need to know it's dead.

If I don't, it could hunt me.

I reach for the coffin's edge, use it to pull myself up. My legs don't want to work. They tremble and twitch as I rise and look inside.

White fabric, torn in many places, smeared with long streaks of wet red and a few light spots of powdery crimson. Loose padding shows beneath the rips.

A bloody, white pillow. Next to it, a limp, white snake.

No, not a snake: a *tube*.

A tube that ends in a long, glistening needle. Its white skin is torn where I bit it, showing some kind of black fibers beneath.

I watch the tube for a little while. It doesn't move. It's dead, because I killed it.

I pick up a piece of the bar that held my waist. The surface is deeply pitted, crumbly with that crimson powder . . . rust, maybe? Rust that ate away much of the metal, making the bar thin and brittle. Had it been solid, there is no way I could have broken free.

My eyes aren't stinging anymore. They've stopped watering. I can see the rest of the room.

There are eleven more coffins. Two parallel rows of six, lined up end to end. A wide aisle filled with a flat sea of untouched gray separates the rows. The thick dust coats the coffins, makes hard edges look like soft curves.

I was in the last one in the left-hand row. I can see it clearly now, see all the detail. It is decorated with intricate carvings: cartoonish people with big noses and huge, wild headdresses; squat pyramids with lots of steps; simple versions of the sun; big cats with exaggerated eyes and tooth-filled snarls.

This room is long and narrow, like it was made specifically to hold these coffins. It doesn't seem that bright in here now that my eyes have gotten used to it—the arched ceiling has only a few lights that work, barely enough to illuminate stone walls that are covered with gray-coated carvings.

At the far end of the room, I see an archway. In that archway . . . doors, maybe? They look heavy and solid, but I don't see any handles.

Something at the foot of my coffin catches my eye. A flat area, about the size of my hand, surrounded by dozens of small bumps, all of it hazed in puffy gray.

I reach out, trembling, and brush dust from one of the small shapes. It's a jewel: deep orange, glowing like frozen fire.

I wipe clear the flat area. It's engraved with seven letters and one period.

M. *Savage*

Is that my name?

I hear something. A small sound. Very quiet, very faint. It makes me think of being trapped in the dark, and then I realize why.

It's a girl's scream, coming from inside another coffin.

THREE

My wobbly legs still can't quite support me. I lean on the coffins to stay on my feet, stumble my way toward the scream.

Each step kicks up a small cloud of dust, as if I am the first person ever to set foot here.

The noisy coffin is halfway up the left-hand row. As I get closer, I can make out faint words coming from within.

"Help me! Mommy, get me out of here!"

I put my hand on the dust-caked lid. I feel tiny vibrations: the girl inside is struggling. I think of that long, bloody needle jutting from the white tube.

With big swipes, I brush the dust from her coffin, accidentally creating a brief fog. The polished carvings gleam under the lights.

I rap my knuckles on the lid; her screaming stops.

"Calm down," I say. "I'll try and get you out."

There is a pause. Then she speaks, the coffin cutting the volume of her words but not the desperation they carry.

"Who are you?"

Who am I? No idea. Somehow, I don't think telling her *I'm Savage* is going to make her less afraid. I don't even have a first name, only an initial, but maybe that will work.

"My name is *Em.* What's yours?"

"I . . . I don't know."

A feeling of relief explodes inside of me, so intense I almost fall down again: *I'm not the only one.*

I have to get this girl out.

"Are there bars holding you down?"

"Something is," she says. "I don't know what, I can't see anything. I can't move. It's so dark in here, please help me!"

"I told you to *stay calm.*" My voice echoes off the stone walls, and I hear how harsh it sounds. She's afraid, she's trapped; yelling at her isn't going to help.

"It's okay," I say in a softer tone. "Listen, you have to break those bars."

"Break them?" Her voice cracks. "I tried, they're too thick!"

"Try harder. I broke mine."

Another pause. I listen to her grunting and struggling, then hear the raw terror carried on her words.

"I *can't* break them, I told you I'm not strong enough. Get me out, please *get me out!*"

I slap the lid, hard.

"Be quiet," I say. "I'll find a way to open it."

Why can't she get out like I did? Is she weaker than I am? Her fear is contagious, radiating from the coffin and coiling inside my chest. At first I was afraid I would die in the dark, but if this girl dies, I will be alone—somehow, that is even worse.

Not knowing what else to do, I push against the lid. Nothing happens. I slide my fingertips under what feels like the edge and

I lift—gently at first, then with what little strength I have. Still nothing. I feel the long seam that runs down the middle, that separates the lid halves . . . too tight to get my fingers in there.

I look around the room. Across the aisle, I see something leaning against a coffin, a fuzzy gray shape maybe as long as my forearm and hand together. Five steps take me to it. I reach down, grab the shape, lift it and shake free the dust.

I hold a golden bar. Jewels of different colors and sizes dot its length. At the end is a C shape: the stubby prongs are silver, not gold. The bar is heavy and solid.

A weapon. I have a weapon.

Suddenly I am not quite as afraid.

I start to turn back to the girl's coffin when something catches my eye . . . the lid of this one, it's as dusty as the others, but it's not sealed tight like hers. It's slightly open, showing a thin line of deep shadow no wider than my pinkie.

I can't look away.

My right hand holds the weapon. My left hand reaches out. I slide my fingers through the there-but-not-there dust, into that shadow, curl them under the lid-half closest to me. The polished wood feels cool against my skin. I grip tight and pull. It moves a tiny amount, then resists. I broke my lid and when I did it opened; maybe if I can wedge the golden bar in that space, I can—

"Em, are you there?" The muffled voice comes from across the aisle, from the girl. Then, bordering on panic: "Did you leave me?"

I rush back to her coffin.

"Sorry, I'm here. I found something I can use. I'm going to try and break the lid and get you out. It will be loud. Hold on, okay?"

"Okay. Just please hurry."

I lift the weapon over my head, then smash it against the lid. It makes a dull thud when it hits, denting the dark material, making the whole lid vibrate off a hovering sheen of dust.

It feels good to hit something. Really good. I swing again, harder this time, feel my lip curl into a snarl as the metal strikes home. Again and again, each time harder than the last, smashing a carving of a big cat, crushing a stepped pyramid, chipping away the polished surface to reveal white wood beneath.

Finally, something breaks: the lid splits down the middle. The long halves slide to the coffin's sides, revealing an older girl with long, thick, curly red hair spilled across her face. Her eyes squeeze shut against the light. Crimson bars pin her down. She's wearing a white shirt that's too small for her, an embroidered red tie, and a short plaid skirt.

She's breathing fast. Her face is wrinkled up and her head is twitching a little, like she thinks someone is about to hit her but she can't see the blow coming and can't run away.

"Em? Is that you?"

I take her hand in mine. Her grip is weak, but her skin is warm and soft.

"It's me," I say. "It's okay."

"Thank you, Em, oh, *thank you*. Can you undo these bars?"

"I can. Stay very still."

A couple of carefully aimed strikes from my weapon are all it takes to shatter the brittle old metal.

She lifts her hands to her chest, rubs at her wrists. The skin there is barely scuffed at all—did she even *try* to fight her way free?

"Hold on," I say, "let me help you out of there."

I set the weapon down.

I help her sit up, help her ease out of the coffin. It's a challenge, because she's so weak and I'm barely stronger than she is.

She puts one foot down to stand, but her legs won't support her—she falls into me, sending us both tumbling. We land in a dust-puffing heap, still holding each other.

We don't move. We lie there for a moment, shivering, clinging together, coughing slightly. She holds me tight, so tight that I know we feel the same way: neither of us understands what's happening, but we are not alone, and for that we are deeply grateful.

FOUR

The red-haired girl squints tightly, making the bridge of her nose wrinkle. So much hair, still draped over her face as if it can shield her from our strange reality. She's trying hard to make her watering eyes adjust. She trembles in my arms, terrified and confused.

"We're safe," I say, trying to comfort her. "We're alone here. Take it easy."

She nods, holds me tighter, but I feel her relax a little. Her hand seeks out mine. And we lock fingers.

I look at our clasped hands: our skin is not the same. Hers is pale, a pinkish tan. Mine is much darker; mine is brown.

Our hands are about the same size. That strikes me as strange—she looks older than I do, almost old enough to leave school. Girls that age are usually so much taller.

School . . . these clothes, did we wear things like this in school? I can't remember. I have a vague image of a few girls looking beautiful and perfect while I looked ugly and stupid, even though we all wore the exact same thing.

Her short plaid skirt shows almost all of her legs. They are long and shapely, not knobby-kneed twigs like mine. Maybe someday I will have legs like hers. The sleeves of her white shirt end just past her elbows. At her chest, the top two buttons are missing, showing the curve of her breasts. She's probably embarrassed by that. I'm embarrassed for her; it makes me uncomfortable.

We lie there, unmoving, dust motes swirling in the air.

Her hair is so long. I reach to my own head, feel that my hair is tied back in a heavy braid. I pull it around and look at it—it's black and thick. The braid hangs down to my waist. It feels so silky, like it was recently brushed.

Someone put me in a coffin and fixed my hair? A shiver slides across my skin.

Maybe it's okay. Maybe Mom brushed it. Or Dad. But if it was them, did they do that right before they sealed me in and left me to die?

The red-haired girl finally opens her eyes a little, blinking slits that show me their color: a deep green.

She blinks away tears. She sniffs, wipes at her nose.

"You saved me," she says. "You set me free. Thank you, Em."

She sits up. She brushes her thick hair behind her left ear, then her right. When she does, I see something on her forehead.

A black circle, as wide as the distance between her eyes, made of a material that clearly isn't her and yet is also a *part* of her at the same time. The dark color stands in stark contrast against her white-pink skin. The outside of the circle is smooth. The inside is kind of jagged, with stubby points sticking inward. Eight of them, evenly spaced apart. Stubby points . . . kind of like . . .

Like *teeth*.

She's a tooth-girl.

I feel a surge of emotion. Tooth-girls . . . they made fun of me in school . . . didn't they? I can't remember my school. And I can't remember why the tooth-girls ridiculed me, only how their words and glares and jokes made me feel: small, unimportant, worthless.

I *hate* her.

No . . . I don't even know this girl. At least I don't think I do. We're in this together. I will not hate her because of some decoration on her skin.

Wait—do *I* have one?

My free hand flies to my forehead. I feel something embedded there. A circle, like hers, but smooth, both inside and out. There are no stubby points, no *teeth*.

Our fingers remain locked. Her skin is warm, the only warm thing in this cold room.

"I'm afraid," she says. "What is this place?"

"I don't know."

My fingertips lightly trace the shape that marks my skin.

She sees me doing that, reaches to her forehead. Her eyes widen with discovery.

"I have one, too," she says. "Yours is a plain circle, but mine feels different on the inside. Bumps or something . . . what are they?"

Teeth, I want to say, *because you're a tooth-girl.*

But I don't say that. I like her, and she seems to like me. I don't want her to know that phrase in case it makes her remember something and not like me anymore.

"They look like stubby bits," I say.

She waits for me to keep going, but I don't know any other way to describe what I see.

She thinks for a moment. She shrugs. "We both have symbols. I don't know what they mean."

"Neither do I."

She looks around the room, taking it all in.

"This isn't the birthday I was hoping for," she says.

"It's your birthday, too?"

She looks at me, doubtful, like I'm playing some kind of trick on her.

"Yes," she says. "I'm twelve."

She's the one who is playing tricks. My instincts were right: the tooth-girl, whatever that is, is already making fun of me. I lean away from her.

"I'm not dumb, you know," I say.

She blinks, confused. "I . . . of course you're not. I didn't say you were." She blushes and looks away, like she knows she said something wrong but doesn't know what that something was.

"Em, I would never be rude to my elders like that."

Elders? What is she talking about?

"You're not twelve," I say. I point at her legs, her breasts. "Look at you. You think I'd be so stupid that I'd believe you're the same age as me?"

Her expression of embarrassed confusion changes to one of total disbelief. She holds out her arms, looks at them, then down at herself.

"I don't understand," she says.

She pulls at the bottom of her shirt, but the material doesn't stretch. Her belly—flat, pale—is exposed. This, too, makes me uncomfortable.

My belly is cold.

I look down at my blood-speckled shirt and realize, for the first time, that it's too small for me. The bottom of it leaves my stomach open to the cold air. My sleeves end halfway up my forearms. No wonder it feels freezing in here: I'm half-naked.

I touch my belly, suddenly self-conscious. This seems . . . *wrong*, like showing bare skin is a bad thing.

The shirt is too tight against my breasts.

Or . . . are my breasts too big for my shirt? I feel them. They weren't this size before . . . were they? No, they weren't. I'm sure of it. I can't remember anything, but I know my body has changed.

The red-haired girl stares at me intensely. I realize I'm touching myself right in front of her. I look away, put my hands in my lap.

She feels her own chest—her eyes widen with surprise. "What happened? They weren't like this before."

I shake my head. "Same with me."

"So, you say you're twelve," she says. "You look nineteen, maybe twenty. You look like a grown woman."

"So do you."

She nods slightly. She looks off, glancing at nothing in particular. Her lips twitch, like she's saying half-words that I can't hear.

"It doesn't make sense," she says finally. "We need more information. Until then, we have to believe what our eyes show us."

She again cups her breasts. She isn't ashamed at all; she's measuring, thinking.

The corners of her mouth curve up in a small grin.

"I can't recall what I asked for, but I'm pretty sure I wasn't expecting *these* as a present," she says. "Maybe it's a good birthday after all. I mean, other than being locked up in the dark."

Her fascination and delight with her body's unexpected change hasn't completely taken the fear out of her eyes. She reaches up, touches one of the carvings on her coffin lid. A jaguar, I think it is, one eye smashed and splintered from where I hit it.

"Some of these images seem familiar," she says. "I can't place them, but . . . well, they're familiar."

"My coffin has them, too."

The red-haired girl wrinkles her nose, shakes her head. "*Coffins* are for dead people. We're clearly not dead."

She stares at my forehead. Her eyes narrow—she's trying to work something out—then she looks away. Does she remember what my circle means? If so, she doesn't share.

She points to the jewel-encrusted rod lying on the ground beside me.

"I think I know what that is," she says.

I pick it up and wipe dust off the metal. I move it closer to her so she can see it better. "Maybe you used a weapon like this before?"

For the first time, the red-haired girl smiles wide. It lights up her whole face. She looks *amazing*. Her eyes gleam with delight. I'm not sure it's possible for a person to be more beautiful than she is right now.

"It's not a weapon," she says. "I think it's a *tool*."

A tool? That never crossed my mind.

She starts to nod, like she's sure she's right, then stops. Her smile fades. She's not sure. She isn't sure about anything.

"Em . . . do you know my name?"

"No. Let's find out what it is."

I stand, take her hand and help her up.

She seemed so tall at first, but I'm only a tiny bit shorter than she is.

I lead her to the foot of her coffin. Just like with mine, there is a flat area surrounded by dust-covered jewels. I brush it clean. Blue jewels frame the engraved letters *T. Spingate*.

"That's you," I say. "I think. Your name is Spingate. Does that make you remember anything?"

She frowns. Her lower lip quivers. Her eyes water, and this time it's not from the light. Her eyelashes are long and dark. I suddenly have a desperate urge to find a mirror. Do I have green eyes like hers?

Spingate shakes her head. "I can't remember anything. I remember my mom . . . sort of. But I can't remember her face."

As soon as she says that, I realize I have no idea what my parents actually look like. Mom and Dad, they're blank spaces. I know the concept of my parents, I know they loved me and I loved them, but their faces, their names . . . nothing.

Spingate sniffs, wipes away tears. She nods slowly, as if accepting things for what they are. She studies our surroundings, taking in the walls, the ceiling, the door-arch.

"Em, do you know what's outside this room?"

"No idea."

She looks at the coffin across the aisle, where I found the weapon.

"That lid isn't shut all the way. Was that one yours?"

I point to my right, to the last coffin in our row. I see my path of footsteps through the dust.

"I was in that one," I say.

Spingate stares down the aisle for a few moments. Her mouth moves a little again. When she does that, it's like she doesn't even know I'm there.

She looks me up and down.

"How did you get all bloody?"

Other than smears of dust, her shirt is clean and white.

"There was a tube in my coffin," I say. "It stabbed me with a needle. That's what woke me up."

Her expression darkens. Maybe she realizes that if I hadn't broken out of my coffin, she would still be in hers.

"But how did you get out? There's no one else here."

I shrug. "I got myself out."

She gives me a strange look, as if the concept is unthinkable.

Spingate's hands reach to her shoulders, rub slowly up and down like she's hugging herself against the chill. She walks across the aisle, wobbling a bit but standing on her own, then kneels at the foot of the coffin with the slightly open lid. She brushes off the nameplate.

"It says *B. Brewer*. The stones are purple. Maybe we can use the tool to open it and see if someone is inside?"

We've been sitting here talking, and I never thought that there might be others trapped like Spingate was, like I was. All these coffins . . . maybe one of them holds a person who knows what this place is and how we got here.

I walk across the aisle and jam the heavy bar's forked end into the small crack, the lid closest to me under the bar, the forked end under the lid farthest away. I push down.

The lid doesn't budge.

I rise to my toes, put all my weight on the bar.

"Em, I can help with—"

"I've got it," I say, my effort turning the words into grunts. I hear a slow creaking coming from the lid. I rise up a little more, then push down as hard as I can, all at once—there is a loud *bang* from the coffin as something gives way.

The lid halves suddenly tilt up, hum as they slide to the sides. Sheets of gray spill off their smooth, carved surfaces.

We look inside: a wave of fear pushes my body a step backward.

Spingate reacts differently—instead of stepping away, she leans forward.

"Maybe you were right," she says. "If that's B. Brewer, I guess in his case it really is a coffin."

FIVE

Brewer is a dead little boy.

A thin line of dust runs up his tiny, shriveled body, dust that fell through the crack between the lids.

The coffin is the same size as mine and Spingate's, but it looks huge surrounding such a small corpse. The skin of his face is dried so tightly to his skull that it's cracked in some places, showing the bone beneath. His eyes are empty sockets. His lips have shrunken back, showing two rows of discolored teeth; it looks like he's smiling.

I feel sick to my stomach.

Brewer is wearing a white shirt and an embroidered red tie. Black pants and a black belt instead of a plaid skirt. Even if he wasn't all dried up, the outfit would have been too big for his little body. Pitted, crimson-spotted bars hold down his hips, ankles and wrists, even though his feet and hands are hidden inside his pants and sleeves.

Spingate points to his tiny forehead, to a symbol—just as

black as ours—embedded in his dried skin. It is a circle with one line down the middle and one running from side to side.

"A cross," she says.

"Or a *T*."

She shrugs. "Maybe a plus sign?"

"Maybe."

A tooth-girl, a circle-girl, a cross-boy . . . and we have no idea what any of it means.

I'm staring at a corpse. That could have been me. These are coffins after all, so why is he dead while I am alive? Looking at him makes me cold in a different way than the temperature and my scant excuse for clothing.

I'd be so much warmer with pants. Did he get to wear pants because he's a boy? If so, that's not fair.

Spingate slowly extends a finger toward Brewer. She pokes his cheek. Dried flesh crumbles and falls away. It's awful, but it doesn't seem to bother Spingate at all.

She grabs the sleeve of his shirt, starts to tug.

My hand locks on her forearm.

"Stop that," I say. "What are you doing?"

"Making a bandage."

"For what?"

She points to my wrists. "You're still bleeding."

I look at them and see she's right. The bars rubbed my skin raw. Small spots of red well up from a dozen tiny tears. Dust packs the wounds, making the blood more sludge than liquid, but it's still slowly oozing out.

"I'm fine," I say. "We shouldn't disturb the dead."

Spingate huffs. "The dead don't care."

She tears two long strips from his shirt, jerking his tiny body in the process. A thick, dry piece of his face falls away, exposing the cheekbone below.

Spingate wraps the strips around my wrists and ties them off.

"That's better," she says. "Should we open the other coffins?"

Nine remain closed. Spingate and I wasted time sitting with each other. We wasted more staring at Brewer.

"Yes," I say. "And quickly."

She holds out her hand toward my weapon. "Can I try?"

That strikes me as funny. She wasn't strong enough to get out of her own coffin, but she thinks she's strong enough to break one open from the outside?

I hand her the jeweled rod.

Spingate takes it, and when she does, that soul-melting smile peeks out again. She's excited, moving quickly, her fear suddenly forgotten.

She moves to the next coffin and brushes dust off the nameplate. The jewels sparkle bright yellow.

"K. O'Malley," she says.

Spingate's fingers trace the yellow jewels. She puts a fingertip on one and pushes: it slides inward until it clicks. When she pulls her finger away, the jewel stays depressed. She pushes it again and it clicks again, then returns to its original height. She moves to the next one, pinches it between finger and thumb and twists: the jewel rotates in place.

Somewhere inside the coffin, we hear a series of small whirs and clinks.

Spingate doesn't know what she's doing, but she's trying things—pressing, then listening, turning, then listening some more. Her lips move a little, making no sound. She points at the jewels, her finger bouncing in the air—she's counting.

She lifts the weapon, touches a pattern of jewels on its shaft, then presses a similar pattern on the jewels surrounding the name *K. O'Malley*. A hidden panel on the side of the coffin slides up fast, revealing the negative space of two small circles.

Spingate laughs, delighted at her success. She stands, then slides the rod's prongs into the circles—they fit perfectly. I hear a click. She lifts the end of the rod.

A deep *thrum* comes from inside the coffin. The lid halves shudder. Dust powders down from them as they slide neatly to the sides.

Inside, lying motionless, eyes closed, is . . . a boy. A sleeping boy, dressed like Brewer but as big as we are. Bigger, even— his shoulders press against the coffin's white fabric, the toes of his black-socked feet touch the end. He has thick, brown hair. His skin is darker than Spingate's, but not as dark as mine.

He is beautiful.

The symbol on his forehead is a circle, like mine, but the right half is solid black. His clean white shirt is far too small for his smooth chest. Some of the buttons are missing. There is no dust on him, none at all. No blood, either. The bars holding his waist, wrists and ankles seem far too tight.

I stare at him. I can't help it. I feel strange. My insides shiver.

"He's breathing," Spingate says, her words a hushed breath.

I need this boy to wake up . . . I need him to see me.

"Give me the weapon—I mean the *tool*. I'll break his bars."

"Just a moment," she says. "We might not have to break any-thing."

The tool is still firmly locked in the coffin's side, sticking up at an angle. She looks at it, then at O'Malley, then at the tool again. She presses a pair of jewels on the handle: nothing happens. She thinks, presses a different pair, then the bars across O'Malley's wrists, ankles and waist split in the middle and snap down, van-ishing inside the coffin's padded lining.

Other than the gentle rise and fall of his chest, he doesn't move. I feel a rush of panic that Spingate will wake him—I need to be the one who does it.

"Go open the other coffins," I tell her.

She looks at me. She seems confused. She looks at O'Malley again.

"Spingate, hurry up about it," I say. "We don't know how much time we have."

She sighs. She likes looking at him, too, and it's hard for her to look away. She does, though. She pulls the tool free and walks to the next coffin.

I stare down at O'Malley. His hair looks so soft. His mouth is slightly open, his full lips moving with each breath. When Spingate smiled for the first time, I thought she was the most beautiful thing that could ever be.

I was wrong.

I hear Spingate brush dust away from a metal plate.

"This one is . . . oh, I'm not sure," she says. "I think it's . . . Air-ah-mov-sky?"

Something about that grabs my attention.

"What are the last few letters?"

"It ends with an *S,* a *K* and a *Y,*" she says.

My breath catches, because I *remember* something. A name. A name of a . . . oh, what is it, it's right there, tickling my thoughts . . . of a *musician.* Yes! A musician, with a name that ended in an *S,* a *K* and a *Y.*

Tchaikovsky.

"It's not *sky,*" I say. "It's *skee.*"

I go back to staring at O'Malley.

"Aramov*skee,*" Spingate says. "Can I open it?"

Why does she keep asking for my permission?

"Sure, go ahead."

I hear her working at something. I reach out a finger, gently touch O'Malley's ribs. He's warm. The contact sends a prickling sensation across my skin. I don't feel cold anymore.

He doesn't respond.

What should I do? What if he doesn't wake up at all?

I hear that *thrum* again, hear Spingate laugh as Aramovsky's coffin opens.

SIX

Spingate opens the rest of the coffins. Five of them contain emaciated little corpses. Three hold living people, sleeping just like O'Malley.

I don't remember my mother's name or face, but somehow I remember going to the store with her. Before she put a carton of eggs in our cart, she would open it, check to see if any were cracked. This room is a carton with a dozen eggs—six broken and ruined forever, six still whole.

B. Aramovsky is a boy with dark skin, a shade almost as deep as the black hair that clings to his head in tight curls. The symbol on his forehead is a circle, same as mine, but with a smaller circle inside. He is tall, even more so than O'Malley; Aramovsky's feet are flat against the bottom of his coffin, while his head presses against the top. His white shirt is tight against his muscles, although he's skinnier than O'Malley and the buttons haven't ripped away.

K. Bello's skin is white. Are people supposed to be that pale?

Maybe she's sick. Bello has long blond hair, so thin that if you walk by her coffin a few strands slowly move as if hit by a breeze. The symbol on her forehead is a single circle, exactly like mine.

The last one, *J. Yong,* is another boy. His tan skin looks smooth and soft. He has thick black hair, as black as Aramovsky's but straight rather than curly. It hangs down to his eyes, covering his symbol. I brush the hair back to see it: a black circle with a solid five-pointed star inside.

Savage, Spingate, O'Malley, Aramovsky, Bello, Yong. Other than Brewer, I don't know the names of the dead and I don't care to.

Broken eggs don't matter.

Everyone—corpses and the living alike—wears the same style of clothing: button-down white shirt, red tie, black pants or a red and black plaid skirt.

And there is something else: everyone is beautiful. Beyond beautiful . . . *perfect.*

O'Malley is the most attractive of the boys, but it's a close thing. All three of them have strong features, square jaws, thick necks, muscular bodies. If they were awake, I bet they could run forever. I bet they could lift anything. They could probably lift me as easily as they can breathe.

Spingate and Bello have curvy shapes, beautiful hair, flat stomachs and firm legs. They are flawless. I can't remember any details of my school, but I am haunted by echoes of feelings I had looking at older girls like them. I felt so awkward. I knew I would never have a body like theirs. Those girls always looked so confident.

Now I have firm legs and a flat stomach, just like Spingate and Bello, just like those girls I can't quite remember. I have breasts, too, but I still don't feel confident because this isn't *me.*

Having the body of a woman doesn't change the fact that I'm still a kid.

Spingate is standing next to Bello's coffin, gently stroking the unconscious girl's hair.

"Em, I don't understand," she says. "Why are they still asleep?"

My past is a vague whisper, shades and hints of events that might have actually happened, or might have been a dream. The only reality I can count on is what happened after the needle struck home.

Pain woke me. Pain, fear and *blood*. There is no blood on Spingate.

"I don't know why," I say. "What woke *you* up?"

She thinks. "A tingling. All over my body."

"Did it hurt?"

She shakes her head, pauses, then nods. "A little. Maybe. No, not really."

I look into O'Malley's coffin. There is no white tube. Maybe one is in there, somewhere, hidden behind the white fabric.

Or, maybe . . . the needle was for me alone.

Spingate suddenly claps her hands, hops up and down. Her red curls bounce.

"A mild *shock*," she says. "That's what woke me. Electricity."

She walks around the room, studying the pictures carved into the stone walls, examining the coffins, even staring up at the ceiling. I don't know what she hopes to find, so I turn my attention back to O'Malley.

I am suddenly afraid he will never wake up. Or what if he's not real at all . . . what if I'm still in my coffin, dreaming? But if O'Malley isn't real, why does looking at him make my throat feel so dry?

"I found something over here," Spingate says. "I think these are controls of some kind."

I nod, but don't look. I wrap my hand around O'Malley's firm shoulder. There is something comforting in the denseness of his body.

I squeeze his shoulder, ever so slightly.

He doesn't move.

Wake up . . . please wake up.

I give him a little shove.

Still he doesn't move.

I lean in, ready to shake him hard. As soon as I do, a thousand tiny needles drive through my skin. My arm moves on its own, yanking my hand away from O'Malley—the second I let go of him, the needle-pokes stop. I look at my hand, not sure what just happened.

"Found it!" Spingate calls out. "Did they wake up?"

O'Malley is twitching a little. His face is no longer peaceful. His brow wrinkles and his closed eyes squint, as if he's beginning a nightmare.

"No," I say. "He's moving, but still asleep."

"I'll give them all a little more."

I hear a buzz: O'Malley sits up like a shot. A button pops from his strained shirt and sails off to land soundlessly somewhere in the dust. He is terrified, confused. His wide-open eyes stare into nothing.

His eyes are blue.

I hear screams of fear and confusion. Aramovsky and Bello are awake. Aramovsky lurches out of his coffin, lands hard in a billowing puff of dust. Bello sits up, her eyes squeezed tight, her hands reaching out blindly to ward off a threat she can't see and can't stop.

Yong rolls out of his coffin, the move fast and graceful even though his eyes are still closed. He lands on his side, hands over his ears, elbows together and touching his tucked-up knees.

I look back to O'Malley.

He squints and blinks against the light, but he is looking right at me.

The survivors are awake.

The eggs have hatched.

SEVEN

They don't know their names. They don't know why they're here. They don't know where we are.

The only thing they know for sure is that today is their birthday.

Aramovsky is the loudest, demanding information more than asking questions. I get the feeling that he thinks maybe Spingate and I were the ones who put him in the coffin in the first place.

Yong keeps glancing at his own arms, flexing them slightly, a smile teasing the corners of his mouth when his muscles strain the white fabric. Between those glances, he glares at all of us like we're not to be trusted, like we know what's going on and we're playacting together to keep him in the dark.

Bello is very quiet—she seems afraid to talk. She's the smallest of us. She looks fragile. I'm sure the boys could have broken out of their coffins if they had awoken to darkness and pain. Spingate, too, maybe, if she hadn't convinced herself it was impossible. But Bello? She would have been trapped in there forever, until she died and shriveled up like Brewer.

O'Malley watches me and Spingate, but he doesn't seem suspicious, or angry. When someone talks, he looks at them the way Spingate looks at the tool or the jewel-controls: he's analyzing, he's measuring.

I tell the others what happened between the time I got out of my coffin and when Spingate shocked them awake. Since she and I have been up for maybe thirty minutes more than they have, it doesn't take long to cover everything.

When I stop talking, I wait for them to respond. They don't. Spingate doesn't make a sound. She pretends to study the jeweled rod so she doesn't have to look at anyone.

"That's it," I say. "That's all we know."

The four newcomers stare at me. I woke up alone, had to figure things out for myself. In a way, they have it harder: they awoke as a blank slate, naturally assuming the people waiting for them would explain what was happening. Which, of course, Spingate and I can't do.

O'Malley scratches at his temple. His deep-blue eyes drill into me.

"So that's all you know," he says. "That's it?"

I nod.

"Then you don't know much."

He doesn't say it accusingly. It's a fact.

"*We,*" I say. "*We* don't know much."

He nods slowly. "We. Yes, *we.*"

There is strength in that word.

Yong shakes his head and looks off, disgusted.

Bello stares at every person in turn, as if she's waiting for someone to do something. To do anything. No one does. Her eyes are striking, green at the outer edges that blends to an orange-brown around the black dot of the iris. Finally, her eyes settle on me.

"So, Em . . . what now?"

I wait for someone else to speak, to know what we should do next. The other five are obviously waiting for the same thing.

"Spingate," I say, "is there anything else on those controls you found? Can we . . . I don't know . . . call for help or something?"

She shakes her head. "I think they were for adjusting the . . . oh, what's the word . . . ah, yes, for adjusting the *environment* in the coffins. I don't think the controls do anything else."

I was afraid of that. "Then we have to leave this room."

Bello wrings her hands together, left clutching right, right clutching left, over and over.

"We should stay put," she says. "We don't know what's out there. We should wait for grownups to come and get us."

Grownups. Like the word *we,* the word *grownups* has power. Grownups would know what to do, would tell us where to go.

Yong spreads his hands, a gesture that takes in the whole room.

"What grownups?" he says. "Do you see any grownups here? I don't. Someone put us in this place, probably those same grownups you're crying for."

"We don't know that," Bello says, her hands wringing faster.

Yong spits into the dust. "Don't be an idiot. We're in a dungeon, there isn't time for your stupidity."

"Stop it," I say, my voice sharp like it was when I yelled at Spingate to be quiet. "There's no reason to be mean."

Yong turns his cold gaze on me. I see his eyes flick to my forehead, see those eyes narrow in thought, like he's almost got something, then that something is gone.

"Sure," he says with a smirk. "Let's all play nice, because that will make things better, right?"

I feel something I haven't felt yet: anger. I don't like the way Yong looks at me, the way he seems to dismiss me.

We hear a grumble, a muffled sound that rolls fast, then slow, then faster and louder.

All heads turn to where that sound came from: Spingate's stomach.

"Oh," she says. Her hands cover her exposed belly. She blushes. "Sorry. I guess I'm hungry."

The last word seems to unlock something in me, reveal a pinching emptiness in my middle. It was there all along, I think, but my brain didn't process it. Maybe I was too busy thinking about all the other things that are wrong to realize that I'm starving.

I see other hands on other bellies. Everyone is hungry.

"Bello's right," I say. "We don't know what's out there. But we know what's not in here—food."

We look at each other in unspoken understanding. Waiting is not an option.

"There's no water here, either," Spingate says. "Water is even more important than food." She looks up and to the left, her nose wrinkling. "I think that's right."

Aramovsky tugs at the sleeves of his white shirt. He fidgets with it constantly, as if on guard against a crease sneaking up on him.

"Why don't *you* go, Em?" he says. "You can find food and water, bring it back for us. We can wait here in case the grown-ups come."

Yong makes a *pfft* sound with his mouth.

"You're a brave one, Aramovsky," he says.

Aramovsky glares at Yong. "It's not about bravery, it's about practicality."

Yong rolls his eyes. "Yeah, that's what it is. Practicality. Then how about you go, Aramovsky? The rest of us can stay and be *practical*."

Aramovsky draws himself up to his full height. He is much taller than the other boy.

"Don't you tell me what to do," he says.

Yong's arms uncross. His hands drop to his sides, curl into fists.

"You volunteer others, but you won't go yourself? Then how about I *make* you go?"

Yong smiles. It's a beautiful smile, the kind that would make me want to follow him around all day from a distance, just to see what he does, see who he talks to. But his eyes . . . they radiate something else altogether. Aramovsky is taller and both boys are packed with muscle, but Yong *wants* to fight—Aramovsky does not. Maybe Aramovsky tried to use his size to intimidate, but it backfired on him and now he doesn't know what to do.

"We stay together," I say in a rush. "We aren't making anyone do anything, okay?"

Aramovsky nods quickly. "Em's right."

Yong again stares at me. I get the impression I'm annoying him.

O'Malley tries for the tenth time to pull his top two shirt buttons together, even though he has to know by now his chest is too big for that. He gives up, instead keeps a hand pressed near his neck, as if he's embarrassed so much skin is showing.

He looks at me.

"Em, why do *you* get to choose what we do? Are you in charge?"

There is no malice in his voice. He's not accusing me of anything; he's asking a question that needs to be asked.

"I don't know," I say.

Aramovsky points at me. No, he points at my forehead.

"Em can't be in charge. She's a circle."

He says that like my symbol has significance. It does, I know it does—*all* our symbols have significance. We can feel it. But from the searching looks on everyone's faces, none of us know what that significance is.

O'Malley shrugs. "If Em doesn't make the decisions, then who does?"

No one speaks. We're kids: someone is supposed to tell us what to do. That's the way things are.

Finally, Yong breaks the silence.

"I'll do it."

His arms are crossed again, his head is tilted slightly to the right. He is a walking challenge, daring anyone to contradict him. Something about his presence promises pain.

"I'll run things," he says. "You all do what I say and we'll be fine."

I don't think he should be in charge. Or Aramovsky, for that matter—something about the tall boy makes me nervous. But who am I to say Yong shouldn't lead? Someone has to get us out of here, someone has to make decisions.

Yong stares at Bello, who looks down instantly. He stares at Spingate; she clears her throat, blushes again, then shrugs. Yong tries to stare at Aramovsky, but Aramovsky won't even meet his eyes. I'm the next target for Yong's burning glare. I try to match it, try to wordlessly stand up to him, but I can't—I look away. Those fists of his . . . would he hit me?

I don't even know if I've ever been in a fight.

Finally, Yong stares at O'Malley.

O'Malley stares right back; calm, not threatening, but not reacting to Yong's intimidation, either.

"Em got out of her coffin on her own," O'Malley says. "No

one else did that. Then she freed Spingate. The two of them got the rest of us out. Without Em, we all might still be asleep. Or, worse, awake and trapped in the coffins."

Yong frowns. He seems confused, as if he expected any disagreement to involve shouting and pushing, not simple reasoning. O'Malley isn't even arguing with Yong, he's simply presenting facts.

"So she got us out," Yong says. "So what? She has no idea what's going on. Getting us out of the coffins doesn't mean she's a good leader."

O'Malley thinks on this for a moment, really considering it, then nods.

"That's true, it doesn't mean she's a good leader," he says. "But she didn't panic. When Spingate called for help, Em helped her. Em told all of us what was happening and didn't pretend that she knew more than she did. Don't you think those are qualities we'd want in a leader?"

Yong says nothing.

I wouldn't have thought those things made me a leader, but the way O'Malley pointed them out makes it sound so obvious.

Maybe Yong wants to argue, but there's nothing to argue against.

"Whatever," he says, and leans on a coffin. He looks away, taking in the aisle of dust as if it bores him only slightly less than we do.

Spingate walks to me, offers me the tool. She doesn't need to say why—the leader should carry it.

"You can be in charge, Em," she says. She looks at Bello and Aramovsky. "Don't you think Em should be in charge?"

A tooth-girl wants me to lead? My blurry memories tell me that's an impossibility, and yet I see it with my own eyes.

Bello and Aramovsky glance at each other. Her hand-over-hand fussing starts up again.

"Until we find the grownups," she says quietly. "Em can be in charge until we find the grownups."

Aramovsky clearly doesn't agree, but he stays quiet.

I take the tool from Spingate. I smile at her. She smiles back.

O'Malley is staring at me. Those blue eyes lock me in, make me feel jittery. When he looks at me, does his stomach tingle the way mine does when I look at him? He defended me. Why? Does he really think I could be a good leader?

He gives me a small smile, then he shrugs.

"I guess it's up to you, Em. What do we do now?"

What do we do? How should I know? I'm in charge, but I realize that in the whole exchange I never *asked* to be in charge. That doesn't seem to matter—everyone is waiting for me to make a decision.

So I make one.

"First, we get out of this room."

I walk to the archway. The others follow close behind. Yong waits until we stand before it, then he joins us.

The archway is made of rust-caked metal, covered in dusty symbols just like the walls and coffins. What I thought might be doors are two slabs of stone, pressed together so tightly the vertical line separating them could be mistaken for a thin scratch. I don't see any handles, any way to open them.

"Promising," Aramovsky says. "Your leadership is off to a wonderful start."

I ignore him.

Spingate steps forward and wipes dust from the archway's right side, revealing sparkling gemstones set into the flaking metal.

Her lips move. I wait while she thinks.

"It's similar to the coffins," she says finally. "I push these three red jewels—"

She presses them, one, two, three, each jewel moving down a tiny bit until it clicks.

Below the jewels, a small panel pops open. Inside are two holes, same as we saw in the coffins.

Spingate claps and jumps up and down, delighted with her discovery.

I look at her, amazed. "How do you know how to do that?"

She bites her lower lip. Her eyebrows go up, then she shakes her head and shrugs.

"I don't know. It seems . . . kind of obvious, somehow." She points to a row of three red jewels on the tool's shaft. "Press those—one, two, three—then use it to open the door."

I pause a moment before doing so. If this doesn't work, if the doors won't open, I have no idea what we do next. Some leader I am.

I press the red jewels: one, two, three. I slide the tool's prongs into the holes, feel a small vibration as something locks tight. The tool has become a handle. I lift it, feel an initial, wiggling resistance. I gradually increase the pressure until something hidden and frozen seems to break free, then the tool rises smoothly and clanks to a stop.

The floor shudders, the walls groan. A light shower of dust rains down from the ceiling.

A loud clang echoes through the air. The door-halves slide open a grinding fraction of an inch, making the entire room vibrate.

Outside our coffin room, the light is brighter.

The vibrations stop. The doors slowly open.

PART II

WORDS AND
WEAPONS

EIGHT

A wave of warm air caresses us.

Outside our open door is a hallway. The walls are white and smooth, but scratched and cracked in places. The ceiling seems to be made from some kind of pale, rough crystal that glows brightly. Like the coffin room, the floor is a field of soft gray.

Bello and Aramovsky hold each other, her head barely reaching his shoulder. Spingate takes a step behind O'Malley, who is watching me, waiting for me to act. Yong lurks in the background, still pretending to be bored as far as I know.

Someone has to go first.

I take a deep breath. I'm the leader, right? That means I have to lead. I pull the tool free.

When I step into the hallway, I am surprised that Yong steps out with me.

That smirk again. "Can't let you have all the glory, can I?"

He pretended to be bored with us, but couldn't let me be the first one out. Yong is strange. Or maybe he's normal. I have no way of knowing.

The hall runs to the left and right, straight and true as far as I can see in either direction. And on both sides, more to the right than the left, bumpy things, all across the floor, just as coated in dust as the floor itself.

Those things are . . .

I think of Brewer, shriveled-up little Brewer.

Those things are . . .

I squeeze my eyes shut. My brain doesn't seem to work. My thoughts feel clogged, my head feels . . . *muddy* is the word that seems right. I can't put the pieces together. I don't *want* to put them together.

As a group, the others step out around me. No one says a word.

Yong turns right, walks to the first pile of bumpy things. He reaches down and picks something up. Dust tumbles from it, tiny waterfalls of curling motes that hang in the air.

He's holding a bone.

Long, white, with bits of dark material clinging to it—scraps of dried *meat*. It looks like he is holding a nightmarish club.

"It's a femur," Spingate says, her words a shocked sigh. "A human femur."

Yong drops it. He looks down, slowly turns in place. He is surrounded by skeletons, by bones—piles and piles of them.

This hallway is full of dead people.

Hands on my arm: Bello, clinging to me.

"Em, this isn't right," she says. "Let's leave this place."

A great idea, if only I knew where to go.

Yong reaches for a round bump near his feet. His hands brush away the gray, then come up holding a human skull covered in tightly dried skin. There is no jawbone. Two empty eye sockets stare out.

He looks at it, adjusts it in his hands. As he does, the stiff flesh along the jaw cracks and crumbles, becomes a puff of descending dust.

And then I understand. The dust . . . it's *skin*. Skin and muscle, eyes and brains and guts that have become nothing more than floating powder. Powder that was in my mouth, down my throat, powder that is all around me, coating everything.

What I thought was a sea of dust is an ocean of death.

Yong drops the skull, then runs back to us, to the safety of the group.

Bello cries silently. O'Malley puts his arm around her.

Everyone is looking at me again, waiting for me to tell them what to do. Even Yong. But I don't know what to do. Who would? I have to think, have to figure out what makes sense.

The hallway really seems to go on forever in both directions. All along it are more archway doors that look like the one we just walked out of. Some of these doors are slightly open; dark spaces with who knows what inside. Others are still sealed shut, the stone gouged and chipped.

Now that I've seen the bones, I can't un-see them. Up and down the hall, lumps in the dust.

Bones are *everywhere*.

Some are full skeletons. Some bones lie by themselves: cracked, broken, splintered. A few of them are blackened, charred—they were *burned*.

Bello's silent cry shifts to a quiet sob. Something about her tears suggests weakness (*crying doesn't fix anything*), makes me want to scream at her to *shut up,* to *stop it already.* But I know she can't help it.

"Where are we?" she says through the tears. "What happened here?"

O'Malley still has his arm around her. If I was the one crying, would he put his arm around me?

He lets go of Bello and walks a few steps to Aramovsky, whispers something in the taller boy's ear. Aramovsky moves to Bello. He puts his arm around her, pulls her in close. Bello rests her head against his white-shirted shoulder.

O'Malley walks to the skull. He picks it up, brushes off what little dust remains. A few crispy flakes of skin crumble away. He turns it in his hands, holds it toward us so we can see the top.

There is a jagged, roughly triangular hole in the curved white bone.

"Someone killed this person," he says. "Hit him, or her, with something heavy. Maybe there was a battle." He squints at it, then at us, at our heads, as if he is comparing the size. "I think these people were grownups. Grownups who slaughtered each other."

How many dead people lie in this hallway? Maybe a hundred? It's hard to tell with the parts scattered all over.

One of the dusty skeletons has something sticking out of it. Is that a handle? I walk to what was once a person, grab the handle and pull it free.

I stare at a flat, pointed piece of metal: I'm holding a knife.

If I put the bottom of the metal handle in the crook of my elbow, the knifepoint would reach to the tip of my middle finger. Where the blade joins the handle, two pieces of thin, strong metal stick out the sides. They are etched with tiny carvings of stepped pyramids and suns. At the very end of the handle, below where my hand holds the grip, is a flat, round disc ringed by tiny red gemstones, with another circle of the same stones inside it.

The circle-in-a-circle symbol: exactly like the one on Aramovsky's forehead.

I'm holding the tool in one hand, the knife in the other.

Bello's nose wrinkles. "Em, is that a sword?"

"Swords are bigger," Yong says. "I think. No, they're bigger."

"Leave it here," Bello says. "That's for *them*. That's for the grownups. We don't need it."

I want to drop it. Not because of her words, but because the knife frightens me. I don't even want it touching my skin. This knife was used to kill. It was used to turn people—people like us—into nothing but piles of bones and puffs of dust.

The grownups killed each other. If any of them are still alive, will they try to kill us, too?

"We might have to defend ourselves," I say to Bello. "We need it."

She shakes her head. "We don't need it. It's a bad thing, please don't bring it."

Yong comes closer to me. His eyes are suddenly alive, burning with eagerness. He holds out his hand.

"Give the knife to me," he says. "I'll take it. You carry the tool."

There is a hunger to his words, something . . . *disturbing* about his need. Just like I know it's a bad idea if he leads, I know he shouldn't have the knife.

"I'll hold on to it for now," I say.

He is standing in front of me, his back to the others. They can't see his face, but I can. His upper lip twitches, twists into a sneer. His eagerness shifts, transforms. His heavy black hair hangs down almost over his eyes, eyes that blaze with hate.

"You'll change your mind," he says quietly. Then, in the faintest whisper: "Or I'll change it for you."

Before I can respond, he smiles, turns and walks back to the others, leaving me alone with the skeleton.

I briefly wonder if I should tell everyone what he said, but I decide against it. We don't need another argument right now. We need to follow Bello's advice and get away from this place.

I look at the doors lining the hallway. Gouged, chipped, scratched. Were people desperate to get inside?

I see one set of doors that is slightly open. If we had come out of our room and turned left instead of right, this archway would have been a few feet down on the right-hand side. The space between the stone doors is barely wide enough for me to slide through if I turn sideways. Coming from inside that room, I see a dim, flickering light.

Does that room have more coffins? I walk toward it, past Bello and the others.

A strong hand lands on my shoulder.

It's O'Malley.

"Em, don't go in there," he says.

He sees me looking at his hand, then pulls it away. His face flushes. He didn't act like that when he put his arm around Bello.

"I have to," I say. "There could be more of us inside."

O'Malley closes his blue eyes for a second, swallows, nods once, opens them.

"Then I'm going in with you."

Those words make my heart hammer so loud I wonder if he hears it.

I'm holding the knife and the tool. I thought the tool was a weapon at first—it's not, but it will still work fine for that purpose.

I hold it out to O'Malley. "Take it," I say. "In case there's danger."

Spingate gasps; she points at the tool.

"It's called a *scepter*," she says. "That word just popped into my head. The tool, that's what it's called."

Scepter, tool, weapon . . . all I care about right now is that it is heavy and O'Malley can use it to smash things.

He takes it.

"I'm with you, Em," he says.

His eyes . . . so blue . . .

I can't look at him any longer, so I face the door. I walk to it and slide my body through the narrow opening.

O'Malley follows.

NINE

The room is dim, illuminated by a single flickering light high up in the arched ceiling.

I point the knife out in front of me. O'Malley holds the bottom of the scepter with both hands, the prongs up near his ear.

Like our room, there are twelve dusty coffins arranged in two end-to-end rows of six. All the coffins are open. The lid-halves aren't folded neatly to the sides—they stick up at different angles, broken; did the occupants fight their way out like I did?

I walk up to the first coffin. O'Malley is right next to me. I brush off the nameplate before looking inside.

Orange stones surround the name *L. Morgan*.

Inside the coffin, dust-covered clothes—a little white shirt, a short red tie, little black pants—covering a tiny, withered corpse.

A corpse far smaller than Brewer.

A corpse so small I could cradle it in both arms.

The skull, the *tiny* skull, is smashed to bits at the center of the forehead. I can't tell what symbol is in that dried, cracked skin, if there was any symbol at all.

O'Malley's shaking hand slowly reaches toward L. Morgan's head. His fingertip gently touches the ridge of bone below the little skull's right eye.

"A child," O'Malley says. "Barely more than a baby. How could anyone do this?"

A baby. Even if L. Morgan had been awake when the attack came, he couldn't have defended himself. The grownup bodies in the hallway . . . maybe those people died in a battle, but that's not what happened here.

O'Malley walks to another coffin. One lid-half remains closed, the other has been torn away, tossed to the floor long ago to become a landing place for dust.

"Same thing here, Em," he says. His voice is ragged, more breath than words. "They ripped the lid off, then they caved in this little girl's face."

I see a pile of bumps in the dusty aisle between the coffin rows. Then another, and another. It wasn't just children that died in here.

There are ten more coffins in this room. They are all open. I don't have to look inside them to know what lies within.

All these little kids, slaughtered where they lay . . . I can't bear this for one second more. I have to get out of here.

"O'Malley, come on."

"But don't you want to—"

"Come on!"

I hurry back to the stone doors. I squeeze through the crack and into the hallway. Spingate, Bello, Yong and Aramovsky are waiting, their eyes wide, their faces carrying an expression I now recognize—the look of someone desperately hoping for good news.

"Well?" Spingate says. "Are there more of us?"

"They were . . . younger," I say. "And they're all dead."

"Younger," Spingate says. "Like Brewer?"

I shake my head. I hold my free hand at my hip, palm parallel to the floor, showing them how tall L. Morgan would have been.

Everyone looks down, as if they expect a child to suddenly appear at my side, my hand on his head.

They are shocked. Even Yong. Despair pulls at his features, makes me forget his constant smirk.

Behind me, O'Malley slides out of the narrow opening. His chest barely fits through the gap; the stone door's edges rip off another button, drag a long, white scratch across his smooth skin.

Bello stares at him hopefully, like she wants him to tell a story different from mine.

"Is it true?" she asks. "Little kids?"

O'Malley nods. "Little kids. Dressed like us. They were murdered."

Murdered.

The word enrages me. We could have died the same way, murdered while we slept. I want to know who bashed in those tiny skulls. I want to find the people who did it, and I want to make them pay.

"It was the Grownups," I say. I hear the hate in my voice. "It had to be. They want to kill us"—I spread out my arms, gesturing to the bones in the hall—"just like they killed each other."

I don't want to look in any of the other rooms. We need to get away from all this death. I stare up the right side of the hall, then the left.

To the left is our coffin room, and where we found the knife.

The right seems to have fewer bones, so that's where we'll go.

"This way," I say, and I start walking.

O'Malley falls in on my right side. The other four follow.

We leave the skeletons behind.

TEN

We are walking uphill.

The angle is so slight I didn't notice it at first, but the hallway slopes gently upward.

We've been walking for hours. At least we think it's hours; we have no way of tracking time. The endless incline is subtle, but it exhausts us, leeches away what little strength we have.

I hold the knife. O'Malley carries the scepter. I tried carrying both for a little while, but the scepter was too heavy.

If we had walked in the other direction, we'd have been going down. Spingate said there's no limit on how far down we could go, how deep into the ground, but *up* can't go on forever.

Can it?

Our coffin room must be far below the surface. This hallway doesn't seem to have an end. The softly glowing ceiling gently curves upward in parallel with the floor. Far ahead of us, the floor and ceiling seem to meet, but no matter how much we walk, that connection always appears to be exactly the same distance away.

No one speaks. The memory of the bone pile and the dead kids stays with us, silences us. We've left that behind, though, for which we're grateful.

Bones aren't the only thing we've left behind: we haven't seen a door in maybe an hour, near as we can tell. We walk through an empty, blank, untouched corridor of dust.

My stomach *hurts*. It pinches. It grumbles, loudly. I hear similar noises coming from the others. We need to eat.

Hungry, tired, confused, afraid—it's wearing on us. Our feet drag across the hard floor, leaving long footprints in the dust.

O'Malley finally breaks the silence.

"There have to be people who are still alive," he says. "We can contact someone, get rescued."

Rescue. Another word of power. Someone to save us. I hope my parents are alive, hope their bones weren't among those hidden beneath the gray powder. I don't remember my mother's face, or her name, but I know I love her. And my father . . . if he loves me, why hasn't he come for me? I feel like he was brave, like he was strong, but I don't know if that's true or if I'm being a little girl, hoping her daddy was the best daddy there could be.

Bello scoots out in front of us, turns to face us and walks backward. For the first time, she seems excited.

"Maybe the people who rescue us will have food," she says.

I remember smelling something . . . my dad cooking dinner. Some kind of meat, maybe? My mouth waters and my stomach rumbles louder.

"Bread," Bello says, her eyes all dreamy. "Hot bread, with butter and cinnamon. All crunchy on the outside and soft inside."

"A sandwich," O'Malley says. "With mustard and pickles and big, fat, salty slices of cold chicken."

Pork chops . . . that's what my dad was roasting. How can I know that and not know his face?

"Cupcakes," Aramovsky says. "Chocolate, with chocolate icing as high as the cupcake itself. And lots of sprinkles."

My mouth waters so badly I almost drool.

"Pasta," Yong says. "With tomato sauce, and so much cheese on top you have to take like three bites before you can even *find* the pasta beneath."

"I don't care what they bring," Spingate says. "As long as it's hot. And more of it than I can even eat. But for dessert, I'm definitely going for one of Aramovsky's cupcakes."

"Me too," O'Malley says.

Bello shakes her head. She's still walking backward. Her eyes sparkle, she stands straight and tall—as tall as she can be, anyway. She's happy: she looks like a completely different person from the sniffling girl I met back in the coffin room.

"You're all wrong," she says. She taps her temple. "You're obviously not a thinker like me. Aramovsky's right about chocolate with chocolate icing, but it needs to be a *birthday* cake. With twelve candles!"

Aramovsky laughs. "You're right, Bello, but are there still sprinkles? There better be sprinkles."

Bello rolls her eyes in mock annoyance. "Of *course* there are. It's your birthday, so you get sprinkles. We all get sprinkles."

Everyone agrees that this is a splendid way to finish our rescue meal.

Smiles, nods, yummy noises . . . it's an almost perfect moment. For a brief instant, we're not in our grownup bodies with too-small clothes and no shoes, we're not surrounded by dust that used to be people, and we're not lost and alone—we're six friends walking together, on our way to a birthday party. There will be cake, there will be games, there will be presents. There will be parents who love us and protect us.

Still moving down the hall, Bello spins in slow circles, letting momentum swing her arms wide.

"I bet our parents are coming to get us," she says. "They have to be looking for us, right?"

"Mine are," Yong says instantly.

Bello nods. "So are mine. But . . . I can't remember them. Yong, do you remember your parents? What they look like?"

He makes that *pfft* noise again. "Of course I remember them."

We all know he's lying. He knows it, too, but no one challenges him, because it's a nice lie, one we'd all like to believe.

Bello's spin slows. The excitement drains from her face—fear owns her.

She stops. So do the rest of us.

There are tears in her eyes. Crying again? Bello is really starting to bother me.

"Our parents," she says. "What if our parents are the ones who put us in the coffins?"

I wondered the same thing. I'm ashamed I considered it, even for a second. I see the others looking down, looking away—we've all had that thought, but Bello is the first to voice it out loud.

No one answers her. She seems to shrink, hunching over a bit, elbows pulling tight to her ribs, hands wringing left over right, right over left. Bello stands still, lets the group pass her by, then she falls in at the rear.

We return to walking in silence. We hear only the sounds of our breathing and our shuffling feet.

And our growling stomachs.

Maybe another hour passes. Maybe two. We keep going because we don't have a choice.

Then, far up ahead, that ever-present meeting of ceiling and floor changes: another hallway, crossing ours. It's something different, which is enough to make us pick up the pace despite our exhaustion.

We reach the intersection. The new hallway leads off to our right for a long ways, but the light from the ceiling is dim. Farther in, it looks like there is no light at all. Maybe a hundred steps away, I see a single archway door in the dimness. It's wide open. Maybe there are more beyond it, but it's too dark to tell.

To our left, the hallway goes a few feet before it stops at a wall, a wall that looks like black liquid frozen in mid-splash—as if it melted, then cooled. Maybe it used to be a door, very different from the other doors we've seen so far.

Spingate steps a few feet into the hallway on the right. She stares down it, tilting her head slightly as if that might let her see a bit farther.

"We've been in the same hall for a long time," she says. "We haven't found anything. So far, I mean. Should we try this new one?"

No one else speaks. Are they waiting for me to decide?

Yong walks to stand next to Spingate. He stares down the new hall just as she did, even tilts his head the same. Then he looks back at me.

"We'll go this way," he says. "That makes sense."

I'm not sure that it does. The hallway to the right is different: it looks *flat*. I don't see the floor-meeting-ceiling illusion I've been looking at for the last few hours, but then again, that could be because there isn't enough light to see that far.

The hallway we're in now seems endless, but it has to lead somewhere; I can't say that for sure about the new direction.

"We're not going to walk down a dark hall," I say. "Besides, we need to keep going straight."

Aramovsky points down the hall to the right. "But that way is flat. Maybe you didn't notice. We've been walking uphill for . . . well, for a long time. My legs are tired."

So are mine. I'd like to give my legs a break as much as he would, but I know I'm making the right decision.

"We go straight," I say again. "If we start making turns, we might not know what direction is what. If we keep going straight, at least we know how to get back to where we came from if we get into trouble. I know it's tiring, but walking uphill is a good thing—every step we take is a step closer to getting out."

I see shoulders droop, I hear heavy sighs. They don't want to agree with me; they want to go the easier way.

"Em's in charge," O'Malley says. He sounds tired. "We follow her lead."

Spingate sighs and shrugs. Bello nods reluctantly. Aramovsky keeps looking down the new hallway as if it's paved with the cupcake of his dreams. None of them want to go my way, but they seem resigned to my decision.

All save for Yong.

"I don't want to follow Em's lead anymore," he says. He crosses his arms. "I think it's my turn to be in charge."

"We don't take *turns,*" O'Malley says. "This isn't a game."

Yong points at me. There's something petulant in the gesture, something mean, and for a moment I see a twelve-year-old bully wearing an adult's body.

"She doesn't know what she's doing," Yong says. He looks at me, holds out his palm. "You tried, Em, but you failed. It's my turn now, so give me the knife."

And just like that, the twelve-year-old is gone. I'm looking at a grown man, a lean, strong man who isn't going to take no for an answer.

He wiggles his fingers inward.

"Give it to me," Yong says. "If you don't, I'll take it from you. You won't like that."

Spingate puts her hands on her hips.

"Quit being a jerk, Yong. Em's in charge, you—"

Yong's hands are so fast I barely see him move: he shoves Spingate, hard. She crashes against the wall and falls to her butt. She looks at him in wide-eyed surprise.

She doesn't try to get up.

Bello and Aramovsky press lightly against each other and back away, watching the sudden conflict.

I should say something, I know it, but my mouth doesn't move.

O'Malley's does.

"That's enough," he says.

Yong isn't the only grown man here. O'Malley holds the scepter in his right hand. He seems uncomfortable with the jeweled metal, like he doesn't really know what he's supposed to do with it in this situation.

He takes a step toward Yong.

"Hitting people is bad," O'Malley says. "Tell Spingate you're sorry."

Yong makes his *pfft* sound. "Or what? You going to make me apologize?"

O'Malley's fingers flex on the scepter. His shirt hangs open: the last button must have popped free.

"I'm not going to make you do anything," he says. "I just . . . we don't hit each other. Em's in charge, okay?"

Yong rushes at O'Malley, cocking his right fist as he does and slamming it into the bigger boy's nose. O'Malley's head rocks back. He drops awkwardly, sitting on his left foot, his right leg sticking out. Yong twists his shoulders, throws a left fist that hammers O'Malley's right eye.

O'Malley drops to his side. The scepter slides from his grip. He doesn't move.

Yong looks at me.

"I'm in charge now, Em." He again holds out his palm. "Give me the knife."

I see him, see the star on his forehead, the sneer on his lips. He thinks he can do anything he wants. He thinks he can push people around.

He thinks he *owns* people.

In that instant, I hate him. I want him to hurt.

He raises his eyebrows in mock surprise. "No? Don't think your turn is over? You led us *nowhere,* Em. I'm hungry and we're going to do it my way. Give me the knife, you stupid circle girl, or else."

Hate him. Hate him *hate him*.

I go cold inside. Cold and calm.

Yong shrugs. "Have it your way."

He strides toward me, confident and dangerous. Spingate is still sitting, staring. Aramovsky and Bello do nothing. Yong cocks back his fist, he sneers in fury and arrogance, he leans forward to punch at me . . .

He stops, fist still hovering in the air.

His eyes are wide, his mouth hangs open.

He looks down.

So do I.

The knife . . . the handle is in my hand, but the blade . . .

The blade is buried in his belly.

ELEVEN

Blazing red spreads across his white shirt, flowing down, mostly, but also rising up, wetness winding through the fabric.

I didn't even feel the blade go in. I didn't. It was just *there,* already inside him, like it had always been there.

The circle-in-a-circle disc on the knife hilt gleams under the ceiling's light, gems flickering the same color as Yong's blood.

The hallway is still. There is no noise at all. I can't move.

Yong looks up, looks at me. There are tears in his eyes. A grown man's face wearing a little boy's expression of fear and confusion.

"But . . . my turn," he says, then his legs stop working. He falls away from me. The knife, still in my hand, slides out of him. He lands on his shoulder, tucks up into a ball like he did when he fell out of his coffin.

I see a spot of blood spreading across his lower back, staining the white shirt wet-red.

The blade went all the way through.

That impossible stillness, that time turned to unforgiving stone, it lasts forever. Then it is gone.

Bello screams, hands covering her face.

Aramovsky takes a half-step behind Bello.

Spingate rushes to Yong, kneels next to him, her knees almost touching his. She leans over him, looks at his back.

"Oh, no," she says. "Yong! Lie flat, let me see the cut!"

Yong's hands clutch at his belly. The hands are mostly hidden by his thighs, but not enough that I can't see the blood covering his fingers.

He lets out a long, low moan. His eyes stay squeezed shut.

Spingate's hair hangs down, gets in the way. She rubs madly at her thighs like she doesn't know what to do with her hands, then slaps a palm hard on Yong's shoulder.

"I said, *lie flat!*"

Bello leans in, her cheeks glistening with tears. "Stop hitting him! *Do something!*"

Spingate shakes her head, again rubs hard at her thighs. She looks up at me.

"Em, don't just stand there, come help!"

The knife falls from my hand and clatters on the floor. Dust instantly clings to the blood that streaks the blade.

I kneel behind Yong's back.

"What do you want me to do?"

"Help me make him lie flat," Spingate says, her voice still rushed but now calmer that someone is doing this with her. "We have to put pressure on the wound."

She reaches under Yong's shoulder and his leg and lifts, while I grab a shoulder and a knee and pull. We roll him to his back. He's still curled up tight, the curve of his spine like the curve of an egg, and I have to hold him in place to keep him from flopping over again.

Yong starts to sob, the vibrations shaking his whole body. His mouth is wide open; a string of spit gleams between his lips.

"It hurts," he says. "It *hurts*."

Spingate puts a hand on his cheek, rapidly pets his black hair away from his forehead.

"Yong, listen to me," she says. "You've been stabbed. I have to look at the wound."

He shakes his head, as if to force her hand away.

"No, no it hurts! Make it stop!"

Spingate reaches up and backhand-flips her red hair behind her. She glares at Bello and Aramovsky.

"Come here and help us!"

Aramovsky rushes over, puts his hands on Yong's knees and gently pulls, trying to open the boy up.

"No," Yong says. "It *hurts*. Go get my mom . . . please go get my mom!"

He's pleading for something we can't give him. His voice sounds wrong: words like his belong to a voice that is higher and thinner than what we hear.

I feel wetness on my knees—his blood, spreading across the floor.

Spingate's upper lip curls in fury. She shakes Yong's shoulders, leans in and screams in his face.

"Relax your legs! Relax them!"

Bello reaches in, yanks at Spingate's arm.

"Stop it, Spingate! You don't even know what you're doing!"

Spingate whips her left arm back without looking, trying to brush Bello off, but her elbow cracks into the smaller girl's mouth. Bello's hands fly to her face. She turns, half bent over, and stumbles away.

I don't think Spingate even knows she hit her.

Aramovsky is patting Yong's knees as he pulls. "Open up,"

the tall boy says in a voice that's both deep and patient. "Open up."

Yong lets out a long moan, one that's chopped up into short bits by his chest-rattling sobs. His eyes are squeezed so tight. Snot drips from his nose, runs down his left lip and cheek.

He finally relaxes his legs, lets Aramovsky and me gently move them out of the way. He is flat on his back, body twitching slightly. His blood-drenched hands remain pressed hard against his stomach. From the chest down, his entire shirt is red.

Spingate grabs at Yong's neck, pulls off his tie and hands it to me.

"Press this against the wound when I get his hands out of the way," she says. "We need to stop the bleeding."

I take the tie.

Spingate again leans close to Yong's face.

"You have to move your hands," she says. "Okay? Move your hands."

Not knowing what else to do, I start petting his head like Spingate did, sliding my palm from his eyebrows back. Blood on my hand smears across his circle-star, gets into his hair.

His skin . . . it's cool, clammy, and not just from the blood. He's sweating.

I look at Spingate. "Do something!"

She tugs at his hands, trying to pull them away from his stomach. "I'm trying," she says. "Can't you see that I'm trying?"

Yong's hands won't budge. Spingate leans over them, pulls harder, but his hands stay in place, clutching so tight I wonder if his fingertips are punching through the skin, causing even more damage.

"Aramovsky," she says, "help me here."

He does as he's told, his black-skinned fingers wrapping

around Yong's blood-covered wrists, pulling them gently but insistently, overpowering Yong's resistance. Yong's fingers clutch at open air.

"Mom . . . it hurts."

Not as much energy in his words now. The *mom* comes out as a long, broken word: *maa-aaa-aahm.*

Spingate rips Yong's shirt open, sending buttons flying. His tan skin is a sheet of smeared red. She wipes her hands down his muscled belly, shoving away the blood, making him almost clean for a moment.

But only a moment, because red wells up out of a stab wound slightly above and to the left of his belly button. Gush, flow . . . gush, flow . . .

Spingate slaps my shoulder.

"Em! The tie!"

I shove it against the wound, so fast he cries out like I punched him there. I press the tie firmly, hoping it will do what Spingate said it would do.

Yong looks at me with unfocused eyes.

"Mom? Please . . . make it stop."

The words are weak. His hands relax, shift from clutching talons to limp fingers.

His eyes close. Did he pass out?

Spingate shakes him again.

"Yong! *Wake up!*"

The tie is already soaked, a wet washcloth that needs to be wrung out, but I keep it pressed in place.

"If he's asleep, he won't fight us," I say. "Why don't you want him to sleep?"

She looks at me, confused. "Why? I . . . I don't know. Just because."

Aramovsky glances at me, his eyes full of doubt. He doesn't think Spingate knows what she's doing. She doesn't, clearly, but none of us do.

Yong's entire body relaxes. His head tilts to the left. Aramovsky lowers Yong's hands, puts them on the floor next to his hips.

Spingate is breathing too fast. She shakes her head. "I'm twelve," she whispers. "I'm *twelve*."

She rubs at her thighs. I see tears dripping down her cheeks.

"Stop it," I hiss. "Crying doesn't fix anything. Help him!"

Spingate looks at me, a fast glance where she catches my eyes, then her hands go back to work. She places them flat on Yong's belly, one on either side of the tie.

"Em, lift it away, slowly," she says, and I do.

The blood burbles out suddenly, like we'd filled a balloon and then opened the end. The brief gush flows down his side. . . .

The gush that follows is much smaller.

I wait for the next one, but it doesn't come.

The bleeding has stopped.

I look at the tie in my hands: red fabric soaked with red, red that drips down onto Yong, onto my legs, onto the floor. Yong's blood has turned the dust beneath my knees from powder gray into a crimson slush.

Spingate blinks, like she just remembered something. She presses two fingers firmly to Yong's neck.

He doesn't react.

Aramovsky and I stare. Out of the corner of my eye, I see Bello coming closer, hand over her mouth, eyes wide, head shaking slightly.

Spingate moves her fingers, tries another spot. A *pulse*—that's what she's looking for, a pulse.

She moves her fingers again, to below his jaw, pressing them in so deep the skin and muscle of Yong's neck billow up on either side.

He doesn't move.

My eyes drift to the stab wound, the wound that I made.

A thin line of blood lies in it, pooled there, unmoving.

Spingate pulls her shaking hand away.

"He's . . . he's gone."

The word turns Yong from a person into a *thing*. I fall to my butt, scoot away, leaving a wide, smeared path through the red slush until my back hits the wall and I can go no farther.

I stare at the frightened little boy who wanted his mother.

Yong is dead.

I killed him.

TWELVE

don't know how long we sit there.

Spingate is crying. So is Bello, and this time I don't think she's being weak. I wonder if I should be crying, too, but no tears come.

Yong's blood is all over my shirt, my plaid skirt. Spingate is blood-smeared as well, with two prominent streaks on her ribs where she tried to wipe her hands clean after he died. I know it's not her own blood, and I know it's not the right way to think about it, but I'm almost glad she's finally dirty.

Aramovsky's shirt is spotless. Not a speck on it, not even a wrinkle.

"It's not your fault, Em," he says. "It was an accident."

"Of course it was," I snap.

But . . . was it?

I was so mad. Those feelings of hate, roiling through me. I wanted to hurt Yong. But if he hadn't rushed at me, if he hadn't tried to hit me, I wouldn't have done anything. So Aramovsky is right—it's not my fault.

Aramovsky stands, walks over to O'Malley, gently tries to wake the fallen boy.

I stare at Yong. I'm waiting for him to move, like this is a game and I've been tricked. He's going to sit up and smile, and everyone will laugh because they are all in on it.

But no one is laughing.

And Yong doesn't move.

Aramovsky helps O'Malley to his feet. Blood runs from O'Malley's nose, and more trickles from a cut over his right eye.

He stares down at Yong.

O'Malley looks at all of us in turn, as if he, too, is waiting for someone to tell him this is a game. I see his eyes flick from Yong to the bloody knife, back to Yong, and then to me.

"Em, what happened?"

I glare at him. He would know what happened if he hadn't got knocked out. Come to think of it, if he hadn't got knocked out, none of it would have happened at all. He can defend me with words, it seems, but not with his fists.

O'Malley doesn't look so beautiful anymore.

Aramovsky puts his hand on O'Malley's shoulder.

"Yong attacked Em," Aramovsky says. "She protected herself and stabbed him."

I'm on my feet so fast I don't recall trying to stand.

"I did *not* stab him! He ran into the knife. It was an accident, Aramovsky. An accident!"

My shouts bounce off the walls. Both Aramovsky and O'Malley lean back a little bit, away from me.

"An accident," Aramovsky says to O'Malley, and nods. "It was obviously an accident, like Em said. I suppose if Yong hadn't put you down, he wouldn't have attacked Em—he'd still be alive."

O'Malley winces. Did it hurt him to hear that? Good, it *should* hurt him.

"Spingate tried to save him," Aramovsky says. "The cut, it was very deep. There was nothing anyone could do."

O'Malley's expression remains blank. He stands there, bleeding. He steps to Yong, kneels in the crimson slush. He stares at the body, but talks to us.

"Why did he attack us like that? He went crazy."

No, he wasn't crazy—he wanted to lead. He wanted it bad enough that he had no problem hitting to get his way. Yong was a bully.

O'Malley stands. He brushes slush from his pants. He sniffs . . . he's crying. Not the noisy sobs of Bello and Spingate, but he doesn't try to hide the tears that line his cheeks.

"This is horrible," he says.

Then he looks at me. "So, Em . . . what now?"

Is he joking? I'm the leader who took us nowhere, who didn't find food, who put a knife in Yong's belly, and O'Malley still thinks I should decide?

Spingate is also looking at me. So is Bello, and Aramovsky.

They are all waiting.

Yes, I am the leader, and I should be. I'm the one making the decisions. I'm sorry Yong is dead, but that wasn't my fault—it was his.

"We go straight," I say.

I reach down and pick up the knife.

"*No*," Bello says, the word almost a scream. "I told you the knife was a bad thing. Leave it, Em, just *leave it*."

I ignore her. My skirt is ruined anyway, so I wipe the blade clean against it, first one side, then the other.

Spingate's stomach rumbles. She hangs her head, her face hidden by thick red curls.

I take a few steps down the hall, until my feet are once again on untouched gray.

The others hesitate.

"Let's go," I say. "We have to get moving."

O'Malley tilts his head down at Yong. "What about him? Do we carry him? Or maybe take him back to the coffin room, so he's not on the floor?"

The question makes our situation hit home: Yong is dead, and I'm going to leave him here. We don't know how far we have yet to walk. We have no food and no water. Our mouths are so dry our lips are starting to crack. We're already exhausted—we can't afford the energy needed to carry a dead body.

He'll be lonely here.

I try to chase away that thought, because it is the thought of a silly little girl. Yong is gone. I didn't like him, but he was one of us. Abandoning his body is wrong, I know it in my heart, but what choice do we have?

"No," I say. "I'm sorry, but we can't take him with us, and we're not going back. He's dead. He stays here."

O'Malley looks down at Yong, as if he wants to argue with me and his reasons for doing so are right there, somewhere on the body. He stares for a long while, thinking, then nods slowly.

"I guess you're right," he says. "But . . . I don't know, shouldn't we bury him or something?"

Spingate stands, flicks red slush from her clothes. "That would be a neat trick, O'Malley. Want to dig right through the floor?"

O'Malley wipes his face with the back of his hand, clearing off both blood and tears.

He looks down the dark hall.

"I can see an archway door," he says. "It looks open. There might be empty coffins inside."

I'd forgotten about that archway, just at the edge of the hall's dim light. O'Malley wants to put Yong in a coffin. I suppose that's better than leaving him here.

"All right," I say. "Do it quick and come right back."

He glances at me, questioning at first, then understanding. I can't touch Yong. I don't even want to be near him.

"Sure, Em," O'Malley says. "Aramovsky, will you help me?"

The taller boy nods.

"We should say a few words first," Aramovsky says. "While everyone is here with him."

Spingate huffs in disgust. "The dead don't care what you say."

She walks to me, stands by my side and waits.

Aramovsky presses his hands together, holds them near his chest. He closes his eyes and tilts his head back. There is something familiar about the gesture, another thing from our past that our memories won't reveal.

Spingate crosses her arms. "We're wasting time."

Bello points at her. "You shut up, Spingate. You think you're so smart, but you couldn't save Yong, could you?"

Spingate turns away as if Bello had slapped her.

"I tried," she says. "I tried."

O'Malley, Aramovsky and Bello are looking at me, waiting for permission.

"Make it quick," I say.

Aramovsky's hands drop to his waist.

"We're all afraid," he says. "Yong didn't choose to be here any more than the rest of us did. We will never know why he attacked us. No one meant for him to die. Today . . . today was his birthday."

The words themselves are meaningless. The way Aramovsky says them, though, the smooth, calm tone of his voice . . . his words are comforting.

We still have no idea what's going on, and this nightmare keeps getting worse, but like the rest of us, Yong was a twelve-year-old kid. It isn't my fault he's dead. Now that I think about it, it isn't his, either—the fault lies with whoever put us in those coffins and abandoned us in this dungeon.

"Thank you, Aramovsky," I say.

Bello can't stop crying. Her eyes are puffy and red. She kneels next to Yong. Her body trembling, she touches her forehead to his. She stays there for a moment. It's heartbreaking to watch. It almost brings me to tears.

But still, no tears come.

She stands. Head hung low, Bello moves past me.

Yong lays alone in a trampled, smeared ring of crimson slush. Now he's just like the Grownups we left behind: a victim of violence, dead because a knife punched a hole in his body.

I wonder how long it will be before he crumbles to dust.

There is nothing else we can do here. I look at O'Malley, tilt my head toward the dark hall.

O'Malley grabs Yong's wrists. Aramovsky takes his ankles. Together, they walk down the dim hall, the dead boy a shallow curve between them, his head hanging limply and jostling with every step.

They carry him away.

Bello, Spingate and I wait. It doesn't take long. O'Malley and Aramovsky come back—without Yong. I don't know if they left him in a coffin, but they left him, and I feel relieved.

The two boys join us. Aramovsky still doesn't have any blood on him, but his expression is different. He's seen something that frightened him, disturbed him.

I look to O'Malley. He won't meet my eyes. I know what he and Aramovsky saw—more murdered children.

"All the coffins had been torn open," Aramovsky says. His voice sounds different, like the last bit of breeze before a gust of wind fades away completely. "We found one where the lid still moved. We put Yong inside and pushed the lid closed. It clicked shut. He is at rest."

I wonder if they put him on top of a skeleton, or moved the skeleton to the floor so Yong could lie alone. I decide I don't want to know.

"Time to leave," I say.

I turn and move down the hall. The others follow. This time, O'Malley stays with them.

I walk out in front, alone.

THIRTEEN

We walk uphill.

We are covered in blood.

Bello's lower lip is swollen and split.

O'Malley's nose has stopped bleeding, but a few drops still ooze from the cut over his eye.

The hallway goes on and on. The dust is endless.

There has to be a way out of this place. There has to be.

My mouth is dry and pasty. I'm so thirsty. I'm not hungry anymore, but I think that's not a good thing. My head hurts.

The others are in the same shape. They shuffle more than walk. They look beyond tired, with dry lips and sunken eyes. Maybe we were all perfect when we woke up, but not anymore.

If we don't find water soon, will we be able to keep walking?

And we need to sleep. If we find any coffin rooms farther up, maybe we'll rest for a while.

Every few steps, I see Yong's wide eyes, the look of disbelief on his face.

It was an accident. Everyone thinks so. There was nothing I

could have done. He ran into the knife. He did. He was going to hit me. Was I supposed to let him?

I look at my hand, the right one, the one that holds the knife. His blood—dry now—is in the folds of my knuckles, mixed in with the dust and tacky sweat that covers me head to toe.

I've never been this dirty. I've never been this sweaty and disgusting. I've never been this afraid, this thirsty, this alone.

I haven't been a good leader, but four people are counting on me to take them to safety. I don't know if I'm twelve or if I'm twenty and I don't think age matters anymore. We are the only ones here.

There is a way out. I *will* find a way out.

Behind me, I hear sniffling. I turn, expecting to see Bello crying yet again, but it's not her—it's Spingate.

I stop. So do the others.

"You did everything you could for him," I tell her. "At least you did something. The rest of us were useless."

She shakes her head.

"It's not that. It's just . . . maybe they're all dead."

Aramovsky puts his arm around her shoulders. "All who is dead?"

"All the Grownups," Spingate says. "I'm so tired. I don't want to do this anymore. But if they're gone, then there's no one left to rescue us."

"We'll be all right," Aramovsky says, then glares at me like I'm the one who made Spingate cry. "Em is our leader. She says she knows what she's doing."

I've said no such thing. Is he trying to make a point? I'm starting to think that Aramovsky says one thing but means another.

Bello's hands come together again, clutching and turning in constant motion.

"What if Spingate is right?" she says. "If there are no Grown-ups, what are we going to do?"

Aramovsky nods. "Yes, Savage, what then? Who is going to take care of us?"

We all saw each other's coffins; everyone knows my last name, but Aramovsky is the first to speak it. Even I haven't said it out loud. I don't like that name and I don't know why. Hearing it makes me uncomfortable. I think he knew that it would . . . so why did he do it?

Because he wants to make me look bad in front of the others.

Anger flames in my chest.

He's challenging my leadership, that's what he's doing. He thinks *he* should be in charge.

My fingers flex on the knife handle.

Cold fury sweeps over me, an urge to teach Aramovsky a lesson—then I recognize that feeling, and when I do it vanishes, replaced by a shudder of realization.

It was exactly how I felt when Yong came at me.

In the shameful calmness that follows, I understand that Aramovsky wasn't challenging me. He was just talking. There is no harm in that. And even if he *was* challenging my leadership, that's okay as long as he's not hitting anyone. If I'm not the right leader, then someone else is. I don't care who is in charge. I want to get out of this place.

"Maybe there aren't any Grownups," I say. "If that's true, then we will survive without them."

They stare at me like my words are as unknown as their first names. Even Aramovsky's glare dissolves into astonishment. Is it really so impossible to think that we can make it on our own?

I point behind them, back the way we came.

"You want someone to take care of us? Were the people who

died back there supposed to do that? You saw what they did to each other. They murdered little kids in their coffins. If the Grownups are all gone . . ."

I hesitate, knowing I am about to say something none of them want to hear. Saying it might make this *real*. Maybe I can't remember anything, but I know that reality is what it is whether we like it or not.

"If the Grownups are really gone, well, then *good*," I say. "We don't need them. We don't need someone else to rescue us . . . we can rescue ourselves."

I feel my face flush, so I turn and start walking again. *Rescue ourselves?* I suddenly feel like an idiot. We don't know where we are, don't know *who* we are. We're kids—we're not supposed to be on our own.

After what I just said, will the others still follow?

Four sets of feet shuffling along behind me answer my question.

Aramovsky falls in on my left.

"Maybe the Grownups didn't do it to themselves," he says quietly. Then, louder: "Maybe . . . maybe it was a *monster*."

The word hits us hard. A word made of shapeless forms, woven from fear. *Monster* is all the things we don't understand, and right now, we don't understand anything.

"Spare us," Spingate says. "There's no such thing as monsters."

Aramovsky looks over his shoulder at her. "Really? And how do you know there aren't monsters?"

"There just aren't," Spingate says. "Monsters are something only babies believe in."

Aramovsky and Spingate start to argue, but I don't hear their words: far up ahead, I see something, a break in the floor-meets-ceiling illusion.

This time, I know what it is.

"There's another corridor up ahead," I say.

Their argument stops instantly.

Suddenly I'm not quite as tired. I pick up the pace, walking so fast I'm almost jogging. I don't care if this new hallway is like the last one—dim, maybe even dark—but we're going that way because I am desperate to see something different.

For the first time since Yong died, I find O'Malley at my right side.

"Em, maybe we should take it this time."

"We'll see," I say.

I don't know why I said that, because I've already made up my mind to do exactly what he wants.

The sound of our footsteps fills the hall with a soft thudding. We close in, kicking up a trail of dust that hangs behind us.

Then, over the sound of our running, I hear something else.

I slow quickly, plant my feet and slide to a stop, my arms out to the sides to keep anyone from running past me.

"Em, *watch out*," O'Malley says as he stutter-steps to avoid the knife blade that almost touches his belly.

I start to apologize, but Aramovsky runs into me from behind. He grabs my shoulders, keeps me from falling forward.

"Sorry," he says. "You stopped so fast."

Bello is on my left, hands wringing. "Em, what's going on?"

I glare at them all, hold a finger to my lips.

They fall quiet.

We stand still. No steps, no words, not even breathing.

In the silence, I hear the noise again. Faint at first, but quickly growing louder. It's coming from the intersection of the new hallway.

It is the heavy sound of footsteps marching in time.

FOURTEEN

want to run, but I stop myself because it won't do any good. There are no doors, there is no end to this hallway, nowhere to hide. As soon as the marchers turn the corner, they will see us.

The sound draws closer.

(If you run, your enemy will hunt you. . . .)

That phrase again, rolling through my thoughts. Whose voice is it? One more thing I can't remember.

And yet I know the voice speaks the truth. As exhausted as we are, as thirsty and as hungry, I don't think we could run very far or very fast. Whoever is coming can either see our backs and know we're afraid, or see the knife and know we are dangerous.

I press close to the right-side wall, knife out in front of me. O'Malley stands a step behind me, at my left shoulder, holding the scepter like a club. I instantly understand he is not behind me because he is afraid, but rather because he is following my lead, staying close to the wall so we are a little less obvious. If danger comes, I know he will try to step out front and face it first, because he is so much bigger than I am.

Maybe he isn't any good at fighting, but that doesn't stop him from standing with me. He's so close I can sense him, feel his body heat. He is sweaty and stinky. His scent, it's new, something different from the way boys smelled back in my limited memories of school. It's distracting—almost as if I like it, but he doesn't smell good. I feel my heart in my throat, pounding all the way into my stomach. Is that because of the danger, or also because of him?

I clench my teeth and readjust the knife in my hand. We're in trouble, I need to focus.

Bello pulls at my left arm.

"Em, let's *go*! What if it's the Grownups?"

I yank my arm away. I don't have time to explain to her that a voice in my head—a memory—is guiding me, and I know its words are true.

"We don't run," I say. "Whoever is coming, we face them."

Bello starts to cry. Of course she does. She moves behind O'Malley to stand with Aramovsky and Spingate.

The marching footsteps sound so close, like the steady beat of a big drum.

A thought grips me: what if Aramovsky is right, what if there *are* monsters? Spingate doesn't know for sure that monsters don't exist. No one does. Visions of claws and fangs and wild eyes flash before me, a horde of beasts flowing down the hall, searching for helpless children to carry away and devour.

But I'm not a child anymore.

And I'm not helpless.

The marchers come out of the hall and turn to their right, away from us.

Not monsters . . . *people.*

Two columns of beautiful people dressed like us, led by the biggest person I've ever seen. They all turn to their right, away from us, so focused on matching their steps that they don't even look our way.

The sense of relief is so overwhelming I almost laugh at myself for believing in Aramovsky's nonsense.

The leader carries a long stick and marches with precise, loud steps. His skin has only a little more color than pale Bello's. Gleaming blond curls cling to his head so tightly they don't move when he walks.

I count nineteen people: two lines of nine, with the big blond in front.

We stay very still. Maybe the marchers won't see us at all.

I almost have time to turn and tell everyone to be quiet, but before I do Spingate shouts out.

"Hey! Over here!"

My heart sinks.

The marching lines stop. They are not so ordered now: Spingate startled them. They shift out of their lines, afraid, some suddenly holding each other.

"Spingate, you idiot," I hear Aramovsky hiss from behind me. "Why did you do that?"

"They're the same as us," she answers. "We can all work together."

The blond boy runs to the back of his lines, puts himself between us and his fellow marchers. He points the stick at us, and I see it ends in a wicked blade; it's not a stick, it's a spear.

He has a circle-star on his forehead.

He raises the spear high.

"Everyone, *follow me!*" he screams, then sprints toward us. Two of the marchers are right behind him, a boy and a girl, both with short, glossy black hair and caramel-colored skin. The rest of them don't move; they stand in the hall, unsure of what to do.

My feet feel stuck to the floor. O'Malley tugs at my arm, urging me to run away, but I can't move. The blond boy charges: he's going to shove that spearpoint into my belly and I will wind up like Yong, on the floor, dead and cold and alone, crumbling away into dust.

I'm going to die and I haven't even learned my first name.

The spear-wielding boy slows, stops a few steps from us. He's looking at me, but *down*—I realize I'm holding the knife out, point first.

Even through my fear, I notice the shape of his face. He is beautiful in a way that is different from O'Malley; this boy is bigger, stronger, his shoulders and neck are thicker. There is a bruised bump on the right side of his heavy jaw.

All our clothes are too small for us, but the blond boy's shirt is buttoned only at the waist; his broad chest stretches the fabric into a wide V. The sleeves are so tight I think his big arms might rip them apart at any moment. With even his smallest motion, I see muscles flutter beneath smooth skin.

He stands there. He had one strategy: *charge*. That didn't work, and now he doesn't know what to do.

Maybe I won't die after all.

"Hello," I say.

He blinks. "Uh . . . hello."

I lower my knife to my side.

"I'm Savage," I say. This time, that seems like the right name to use.

The boy sets the butt of the spear on the floor and angles the shaft back until the blade points straight to the ceiling. He looks at me like he doesn't know what to make of me. He's not angry, not suspicious . . . he's more *confused* than anything else.

"You didn't run," he says.

I shake my head. "No, I didn't. What's your name?"

He pauses a moment, maybe waiting for me to change my

mind, to suddenly turn and sprint away from him. When I don't, he shrugs.

"I think my name is Bishop," he says.

He *thinks* that's his name? He doesn't know any more than we do.

"R. Bishop," he says. "That's what was written on my cradle."

"Cradle?"

The word makes me think of babies, even smaller than the little ones we saw in the other room.

He nods. "We were lying in them when we woke up."

"Oh," I say. "You mean the coffins."

He stares at me, then smiles. "*Coffins?* That's not very happy, now is it?"

I realize that he's the only one in the hallway not wearing a red tie.

His eyes are a strange color: yellow, a bit darker than the curly blond hair matted to his head. His eyes catch the light, almost seem to glow.

That symbol on his forehead . . . he's a circle-star, like Yong was. The two hard-eyed people behind him, the boy and the girl, are also circle-stars. Will they try to take over like Yong did? Will they hit people to get what they want?

Bishop looks past me, taking in the others. "Are there more of you?"

I almost say, *There were six of us,* then Yong's dying face is all I can see.

"Just five," I say, forcing the vision away. "There's nineteen of you?"

He looks back down the hall, realizes that only two of his marchers came with him. He shakes his head in disgust.

"Depends on how you count," he says. He leans close to me,

speaks quietly. "Most of them aren't worth much of anything, except for El-Saffani here." He gestures to the boy and the girl.

They talk, the girl first, then the boy. "We are strong—"

"—stronger than the others—"

"—except for Bishop."

Their eyes look exactly alike, dark-lined with heavy eyebrows and deep-brown irises. They are lean and firm, built for speed rather than pure strength. The boy is slightly taller than the girl. They both still seem ready to fight even though their leader is relaxed and smiling.

Two people, but he only said one name.

"Which one is El-Saffani?" I ask.

"They both are," Bishop says. "That's what was on their cradles, *T. El-Saffani* and *T. El-Saffani*."

They're twins.

Bishop's eyes take in my clothes, twitch over to Spingate's shirt, Bello's lip, O'Malley's cut.

"How did you all get so bloody? Was there a fight?"

The rest of the marchers are slowly coming closer. There is no blood on their shirts. None on Bishop or El-Saffani, either. This group has had an easier time than mine, it seems.

"An accident," I say, and glance back at the others—especially Spingate—silently telling them to stay quiet. The new people don't need to know about Yong, at least not right now.

Bishop shrugs. He smiles wide, a smile that would be more at home on the face of a little boy than on the face of a grown man. His chest puffs up, straining the last button of his too-small shirt.

He raises the spear high until the point almost touches the glowing ceiling.

"Savage, I like you. You and your friends can join my tribe."

Tribe: a word of power.

He charged us, screaming, furious, weapon in hand—ready to attack, I'm sure of it—and now he acts like this is recess and we're all pals?

"Why are you raising the spear?" I ask.

My question confuses him for a moment.

"That's how we make announcements," he says, as if that is completely obvious. "When you raise the spear, everyone has to listen. Those are the rules."

O'Malley takes a step forward, stands shoulder to shoulder with me. He seemed so big when I first met him. But compared to Bishop, O'Malley doesn't look that big at all.

"Join *your* tribe?" O'Malley says. His blue eyes narrow. "Maybe you should join *our* tribe."

Bishop stares at O'Malley like those words make no sense.

"But I've got the spear. That means I'm the leader." He holds it up, not threatening, but rather showing it to us as if we had somehow missed seeing it altogether.

O'Malley gestures to me.

"So?" he says. "Savage has the knife."

Something about all of this makes my stomach churn. *Spears and knives. Tribes.* The beginnings of an argument . . . an argument about who should lead. That's how it started with Yong. Things are heading in a bad direction. I have to do something to prevent that.

"No one needs to join anyone else's tribe," I say.

My words confuse Bishop even more. He's getting mad.

"Someone has to be in charge," he says. "There have to be rules. That's how things work."

His fingers flex on the spear handle. I know, somehow, that if R. Bishop gets angry enough, my friends could get hurt.

A girl gently pushes through the marchers. Her skin is pale, but without Spingate's pinkish hue. The tone is hard to define, a brown-tan that borders on white, but is clearly not. She is my height—does my skirt look as short as hers? Her long muscles flutter with even the slightest move, especially on her powerful legs. Her hair is unlike anyone else's: long, kinky curls that puff out wider and wider before they end at her smooth, toned shoulders. She's not smiling now, but when she does, I know it will be stunning.

She has a circle-star on her forehead.

There is no blood on her shirt, but there is a big, bluish bruise on her right cheekbone. Other than that, she appears to be fine—except for her lips, which are dry and chapped just like ours.

I realize that all the new kids have dry lips, even Bishop.

"Do you have any water?" the girl asks.

Bishop scowls at her.

"Shut up, Latu. I do the talking."

She glares back at him, defiant. "Maybe you should do less talking and more leading, Bishop. We're thirsty."

He sighs. "Do you want what happened last time to happen again?"

"I don't know," Latu says. "Do you?"

She is solid and could probably beat me to a pulp, but Bishop is nearly twice her size. Anger pours off her: so does fear. Has she already fought him and lost?

"I'm a good leader," Bishop says. "You don't see blood all over *our* shirts, do you?"

Bishop is trying to act like Latu doesn't bother him, but he's not a convincing faker. He's getting angrier by the second. El-Saffani watches him, as if the twins are waiting to see what he does. They are wound up tight. They look ready to attack, just like Yong was. Are all the circle-stars like that?

I need to get Bishop thinking about something other than O'Malley and Latu.

"Bishop, where did your group come from?"

He points behind him, to the new hallway. "From there."

Obviously they came from there. That's not the information I was hoping for.

"We keep turning," says boy El-Saffani.

"Bishop said it's good to turn," says girl El-Saffani.

Another boy laughs, a cutting sound that makes me feel stupid even though I have nothing to do with their group.

Bishop turns, stabs a finger toward the source.

"Shut up, Gaston. I told you not to laugh at me."

A boy slides through the marchers packed in behind Bishop and Latu. He's small, even smaller than I am. His white shirt fits perfectly. All the buttons are buttoned, his sleeves are the right length, and his red tie is nice and neat. His left eye is puffy and bruised.

His symbol is the same as Spingate's: a jagged circle.

"I'm not laughing at you, Bishop," Gaston says. "I remembered a joke, that's all. It's really funny. It goes like this. Once upon a time there was this really big, really *stupid* kid that liked to hit people. He kept making all of these turns without knowing where he was going, and—"

Bishop takes a step toward Gaston. Gaston moves fast, melts away behind the bigger kids in his group and is instantly out of sight.

"That's what I thought," Bishop says.

He glances back to the intersection. When he and his friends were marching, he was so self-assured, like he was carved from confidence. A little bit of teasing, and now he seems full of doubt.

"Maybe we should go back," Bishop says quietly. "There

were a couple of turns where we . . . maybe we should try that way again."

Latu shakes her head, shakes it hard.

"I'm not going back," she says. "I'm *not*."

Her wide eyes burn with fierce determination born from true terror.

I see nods of agreement among Bishop's group, faces filled with fear. Even El-Saffani's cold expressions shift into something normal—they are children again, little kids terrified by something they want to forget.

"What did you see?" I ask, even though I suspect they saw the same things we did.

Bishop licks his dry lips. He stares absently at the wall.

"Rooms," he says. "Rooms filled with skeletons. Some of the bones looked like they'd been cut into pieces."

I nod. "That's what we saw, too."

He continues talking as if I said nothing at all.

"There was one strange room. We got to it through a door in the floor. Went down a ladder. Gaston was the only one who could get it open. That room and some of the others had these . . . uh . . . Gaston, what did you call them?"

Gaston slides out of the crowd again, but keeps his distance from Bishop.

"Pedestals," he says. He holds his hand at his sternum, palm down, showing how tall they were. "Made of white stone. The way they were placed in the rooms, they seemed . . . important. Like a really important statue is supposed to rest on them, you know? But all the pedestals were cracked or broken—except for three that were in the room with the ladder. But that place . . ."

His voice trails off. He looks afraid, more afraid even than Latu.

"Something in the room scared you," I say. "What was it?"

Gaston starts to talk, then stops. He looks at Bishop, who won't meet his eyes. Maybe these two don't like each other, but something happened down there that unsettled them both.

"A body," Gaston says quietly. "All shriveled up, just bones and skin. It was facedown, sprawled out. It had clothes on that I think were white, but the . . ."

He pauses, rubs his face, then continues.

"The *juices* stained the clothes, made the cloth different colors. The body had some kind of metal shackle on one arm, with a thin point sticking out of it, but the shackle wasn't chained to anything." He nods toward Bishop's spear. "That was in the dead guy's back, shoved through so hard it stuck in the floor."

Bishop got his weapon the same way I got mine—out of a person that died from it.

For some reason, I want to make this smaller boy feel better. Maybe he's embarrassed he was afraid, but there is nothing to be embarrassed about.

"We saw dead bodies, too," I say. "Bodies are frightening."

Gaston glances upward, thinking, then shakes his head.

"No," he says. "Well, yes, the body was all shriveled up and disgusting and scary, but it wasn't that. It was the room itself. Just Bishop and I went down. It was really dark, and round, and . . . well, there was something *wrong* with it, is all."

"Haunted," Bishop says quietly. "It's haunted."

Gaston rolls his eyes. "Bishop, there's no such thing as ghosts. What are you, ten years old?"

Bishop snarls at him. "Oh yeah? If there's no such thing as ghosts, then why did you scramble up that ladder so fast, huh? You almost peed your pants."

Gaston says nothing. I can tell he wants to give an explanation, tell everyone what exactly was wrong with the room, but he can't. I get the feeling Gaston thinks he knows everything.

When there is something he doesn't know, something that he *feels* instead of sees, it bothers him. I will have to remember that.

Latu crosses her arms. "Enough talk. I'm not going back. I don't want to see any more bones."

Bishop shakes off his memories of the strange room. He forces a smile. Once again he is the big-chested, broad-shouldered, brave king of the playground.

"We missed something is all," he says. "There's probably bones all over this place. We *are* going back. When we get to the hall that leads to the haunted room, we'll go the other way. Simple."

Before meeting the marchers, I knew I wanted to travel down the new hall. But Bishop's group came from there, and they didn't find any food or water. They also seem to be a bit lost—same thing could happen to us if we go that way. And I have to agree with Latu: I don't want to see any more bodies. Maybe it's best if I stick to my original plan.

Up can't go on forever.

I start to point down the long hall behind me, then realize I'm using the knife to do that. I stop myself and use my free hand instead.

"We came from that way. We're following this hall until it ends. I think if we turn too much, we won't know which way we're going."

The El-Saffani twins look at each other. The rest of Bishop's friends exchange glances. Is it possible this never occurred to them?

"We'll keep going straight," I say. "You are all welcome to join us if you want."

Bishop's expression changes. He looks at me with admiration, but also something else . . . like I have challenged his authority, and he has to do something about that.

He steps closer. He's a full head taller than I am. I have to look up to meet his strange yellow eyes. O'Malley bristles; he's as wound up as El-Saffani.

Bishop smiles down at me.

"You are brave," he says. "You didn't run. Almost everyone runs from me. Our groups should stay together. There is strength in numbers. You and your friends will come with us."

He thinks I'm brave? It's almost funny. The biggest person I've ever seen rushed at me, screaming, thrusting a spear: I couldn't even move, and he mistakes that for courage. Well, whatever he thinks, we're not going to start blindly wandering around this place.

I square my shoulders and stare up at him.

"I told you where we are going, Bishop."

That half-confused, half-angry look comes over his face again.

"But I carry the spear. That means I'm in charge."

O'Malley leans in. "Maybe someone else should carry it."

Bishop smiles at him. It is a very different smile from the one he gave me.

"You could take it out of my hand," he says to O'Malley. "If you do, then *you're* in charge."

O'Malley holds the scepter at his side. He nervously grips and re-grips the jeweled shaft.

Bishop glances down at the scepter, almost eagerly, like he hopes O'Malley will take the first swing.

"I like Savage," Bishop says. "I don't like you. What's your name?"

"O'Malley."

"That's a pretty weapon, O'Malley," Bishop says. "Nice and sparkly."

This is going to end in blood. Just like with Yong.

I can prevent a fight—all I have to do is let Bishop lead. All I have to do is say the words, and no one will get hurt.

But I can't, because I *want* to be the leader.

Still smiling at O'Malley, Bishop closes his eyes. "Why don't you hit me with your sparkly weapon? I'm not even looking. You'll probably knock me out with one shot, then you can take the spear."

Bishop is daring him. I see O'Malley considering it, brow furrowing, eyes flitting from the bridge of Bishop's nose to his temple to his jaw, looking for the best place to strike. Beads of sweat break out on O'Malley's forehead, darkening the dust coating his skin. We're about to slide into a huge fight. He's going to swing, blood will spill, blood all over. . . .

Then, O'Malley visibly relaxes. The stress vanishes from his features. His face is once again blank, expressionless.

"I have a better idea, Bishop," he says. "You insist on all of us staying together, so why don't all of us decide who gets to be in charge?"

Bishop's eyes open. His smile fades.

"How can *everyone* decide? That's the point of having a leader in the first place, to make decisions. Isn't it?"

O'Malley nods. "That is the point. But sticking together was *your* idea, right?"

Bishop looks suspicious. "Yes, but I still don't know what you're saying."

Gaston crosses his arms, grins.

"He means we take a *vote,* Bishop," the boy says. "That way no one gets hurt."

Bishop glances at the others in his group. This situation is getting away from him, and he knows it. It's not that he's stupid, because I can tell he's not, but at the same time, he's not as smart as O'Malley. Not even close.

Bishop thinks for a moment, then nods.

"All right, fine, we can vote. I organized eighteen people. Savage, you organized four. So I win the vote." His chest puffs out. "I am the leader."

Gaston shakes his head. "The only reason you were in charge in the first place was because if we didn't agree with you, you hit us. You didn't *organize* people, you oversized idiot, you *bullied* them."

I glance around at the other new faces. No, no one has blood on their shirts, but through the caked-on dust I see a few bruises, a few puffy lips. The bruise on Latu's cheek . . . it's about the size of Bishop's big hand if that hand formed a big fist.

Bishop seems annoyed, exasperated, like he can't fathom why everyone doesn't understand basic facts.

"I made decisions," he says. "If someone doesn't make decisions, then no decisions get made."

In that instant, I know Bishop and I are more alike than we are different. Someone has to make decisions—but that someone shouldn't be him.

Gaston points at me. "She has a plan. You have us wandering around, but everyone is too afraid of you to say anything."

I see some of Bishop's friends nodding. Only some, though— there are several with circle-stars like his, like Yong's, like El-Saffani's. None of those people agree.

I glance at O'Malley, my eyes asking him if I should say something. O'Malley shakes his head ever so slightly, barely a twitch left, then right. His blue eyes stare hard into me. He wants me to let everyone keep talking.

So I remain quiet.

Bishop gestures down the hall. "All Savage is doing is walking straight. Where's the adventure in that?"

Now the other circle-stars nod. They want adventure, too. I

count quickly: including Bishop, El-Saffani and Latu, eight people have circle-stars. There is one girl with the circle-cross, like Brewer, one more boy with the jagged circle like Gaston and Spingate, two half-circles like O'Malley, and six empty circles like Bello and me. Aramovsky is the only circle-in-a-circle— I wonder which way he'll vote.

Bishop turns to face his friends. His shoulders draw back and his chest sticks out. He talks to them, not in a shout but not far from one.

"Who wants to walk straight? That's dumb. The more we turn, the more area we cover. Come on, we're going to find something soon. We missed something is all. We'll go back and turn a different way."

The members of Bishop's group who do not have circle-stars stare down, glance around the hallway, cast their gaze anywhere but at him. They won't meet his eyes.

I finally understand why O'Malley wants me to keep quiet— Bishop is losing the vote all by himself. But I can't rely on that, I have to say something. If I can get these people on my side, I can end this without a fight. If, that is, Bishop actually accepts the vote.

"We don't need *adventure*," I say. "We need to get out of this place."

I see faces change instantly, I see wide-eyed admiration.

Gaston raises his hand. "I vote for Savage," he says, still glaring at Bishop. "Who else votes for Savage?"

Bello, Aramovsky, O'Malley and Spingate raise their hands. So do Latu and everyone in Bishop's group that is not a circle-star.

Gaston points at each, counting slowly and loudly. *Too* loudly, as if he's enjoying what is an already obvious result.

"That's sixteen for Savage. Now, raise your hand if you want Bishop."

Seven arms go up, including Bishop's. He has lost, but all the circle-stars except for Latu voted for him. They glare at me: four boys, two girls. The circle-star boys are taller than most of us, thick with muscle. The girl circle-stars are toned and lean—they look like they could probably beat O'Malley or Aramovsky in a fistfight.

Without the knife, I wouldn't stand a chance against any of them.

If the circle-stars ignore the vote and follow Bishop, it's going to be a problem.

I realize that I didn't vote, but it doesn't matter.

Gaston nods. "Sixteen votes for Savage, seven for Bishop." His mouth twists into something that is half smile, half sneer. "Savage won. She's the leader. Bishop, give her the spear."

Bishop's eyes narrow. His cracked lips flatten, his nostrils flare. At that moment, he is even more frightening than when he ran at me, screaming. Violence bubbles under the surface. For a second, I wonder if he's going to stab the spear into Gaston's belly.

"It's mine," Bishop says. "The spear is mine."

O'Malley points at it. "You said the leader carries the spear. Em is the leader, so give it to her."

O'Malley's words sound far different from Gaston's. There is no malice or arrogance in O'Malley's voice, just an infuriatingly calm delivery of what everyone already knows.

The spear shaft starts to shake: Bishop is squeezing it so hard his arm trembles. He likes being the leader.

And, I realize, so do I.

For a long moment, I am sure this will erupt in a battle that ends with our bones scattered across the hallway. Then Bishop closes his eyes. He tilts the spear toward me.

I take it. I can do this. I can lead us.

I hand my knife to O'Malley. O'Malley hands the scepter to Spingate. Gaston seems to see the scepter for the first time; his eyes go wide with recognition.

Bishop shakes his head, then nods. He lets out a big, cheek-puffing breath. The pending violence inside him evaporates. He's already over it. His face shows whatever he is feeling as plainly as if he's speaking it out loud.

"Okay, Savage, you won," he says. "Fair is fair. You're the leader. So, what now?"

I heft the spear in one hand, feeling the weight. Maybe I should make the scepter the symbol of leadership again: a tool rather than a weapon. But no, Spingate knows how to use the scepter better than I do, and a part of me realizes that there has to be *something* to signify who is in charge.

I was the leader of four other people. Now I am the leader of twenty-three. Everyone seems to want to follow me, and I don't know why. Whatever the reason, I will not let them down.

Not sure of what I'm supposed to do, I mimic what Bishop did; I raise the spear.

"We go straight," I say.

I walk.

They follow.

FIFTEEN

We walk uphill.

And we walk, and we walk, and we walk.

It doesn't make sense—even if our coffin room was far below ground, shouldn't we have made it to the surface by now? And we still haven't seen any windows, any hint of the outside.

My feet hurt. They were numb from the constant walking, but when we met Bishop's group we stopped for a bit: it was like blood flowed into them again. My feet thought they were getting a rest. Now that I've put them back into action, they are not happy. It feels like my bones will soon wear right through muscle and skin.

I hear the others talking behind me, my group and Bishop's marchers alike, saying out loud the same things that run through my head. They know they have families, but can't remember any faces. They know they went to school, but can't recall what classes they took, their teachers, their classmates . . . no specifics of any kind.

They want to know what their symbols mean.

They want to know their first names.

As we walk, I try to meet some of the new people. There is K. Smith, the only circle-cross, a girl so thin she looks like she's on the edge of starvation. She has stunning gray eyes, olive skin and short brown hair. She's the tallest girl among us, almost as tall as O'Malley.

G. Beckett has tan skin and strawberry-blond hair. His symbol is a jagged circle, like Spingate's and Gaston's. Beckett doesn't say much. He seems younger than me—not in size, but rather in the way he carries himself.

There are six empty circles besides Bello and me: E. Okereke, a boy with the blackest skin of any of us; Y. Johnson, a girl with dirty-blond hair who won't look anyone in the eye and mumbles to herself; R. Cabral, a girl who looks anyone and everyone in the eye but says nothing; and O. Ingolfsson, a squat blond boy who looks as strong as Bishop, although he isn't as tall and clearly isn't as coordinated. The last two circles are J. Harris and M. D'souza, a boy/girl pair who go out of their way to avoid talking with me.

The circle-stars hate that I won the vote. Most ignore me. The bald, brown-skinned girl, Y. Bawden, will answer my questions, but she doesn't trust me. At least she isn't openly hostile: U. Coyotl—whose tan skin has a reddish hue that looks like his mother gave him a bath and scrubbed him way too hard—and W. Visca—a big boy with light pink skin and blazing white hair—all but snarl at me every time I look at them.

The person who surprises me the most, though, is Bishop. I expected him to carry a grudge, maybe plot a way to take back the spear or fight me for leadership the way Yong did. Bishop does none of that. He's happy. He's talkative. In fact, he won't *stop* talking. His constant chatter is the only thing that raises everyone's spirits.

Time drags, as do our feet. I honestly don't know how much longer we can go on.

It is maybe five or six hours after I got the spear that the first of us falls: a half-circle girl named Q. Opkick.

Before I can reach her, Bishop already has her over his shoulder. He's smiling, nodding, like someone passing out from lack of food or water—or both—is the most normal thing that could happen.

More will fall, and soon. All we can do for Opkick is press on, so we press on.

My feet . . . they hurt so bad.

Perhaps an hour later, I almost fall myself. I stumble, but O'Malley catches me, rights me. He does that strange thing again, where he can kind of speak to me with his eyes. Those eyes say: *Don't fall—if you do, we're lost.*

I nod. I can keep going.

And then, finally, far up ahead, our hallway . . . it *ends.*

I move faster. So do the others, headaches and thirst and dry mouths forgotten. When Bishop had his group marching in step, it made a sound like the steady beat of a big drum. I don't make anyone march: as we quicken our pace and break into a run, it sounds like rolling thunder.

The hallway ends in a dusty, rusted archway blocked by two stone slabs, a thin line down the middle separating them.

A door.

We stop. We stare. It could be nothing. It could be everything.

Is this it? Did we make it? Does the door lead us out of this horrible place? Does it lead to food and water and people, maybe our parents?

"Bishop," I say, "give Opkick to someone else. I need you up front with me."

O'Malley glances my way, a sour expression on his face. He doesn't like that I want Bishop up front, but that's stupid—Bishop is the biggest and strongest of us, of course he should be the first through.

Bishop joins me at the door. El-Saffani is at his sides. The twins came without being asked. Where Bishop goes, they go.

I look back to Spingate.

"Open it," I say to her.

She nods rapidly, excited at this new puzzle she must solve. She brushes dust off the metal frame, exposing embedded jewels. She studies the archway for a moment. I see her lips moving. She starts pressing blue jewels. She shakes her head—she got it wrong.

Gaston joins her. He points at a pair of yellow jewels. Spingate nods, presses them. Then she presses a green one: a hidden panel pops open.

Inside the panel, two dark holes.

She looks at me, asking for permission, as always.

I glance at Bishop. I have a connection with him that isn't there with O'Malley. I can't explain it. It's something I feel in my stomach, in my bones. O'Malley is smart, he helps me keep things organized and calm, but Bishop is like me in one key way: he *wants* to lead. He and I are willing to make decisions and take responsibility for them.

Bishop grins at me. Perhaps behind this door is the adventure he seeks.

He's ready.

So am I.

I nod at Spingate. "Open it up."

She slides the scepter's prongs into the holes. They click home. She lifts.

The hall groans and shakes.

With a grinding sound so loud some people cover their ears, the stone doors begin to shudder.

SIXTEEN

The doors slide open a crack, then stop. Hot, humid air billows out. So does a stench, something rich and awful.

Spingate runs to me.

"Em, the air is *damp*. That means there might be water in there!"

I nod. I'm not sure if she thinks I'm stupid, or she says whatever crosses her mind no matter how obvious it might be.

The doors slowly slide wider.

It's dark inside, pitch-black, the hallway's light creating a widening rectangle of brightness on the floor beyond.

For a moment, I hope I am seeing an illusion, or that my eyes are playing tricks on me. I want to see grass and trees. I want to see the outside. What I want doesn't matter though: reality is what it is, and the reality I see before me is just another room.

Little Gaston's face wrinkles up. He waves a hand in front of his nose.

"Oh, that's *awful*. Bishop, if you're going to fart, couldn't you at least walk to the other end of the hall?"

Bishop turns toward him. Gaston melts away again. Snarling, Bishop goes to give chase, but I grab his arm.

"Stay with me," I say. "We don't know what might come out of there."

His pale face flushes. He knew better than to let Gaston get to him at a time like this. Bishop steps to the widening space between the doors, his knees bent, his hands out in front of him and ready to take on any danger.

I hear kids moaning from the smell pouring out of the room. I think I know that odor, something from school . . . I wish I could remember. If I ever find the people who made us forget everything, I swear to Tlaloc, I will stab them all.

Tlaloc? Who is Tlaloc? That's a name, like *Tchaikovsky* was a name, but I don't think Tlaloc is a musician. I don't know who it is, but at least the name gives me a bit of hope that maybe my memories will come back.

The heavy doors are halfway open when the right one grinds and slows. It starts to shudder up and down, the floor bouncing under our feet each time it descends. Then it lurches and comes to a stop with an ear-splitting crunch.

The left door keeps going. It slides all the way into the wall, making the hallway vibrate one final time.

The right door, obviously broken, tilts away from us at a slight angle. The area beyond the opening is completely dark except for the hallway's light, which plays off a hard floor littered with bits of metal and streaked with some kind of dirty grime.

O'Malley leans close to me.

"Em, what do we do?"

We can either turn around and leave, or we can enter a dark, stinky room so humid that just standing outside of it is already making me sweat. But like Latu said, I'm not going back.

"We need light," I say. I turn to Spingate. "Any ideas?"

She clutches the scepter in both hands, holding it to her chest. She shakes her head.

Bishop silently steps into the dark room, El-Saffani at his sides. It annoys me he went without my say-so, but only a little.

The metal bits are springs, bars both round and flat, screws and nails and random pieces that used to be part of who knows what. Hanging down from somewhere above the archway, I see white cloth—banners of some kind, perhaps?

Gaston steps in front of Spingate and faces her. He's staring at . . . is he staring at her breasts? Spingate notices it, too—her cheeks redden and she looks at me, silently asking me to do something about it.

"Gaston," I say, "you're being rude."

He looks at me, confused. Then his eyes widen with under-standing.

"Oh, no, I'm looking at the scepter." He grins up at Spingate. "But don't get me wrong, you've got really nice boobs."

I can't believe he said that. Spingate is flustered and doesn't know what to do.

Gaston holds out his hand toward her. "Can I see the scepter? I feel like it . . . we need light, and it should"—he struggles to find the right words—"you know what I'm saying?"

She shakes her head, still flustered at his comment, then her eyes narrow. She looks at the scepter anew. Her lips move for a few seconds, and she nods.

"Yes, I think I know what you mean," she says. "It should . . ."

Her voice trails off. She keeps her grip on the scepter's bottom end, but tilts the top toward Gaston, letting him hold the prongs. They lean in together, hovering over it, examining it.

From inside the dark room, Bishop calls to me.

"Em, it's safe to come in."

I'm excited and bothered all at once. Excited because it feels like Bishop is looking out for me, checking for danger to keep me safe. Bothered because I'm in charge and he went in without asking or being told to do so. That's not how things are supposed to work. So did he do it because he wants to protect me, or because he doesn't respect me as the leader?

No, I'm being ridiculous. If Bishop was trying to protect anyone, it's probably Spingate. I see the way the boys look at her. And this isn't about my leadership, either—if I'd had time to think about it, I would have asked Bishop to go first anyway: he's bigger, faster and stronger than everyone else. I know it, he knows it. He did what I would have asked him to do . . . only I didn't ask.

Bishop leans out of the dark room. "Em, come on. And watch your footing, it's slick."

I step through the opening. O'Malley comes in with me.

My eyes adjust quickly to what little light there is. This place is bigger than our coffin room. It's quite a bit wider, and so long the end of it is lost in thick shadows. There's nothing much here other than the bits of metal scattered across the floor.

I take another step and my foot slides, almost making me fall.

"Told you to be careful," Bishop says.

I kneel and put my fingers to the floor. It's all greasy.

"What is this stuff?"

O'Malley points to the jammed door. "Gotta be from that."

The top of the stone door cracked through the archway, bending the metal and ruining the wall. The door must weigh a lot. It looks like it might tear through at any second, fall flat and smash whatever happens to be beneath it.

"Stay away from the door," I say, loud enough for everyone to hear. "It's dangerous."

I feel the cold grease soaking through my socks.

"The stuff is all over the place," Bishop says. "The entire

floor is covered in it. I think it helps the door open. It must have leaked out, which is maybe why the door jammed."

I wonder how long it has been since someone came down here to fix the things that need fixing. Maybe this room isn't important to whoever runs this place. Why fix something if no one is using it?

Everywhere I step, greasy dirt crunches and slides under my tired feet. I examine the walls: stone, with a line of carvings running along them. It's too dark to see details, but my fingertips recognize rough outlines: suns, jaguars, stepped pyramids, faces with big, flat noses.

It stinks so bad in here. I know this smell . . . if only my brain could make the connection.

A glance back out the door shows the others grouped together, staring into the room, hoping we find something to eat or drink. The white shirts of Bello and Aramovsky merge with the white shirts of Latu, Ingolfsson, Beckett and the others. There is no difference between my people and Bishop's—we are all in this together.

Except for the circle-stars, I remind myself. They are different.

The room's darkness seems to come alive. It swirls around me, envelops me. Circle-star . . . Yong . . . his face so close to mine, his eyes wide. He knew he was going to die, he *knew* it and there wasn't anything he could do but wait for death to come, wait in agony, crying out for his mother.

The hand on my shoulder makes me scream.

Bishop steps back, surprised, holds up both hands, palms out.

"Sorry, Em," he says. "I called your name but you didn't hear me. Are you okay?"

I nod quickly. I see El-Saffani looking at me. Maybe *scowling* is a better word. Do they think I'm weak?

"I'm okay," I say. "What did you want?"

He points up, to the banners.

"Did you see what's on those?"

I look at them. At first, they are subtle variations of darkness and shadow, as gray as ash, but after a few seconds patterns form. The banners . . . no, *flags* . . . hang from poles mounted in the wall above the archway. Maybe a dozen flags, all white or perhaps light gray, and they all have the same symbol: an empty circle.

"Same as yours and Okereke's," Bishop says.

I would give anything to know what our symbols mean. Do they define who my people were? Maybe my "tribe," as Bishop would say? Was this room for my tribe?

Alone, I walk deeper into the dark room, leaving the cracked archway behind. I still feel a slight pull against my legs—I'm walking uphill. As it has been from the beginning, that pull is very small, so tiny it's barely noticeable, but step after step, minute after minute, hour after hour . . . it's getting to me. It's driving me nuts.

I led us here. I led us to nothing. I hoped so badly those doors would open to the surface and we would be out. This is all too much . . . my decisions haven't produced anything good.

You tried, Em, but you failed.

"Shut up, Yong," I whisper. "Please shut up."

I want to cry, but just like before the tears don't come. Crying doesn't fix anything, isn't that what the voice in my head told me?

Have to focus. Everyone is counting on me to keep them safe.

There's something off to my left, by the wall. A few steps take me to it. It looks like a column of white stone, cracked in the middle, the top half lying broken and crumbled on the greasy floor. I recognize it from Gaston's story about the haunted room—it's one of the chest-high pedestals he talked about.

I wonder what rested on the flat top before someone smashed it to bits.

A boy approaches. I sense him before I see him: O'Malley, there in the dark beside me.

"Em, the others are getting upset," he says quietly. "They want to know if they're supposed to come in or if we're going back."

I'm upset, too, but does that even matter to him?

"Go back to where?" I say, unable to hide the frustration that drips from my voice. "To our hallway of bones, or to Bishop's haunted room?"

I can barely see O'Malley's face.

"Well, we can't go forward," he says. "It's too dark."

No, we're not going back. Not while I am the leader. All this effort can't be for nothing. Sooner or later, going *up* will take us *out*.

"We go straight."

O'Malley pauses, perhaps trying to choose the right words.

"The others aren't going to like it," he says.

I laugh, an evil, dark-sounding thing that would make me doubt any leader who made it.

"O'Malley, *I* don't like it. But we don't have a choice."

We hear a commotion behind us, back by the broken archway.

"Em! Come here!" It's Spingate, silhouetted by the hallway's light. Gaston is with her. He's holding the scepter, but that's not what he's looking at.

"Hey," O'Malley says. "Is that little guy staring at Spingate's—"

I grab O'Malley's arm and pull him along, cutting him off. "Come on, let's see what she wants."

Careful steps along the greasy floor bring us back to her. Spingate's face is alive with joy. If we could turn her excitement into light, there wouldn't be a shadow in the place.

"Look what Gaston and I found," she says. "Gaston, show her!"

He holds the scepter upside down and touches a series of gems. A tiny cone of flame suddenly hisses out the end, so bright I hold up a hand to shield against the powerful light.

He shuts off the flame. Ghost images dance in my vision. The room is pitch-black once again.

"It's a torch," Gaston says. "For welding things, I think."

Spingate again jumps and claps. I'm going to have to have a word with her about that. The way her . . . her *parts* bounce around when she jumps, it's distracting even to me—I can't imagine the effect it has on the boys.

"So we can use the scepter to light the way," I say. "That's great."

Gaston gives a wincing half-shrug. "Well, I don't know if that's a good idea. The fire has to burn fuel, and we don't know how much fuel the scepter holds. We shouldn't use it for light, or it might burn out and we won't have the flame if we need it."

I sigh. This is so annoying.

"Then what are we supposed to use it for, Gaston?"

He purses his lips. "To set stuff on fire? Maybe the grease on the floor will work as fuel. If we soaked our clothes in it, found some sticks or something, maybe we could make torches."

Spingate crosses her arms. "What, and have all of us be naked?"

Gaston grins. "If that's the only way, that's the only way." He gestures around the room. "Do you see any other fabric around here?"

There is a pause, then I look up. Bishop and O'Malley do the same.

The flags.

"Bishop," I say, "do you think you can get those down?"

He nods.

"That tall boy in your tribe," he says. "What's his name?"

"Aramovsky?"

"Aramovsky," Bishop repeats. "Will he let me and Visca lift him up? We'll have to get our hands under his feet. He might fall a couple of times, but hopefully it won't hurt him too bad."

Aramovsky heard his name. He cranes his head, peering into the room, wondering what's going on.

I look at the floor. The light from the hallway reflects off the smeared grime. I smile. He isn't going to like this, but I won't give him a choice.

"Aramovsky, get in here," I call out. "Time for you to finally get dirty."

SEVENTEEN

We walk uphill. We carry torches.

Aramovsky didn't get dirty. He didn't fall, not even once. Figures. With the help of Bishop and Visca, he ripped down the flagpoles. I hate to admit it, but Aramovsky did a good job.

Spingate and Gaston used the knife to cut the flags into long strips, then rubbed them in the greasy dirt and wrapped them tightly around the ends of the flagpoles. Gaston used the scepter to set them on fire. Flames lick up from the fabric in soft, pulsing waves that are hypnotic if you look at them too long.

Bello was smart enough to keep one flag whole. She tied the corners together to make a kind of bag that holds the extra grease-soaked strips. Okereke volunteered to carry the bag. Of all the circles from Bishop's group, I like Okereke the most, probably because he seems to be the hardest worker.

We move through the long room, three abreast. Torchlight makes shadows that twitch and jump. The darkness seems to be a living thing waiting to pounce on us and swallow us alive.

The room ends at a narrow, stone-walled hallway. Bishop and

El-Saffani lead us in, Bishop carrying a torch. I'm in the second row, several steps behind them. O'Malley is on my left, knife in hand, and Latu on my right, also carrying a torch. The rest of the group follows after, a long procession of flickering flames lighting up frightened faces.

If I ever get to sleep, if I have nightmares, I know they will happen in a place that looks like this.

Bishop isn't that far ahead. He and El-Saffani stop, wait for me, and I soon see why: an open archway on the left and another on the right. Past those, two more of the same on either side. The flickering torches seem to make the archways waver like the twitching mouths of giant, bloodthirsty monsters.

"I think we should look in these rooms, Em," Bishop says quietly. "It's not a good idea to leave unchecked areas behind us."

O'Malley shakes his head. "If we look in every room we find, all our torch-strips could burn out and we'd be left in the dark. Better to keep going straight as fast as we can."

Aramovsky was in the row behind me. He comes closer, eager to be part of the group that's making decisions.

"O'Malley is right," he says. "We're tired and hungry and thirsty." He half turns, so the people behind us can hear him clearly. "We don't want to waste time playing games, Em. We want *food*."

I hear grumbles of agreement, see scowls on more than a few faces. They are losing patience. They elected me leader—did they think I could use the spear to make food and water appear out of nowhere?

"Be patient," I say to them all. "We're going to get out of here, but I need you to be patient."

I'm going to get us out of here? I'm surprised at how convincing I sound.

Bishop and O'Malley both made good points. The darkness and shadows make this area feel dangerous, though, and my instinct tells me that when it comes to danger, I should trust Bishop.

"We'll check the rooms," I say. "There might be water. But we need to do it quick, so we can keep moving forward."

Bishop nods. "El-Saffani and I will make it fast. Everyone stay here."

Before I can answer, Latu speaks.

"You take the ones on the left, we'll take the ones on the right," she says to Bishop. "Faster that way."

Bishop stares at her. The shadows dancing across his face make him look much older. Almost . . . grown up. He starts to speak, stops—he's not in charge anymore. He glances at me, waiting for me to decide.

"We'll take the rooms on the right," I say.

Bishop purses his lips, then nods. "All right."

He waves someone forward. It's a circle-star boy with skin almost as dark as Aramovsky's. Farrar, I think his name is. If it weren't for Bishop, Farrar would be the biggest person in our group. Everything about him is wide, from his shoulders to his chest to his head—even his nose, which is short and flat.

"Keep everyone here," Bishop tells him. "We're going to look at these rooms."

Farrar nods once. He stands straight and tall, round shoulders back, big chest out. He might as well *be* a wall that blocks off the hallway. He accepts his orders, but doesn't even glance at me. My anger wells up again. Maybe it will take a little time to figure out how this works with Bishop, but when it comes to the circle-stars, he gives the orders and they listen. Except for Latu— she seems to be on my side.

But there shouldn't be *sides*. I have to keep reminding myself of that.

Bishop grips my shoulder with his free hand. "Be careful, Em. If you need help, just yell. Farrar or I will come."

With that, he turns and walks into the room on the left, El-Saffani right behind him.

O'Malley huffs. "Like we need his help."

I hope we don't, but I'm glad we'll have it if we do.

Latu, O'Malley and I enter the first room on the right. The layout looks familiar. Above is an arched ceiling decorated with carvings that shift and jitter in the torchlight. There is an aisle down the middle, as there was in our coffin room, and what might be coffins on either side, but they are different from ours. Where we had two rows of detailed, wooden coffins lined up end to end, with space between them, these are plain and white, lined up side to side and packed one against another, the far ends pressed against the wall. At the end of the aisle is another one of those white stone pedestals, this one broken into a dozen pieces.

These coffins aren't covered. I can't see into the ones at the far end of the room, but the ones close to us are empty. The ends of these coffins don't have carvings and jewels, they don't have nameplates—all they have are two flat metal discs, each the size of my fist. All the discs are scratched and dented, as is the white material around them—like someone with stiff boots kept kicking the discs harder and harder.

Latu walks toward the end of the room, her torch held up high. She looks down and left, down and right, over and over again. She reaches the wall, then jogs back.

"Empty," she says. "All of them."

O'Malley kneels, runs his hand over the end of a coffin. He taps it with the point of the knife.

"Latu, put some light on this," he says.

She tilts the torch close to him. I notice the light is starting to fade: the flame is slowly burning out.

O'Malley puts his finger into a deep gouge.

"Look at this scratch," he says, then runs his finger along it. The white material is torn and splintered. It's not wood and it's not metal. I should know what it is, but—like almost everything else—I can't place it.

O'Malley stands. Latu holds the torch over the coffin. More scratches on the inside, both where someone would lie and on the walls that separate it from the coffins on either side. On the flat bed, there are metal fasteners of some kind, but nothing fastened to them. The fasteners are scratched and rusted over.

Cracks, breaks, crumbled bits . . . so much damage.

"Looks like someone got mad at it," O'Malley says. "Got mad at all of them."

"No padding," Latu says. "Ours had padding. Did people lie in there on that hard bottom?"

O'Malley shrugs. "If these are even coffins at all. We don't know if they are."

But we *do* know.

Why are these different from ours? Why are they packed in like this?

Latu sees something. She reaches into the coffin, tugs at one of the fasteners. It rattles in complaint, then she stands. She holds her hand out for us to see.

It's a tiny bit of dirty white cloth.

O'Malley takes it from her, holds it close to his face, squinting to see it in the fading torchlight.

"Looks like the same lining that was in our coffins," he says.

He offers it to me. I take it. It's hard to tell from this small sample, but I think he's right.

Memories of my coffin flare to life. Waking up in the dark. The white fabric splattered with my own blood. I can remember nothing from before I woke up, but everything after—including some things I'd much rather forget.

Latu leans down, wipes her hand on the coffin's hard, flat bottom.

"So where's the rest of the cloth?" she asks. "Where's the padding? Did someone take it out?"

I don't have the answers to her questions. Neither does O'Malley.

"Let's check the other rooms," I say.

We turn to go, but on the way out Latu sees something else. She reaches into another coffin, picks something up, holds it near the torch for all three of us to examine.

A thin shard, a pale yellow splinter. It's the wrong color to have been part of the coffin. I know I've seen this material before, though, and recently.

I take it from Latu, pinch it between thumb and forefinger. I look closer.

A coldness washes inside my chest as I realize what it is.

"Bone," I say. "A little piece of bone."

I look in the coffins again, as if I might have missed seeing bodies, but there is nothing in any of them.

O'Malley takes the splinter from me, stares at it.

"You're right," he says. "So where's the rest of the skeleton this came from?"

One more thing we don't know.

I take it back from him and toss it into a coffin.

"Next room," I say. "Come on."

EIGHTEEN

ishop and El-Saffani found the same thing we did: two long rows of empty, beat-up coffins.

Latu's flame flutters out. Bello wraps another strip of flag around the pole as Okereke watches, holding a torch of his own. He uses his to light ours as Bello starts wrapping Bishop's flagpole with a new strip.

Latu, O'Malley and I enter the second room on the right.

This one isn't any different. We find a few tiny scraps of fabric, a few broken bits of bone. We count the coffins this time: twenty-four on each side. If all six rooms are like this, that's space for almost three hundred people.

So where are they? At the very least, where are their bodies?

I stand in the middle of the room, holding the spear, as O'Malley and Latu move down the aisle. He checks the coffins on the right, she the left. This room also once had a pedestal, but it's been smashed into a hundred white pieces. Only the flat top remains intact. Mostly, anyway.

"Hey, Latu," O'Malley says. "That bruise on your cheek, that come from Bishop?"

She nods, keeps looking in the coffins, one after another.

"Yes, but I hit him first."

O'Malley stops checking. "What? How did *that* happen?"

"I woke up in a room with Johnson and Cabral," she says. "The other cradles had dead little kids inside."

Even in the torchlight, I can see the hard muscles in her arms.

"I bet you broke out of your cradle first," I say, using her word for the coffins. "Then you broke out the other two. Am I right?"

Latu looks back at me.

"When I woke up, my cradle was already open," she says. "Same for Johnson and Cabral. Our room door was open, too."

Why did their coffins open and not ours? And how could their room door be open, when we had to use the scepter to get out?

"We wandered the hall for a little bit," Latu continues. "Then Bishop found us." Her eyes narrow at the memory. "He had the others with him. He rushed at us, like he did with you. Johnson and Cabral ran. I didn't."

I wonder if she stood her ground because she was so terrified she couldn't move, like me, or because she is actually brave.

"He rushed you," O'Malley says, amazed at the story. "That's why you hit him? To keep him from tackling you?"

Latu shakes her head. "No, he stopped before he got to me, like he did with Em. He told me I had to join his tribe. I didn't like the way he talked and I didn't want to join his stupid tribe, so I punched him."

She's not brave, she's out of her mind.

O'Malley starts to laugh. "That bruise on his jaw? That's from you?"

Latu nods. "I shouldn't have done it. I didn't think. I hit him, and he hit me back so hard I fell down. I . . . I don't remember ever being hurt like that before. He asked if I was done fighting. I said yes, and he helped me up."

O'Malley goes back to looking inside the coffins, sometimes reaching his hand in and swishing it around, feeling for whatever might be in there.

"Then what happened?" he asks.

Latu also returns to searching the coffins.

"Then nothing," she says. "We got into a fight, I guess, and he won. So Johnson, Cabral and I joined his tribe and we wandered all over this stupid place for I don't know how long."

I see the torchlight play off her tongue as she licks her dry lips, which reminds me of how thirsty I am. It's so humid in here my shirt clings to my body—there has to be water somewhere.

Bishop hit her, true, but she hit him first. He didn't hit me. Or O'Malley. Does Bishop have more control over himself than Yong had? For that matter, Latu hit Bishop—does she have *less* control? I already feel connected to her, like we were close friends before the coffins and we just can't remember it, but if she's that unpredictable, is it smart to trust her?

O'Malley finishes with his side of the room and walks back to me. Latu does the same. O'Malley grins at her.

"Your bruise looks like it hurts," he says. "But I bet it was worth it to punch that jerk."

She smiles back at him. "Yeah, it was."

We go back into the hall in time to see Bishop and El-Saffani enter the last room on the left. Latu's torch is already fading a bit, but enough burning cloth remains to see what's in the last room on the right before we have to tie on another greased strip.

I look back down the dark hall. Farrar still blocks the way, flickering torches lighting up the scared faces and white shirts behind him.

O'Malley, Latu and I enter the last room. It stinks in here like it stinks in the hall, and in the rooms we searched. Without a word, Latu moves to the left, O'Malley to the right, each checking the coffins on their sides. Maybe this is the room with water, or maybe there are more weapons to be found.

I hear something.

O'Malley and Latu hear it, too. They stop. Our ears seek out the sound . . . a scraping, a snorting . . . the rattle of a coffin wall as a body bumps against it.

It's coming from the last coffin on the left.

Is it a kid like us? Or is it something else?

I don't know what to do. I'm frozen once again. So is O'Malley, the torchlight sparkling against the whites of his wide eyes.

Latu slowly creeps forward, toward the sound.

We should go get Bishop, get more circle-stars. I should say something, but my mouth doesn't want to work any more than my feet do.

She's five coffins from the last one . . . then four . . .

O'Malley moves to stand next to me, the long knife held out in front of him.

Three coffins . . . then two . . .

A deep *snort*.

That sound—it's not a kid like us. It's not an adult. It's not *human*.

Something moves, pops up out of the last coffin, something with shiny eyes, something covered in black, greasy hair that reflects the torchlight, and I know monsters are real—because that *is* a monster.

I take a step away. O'Malley takes two. Latu slowly backpedals, her torch angled toward this sudden threat.

We look at the monster. The monster looks at us.

An old memory flares to life, but not just from what I see—it's also from what I smell. That awful odor that I couldn't identify. It's from when I was little, at school . . . no, not *at* school, on a field trip with people *from* the school, a field trip to a special place.

To . . . to a *farm*.

The awful smell is animal droppings.

The black-furred thing standing in the coffin, it's not a monster at all.

It's a pig.

NINETEEN

The pig is just tall enough that its head hangs over the coffin wall. It's not very big. It's black, or at least its head is, because that's all we can see. Is that the color of its fur, or is it completely covered in grease and dirt? So hard to tell in the flickering torchlight, which makes the animal's black eyes waver with glimmering reflections.

"I can't believe it," O'Malley says. "That's a pig. I think I've seen one before."

Latu keeps backing up until she stands next to us. "Em, what do we do?"

I have no idea. What is a pig doing here?

My heart kicks so bad I feel it in my throat. When that black head popped up, I was sure Spingate was wrong and Aramovsky was right, that monsters were real and one was about to attack us.

"A farm," O'Malley says. "I saw one on a farm."

His words are light and dreamy, like the word *farm* is a discovery to him, a happy memory come to life.

Latu leans close to O'Malley without taking her eyes off the pig, which is still looking at us.

"What's a *farm*?" she asks him.

"A place where they grow food," O'Malley says.

My hunger pangs and pains return all at once, rush back with more intensity than ever before.

"*Food,*" Latu says. She shakes the torch in the pig's direction. "Is that thing *food*?"

The tone of her voice is full of want, full of need.

"Yes," O'Malley says. His voice doesn't sound dreamy anymore—it sounds *hungry*. "Yes . . . pigs are definitely food."

The pig grunts. Its right ear twitches. It's staring at me. The pig is food, food that's still *alive*. I don't know what this animal is doing in here, but it isn't hurting us. If we're going to eat it, it has to die. Hasn't there been enough death in this place already?

But we don't know if we'll find food somewhere else. There are twenty-four of us, so many mouths to feed. Reality is what it is whether we like it or not: the reality is that we're starving.

Before we can eat that pig, someone has to kill it.

"O'Malley," I say, "go get Bishop."

He quietly turns and walks out of the room.

Latu nudges me. "Em, give me the spear. I'll kill it right now."

"Do you know how to kill a pig?"

"No," she says. "I'll . . . I'll stab it until it stops moving."

She doesn't want to kill the pig, I can tell by her voice, but she knows what must be done and she's willing to do it.

"Wait for Bishop," I say.

"Em, give me the spear before the thing runs away!"

Latu's yelling spooks the pig. Hooves paw at the coffin wall, filling the room with deafening noise, *clak-crack-clak*.

Behind me, I hear heavy footsteps rush into the room. It's Bishop. He takes one look at the situation, then shouts at me.

"Em, give me the spear!"

The pig leaps out of the coffin and into the aisle. It hits the ground running, charges straight at me, squealing so loud it hurts my ears. I thrust the spear out in front of me, more to protect myself than to stab the animal. The little head bobs left and then the pig is running right, brushing against my left leg as it shoots past, too quick for me to react in time.

I turn to give chase—and almost drive the spearpoint into Bishop's chest. He twists at the last moment, so *fast,* his hand grabbing the shaft as the blade hisses through the empty air where his heart had been a split second earlier.

O'Malley and El-Saffani have a chance at the pig, but scoot out of its way instead of diving on top of it—the pig scampers out of the room.

Bishop yanks the spear from my hands. Two steps take him into the hall. I give chase instantly, my legs finally my own again.

I see Bishop start to throw—the image burns into my eyes, my brain, my forever memory. His right arm cocked back, muscles straining the fabric of his shirt, the spear shaft balanced in his hand, the blade tip near his neck. His left hand extended, fingertips pointed down the hall, the straight arm a perfect continuation of the spear's line. His bare chest, sweaty and gleaming in the torchlight, every fiber of him taut and fluttering. He is all the motion that has ever existed. He is a gemstone sculpted to look like a person: hard and permanent and flawless.

His right arm whips forward, driven by the twist of his shoulders and hips. My eyes follow the spear down the hall. It flies fast, far and straight. The tiniest bit of torchlight reaches out, and I see a glimpse of a black-furred leg before it is swallowed up by shadow.

The spear follows it, vanishes from sight.

A squeal of pain echoes from the darkness.

Bishop grabs a torch from Bello—I hadn't even noticed her there, her or Okereke and his flag-bag full of oily strips—then sprints after the pig. El-Saffani follows him, as does Latu.

I glance back down the hall, see Farrar standing still and firm in front of fading torches, see the kids packed in behind him. We're getting too spread out, and everything is happening so fast.

We found a pig—what else will we find?

"Bishop, STOP!"

He stumbles, surprised, then turns and looks at me. El-Saffani and Latu stop as well, their bodies seemingly desperate to rush down the hall despite what their brains tell them to do.

"Em, I hit it," Bishop says. "It's dead! Come on!"

He's so excited. He's a bright-eyed little boy on his twelfth birthday, and this game was his present, the best present he could ever imagine.

Another pain-laced squeal echoes along the stone walls. The pig sounds farther away—obviously, it's not dead.

Bishop snarls and smiles all at the same time.

"It's *wounded*," he says.

The best game he could ever imagine just got better.

He's coiled so tight he's almost shaking with intensity. I instinctively want to back away from him, point the spear at him in defense like I pointed it at the charging pig. I force myself to stand firm.

"Em, come on," he says. "Let's go after it!"

He's asking me to come with him. He took the spear, ripped it right out of my hands, but not because he wanted to be the leader. At that instant, he didn't care about what the weapon symbolized; he used it for its true purpose.

The spear is for killing.

No matter what I tell Bishop to do, I know he's going after

that pig. If I tell him to stay, he'll go anyway, and everyone will know my leadership can simply be ignored. That could hurt us even more than thirst or hunger. I have to keep control, I have to keep us united.

If people don't have faith in me, we will all lose.

"Bello, give half the torch strips to El-Saffani," I say. "Then you and Okereke take the rest back to Farrar and the others, wait for me there."

O'Malley shakes his head. "Em, everyone needs to stay together. We can't go chasing around in the darkness, we can't get separated. The others are going to get upset."

He's right. People are already antsy. If I leave them with Aramovsky . . .

"O'Malley, you go back with Bello," I say. "Tell everyone we're trying to get food." I hold my hand toward him, palm up. "Give me the knife."

He looks at my hand, then doubtfully at Bishop.

"I should go with you," O'Malley says.

"Give me the knife," I repeat. "Keep everyone calm."

O'Malley shifts from one foot to the other.

"Going after the pig is dangerous," he says.

"O'Malley, the *knife*."

He hands it over hilt-first, scowling at me and Bishop both.

I turn to Latu.

"Go with O'Malley. We'll be back as soon as we can."

She shakes her head. "No, I'm going with you. I want to be part of the hunt."

This is the girl who punched Bishop in the face. I see the same look in her eyes I see in his: she's going to go no matter what I tell her. I'm getting frustrated: I don't know how to control the circle-stars, I don't have time to argue with her, and I can't lose that argument while everyone is watching. If Bishop can ignore me, if Latu can, then what's to stop Visca, El-Saffani and the other circle-stars from going their own way?

"You stay at my side," I tell her. "You protect me, agreed?"

Latu nods hard enough to make her frizzy hair flop back and forth.

O'Malley's face wrinkles in anger. "What? Why does *she* get to go?"

Because Latu won't do what she's told, and you will.

"Just keep the others calm," I say.

Bello hands Boy El-Saffani an armful of rags. Latu grabs one, wraps it around her still-burning torch. She does it so fast that she's finished before it's fully aflame. Bishop quickly tries the same move, hisses in pain as fire singes his skin.

He sucks at the burned finger, looks at me with eager eyes and nods.

We're ready.

I nod back.

Holding the torch, Bishop heads down the hall, El-Saffani at his heels.

I run after them, Latu at my side.

If I look back, I know I'll see O'Malley staring at me—so I keep my eyes forward.

I don't know if this is the right decision or not, but the decision is made.

The hunt is on.

TWENTY

We hunt.

I run with the circle-stars. Torchlight plays off hallway walls lined with patterns and carvings of the usual symbols, but new ones as well—people with shovels, people harvesting crops, people moving things, people working together to build and create. It all flies by as we run, making the tiny images on the walls seem to sprint in the opposite direction.

Bishop is out in front, and for this, at least, there is no question as to who is the leader. He slows and stops. The rest of us do as well, following his every move.

The spear lies on the hallway floor.

He picks it up. He has the torch in one hand, the spear in the other. There is blood on the blade.

Bishop offers the spear to me. I reach to grab it, but I'm already holding the knife. I can't carry both weapons, and right now Bishop's ability with the spear is the most important thing.

"You take it for now," I say. "Give it back when we're done."

He nods. He doesn't care who is in charge—he's focused on the hunt and nothing else.

Bishop hands his torch to Boy El-Saffani, then kneels and puts two fingers to the floor. He lifts them, looks at them, and we all see what is on his fingertips.

Blood, flecked with dirt.

"We can track it," he says.

He heads down the hall. We stay close behind.

This is *exciting,* and that surprises me. I came along to maintain an illusion of control, but my skin feels electric, my senses seem sharp. I don't remember who I am or what I was, but in my heart I know nothing I did before could possibly make me feel this alive.

How can I feel this way? Bishop is going to find this animal and kill it. We're going to cut it up . . . we're going to *eat* it. The very thought disgusts me, yet killing the pig is something we must do to survive.

Bishop runs at a half crouch, eyes fixed on the hallway floor. The pig's blood trail is easy to follow, with a new spluttery streak every few steps. The poor thing must be terrified.

We move quickly. The circle-stars make practically no noise. My steps seem loud and clumsy by comparison. Girl El-Saffani keeps flashing me dirty looks because of it, and Latu isn't that pleased with me, either. I don't think they are doing anything special to stay silent—it comes naturally to them.

The hallway opens to a wide, round space. Archways line the curving wall. Ten, maybe twelve of them. At the far end of the room, barely visible in the torchlight, I see the hallway continue— maybe *up* can't go on forever, but it still shows no sign of ending anytime soon.

What do we do now? There are only five of us; it will take a long time to look in all these rooms, and if the pig kept going down the hall we'll lose it if we stop to check even one of them.

I glance at Bishop to see what he's thinking, but his attention remains firmly fixed on the floor.

"I know where it is," he says, then jogs to an archway on our right.

We run after him. I glance down as I go, see Latu's torchlight flicker off a thin streak of blood that shows the pig's path as clearly as someone standing there, pointing and shouting *It went this way!*

I hear the grunt of an animal. I stop in my tracks. That didn't come from up ahead, where Bishop is going. It's hard to tell in this big room, but . . . did that come from somewhere off to the left?

"Bishop, wait!"

Latu pauses, but Bishop and El-Saffani either don't hear my order or they ignore it. Latu is looking back at me, torch in hand. Her face pleads with me to get going before Bishop leaves us behind.

I run to catch up.

Bishop pauses at the archway. The stone doors are partially open. They sit at funny angles, like they are broken and will never close again. There is enough space for us to slide through.

We enter.

Our torchlight reveals a stone dome and the largest room we've been in yet. If I stood on Latu's shoulders while she was standing on Bishop's, I could probably touch the ceiling with my fingertips. In the middle of the room is a circular stone, the flat top about waist high. It's big enough that if I lay on it, I could spread my arms and legs wide and my hands and feet would barely hang over the edges.

A grunt and a squeal: no question this time, it came from inside the room. There, against the wall on the other side of the circular stone—the wounded pig. It sees us and starts sprinting madly, racing along the wall's curve in a hoof-clicking panic.

Bishop takes a hop-step toward it, twists his hips and shoulders: the spear again sails through the air.

He misses.

The blade sparks when it skips off the stone floor just behind the running pig. The spear clatters against the wall.

Bishop roars and sprints at the pig. El-Saffani angles left, trying to cut off the animal, while Latu positions herself in the room's narrow opening, blocking any way out. The circle-stars didn't communicate with each other, yet they act as one, four people who instantly work together like they've done it a hundred times before. I have no idea what to do, so I stay near Latu.

The pig pauses, its head flicking side to side as it looks for somewhere to run. Bishop launches himself at it—the pig hops over his outstretched arms and darts away. Bishop grunts in pain when he crashes to the stone floor.

The twins rush the pig at the same time, but they might as well be trying to catch the air itself. The solid animal bobs left and right as it slips through the grasp of Boy El-Saffani. Girl El-Saffani snatches at its rear ankles: she grabs the right one, but is yanked off-balance as the pig powers along on three remaining legs. She stumbles, trips and lands hard on her shoulder.

The pig barrels straight at Latu and me.

Latu is still blocking the exit. She waves her torch back and forth; the whipping flame makes shadows lengthen and shorten, lengthen and shorten.

The pig stops, confused by the fire.

"Em, *stab it*," Latu screams. "Stab it now!"

The long knife, I forgot it was in my hand. I have to kill the animal. We have to eat, there isn't any choice. . . .

The pig glances back at Bishop, who is scrambling to his feet, then at Boy El-Saffani, who is closing in—then at Latu. I can almost see the pig make a decision of its own: better to face the fire than to be trapped in this room.

It rushes at Latu. I step between her and it, thrust out with the blade. The pig sees my attack and scoots to its left, so *fast*. I whip the knife sideways and feel it dig in deep, but it flies out of my grip, spins through the air and clatters on the stone floor.

Squealing in pain and terror, the pig launches itself at Latu, slamming into her and knocking the torch from her hands. Latu tumbles backward, grabs the pig in both arms as she falls. Pig legs thrash, trying to find purchase, but Latu has her arms wrapped tightly around the animal's thick middle.

"Em! Help me hold this thing!"

I move to grab it, but the pig moves faster.

It twists its neck and bites down hard on Latu's shoulder. Her scream echoes off the dome roof. The pig thrashes its head side to side. Latu's feet kick, she tries to push the pig away, but the animal won't let go.

I am on it before I know it, punching and shouting, my fists slamming hard into the solid body, splatting against greasy, stinking fur.

The pig scrambles away, hooves clattering on stone. It sprints for the hallway that leads deeper into unexplored areas—in seconds, it is lost in the shadows.

It's gone.

Latu moans. Her right hand clutches her left shoulder. Blood seeps through her fingers, spreads across her white shirt. I grab her, try to sit her up.

"Latu! Are you okay?"

A stupid thing to say, but I don't know what to do. Blood is everywhere. Her face is a scrunched wrinkle of agony. Her lips curl back, and she forces her words through clenched teeth.

"Go . . . *get it,*" she says. "*Kill* it."

I try to see how bad her wound is.

"I'm staying with you."

Her eyes pop open, go wide with sheer fury.

"Em, *kill it* before it gets away!"

Bishop stumbles past us. He's limping, favoring his right knee. The knife is in his hand.

I look back through the broken archway doors. A fading torch lies on the floor. In the fluttering flame's light, I see Boy El-Saffani trying to help Girl El-Saffani to her feet. She's struggling to get up but her arms and legs seem weak and uncooperative.

Bishop limps off after the pig. He doesn't have a torch. He's going to get lost in the darkness.

Latu's bloody hand locks down on my wrist.

"Em, I'm okay, just *go.*"

I grab her torch from the floor and scramble to my feet. I chase after Bishop.

It's not hard to see where he's going: a trail of pig blood lines the way. The gleaming liquid looks more black than red under my torch's glow. I see him up ahead, limping along.

"Bishop, stop! Come back, Latu's hurt."

He keeps going, taking two steps with his left foot for every one with his right. His bare feet slap against the blood-covered stone, leaving red-black footprints that mark his path. Sometime in the past few hours, I don't know when, he took off his socks and left them behind.

"Bishop! *Stop!*"

He does, and whirls toward me. His face is something I barely recognize, a mask of insatiable rage.

"It's *getting away*," he says. "Either come with me, or give me the torch so I can go on my own."

Alone? He's not thinking clearly. He's too consumed by his anger, his lust for the hunt. Right now all that matters to him is catching the prey. That is more important than staying with the group, more important than Latu . . . more important than me.

He holds the knife in his right hand, down low, close to his thigh. He thrusts his left hand toward me, fingers outstretched: he wants the torch.

"I'll go in the dark if I have to," he says.

He's gone mad.

I know I should go back to Latu, get her to the others, but I can't leave Bishop now. I *can't*. If he goes alone and something happens to him, I would die.

"I'm coming with you."

I jog ahead of him down the hall. He limps along, his face a snarling scowl of total focus.

If I can't talk him out of it, at least I can try to keep him safe.

The hall is the same as before, with carvings lining the walls. We pass archways both open and closed, but the blood trail enters none of them.

Bishop doesn't even look at me. He is obsessed, controlled by the thought of chasing down that pig. There is something basic about Bishop that excites me, that makes my soul shake. A word comes back to me from my days in school.

Primal.

That's what Bishop is: *primal.*

Whatever he did to his leg is beginning to ease. He starts running left-right, left-right, although he winces and dips a little each time his right foot slaps down. He picks up speed. I almost have to sprint to keep up with him.

The blood trail . . . it's thinning out.

"No," Bishop says, the word full of loss. "If we lose the trail now, we might never find it."

My torch is starting to flutter: it's almost out. Soon we'll be in the dark, and Bishop either doesn't notice or doesn't care.

"We can't be that far behind," he says. "It's lost a lot of blood—it will slow down soon, then crawl away somewhere to die."

There is no doubt in his voice: he knows exactly what he's doing. But if he's really like me, like Bello and the others, he's only *twelve*. How can he be such an expert?

"Bishop, I can barely even remember what a pig is, and you know how to hunt one?"

He looks up from the blood trail, glances at me without breaking stride. "What's a *pig*?"

"The animal we're chasing."

He shrugs and returns his focus to the hallway floor.

Realization hits home, and with it comes a shiver: Bishop doesn't know how to hunt a pig, he knows how to *hunt*. I don't think he cares what we're after, as long as he catches it.

The trail stops.

Bishop looks around frantically. "Em, help me find the blood! There has to be more here somewhere."

I drop to my knees, hold the fading torch close to the ground. It's more glow than flame now . . . I'm going to be in the dark again.

Ahead and to the right, something catches my eye. An archway, stone doors sealed tight, but at the bottom I see a wide black spot.

"Bishop, look!"

I crawl forward, stick the torch into the blackness. Yes, it's a *hole*.

A hole streaked with blood.

Bishop dives to the floor and starts crawling through. He grunts and growls, trying to force his body into the hole. The sounds he's making . . . If I closed my eyes and just listened, I don't know if I could tell the difference between him and the pig.

"Bishop, stop it—you won't fit through there."

I can't see his head anymore. His shoulders seemed jammed. His bare, bloody feet push at the floor. He wiggles and thrashes. Then his shoulders slide through, and he's gone.

"Em, get in here!"

I slide the torch into the hole, then follow it. I crawl through easily, grab the torch and stand.

Bishop's white shirt is in shreds. He pulls it from his broad shoulders and tosses it aside. His sweaty, hairless chest gleams in the torchlight. I'm consumed by an urge to reach out, to touch his skin, to see if his muscles are really as firm as they look, to trace a finger along his collarbone. . . .

I shake my head, try to clear my thoughts. What's wrong with me? Why would I want something like that, something . . . *shameful*? The pig, Bishop's obsession with it, that's what I have to focus on.

The torch sputters.

Bishop and I watch, helpless, as the light flutters out completely.

All is black.

Just like the coffin, just like when I was trapped and that thing was biting me. We're going to die here, stuck in the darkness. I hear my own breathing, so fast, but I feel like I'm not breathing at all—my chest is tight and no air is coming in. It's not fair, I fought my way out of the dark once already, I can't go without light I can't I—

"Em, open your eyes."

—can't breathe I can't breathe I can't breathe. I'm trapped in the dark in a coffin where no one will come save us and Mom and Dad *abandoned* us and left us to die left us alone, I have to—

Strong hands grip my shoulders. *Warm* hands, hands gritty with dirt and slick with sweat.

"Em, *calm down*."

It's Bishop, talking to me, holding me. I draw in a big, slow breath, and this time I feel the air go in deep.

"That's better," he says. "Now open your eyes."

I didn't even know they were closed. I open them, expecting endless, mind-numbing dark . . . and am surprised that there's enough light to make out the shape of Bishop's face. He's close. Close enough to kiss.

He lets go of my shoulders. He points to his right.

At first I don't understand what I see. It looks like a wall with hundreds of little bright spots, like tiny, glowing jewels. But it's not a wall . . . it's a mass of curved bars, twisting in and around each other. There is depth to it. The bright spots, they aren't jewels . . . they are spaces, showing light coming from the other side.

Bishop walks to this strange wall. I follow him.

They aren't bars . . . they are *plants*. Dead wooden stems with rough bark, each as thick as my wrist. Here and there I see a few brittle, brown leaves. Some withered stems grow along the floor, reaching into the room as if they sought sunlight, and, finding none, simply died.

I grab one of the curving plants, feel the rough bark against my skin. I give it an experimental shake. It barely moves. The stems have grown together, fused with each other into an impenetrable weave that might as well be a cage. The weave is so thick I can't quite see all the way through it—whatever lies beyond looks like a big, brightly lit space.

"Bishop, what is this?"

He shakes his head. "I'm not sure. The word that comes to mind is *thicket*. Do you know that word?"

I don't. It means nothing to me, the same way *pig* meant nothing to him.

Bishop kneels, hands exploring the stems. I see white spots among the brown. I kneel next to him and take a closer look. Some of the stems have been sliced through: the spots are pale wood that lies beneath the bark.

He touches a severed branch.

"I don't get it," he says. "If someone cut through this, why cut so low?"

That trip to the farm . . . something about that memory flares to life. A man . . . an old man, wearing a funny hat, talking to me. No, to *us,* to the class. Something about what a pig can eat . . .

"Not *cut*," I say. "*Gnawed*. The pig did it, Bishop."

As if to confirm what I said, Bishop reaches in a little farther, touches another gnawed bit of white wood. When he pulls his fingers back, there is blood on them.

We both see it at the same time. The gnawed branches outline a half-circle of empty space—a tunnel that leads deeper into the thicket.

Bishop looks at me.

"If the pig made it through, so can we," he says.

He doesn't ask for permission, doesn't wait to hear what I think. He lies flat, and he starts in.

TWENTY-ONE

We crawl across dirt.

The little tunnel's sticks scrape at my arms and shoulders, snag on my shirt and snarl in my hair. I didn't realize that my ponytail has been coming apart. It's hard to keep the hair out of my face. I must look like an even bigger mess than I thought.

Bishop struggles to crawl through. He's much bigger than I am. The sharp edges tear into his bare skin. I'm behind him, his feet not far from my face. We're both flat on our bellies. Twice I see him tangle in the thicket, gnawed wood stabbing into him, and I know the pain will make him turn back, but he snarls and growls, either forces his body through or uses the knife to cut away the offensive branches. He presses on.

He is big and fast and strong, but he is also *tough*. He doesn't ignore pain as much as he endures it. He will not quit. The twelve-year-old me looks up to Bishop, wants to be like him in that way.

At any point since the vote, he could have taken the spear

from me and claimed leadership. I couldn't have stopped him, yet he hasn't done that. He's been true to his word.

Is he my friend? I feel that he is, and I am grateful for it.

When our torch went out, I thought the darkness would eat me up and swallow me down. But ahead of us, light, coming through the thicket. No, not just ahead of us—light filters down from above.

I stop crawling.

Plants . . . light.

Is it *day*light?

And that awful smell, the pig crap, it's gone. The air here smells fresh and clean.

Have we made it? Is this the way out?

I scramble to catch up to Bishop. He's grunting, forcing his way past another tangle. He wants through so badly he's willing to pay for it in pain, in blood.

And I wonder: is blood the true cost of all things?

He crawls free and stands. I speed up, unable to control myself, feeling the cold dirt scrape against my belly and thighs. I try to rise too early and am rewarded with a small, jagged branch digging deep into my shoulder.

"Ow, *ow*!"

"Hold still for a second," Bishop says. He snaps the branch off the thicket, then gently pulls the bit of wood out of my skin.

"Are you okay?"

If his expression wasn't so serious, I'd think he was mocking me: bleeding scratches cover his shoulders, arms and face.

"I'm fine," I say. "Thank you."

He smiles.

I look out at a sea of green. Grass and trees, the first living things I have seen other than my friends and the pig. Then I glance up, and anguish overwhelms me. My heart cries out for someone to make it all stop, to finally *let us go*.

This is another room. Different, massive, but still a room: we are not outside.

The ceiling glows brightly. I have to shield my eyes to look at it. Unlike the hallways, the ceiling here is arched, as if we're standing inside the end of a long, wide pipe. It curves high above. I doubt I could touch the top of it even if twenty of us stood on each other's shoulders.

Thick groves of trees line the sides, reaching up to the bottom edges of the ceiling arch. On some of those trees, I see bits of color in different shapes.

It's . . . it must be fruit.

Food.

If we can eat it, we are saved.

Before us is a wide clearing of knee-high green that leads up to something just as beautiful as the fruit: *water*. It's a spring bubbling up out of the ground, a sparkling, glorious, living jewel that rises as high as my face before tumbling down into tall reeds. The reeds run down the center of this room, a wide swath of them that is oddly rectangular in shape. At the far end of that rectangle, more grass, and beyond the grass, a line of trees that are so tall I can't see past them, can't see how far the arched roof goes.

"Food and water," Bishop says. He looks at me, astonished. "Savage . . . you did it."

I shake my head slowly. "But I didn't get us *out*."

"You will," Bishop says. "I know you will."

I look behind us. Here, the thicket is far different than it was in the dark room. Leaves cover it, making it look like a sloped, uneven blanket of deep green that lies comfortably under the shade of fruit trees. The thicket spreads left and right into the dense woods that line either side of this huge room. Through some spots, I can make out a stone wall.

We must have crawled through a hole in that wall.

Bishop stares at all of it, wide-eyed and smiling.

"This place, Savage . . . this place will keep us alive. We can rest."

That word, *rest*, it triggers something inside me. I'm hungry, thirsty, and so tired. I haven't slept since I came out of the coffin.

But I can't rest yet.

"We need Spingate," I say. "Maybe she can figure out if the fruit is safe to eat."

Bishop shrugs. "If it's not, does it really matter?"

He walks to a nearby tree dotted with blue, fist-sized fruits. He reaches up, pulls at one of them. The branch bends for a moment, then a stem snaps free and the branch springs back into place with a rattle of leaves.

I start to speak, to tell him to wait, but I say nothing. Bishop is right: if the food or water is poisonous, what difference does it make if we die from that or from starvation and thirst? I'm exhausted, drained. So is Bishop. So are the rest of our people. I'm not even sure if I have the strength to get back to them and bring them here. If we don't eat and drink what we see before us, we're finished anyway.

Bishop puts the blue fruit to his mouth. He bites down—it sounds crunchy. He chews. A bit of clear juice squirts out of his mouth, runs down his chin. He reaches up, snaps off another piece of fruit. With a wet smile, he offers it to me.

I take it. The fruit is firm and light, its surface cool to the touch.

Maybe it will kill me. If so, I don't care.

I take a bite.

Flavors explode across my tongue: *sweet, cool, tangy*. I know that I have never, *ever* tasted anything this good. I chew madly as I take a second bite, then a third.

Bishop pops the last of his blue fruit into his mouth. His teeth crunch noisily on hard seeds even as he reaches for a different tree, a different fruit, one that is long and purple. Then he stops: something has caught his attention.

Knife in hand, he walks out into the knee-high grass. I see the deep scratches in his back, crisscross lines leaking blood. There are rips in his pants. I can see little glimpses of his thighs.

My face flushes hot, and I look away. His pants are the only clothes he has left. If those go, he'll be naked. A grown man, *naked*. My stomach feels queasy, and I don't think it's from the fruit.

The grass seems to close in behind him. He bends, touches something, straightens, rubs his thumb and forefinger together.

I see redness on his fingertips.

He continues on, moves closer to the bubbling column of water. His limp is almost gone.

Finally, he stops. He stares down. He doesn't have to call for me, because I know what's there.

I walk to join him. The stiff grass feels sharp against my shins and knees.

Near Bishop's feet, the pig lies on its side. Grass is flattened around it, pushed down by its body. In this bright, clear light, it's like a different animal. Black fur gleams. Ears twitch, flicking this way and that as if the pig hopes to hear someone coming to save it.

Poor thing . . . there is no help in this place, something I've already learned.

Bishop's spear throw opened up the animal's thigh, an awful gash that makes me wonder how it could run at all. There is also a slash on its upper flank, a straight line that starts at the neck and ends past its shoulder.

That cut was mine.

Blood oozes across the black fur, blood that is littered with dirt and small sticks, dotted with crumbled leaves.

Yes . . . blood *is* the price of all things.

The pig's ribs and stomach rise and fall in a ragged rhythm. Every breath in is a sucking snort, every breath out comes as a thin whine of misery. The pig's legs twitch, like it would run away if it could just find the strength to rise again.

Worst of all are the animal's eyes. They are brown with big, black pupils. They flick to me, to Bishop and back again, over and over. The wide eyes show obvious terror—they look almost human.

We stare at it for a moment.

"I had a dog," Bishop says finally. "I can't remember her name."

I don't know what to say to that, so I simply nod.

"The pig is dying," he says. His voice is small, quiet, not at all at home in a body his size. I understand why. This was a game to him. Now he's looking at a frightened, exhausted, bleeding animal.

It's not a game anymore.

Despite its wounds and the filth covering its fur, in this light, I find the pig beautiful. The wet nose, the wide eyes . . . if we had seen it here, in this clearing, running and scampering and full of life, would we have tried to kill it?

Part of me wants to say *Of course not,* but I know that part is from the little girl I used to be. Twelve-year-old Em—well-fed, well-rested, *safe* Em—would have wanted to make the pig a pet.

If I had understood how this hunt would end, I would have

stopped it. We were hungry; now this animal will die in a place with more food than we could ever eat. This is awful. The pig did nothing to us.

"It's in pain," I say. "We have to help it."

Bishop's face is pale. He knew how to hunt; he didn't realize what he would have to do when that hunt was over.

"We can't help it," he says. "It's wounded real bad. It will be dead in a little while. Maybe an hour, maybe more."

I shake my head. "That's not what I meant by *help it*, Bishop. You have to end its suffering."

He looks at me, a tortured expression on his face.

"You mean kill it *now*? Why? It's going to die anyway. Why can't we let it die?"

Why? Because I don't need memories to know right from wrong. Because Bishop insisted on hunting this animal to exhaustion. Because if I was a better leader, I would have stopped him from hunting it in the first place. Because Latu was hurt and we should have stayed with her. Those and a hundred other reasons, but there is one reason that stands out above all others.

"Because it's not *humane*," I say.

The pig lets out a high-pitched whine. It tries to get up, but can't.

I feel a cool tickle on my cheeks. I touch there, look at my fingers . . . *tears*. I couldn't cry for Yong, but I can cry for a pig?

The knot in my chest is as hard and tangled as the branches we crawled through to get here. Just as sharp, just as jagged.

That voice in my head stirs, the one that said *Crying doesn't fix anything*, the one that told me to *always attack*. It's a man's voice, swirling up from somewhere in my hidden memories.

It says, *Choices have consequences*.

The voice is right.

"You wanted to hunt it," I say to Bishop. "So finish the hunt."

He says nothing. The pig continues to whine, each small sound a pointy stick jabbing into my soul.

Knife shaking in his hand, Bishop kneels next to the pig. It tries to lift its head. Its hooves twitch—it wants to run because it knows what is coming, but it has nothing left with which to fight. Even now, with blood seeping onto the grass, this animal wants to live.

In that way, it is no different from us.

We know the pig can bite. Bishop isn't taking any chances. His free hand shoots out, pinning the black furred head to the ground. Bishop leans forward, using his weight to hold the animal still. The pig squeals and grunts, breaths ripping in and out. The legs kick a little bit more, then it stops struggling.

Bishop presses the knife's edge against the pig's thick neck.

I wait.

I wait some more.

The pig's eye looks up at me.

"It's terrified," I say softly. "It's hurting. Please, finish this."

The knife hand trembles.

I see the muscles in Bishop's shoulders twitch and bunch up. He's trying to cut, but his hand won't obey.

He lets out a soft little moan.

Bishop knows how to hunt. He knows how to throw a spear. He knows how to hit people and how to yell and scream.

But he doesn't know how to kill.

He lets go of the pig's head and sits back on his heels.

The animal is still breathing. Each breath is a spasm of torment. I can't let this continue.

"Give me the knife."

Bishop's head snaps up. He looks at me like I am a total stranger. "Just let it die on its own."

I hold out my hand, palm up. "Give it. You've never killed anything before."

Bishop stands. A wave of anger visibly washes over him. He leans toward me, trying to intimidate whether he knows he's doing it or not, but his anger isn't because of me—he's frustrated, furious with himself, and will take it out on anyone or anything.

"No, I've never killed anything before," he says. He sneers. "Have *you*?"

I look into his eyes, and I nod.

There is a moment of disbelief, then his anger drains away. He knows I am telling the truth.

"What did you kill?"

"A boy," I say. My voice sounds like it belongs to someone else, someone incapable of emotion. "His name was Yong. He attacked me."

It was an accident, I didn't mean to do it, he gave me no choice.

Bishop is stunned. He is the biggest, he is the strongest, he is the loudest. And me, tiny little me, has done something to another human being he can't even do to a wounded animal.

"You killed," he says. "A *person*. You killed a person? You can't . . . I don't understand. But . . . *how*?"

While he stammers, the pig suffers. We've talked long enough.

I hold my hand out again.

"I killed him with that knife," I say. "That's how. Now give it here."

He offers it to me. He forgets to do it hilt-first. I reach around the blade and take the knife from him.

I kneel next to the pig.

"Hold it down," I say.

Bishop kneels, again presses the big head to the grass.

I put my hand on the pig's shoulder. It's warm. I can feel the *thump-thump* of its panicked heart pounding through its body. Yong died because I stabbed him in the belly, but it took a long time. I can't do the same to this animal; it has suffered enough.

I slide my hand to the thick neck. The muscle there is so firm, almost as solid as wood.

Something tells me this is where I should cut.

I rest the knife's edge against it.

"Em, don't," Bishop says in a voice so quiet I barely hear it even though he is right at my side.

It would be easier to let the pig die a slow, agonizing death. But I'm not going to do the easy thing . . . I'm going to do the *right* thing.

The pig's eye swivels: it looks at me.

"I'm sorry," I say.

I lean in and slice the blade forward.

Filthy black fur and the muscle beneath it part with no resistance. There is a frozen moment where the cut sits deep and empty, then it fills with blood. I push down harder as I draw the blade back.

Blood spurts out onto the grass, splatters across my face and arms. The pig kicks hard, as if realizing—too late—that this is the end. Bishop throws his body on top of it, weighs it down. The pig twists and tries to bite. Bishop's hands clamp tight on the animal's muzzle.

The pig squeals louder than ever before, and keeps squealing. I want it to die, *please* die, I need that sound to *stop*.

Bishop is crying, big sobs that shake his big body.

I'm crying, too.

I slice forward again, then back again, pushing down with all my strength.

The pig's squeals fade, turn into soft grunts.

After a moment, the animal falls silent.

The pig's eye is still looking at me, but there is no longer any life in it.

I'm numb. I didn't think it would be like that. I didn't know what to think, I'm not sure if I thought at all . . . but not like that.

I don't know how much time passes before Bishop slides off. He sits next to me. He takes me in his bloody arms and squeezes me tight. His forehead presses against my neck. I drop the knife and I hold him.

We hear footsteps approaching. We both look up: El-Saffani is there. The twins stare down at the pig, stare at the two of us sheeted in blood.

Bishop and I get to our feet.

The twins talk together, first the boy, then the girl.

"We followed the trail—"

"—the bloody footprints made it easy—"

"—and found where you went through the hole in the door."

Their heads angle down at the same time. They look at the pig, then at Bishop, their eyes bright with astonished admiration.

"It's dead—"

"—you killed it, Bishop—"

"—you are so brave."

Bishop shakes his head.

"I tried, but I couldn't do it," he says. "It was Em."

The twins turn their gaze on me. They still have that hard stare, but now there is something different about it—I am no longer the enemy.

Bishop could have lied, could have said he killed the pig and they would have believed him, but he didn't. He told the truth, instantly and without hesitation.

The pig is dead, yet the horrific squeals still echo in my head alongside Yong's cries for his mother.

My body, my mind and my spirit, they are all spent. I can't think. I can't even *feel,* and I don't know if I will ever feel again.

We have food. We have water, probably, but something nags at me. Something is wrong.

I stare at the twins, trying to figure out what it is.

Then it hits me.

"Where's Latu?"

"Back where she got bit—"

"—she said she was fine—"

"—she told us to come after you."

My fists clench instantly, so hard my fingernails are daggers punching into my palms.

"You *left* her?"

The twins look at each other. They are little kids again, kids who suddenly realize they've done something bad.

"She wanted us to help you get the pig!"

"Because everyone is so hungry!"

"She has a torch—"

"—with extra rags—"

"—*she said* we should go!"

They left her, alone and wounded.

I hear an animal grunt. The noise spooks me, makes me look down at the pig to see if it has suddenly come back to life. No, there is no life there, and never will be again.

A second grunt. My eyes flick up at the sound: there, to the left, just past the tall grass in a cluster of trees that are heavy with red fruit.

A pig.

There are more of them?

A second pig head appears.

Then a third.

I feel cold inside, icy and brittle—how many pigs are there?

The third one grunts.

That grunt rolls around my exhausted brain, looks for a connection. Back when we were chasing the pig in the hallways, I heard a grunt like that—a grunt that didn't come from our quarry.

That trip to the farm, what the man in the funny hat said . . . more of his words flash through my mind, and when they do, I realize why all those coffins were empty.

"Latu," I say.

I snatch up the knife from the grass and I sprint for the thicket.

TWENTY-TWO

Sharp branches scratch my face, my arms and my legs, snag in my hair. The pain doesn't matter. I have to get to her as fast as I can.

I'm through the thicket and in the room on the other side of the wall before I realize I didn't bring a torch. That doesn't matter, either—I'm not going back.

I crawl through the hole in the stone door and emerge to total darkness. That awful smell is here, but I barely notice it. Left hand on the wall, right hand holding the knife, I run. The hallway is straight and I was just here; other than pig's blood, there's nothing on the floor to trip me up.

Is Latu's torch still burning? Did El-Saffani leave her enough greased rags? I'm desperate to see the light of that torch, to see her—I want it so bad I try to wish it into existence.

Faster . . . I must run faster. I try to sprint, but my body simply won't let me go full speed through the absolute black, as if I might run into something new, something I didn't see on the way here.

How could the twins have left her alone?

But it's not El-Saffani's fault. I left, too, chose to go with Bishop instead of staying with my wounded friend. She was *bit*, her shoulder all torn up and bleeding . . . why did I go with him? I wish I could take that decision back.

Without light, there is only sound: my wet, filthy socks slapping against the floor, my fingertips sliding along the wall, my rapid breathing that can't suck in air fast enough to help my burning lungs and screaming muscles.

Latu will be all right. She has to be. She *told* me to go, she said she would be fine.

Up ahead, a pinpoint of flickering yellow stands out like the brightest star in the night sky. It's still far off down the long, straight hall, but I've almost reached her.

The light grows brighter, larger. It's from a torch—a torch lying flat on the floor. Past the torch . . . is that Latu? Lying on her shoulder, maybe? I can see she's moving a little and my heart explodes with relief. She could still be in trouble, but if she's moving she's not dead.

Almost there. She's twitching a little. She's *alive*.

"Latu! Are you okay?"

At the sound of my voice, she stops moving.

Motion from something by her legs. Something black.

Six round, glistening spots pop into existence, dance in the torchlight.

Eyes.

Pig eyes.

Latu wasn't moving at all. The pigs were moving her.

No . . . this can't be happening. That slice of memory from my trip to the farm becomes clearer. The man in the funny hat was telling us that pigs will eat anything—grass, dirt, bugs, crops, meat, cloth, wood . . .

. . . even *bone*.

That's why the coffins were empty, and that's why the pig was in the coffin. It was looking for food.

Newfound strength floods me. I scream with rage and hatred and fury, a scream that would make even Bishop turn and run. I rush at them, at her, at the torch, sprinting and waving my knife in front of me. The pigs scamper away, grunting as they vanish into the darkness.

I reach Latu. I stop.

Tears blur my vision. I shouldn't have left her. I want that moment back I want it back please let this not be real. . . .

Wishing won't help, and crying doesn't fix anything, because reality is what it is.

Latu's dead face stares up at nothing.

I am standing in a pool of her blood.

The pigs ripped her to pieces. Her shirt—what's left of it—is a mess of red-soaked white.

They tore open her stomach.

They shredded her shoulder, the bitten one, chewing away so much muscle that I'm not sure if the arm is still attached or if it's just lying in the right position to make it look like it is.

Parts of her are scattered about the hallway, lying among the bloody hoofprints of her killers.

They ate her feet. Her *feet*. Sticks of red-smeared broken white jut out from where her ankles used to be. I see gnaw marks on the bones.

The pigs murdered her.

The pigs *devoured* her.

The pigs are food for us. We are food for the pigs.

Did Latu scream? Did she fight? I will never know.

I lean against the wall. My shoulder presses into a carving of a man harvesting wheat. I close my eyes.

I want to go to sleep. I want to go to school. I want to take a bath and put on clean clothes. I want Dad to cook me dinner. I want O'Malley's sandwich, Yong's pasta with cheese, I want Aramovsky's cupcake.

Why won't someone come for us?

Because . . . because we're not loved. That has to be why. We are discarded. We are unwanted. Our parents, they left us in this nightmare. They left us *alone*.

It stinks in here. It smells of pig shit and death.

I use the backs of my hands to wipe away tears.

Latu's dead eyes are looking at me. I know they are. Looking at me, blaming me.

My tears come faster, harder, making my sight shimmer, making Latu waver. Her face, it changes.

Now it's Yong.

How many more will die, Em? he asks. *How many more like Latu and me?*

"I don't know," I say. "I don't know how many."

I wipe the tears away again, harder this time, and look down at the body. It's not Yong. It's Latu. And she can't talk to me, because she's dead.

Things could have been different. I can't remember school, but I know I used to go to one. What if I'd met Latu in class? We could have sat at the same table at lunch. We could have played together at recess.

I would have invited her to my birthday party.

She would have invited me to hers.

Is it still our birthday? I don't know. There is no day down here. No night.

Latu and I would have been friends. Best friends.

We would have been *kids*.

But we're not kids. We have been thrust into these older versions of ourselves. This body . . . I'm different in it. I can't remember details, but I didn't cry this much before. I know I didn't. I never wanted to touch a boy's chest. I never got so angry I wanted to hurt someone, like I wanted to hurt Yong.

Is it my fault Latu is gone? Yes. And Bishop's fault? And El-Saffani's? Yes, even Latu's fault, too, because she insisted on coming when I told her to go with O'Malley. Choices have consequences. We all own a piece of the blame—but only a small piece, because we wouldn't have made those bad decisions if someone hadn't put us down here in the first place.

The people that did this to us, they are the ones responsible. Latu's death is on their hands. So is Yong's. All the pain and hunger and thirst, all the blood, it's their fault.

I want to find out who they are. I want to make them pay.

Footsteps echo down the hall. Human footsteps.

Moments later, I see the torchlit faces of Bishop and El-Saffani. They stand there, shocked, staring down at Latu's mutilated body.

Bishop looks at me. "Pigs?"

I nod.

"It's horrible, she—"

"—must have screamed so much."

If I yell at El-Saffani for leaving Latu alone, it won't make any difference. It won't bring her back, so I stay silent.

I squat down on my heels. I don't kneel, because I don't want Latu's blood on my skin. I reach out and take her left hand. It's free of blood, somehow, and it's still warm.

"I'm sorry," I tell her.

I realize I said those same words when I cut the pig's throat, and that infuriates me. The people that put us here . . . I want to cut *their* throats. I want to kill them all.

I rest Latu's hand on her chest. I don't touch her right hand, because two of the fingers have been chewed off.

When I stand, I look away, and I will never look at her body again. I choose to remember Latu with her frizzy hair flying because we're on a swing set, side by side, laughing in the sunshine during recess as we dare each other to go higher and higher.

"Bishop, take Latu into the dome room," I say. "Put her on that stone circle, and bring me the spear."

He pauses for a moment, then bends to scoop up my friend. I don't watch.

"El-Saffani, put a new rag on Latu's torch and give it to Bishop," I tell the twins. "Fix your own torch as soon as you're done. Divide the remaining rags into two piles. Bishop and I will take half, you'll stay here with the rest."

The twins glance at each other, afraid, doubtful.

"We're staying here—"

"—and you're leaving us?"

"That's right. Bishop and I are going to get the others. You guard the door—don't let any pigs get near Latu's body."

Bishop comes out of the room. He hands me the spear. I take it, then offer it to the twins.

"If the pigs come near you, kill them," I say. "The spear is long, so you can stay inside the door and stab them from a distance. The doors are narrow enough that they can only enter one at a time. Even if there are a hundred pigs, you should be able to hold them off until Bishop and I return with the others. Then we're all going to the garden."

The Garden. That name is as good as any, and it fits.

Girl El-Saffani starts working on Latu's torch, leaving Boy El-Saffani to take the spear with a trembling hand. He looks at it as if he can't believe he's holding it.

"Shouldn't we all stay together?" he asks.

We should. I know we should. There is strength in numbers.

But if we leave Latu, the pigs will eat her up. I won't let that happen.

"Stay here," I say, more firmly this time. "When we come back, we will take Latu's body with us. We're going to bury her."

My friend Latu will not wind up as a pile of dusty bones.

Any of these three circle-stars could ignore my commands, but they don't. They look at me like I'm different. Well, I am different—I am the one who kills.

Girl El-Saffani finishes with Latu's torch. It flares to life. Torches are always brightest when the fire first starts.

I flip the knife in my hand, offer the hilt to Bishop. He's stronger and faster, it makes sense for him to have the weapon.

He shakes his head, like he's not worthy of holding the knife. He is ashamed.

"Then I'll carry it," I say. "You take the torch."

He does.

Bishop and I head down the hall at a fast jog.

We're going to get our people.

TWENTY-THREE

We rest.

Everything is different.

Bishop and I reached the others with no further problems. We didn't see any pigs.

O'Malley had kept everyone calm. The second I told them about food and water, they were ready to do whatever I asked.

Then I told them about Latu. I think some of Bishop's marchers didn't believe me, didn't believe that she was dead. That, or maybe they didn't understand what death really meant.

When we got back to El-Saffani, I wanted to make it clear how dangerous this place is. I made everyone go into the dome room and look at Latu's body—then they understood death just fine.

While Bishop and I were gone, El-Saffani heard grunting and snuffling out in the darkness, but the pigs didn't try to enter the dome room. That disappointed me a little; I'd hoped that more of them might be dead.

Bishop took the last flag—the one Bello and Okereke used to

hold the greased rags—and rolled Latu's body in it. He carried her over his shoulder like she weighed nothing.

It seemed to take no time at all to reach the Garden. One by one my people crawled carefully through the scratching tunnel. I told everyone to stay close to the thicket. Bishop must have said something to the circle-stars along the way, or El-Saffani did, because Visca, Farrar, Bawden and Coyotl made sure no one ignored my orders.

As people wandered, ate, stuck their faces in the bubbling spray of water or just gawked at the size of the Garden, I stumbled to the tree where Bishop picked me the blue fruit. I sat down. I haven't been able to get up since. I don't *want* to get up.

Bishop and El-Saffani carried Latu to another tree. They buried her beneath it. They dug the hole with their hands, wouldn't let anyone else help them.

Aramovsky said a few words, but Latu's grave is far enough away from the blue fruit tree that I couldn't quite hear him. I don't know if his words had meaning, or were just random thoughts, like when Yong died. It doesn't really matter, though. As Spingate said, the dead don't care—and neither do I.

I wanted to bury the pig, too, but Spingate and Gaston quickly talked me out of it. They said we need meat as well as fruit. Gaston built a fire. People are cooking the pig. It smells amazing.

Hard to believe I cried when I sliced that stupid animal's throat. When it's done cooking, I'm going to eat it, and I'm going to enjoy it.

I want to kill *all* the pigs. Their squeals and their human-looking eyes won't ever bother me again. They killed my friend. They will kill more of us if they get the chance. That means to be safe, we have to wipe them out.

If it's us or them, I choose them.

Spingate brought me water. We don't have any bowls or glasses, so she soaked a shirt and wrung it out over my mouth. It was cool on my tongue. My throat rejoiced. The more I swallowed, the more my body relaxed.

I hope it was a shirt that didn't have blood on it.

My eyes are so heavy. I'm not quite asleep, not quite awake. I have never been this tired.

I'm vaguely aware of someone sitting down next to me.

"Em, are you okay?"

It's O'Malley. I like his voice.

"Fine," I say. "I'm fine."

I don't sound fine. I sound like my imaginary conversation with Yong will soon be real, because I'll be as dead as he is.

My eyes flutter partway open. Off to the right, I see a little tree with orange fruits. I can't turn away from it, not even to see O'Malley's face. He's very pretty to look at, but those orange fruits are pretty, too.

"Farrar said we should set up a perimeter," O'Malley says. "For the pigs. Just in case. I did that while Bishop buried Latu. I have Farrar, Bawden and Coyotl watching. They'll do that while the others rest, then I'll have them switch off. We're safe, Em."

"All right," I say.

I feel a warm hand on my forehead, stroking my hair. It's very nice.

"You can sleep now," O'Malley says. "You need it. We'll figure everything out later."

His voice sounds rough, weary, like he's not doing that much better than I am.

O'Malley walks off. If I sleep, is he in charge? I think so. I hope he doesn't mess things up. But hey, if no one dies? Then he's better at the job than I am.

My eyes close. I force them open one more time. I can't really see that much, though. Everything is a blur.

I hear a sound that I thought I might never hear again: people laughing.

No one is being disrespectful to Latu, it's just that we have food, we have water. We are *safe*.

Laughter. It's a good sound.

My eyes close.

PART III

FOOD AND SHELTER

TWENTY-FOUR

A piercing scream snaps me awake.

So bright, hard to see. My hands search the ground around me, seeking out the spear, but all I feel is cool dirt and soft plants. The spear isn't here, where is it *where is it?* The pigs, coming for me, coming to tear out my insides and eat my bones, coming for all of us, and—

The scream again . . . followed by a laugh.

My vision adjusts. I look around. My friends are sitting under trees or lying near the reeds. They are eating, talking, sleeping. Everyone is calm.

There is no danger.

The scream, it came from Spingate. She's in the tall grass, wrestling with Gaston. They are laughing.

Under a tree to my right, Aramovsky is standing, talking to a group of people who sit around him in a semicircle. Opkick, Johnson and Cabral, if I remember their names right. By the bubbling spring, Bello and Ingolfsson are making neat piles of fruit. I see O'Malley talking to Borjigin, a half-circle who carries himself more like a girl than the boy he is.

And farthest off, past the long rectangle of reeds that stretches away from me, I see three muscular backs. None of them are wearing shirts. I don't even need to see their faces to know who they are: the dark skin and thick neck of Farrar, the white hair and pink skin of Visca, the wide shoulders and crisscross scratches that can only belong to Bishop. They stand there, in the tall grass, staring out into woods that stretch far away down this long room.

They are guarding against pigs, against the next danger we might find.

I notice that a few others have also abandoned their shirts. Coyotl, Bawden, El-Saffani . . . all the circle-stars. Girl El-Saffani and Bawden don't seem to care that their breasts are exposed, but it makes me very uncomfortable. They should be covered up, like all the other girls are. Do they think being circle-stars makes them different? I guess the answer is that they *are* different. Without their shirts, the circle-stars look like a group— a group separate from the rest of us.

That worries me.

Bello sees me. Her face lights up. She hops to her feet and rushes over. The way the arched ceiling's light catches her blond hair makes her look like she glows from within.

"Em! You're awake. I was worried about you, you slept a long time."

"I did? How long?"

She frowns, shrugs. "Who knows?" She points to my shirt. "You were so out of it you didn't even wake up when we took that off you."

My shirt . . . most of the blood is gone. The dirt, too. Faded stains remain, though, pink where the blood was, light brown from the dirt, faded green from grass stains. The shirt feels a little stiff, as does my skirt.

My clothes feel *clean* . . . and so does my skin.

I look at Bello, confused.

"We washed you," she says. "Me and D'souza. She's a circle, like us."

My hands automatically cover my breasts, even though my shirt is buttoned all the way up.

"You took my clothes off?"

Bello pats my shoulder. "It's okay, the other girls sat in front of you so the boys couldn't see. We washed your clothes and wiped all that gunk from your body. You had lots of scratches. Smith cleaned those. She wouldn't let anyone else touch your wounds. She cleaned up Bishop's, too."

Smith. The tall, skinny girl. The circle-cross.

My hair feels different. I pull the braid around in front of me: it's been redone. Someone tied off the end with a strip of white fabric, torn from a boy's shirt, no doubt.

"We fixed your hair," Bello says. "Even that didn't wake you up. You must have been really tired."

I slept through them undressing me, cleaning me and braiding my hair.

"Maybe *tired* isn't the word for it," I say.

Bello nods. She looks so relieved, like she thought maybe I was going to die. She leans in and hugs me.

I hug her back. It feels so good to hold her.

People saw me naked. I don't like that. Maybe it's silly to feel that way considering all we've been through, but no one should take off someone's clothes without their permission. That's creepy. I know Bello and the others were trying to be nice, though, and it's good to feel clean again, so maybe now isn't the time to say anything about it.

Bello leans back.

Ah, I should have known . . . she's starting to cry.

"Oh, Em, you look so much better now," she says. These tears are from happiness, apparently. "Are you hungry?"

Since I fought my way out of the coffin, what have I eaten? Just the one piece of blue fruit, I think.

"I'm starving," I say.

"Let me get you something." She hurries away.

I stand on weak legs. I lean against a tree trunk for balance. Every muscle in my body aches.

O'Malley glances my way, as if to check on me. He sees I'm up and his face breaks into a wide smile. I don't think I've seen him smile like that before—he is so handsome. Even from a distance, his blue eyes shine like gemstones.

I realize he's holding the spear.

He jogs toward me. Spingate and Gaston see me, too. They stop their wrestling game and scramble to their feet.

Aramovsky notices the commotion, then notices me. He gives me a funny look, then goes back to talking to the people seated around him. I wonder what he's saying.

O'Malley is still smiling when he reaches me.

"Em, I'm so happy you're awake," he says. "We were beginning to worry."

Spingate runs in. The scepter bounces against her right hip, held there by a loop of white fabric that hangs down from the left side of her neck—made from another circle-star shirt, probably.

She wraps her arms around me, squeezes me tight.

I wince, cry out from unexpected pain.

She lets go quickly. "Oh, I'm sorry! Did I bump your scratches?"

I laugh, a little embarrassed. "No, I hurt all over."

Gaston grins. He points a single finger, reaches toward me slowly, and gives me a firm poke in the right shoulder. The sore muscle there barks with dull pain. I twist my shoulder away from him.

"That hurt," I say. "What did you do that for?"

He laughs. "To see if it would hurt, I guess."

Spingate scowls at him. "It's not funny to hurt people, Gaston."

"I know, I know," he says. "Sorry, Em."

Gaston is strange. Likable, but strange.

I notice that his clothes are still dirty. So are Spingate's. No, that's not right—all the blood is gone from her shirt. So she cleaned it, then got dirty again? It's dust, mostly, but also grease streaks and a few flakes of rust. That isn't just from playing in the grass. While everyone was either sleeping or cleaning, Spingate and Gaston were doing something else.

I reach out and brush a bit of rust from her sleeve.

"Where did you two go?"

Her eyes widen. Her face reddens.

"Uh . . ." is all she can say.

Gaston grins. "We took a torch and explored more of the straight hallway."

This news catches O'Malley by surprise.

"You did *what*?"

"We ex-plooooored," Gaston says, drawing the word out like he's talking to a stupid person. "We followed the hallway to see where it goes. Does that answer your question, O'Malley, or do you need me to find another way to explain what *explored* means?"

"I know what it means," O'Malley snaps. "In this case, it means *We snuck away and went off on our own without permission*."

Gaston rolls his eyes. "Oh, I see, without permission. Hey, everyone, I found my dad! Turns out his name is O'Malley. You know, come to think of it, all that fruit I ate is giving me gas. When I need to take a crap, can I just go, or do I have to get your *permission* first?"

O'Malley is getting angrier, which obviously makes Gaston happy. Why does he have to poke at people?

"This isn't about permission," I say. "It's about staying safe. We can't get separated. Didn't you see Latu's body?"

Gaston looks at me for a moment, then down. Yes, he saw Latu's body, and yes, that image stuck with him.

"Maybe we shouldn't have gone off by ourselves," he says. "But we can't stay here forever. I wanted to see how far the hallway went, in case there was trouble, so we'd know how long we'd have to be in the dark. I thought I'd get some work done while you slept, so you don't have to do everything."

There is no sass in his words, none of the condescending tone he uses to talk to the bigger boys. He respects me. That thought fills my heart with warmth. For reasons I can't explain, Gaston's opinion of me is important.

O'Malley is fuming. "You weren't supposed to leave, Gaston. You either, Spingate."

"Yet leave we did," Gaston says. He glances at Spingate, grins. "And we discovered *all sorts* of neat things."

She turns even redder, something I wouldn't have thought possible. She's glaring at Gaston like she wants to choke him. Does she think I'm going to yell at her or something?

"Spingate, relax," I say. "So you guys explored, it's not the end of the world. Just promise you won't go off alone again, okay?"

She nods quickly. "I promise. So does Gaston."

Gaston sneers. "I didn't promise anything, so—"

"*Gaston,*" she barks, turning on him. "You promise Em and you promise right now!"

He rolls his eyes again, but not with the same defiance he showed O'Malley.

"Fine, whatever," he says. "I promise."

Why is Spingate so flustered by this? I feel like I'm missing something, but they both made it back okay.

"You said you found things," I say. "Like?"

"Light," Gaston says. "Maybe ten minutes away from the Garden, the hallway ends at another archway door. Spingate opened it with the scepter. Past it is the same kind of hallway where we all met—white walls, glowing ceiling, the same thing."

I have mixed emotions about that. The fact that if we keep going straight there will be light is good, because we don't have many torches left. But I was hoping he'd found something else.

"More hallway," I say. "No way out of the dungeon? You're sure?"

He shakes his head. "Not that we could see, but we didn't go past the archway. We sealed it up again and came back here." He grins. It's a very self-satisfied expression. "Yep, came right back. We didn't stop to do anything else. Anything at all."

If Spingate gets any redder, people might mistake her for Coyotl. What is wrong with that girl? Maybe she's tired. She looks like she hasn't slept at all.

"Anyway," Gaston says, "the hall goes straight and it goes uphill, which we all know Em loves so darn much. Once we've all had a nice rest, we can get going again. Because we can't stay here."

O'Malley huffs. "You already said that, Gaston."

The smaller boy nods. "And watch me say it a third time." He points to his mouth. "*We can't stay here.* Don't just hear it, O'Malley, *understand* it."

Why is Gaston being so annoying about this?

"Of course we can't stay," I say. "Everyone knows that."

Gaston smiles and crosses his arms. Spingate shakes her head.

I look at O'Malley. "Do people actually *want* to stay here?"

He shrugs. "Some of them."

"You told them we couldn't, right?"

"Em, everyone is so tired," he says. "They're happy they can finally rest. If some of them think we're going to be here awhile, with plenty of food and water, that *keeps* them happy. Sometimes it's better to let people think what they want to think."

That doesn't make any sense.

"It's always better to tell the truth," I say.

O'Malley glances at Spingate and Gaston, like he wants to say something to me but won't while they are around.

"Sure, Em," he says, his tone flat. "I'm sure you're right."

What does he mean by that? O'Malley is hard to read. In that way, he's the opposite of Bishop. I can tell what Bishop is thinking simply by looking at him. But O'Malley? His thoughts are his own.

He offers me the spear. "Here you go," he says.

I take it. I wonder if it even means anything anymore. The circle-stars accept me as leader with or without it, and maybe we're past the point of needing symbols.

We can't stay, but we don't have to leave this very minute, either. I look out at everyone. I see smiles, I hear laughter. Spingate and Gaston were *playing,* for goodness sake.

It's nice here. We could all use some nice.

No one is acting like nothing has happened and that this is normal. Everyone has changed. When we first woke up, I could think of Spingate and O'Malley as little kids in adult bodies. Not anymore. The ordeal has affected them. It shows on their faces. No one has forgotten what we've been through, but here in the Garden, things seem . . . better.

It feels like the hardest times are behind us.

Bello returns with a handful of steaming meat, so hot she's tossing it from her left hand to her right, giggling at the pain. I look in the direction she came from, and see thin smoke rising up. Okereke and Ingolfsson are poking at the blackened, sizzling remains of the pig. The air above it shimmers with rising heat.

Bello offers me the wet, greasy chunk of meat. It smells *amazing*. I lean the spear against the tree and take it from her. Now I'm the one flopping it from hand to hand, laughing as the scalding-hot meat seems to sizzle my skin.

"Go on," Bello says. "Try it."

I open my mouth to take a bite, then pause. This pig was rooting through coffins. That means it probably fed on bones, *human* bones. I don't know much about how these things work, but does that mean the pig meat I'm about to eat is made up, at least in part, from people?

Maybe. And maybe I don't really care.

I take a big bite. Hot juice squirts across my tongue. I wince and laugh, my mouth full. The meat is rich and delicious. It's not just the taste, which is amazing, it's that Bishop and I hunted this animal and killed it. We killed it to provide food for everyone. For reasons I can't explain, that knowledge fills me with a peace I have not yet felt.

Pig . . . pork . . . *pork chops*. That's what my dad used to make, at least as far as I can tell from my spotty memories. Did he leave me in this place, or did someone take me from him?

I would give anything to know what he looked like.

Bello runs off to her piles of fruit. I take another bite of pig before I've even swallowed the first. She returns with a double handful of food: one of the round orange fruits, a long green one, and a purple one that's curved like a shallow C. I can't wait to eat them all.

"The purple one is best," Bello says. "It's very sweet."

Everyone nods in agreement.

"Those are so good," Spingate says. "They make me think of ice cream."

Ice cream? I remember what that is. I gulp down the mouthful of meat, then take a big bite of purple fruit. It is cool and soft, sugary and sweet, so delicious I need to close my eyes and focus all my attention on how it tastes, how it feels in my mouth.

"See?" Spingate says, delighted. "Good, right?"

I nod even as I take a second bite. I tilt my head back and chew, savoring the moment.

The green fruit is next. It's very spicy and it makes my tongue burn a little, but the flavor is incredible.

O'Malley points to the chunk of pig still in my hand.

"Squirt some of the green stuff on there," he says.

I do, squishing juice from the green fruit onto the meat before taking another bite. Each of these foods is amazing on its own, but together, they are perfect.

Spingate peels the orange fruit for me. It has a thick, soft hide, with orange pieces inside that I can pop in my mouth one at a time. Cool and bright, they taste like sunshine.

The others seem content to watch me eat, which I do until my stomach is so packed it's hard to take a full breath.

I am happy—until I hear another boy speak.

"Well, isn't this nice."

It's Aramovsky. He must have crept closer while I was eating. I wonder if he washed his shirt like everyone else did. Not that I'd be able to tell—the boy never seems to get dirty.

"Good to see you awake, Em," he says. "It's nice you can smile and laugh when the dirt is still fresh on Latu's grave."

Everyone stares at him in disbelief. Everyone except me. I look at the ground, because he's right. How can I enjoy myself when Latu is dead?

"Aramovsky, you're a real jackass," Gaston says. "Em finally gets a moment to relax, and you have to say something horrible like that?"

The tall boy tilts his head, like he heard something he didn't quite understand.

"I didn't mean it to sound cutting, Gaston," he says. "Since Em has been the leader, two people have died. If I was the leader, I imagine those deaths would haunt me so badly I could barely function, but here she is, eating and laughing, carrying on like nothing happened." He shrugs. "Perhaps a short memory is a good thing for a leader to have."

I'm not hungry anymore. I let the fruit and meat slide from my hands.

Spingate looks at the dropped food. She sneers, strides to Aramovsky and stabs a finger in his chest.

"You ate your fill of meat, Aramovsky. And fruit, and drank plenty of water. Know why? Because Em found this place." Her hand sweeps from left to right, gesturing to the expanse of the Garden. "You point out that two of us are dead. You like numbers? I like numbers, too, so how about the number *twenty-three*. That's the number of us that are still alive, you ungrateful idiot. Em did a good job."

"No . . . I didn't."

My voice is flat and emotionless. I feel numb inside again. Spingate is wrong. If I had been a better leader, Latu would be here, eating fruit that tastes like ice cream. Yong would be here, too. He'd pretend to be bored, and he'd huff a lot, I'm sure, but at least he'd be *alive*.

Through the fruit trees, not that far away, I see the place where Bishop and El-Saffani buried Latu.

"Latu was brave," I say. "Much braver than me."

I see the others trading glances—they think I'm the brave one. They don't even know what a pretender I am.

Aramovsky smiles. "You haven't visited her grave yet, have you?"

I shake my head.

"Then come with me," he says. "Pay your respects, and see the price of failure."

Through all of this, O'Malley stayed still and quiet, but those stinging words seem to be too much. He steps forward, stands chest to chest with Aramovsky.

"Shut your mouth," O'Malley says. "You don't talk to Em like that."

Aramovsky holds up his hands, palms out. His body says he doesn't want to fight, but his eyes sparkle.

"So *angry*," he says. "I wasn't saying the failure was Em's. I wonder why you thought that's what I meant?"

O'Malley's hands ball into fists. If Aramovsky keeps playing word games, he's going to get hurt.

"That's enough," I say. "Everyone stay here, please. I'm going with Aramovsky to see Latu's grave."

O'Malley looks at me in disbelief. "Em, he doesn't know what he's talking about. You didn't *fail*. Latu's death wasn't your fault."

He's wrong about that, just like Spingate was.

"Come on, Aramovsky," I say. "Let's go."

Together, he and I walk to Latu's grave.

TWENTY-FIVE

The mound of dirt is about as long as I am, about as wide as I am, because Latu was about the same size I am. It could have been me in there. Still could—we're trapped in this building, or dungeon or whatever it is, forever stuck in this place of death. There might very well be a shallow grave in my future, too.

Her grave is under the shade of a fruit tree, which is nice. I think Latu would have liked to lie in the shade.

Someone wove a circle-star out of thin branches and laid it on the dirt. It's very pretty.

"Who made that?"

"Bello," Aramovsky says. "She and Ingolfsson spent hours on it. These trees all have soft branches. They don't make very effective weapons, apparently, because they bend easily. But that means they're good for making symbols."

We stare at the mound for a while. I'd say something, but what good will words do? Spingate said, *The dead don't care what you say,* but maybe the words you speak at a graveside aren't for the dead at all. Maybe those words are for the living.

Aramovsky sighs. "Such a loss. At least we were able to bury her. Will we be going back for Yong's body, so we can give him a proper burial as well?"

The question makes me instantly angry.

"Of course not. We can't go back now."

"As you say. You are the leader, after all."

He makes it sound like leaving Yong's body behind was my choice, when we had no choice at all. Not only does Aramovsky say one thing and mean another, he asks questions when he already knows the answers.

I stare down at Latu's grave. Dirt, flesh, bone, and a little marker made of soft branches. This is all that is left of her.

"You told me to come look at the price of failure," I say. "Then you said it wasn't *my* failure. Do you mean that Latu failed?"

I see his eyes flick to my spear. I realize how threatening my tone sounds. I didn't mean to sound like that, but I hope he heard it—if he intends to talk bad about my friend, he should choose his words carefully.

"The failure is all of ours," he says. "We have failed to give praise and thanks to the gods." He gestures to the grave. "This is the price of that failure."

I don't understand what he's saying. Gods? Maybe he's confused.

"Pigs killed Latu," I say.

He nods slowly. "Yes, it was the pigs. And who do you think sent the pigs?"

I start to answer him, then stop. *Gods,* another word of power, like *Grownups, rescue* and *tribe.* It pushes at the mud masking my memory. *Gods* means something more powerful than teachers or even parents.

Aramovsky is being strange, but there is some truth to what

he said. I'm sure gods aren't involved, but Latu's "killers" aren't here by accident. Someone put *us* in this dungeon, which means someone put the pigs here as well.

"I see this idea troubles you," Aramovsky says.

"It doesn't *trouble* me. I'm just thinking."

He smiles softly.

"We need to pay tribute to the gods, Em. Now is the time for you to order everyone to come together, so that I can lead them in prayer."

That look on his face. So smug. He thinks he knows everything.

"Do you actually remember something, Aramovsky? Do you remember where we came from? Why we're here?"

His smile fades. There is no kindness in his eyes. He wanted me to believe he knew the right thing to do, and when I don't, he's angry at me for it.

He acts so superior, but he hasn't *done* anything. Hasn't fought. Hasn't hunted. Hasn't bled.

"Well?" I say. "Do you remember, or are you making this all up to sound important?"

His lip twitches into an almost-snarl.

"I don't pretend to remember everything," he says. "But I know we are weak. In this time of need, we need religion to see us through."

Religion . . . the word bounces around the edges of my knowledge, teasing me with its importance. Religion was a part of school, part of my life with my parents. I know this, I *feel* it, but can't recall any details of what our religion was or why it mattered.

I do remember an emotion though: *hatred*. I hate religion. I don't know why, I just know that I do. Right now, that is all I need to know.

"We're not going to pray," I say. "We're going to rest up and then we're going to get out of here."

Aramovsky shakes his head at me sadly. The way he does it makes me feel like he's an adult and I'm still twelve.

"The gods are angry at us," he says. "You need to listen to me before someone else dies."

"Is that why you brought me to Latu's grave? So you could tell me this nonsense?"

His eyes narrow. I bet he'd like to squash me, but he can't because I have the spear. And, maybe, because he is afraid of me. Afraid because of what I did to Yong.

"Be careful, Em," he says. "Be very careful calling the gods *nonsense.*"

"Or *what*, Aramovsky?" I take a step closer to him.

He instantly takes a step back. His fear feeds me in a way that is different from how food feeds me, and yet it seems equally as important, equally as necessary. I know feeling this way is a bad thing, but I can't stop myself.

"If I'm not *careful*, Aramovsky, what are you going to do about it?"

The fear flutters across his face, then he seems to get control of it. The smug smile returns.

"It's not my actions you have to worry about." He glances at the mound of dirt. "Let's hope the gods understand. Let's hope they are more forgiving of you than they were of Latu."

My thirst for his fear turns sour in my chest, then changes to dread.

What if he's right?

What if we really should be praying?

No. He was wrong about monsters, and he's wrong about this. He's trying to control me, and he wants to use his *religion* to do that. *Religion* isn't just a power word—the word is power itself.

Something pinches in my stomach. At first I think it's caused by this conversation, but it's not . . . my belly feels bloated, odd.

"We're done talking about this," I say. "And don't let me catch you using Latu's death to spread lies about your gods to the others."

"Or what, Savage?" he asks, mimicking my words. "Do you think the gods are going to strike me down for talking about them?"

Now it is my turn to give the smug smile, my turn to mimic him.

"It's not the gods you have to worry about, Aramovsky."

His face goes blank. That lovely fear is on him again.

I leave him standing at Latu's grave.

TWENTY-SIX

Oh, all that fruit I ate . . . my belly is not happy with me. I feel a strange pressure on my insides. When I realize what it is, I cover my mouth and laugh—I have to pee.

I find Bello nearby, sitting by the reeds and the spring of bubbling water. She's sitting on something . . . a low wall? Yes, a stone wall that divides the reeds from the grass. The grass is tall enough that I didn't see it before.

She's laughing with two other circles: D'souza, a brown girl with black hair, and Ingolfsson, the muscular blond boy who looks as wide as he is tall.

The three of them smile at me. The ceiling's light plays off their cleaned shirts. Their ties are even knotted and proper.

My tie is gone. I didn't realize that till now. I wonder when I lost it.

They look at me like I have something important to say. This is so embarrassing. I lean in close to Bello and whisper.

"I have to *go*."

Her eyebrows rise, and she laughs.

"Oh, right, of course. Sorry, Em, I should have thought of that."

She stands and brushes off her skirt.

"I'm going to show Em around," she says to D'souza and Ingolfsson. "You guys keep washing the fruit, okay?"

They nod, go back to gently wiping fruits until the skins shine. I thought the fruit looked clean enough when it was still on the trees. We'll have to figure out how to take a bunch with us when we leave.

Bello slides her arm into mine and leads me away through the knee-high grass.

She leans in and whispers as we walk.

"I have to go, too," she says. "I can't get enough of those purple fruits. I should have told you, they give you the poops."

She leads me away from the thicket where most of our people are. The tall reeds are on my right. That stone wall Bello was sitting on, it continues here, divides the reeds from the grass. Now I understand why the reeds have a rectangular shape: they are on one side of the stones, the grass on the other.

I point at the wall. "What is that for?"

Bello shrugs. "Spingate thinks it used to be the edge of a pond or something. The wall held the water in. But no one's been taking care of it, so the pond filled in with plants or something."

On our left is the forest that lines the room. On the other side of the reeds is more grass, then the same thick line of trees.

If I was to walk from one side of this room to the other, I suppose that would take about two hundred steps. That's how wide it is. I can't say how long it is, because past the grass beyond the pond's end, the forest comes in from both sides, meeting in the middle. The trees are thick and tall; I can't see through them. It looks like the arched ceiling goes on for a long way past the tree line, though. This room might be five hundred steps long, it might be a thousand, it might go on forever.

I see Visca, Farrar and Bishop standing in the grass, facing the tree line. They are the "perimeter" O'Malley was talking about. I'm close enough to them that I can see the scratches on Bishop's back. They are still red and angry, but the bleeding has stopped. Smith seems to know what she's doing when it comes to wounds.

The three boys stand in the light, as if they are a wall that will stop the forest from belching out some new evil to attack us. Even though the ceiling above is blindingly bright, the forest's deep shadows could hide an endless number of threats.

"Bello, has anyone seen any pigs?"

"A few," she says. She points into the woods beyond Bishop, Farrar and Visca. "In there. But they haven't come out. There must be too many of us."

Too many, and we're not so wounded we can't defend ourselves.

We won't stay in the Garden for long, I know that, but maybe long enough to organize hunting parties. We could go into the woods, chase the pigs down. I don't know how many there are. There could be hundreds. But if we butcher every last pig, then I'll know for sure we got the ones that ate Latu.

Kill them all . . . wipe them out.

The thought fills me with a strange kind of joy.

"Em? Are you okay?"

Bello sounds concerned. I didn't realize that I'd stopped walking. I was staring into the woods. Staring, and thinking of a line of dead pigs, gutted and strung out across the grass. That thought made me happy.

"I'm fine," I say, but I know thoughts like those—and the fact that I reveled in Aramovsky's fear—mean I am not fine at all.

"Well, come on then," Bello says.

We start walking again.

I notice a few dark spots up on the ceiling. Irregular circles of varying sizes, some of them mushed together to form interesting, random shapes. Is it some kind of mold, maybe? I squint against the brightness, look closer—it's not mold. There's nothing *on* the ceiling: those dark areas have simply stopped shining.

More mysteries for Spingate to figure out, I guess.

Most of the ceiling glows bright as day. If only that light actually came from the sun, all we would have to do is punch through and we would be outside. We would be free. I would run so far, so fast, and I would never look back at this horrible place where Grownups kill each other and murder little children.

I turn my attention to the grass. The knee-high green blades sprout up through a thick mat of dead brown. These plants have grown, then died and fallen, over and over again. Maybe the grass was once nice and neat. Maybe Spingate is right and the pond once had open water instead of reeds. If so, that time is long past.

A stinging bit of pressure flares up below my belly.

"Bello, I really have to go."

She grimaces. "I know, me too." She points off to our left, into the trees.

"We've been going in there," she says. "It's inside the perimeter, but away from where people eat. The circle-stars patrol it pretty regular, make sure there's no pigs. And also the underbrush is thick enough that the boys can't see us when we make our business."

The boys . . . they're watching the girls? I know that's supposed to make me angry or concerned, but I wonder if O'Malley wants to look at me. I wonder if he watched me while I slept.

No, he wouldn't watch *me*. Maybe he would watch Spingate

or D'souza—I think they are the prettiest of us all—but not me. I'm too short. I don't know what I look like, but there is no way I am as beautiful as they are.

Bello leads me toward the trees. The grass ends abruptly where the tree shadows begin, giving way to vines and some other small plants that grow closer to the ground.

A few steps past the grass line and in the shade beneath the leaves, I see a fallen log. It is brown, rigid, no leaves left on its dry branches. It's a skeleton, a wooden version of the stripped bones we saw back in the hall. How long has it been here? I see more logs. Some are crumbling, a darker brown that is disintegrating into little pieces. There are scraggly bushes and smaller plants growing from and near the rotting logs. Vines climb over everything, even up the trunks of living trees.

This whole place looks . . . *wild*. It doesn't make any sense. We're still underground, I'm sure of it. How can such a wild place be in the middle of a dungeon?

As my feet leave the grass and step onto the vines and creepers, I get the feeling that someone is watching. I turn quickly; out in the grass, Bishop is staring at me. I expect his face to flush red because I caught him looking, but instead he smiles. I feel tingly. He should be embarrassed, but I'm the one that gets a hot face and has to turn away.

A pain in my lower parts reminds me I still have to pee, have to pee *bad*. I need to find a place where no one can watch.

I follow Bello into the woods. It isn't dark in here, because a bit of light filters through the leaves, yet the shadows are plentiful and deep.

We weave around tree trunks, edge past bushes, trying to make sure no one can see us. Branches catch on my shirt; I move gently, and they slide free. The dead leaves are thick, a soft mat that can't completely protect me from the broken sticks poking my feet. This underbrush is dense. I'm glad the circle-stars come through here, as Bello said, because this looks like a good spot for pigs to hide. If we stay in the Garden much longer, I'll make sure we find a better place to do our business.

Bello moves a little to the right; I go a little to the left.

The woods end at a wall. It's green and lush, the same thick branches that make up the thicket Bishop and I crawled through to get here. At the top of the wall, far higher than I can reach, the arched ceiling begins the sprawling curve that will take it up, away and across.

I slowly reach my hand through the thicket. My shoulder is starting to press against the stems when my fingertips hit cool, damp stone.

Stone, just like all the archway doors, just like the dome room and our coffin room. Maybe the walls aren't made *of* stone, maybe the halls and rooms were carved *from* it. And the way we're going up and up and up . . . maybe this whole strange place is inside a mountain.

Something hits me: that walk alongside the pond . . . that didn't feel like we were walking uphill. The incline has always been so slight it is barely noticeable, but when Bello and I were walking through the grass, that felt flat.

All this time, I believed that a step *up* was closer to a step *out*, but if we really are in a mountain, maybe the way out is actually *sideways*?

It hurts my head to think about it. I'll talk to Spingate after I pee. I swear, it feels like I've never gone in my whole life.

I'm surrounded by trees and bushes, bathed in shadow. I look around, but don't see Bello. For the first time since Spingate came out of her coffin, I am alone.

I rest my spear against a tree, slide up my plaid skirt and pull down my underwear. I realize that Bello probably washed those, too. I can't believe the girls saw me naked! What would my mother say if she—

Movement on my right.

I rush to cover up, thinking one of the boys followed us in here; I relax when I realize it's only Bello. She's a little ways away, doing the same thing I'm doing. Through the branches and underbrush, I see her smile a big smile that crinkles her eyes and makes her too-white cheeks rise up high, then she looks away. I can tell that she's embarrassed, just like I am.

Here in the Garden, Bello is a completely different girl than she was in the endless hallway. Maybe some people are meant to walk up front and face danger, while others are made to walk in back, where it is safe.

Still, I don't want her to be able to see me doing my business. I scoot a little to my left, putting a tree trunk between us.

Finally, a moment to myself. In that quiet instant, I can hear laughter from our group echoing out across the grass and into the woods. They are happy, they are safe.

I love that sound.

Movement on the right again draws my eye, but this time I don't look. I'm sure Bello wants her private time as much as I want mine. I hear a branch move, leaves rattle.

Then I hear something else: a muffled scream.

I look around the tree trunk. Through the leaves, I see Bello, see her wide, panicked blue eyes . . .

. . . and see something black clamped over her mouth.

She's yanked backward—Bello vanishes into the underbrush.

TWENTY-SEVEN

pull up my underwear and grab my spear. I run toward her, screaming as I go.

"Bishop! *Help!*"

Broken sticks and sharp twigs drive into my feet, but I ignore the pain. I reach the spot: Bello was here seconds ago. I stare at the thick underbrush, unable to see through it. Part of me says, *Stop, wait for help,* but Bello is in there—something *took* her.

I have to save my friend.

I charge straight into the tangled plants. Branches snag my clothes, scratch my skin. The pain is distant, a faraway thing. I crash through a thick bush. I see glimpses of Bello's white shirt as she's pulled deeper and deeper into the wooded darkness alongside the thicket wall. I rush after her. My foot catches on a vine-covered log and I tumble forward. As I go down, I see her face clearly, see what is covering her mouth:

A hand, long and bone-thin and gnarled, wrinkled pitch-black skin. A black arm is wrapped around her waist.

I land face-first, kicking up a cloud of dead leaves. I scramble to my feet. I see another flash of her shirt as she again vanishes behind dense branches. I snatch up my spear and I'm moving. Something has my friend . . . not some*one*, some*thing*.

(Kill your enemy, and you are forever free.)

I yell for Bishop again, then I point the spear tip forward and I charge in. That thing that is hurting my friend: I will cut it to pieces.

I will *kill* it.

From the left, something slams into me, sends me stumbling— I bounce off a tree trunk and tumble down in a flurry of sticks and dried leaves. The world spins. I taste blood in my mouth.

"Don't damage her!"

A new voice, a voice that promises murder, a voice I've never heard before and have also heard a hundred thousand times. The voice of a woman, of a *Grownup*. Something about that voice whips hard against the brain-mud suffocating my past— for a moment I can almost remember, then that moment is gone.

Where is my spear? I don't see it. My hands whip across the leafy ground once, twice, but I don't feel it.

Weaponless, I jump to my feet, turn to face this new threat.

I see a nightmare.

Two nightmares, a few short steps away. They are people but *not* people. Deeply wrinkled, coal-black skin covers spindly arms and legs. They have big red eyes, round and shiny, but no mouth—leathery flesh-folds dangle where a mouth should be. One is almost my height. The other is taller than me, with a jagged, dark-blue scar zigzagging down its chest.

There is something wrong about them, something that makes me want to turn and run, that makes me want to tear out my own eyes so I don't have to look at them, jab sticks in my ears so I don't have to hear them.

Bello isn't here . . . more of these *things* must have dragged her away.

The smaller one points at me. "Take her," she says in that voice I know but do not know. "Quickly, *take her!*"

The scarred one reaches for me. My hands ball into fists. I am afraid, yes, *so* afraid, but also enraged. It has to be them, the ones that put us down here, the ones that murdered those little children, the ones that let Yong and Latu die.

It grabs my left wrist and pulls me toward the thicket wall. I stumble, then plant my feet and yank back hard, jerking the monster around suddenly as if it didn't expect me to resist at all. I kick at its shin: where my foot hits, I feel something break.

The monster lets go of my arm, hops on one leg to keep its balance. The other leg is bent in at a funny angle below the knee.

"You *bitch*," it says. A man's voice, growling and hateful. "You always were a bitch, Savage."

If it has lips, those lips are hidden by the disgusting folds of skin hanging where a mouth should be.

It raises a trembling arm. There is something metallic ringing its forearm below the elbow, like a thick bracelet, and jutting from that bracelet is a metal rod that ends behind its bone-thin hand. Spindly fingers clench into a fist: the rod's metal tip is pointed right at my face. On the bracelet, a white jewel begins to glow.

The smaller monster grabs the scarred one's wrist, shoves the arm down.

"Don't shoot her," she says. "Just *take* her!"

Shoot her? That bracelet is a weapon?

Something heavy rips through the underbrush to my right, and suddenly Bishop is there, standing between me and the wrinkled monsters. Fresh scratches crisscross his bare arms and shoulders. A snarl twists his face into a mask that frightens me even more than these disgusting creatures.

He's holding my spear.

Bishop roars and lunges forward: the blade drives deep into the scarred monster's chest.

Everything stops.

Bishop's rage-face melts away, replaced by that confused look I saw when we first met. He's still holding the spear shaft in both hands.

Part of me sees the smaller monster scurrying off, vanishing into the trees, but I can't look away from what Bishop has done.

The scarred monster stares at the metal buried dead-center in its chest.

"No," it says. "No . . . I gave up everything."

Bishop makes a noise that is more a whimper of fear than a battle cry. He realizes what he's done, and it horrifies him. He yanks back, pulling the blade free. Thick, grayish-red liquid covers the metal. Bishop shakes his head slightly, automatically, as if he doesn't want to believe this is happening.

The creature drops to its knees. It sags to its right side. It doesn't move.

Bishop grabs my upper arm.

"Come on, Em! There could be more of those things!"

I try to wrench free, but Bishop is too powerful. All my strength barely moves him.

"They took Bello," I say. "We can't leave, we have to find her!"

He looks around quickly. I see what he sees—forest growth so thick that one of those black things could be five feet away and we wouldn't know it. We could be surrounded.

Bishop is overwhelmed, doesn't know what to do. His hand squeezes harder; it *hurts*. I don't think he knows how strong he is.

"Bishop, let go of me!"

He does, then shakes his head. "We can't go after Bello yet—we have to warn the others."

The others . . . are there more monsters in this sprawling room, closing in on Spingate and Gaston, O'Malley and Aramovsky?

I hear heavy things plowing through underbrush: more monsters coming to take us away. My chest turns to liquid and I cannot move.

Bishop spins to face the oncoming noise, blood-slick spear pointed out in front of him.

Farrar and Visca erupt from the tangled branches. Farrar sees us, moves to us, his eyes wide and his fists clenched tight.

"Bishop, what happened?"

Visca sees the fallen monster, takes a step away from it as if it were a spider about to strike.

A choked breath finally forces itself into my chest. I did it again—fear consumed me, and I *froze*.

Visca rushes to my side, his eyes flashing in all directions, searching for threats. "Em, I saw Bello come in here with you—where is she? And what is that thing on the ground?"

That thing is a monster, and Bishop is right: there could be more of them. Hundreds more, hiding in the shadows around us, slinking through the trees.

Visca and Farrar look to Bishop, waiting to see what he does, but Bishop is a mess. His hands flutter on the spear shaft. He can't stop glancing at the horrid corpse, at the red-gray fluid oozing onto the brown leaves and rotted fruit.

When Bishop doesn't answer them, Visca and Farrar turn to me.

They are waiting for someone to tell them what to do.

We either run blindly through the shadows and underbrush, hoping to find Bello, or we return to the others, warn them, maybe get more circle-stars and come back here with better numbers.

I have to make a decision, and I have to make it now.

"Come with me," I say, then I turn and run, away from the shadows and toward the clearing's light. I hear the circle-stars following close behind.

The trees thin. Leaf-strewn ground gives way to vines and creepers, then knee-high grass.

At the end of the overgrown pond, close to our thicket tunnel, I see people clustered together, terrified by the screams. O'Malley stands in front, knife in hand, flanked by Bawden and Coyotl on one side, El-Saffani on the other. O'Malley is clearly afraid, but ready to protect D'souza, Smith, Beckett, Borjigin and the others, people who cower behind this line of defenders.

I sprint along the pond's grassy edge, reeds whipping by on my left. As I run, I look to the woods lining either side of the Garden—so many trees, so many places for the monsters to hide, to sneak in, to grab more of us.

I can fight, so can the circle-stars, but what about everyone else? What if they can be taken as easily as Bello was? I need fighters by my side, not more victims to rescue. I need to get the weak ones out of here, get them out of the way.

After I found Latu's body, I swore I would never leave anyone alone again. When I reach O'Malley and the others, I know I am about to go back on that promise. I already hate myself for it, but I've made my decision.

"Everyone, to the thicket tunnel. Right now!"

They don't know what's happening, but they move just the same. As we run to the thicket, I call out more orders.

"Farrar, El-Saffani, go through and make sure nothing is waiting to surprise us in that room. We'll all gather there before we go into the hallway."

The three circle-stars instantly sprint ahead. Farrar throws himself to the ground first and starts in. By the time the rest of us reach the thicket mouth, the twins are already well on their way.

Do we have torches? I almost call out and ask Bello, but she's gone.

"Okereke, how many torches are left?"

"Seven," the boy shouts back.

That will have to do.

"Gaston, Spingate, you go in next," I say. "You'll be out front in the hallway, with me."

Spingate shakes her head.

"Seven torches isn't enough to get us back to the broken door," she says. "We'll be stuck in the dark."

"We're not going back. We're going to the archway you and Gaston found."

"But we don't know what's there," she says. "We told you, we didn't go past the door."

"*Light* is there, and that's enough for now."

I can't help but give Gaston a look that tells him he did well—his decision to explore might wind up saving lives. He sees the nod, understands it, gives me a firm one in return. Just as his respect is important to me, mine is important to him.

He crawls into the thicket tunnel. Spingate follows.

I point to the last four circle-stars in turn. "Bishop, Visca,

Bawden, Coyotl, watch our backs. Make sure nothing comes after us. Everyone else, into the thicket tunnel and stay in the room until I get there. *Move!*"

O'Malley waves them in one at a time, making sure they don't jostle each other trying to get through.

I turn and stand next to Bishop, both of us looking out at woods that seem to surround us on all sides. The monsters caught Bello by surprise, but now we know they are here—and we know they can die.

Bishop glances at me. "Do we go after her?"

I want to, and I also don't. I'm afraid to go back into those woods, which is what we have to do to find her, if she can even be found at all. I could take Bishop, Bawden and Coyotl, we could go back in . . . but if I do that, I'm leaving the others with fewer people who can fight.

"We're getting everyone to a safe place first," I say. "A room with one way in, where a couple of circle-stars can protect them. Then we'll come for Bello."

He nods. He doesn't want to go back into the woods, either, but I know that he'll do it.

O'Malley's hand on my shoulder.

"Everyone is in. What's going on? What happened to Bello?"

Do I tell him? Do I tell anyone who doesn't already know? The truth might make them panic. Right now people are afraid, but they are listening to me. All that matters is getting the weak somewhere we can better protect them.

"Trust me, O'Malley. I need everyone to move fast and stay together. Help me do that."

His blue eyes stare at me, blaze with a desperate need to know, but he pushes that need away. He crawls into the thicket tunnel.

"Visca, Coyotl, you're next," I say. "Then Bishop. I'll go last."

The words are barely out of my mouth before Bishop grabs my shoulders, turns me, and gently shoves me to the tunnel mouth.

"Go now, Em. We'll be right behind you."

He'll be the last one in. He's not going to discuss it.

I crawl into the thicket tunnel. I force myself not to rush, not to come out with new scratches. If I want everyone else to stay calm, I need to be calm myself.

The small room is lit by seven burning torches. I should have given orders not to light them until we were in the hallway. We've lost precious minutes and I hope we're at Gaston's archway before that matters. People are packed in tight. The air smells of burned cloth.

I wait for the last of our circle-stars to join us, then send Farrar and Visca through the hole in the door to make sure the hallway is clear.

It is.

One at a time, we crawl through the hole. Gaston and Spingate are up front with me. Even if it's a straight shot, I want them at my side because they've been this way before.

I look back for Bishop, but can't see him through the flames and the frightened faces. He will bring up the rear, protect us if the monsters try to chase us down.

Each second we wait is a second of torchlight wasted.

"Everyone, *stay together*," I shout, loud enough to be heard even back at the end of the group. "We're going to move fast, so don't lose track of the person in front of you. El-Saffani, lead the way."

The twins jog ahead a few steps. They are ready to take on any danger.

"All right," I say, "let's *move*."

We run uphill.

Doubts grab at me almost immediately. What if the monsters aren't only in the Garden? What if they're in this hallway as well? What if they are hiding in the rooms we might pass, waiting to grab us? Our torches dent the darkness, they don't chase it away—we might not see the monsters coming.

I should tell my people what I saw, so they can be on guard. I should . . . but still I do not. If I tell them what happened to Bello, will they panic at every flickering shadow? If I stop to explain, will we have enough light to make it to Gaston's archway?

So many decisions to make, coming so fast, and there are no easy answers.

The hallway rushes by. Carvings move like real life as torch shadows dance across them. I see archway doors in the walls— some open, some closed—but we don't have time to look inside. I keep us moving forward and hope for the best.

The fear I felt in the woods creeps back into my chest. Am I running to keep everyone safe, or because I am terrified of those creatures, because my wrist still feels cold where the scarred one grabbed me?

I try to push those thoughts away: I made my decision and I will see it through.

The hall reeks of fear: we are animals fleeing for our lives, no different than the wounded pig. I don't have to tell people to keep up, because they are all sprinting as fast as they can. Our collective footsteps thunder through the hall.

Before long, the hectic pace starts to take its toll. My body begs me to rest, to *breathe*. The monsters could be right behind me, coal-black wrinkles and red eyes and no mouths, ready to grab me and drag me into the darkness.

El-Saffani stops. Gaston's archway door. The stone halves are two giant fists smashed together to block our way. Our torches are all starting to flutter: we made it just in time.

Spingate slides the scepter out of her makeshift holster and goes to work.

I cup a hand to my mouth and shout to the rear of the group. "Bishop, see anything?"

"Nothing," he calls back through the flames and frightened faces. "I think we're all right."

The stone doors grind open. Beyond it, a white hallway with a glowing ceiling.

I lean in near Spingate. "Close it after everyone is through, then come back up front with me."

I turn to face the others. So much *fear*.

In that moment, I finally understand why I am the leader. I know why these people voted for me. We have had all we can take, yet we keep fighting. Everything could crumble to bits at any second, but that won't happen because I refuse to let it happen. These people, they are *my* people, and I will help them survive.

"If you're scared, if you're tired, look to me! We will not stop. I will lead you to safety. Follow me a little farther. Let's move!"

A new mood sweeps over them. I see their faces harden, I see them prepare themselves to do what must be done. Someone has to be the example, and right now that someone is me.

El-Saffani darts out ahead. I run, my feet kicking up fresh dust. Our people follow.

We need a room that is easily guarded. I'm tired but I can't show it. Keep going, legs—*keep going*. Get these people somewhere safe, rest for a bit, then go back for Bello. She is alone and the monsters have her.

A little bit more . . . a little bit . . .

My muscles scream, my lungs burn. I'm ready to collapse when Spingate and Gaston catch up to me.

She points ahead. Archways on both the left and the right. Some are open. We'll be able to defend those.

We've done it.

As we close in, El-Saffani stops. I catch up to them, breathing so hard my mouth hangs open.

The boy points to the ground.

"Footprints in the dust, Em—"

"—and dead people, lots of them."

Piles of dusty bones. The Grownups' war happened here, too, just as it did where we first woke up.

I see the footprints. Are those from the wrinkled monsters? Or are there more kids like us down here somewhere?

I stop and put my hand against the wall to keep from collapsing. I can't move another step.

"O'Malley," I say between gasps, "count us. Are we all here?"

He's barely even breathing hard. How can he run so fast and so far yet not be exhausted? He stands tall, looks back, his finger bobbing in time to the numbers in his head.

Bishop comes up from the rear, gently pushing past everyone so he can stand next to me. His bloody, bare-skinned chest heaves. He's still holding the spear. Even as tired and afraid as I am, I look at it. He looks at it, too—a little longingly, perhaps—then he offers it to me.

With a shaking hand, I take it. The blade remains covered in red-gray smears.

Bishop nods. I am still the leader . . . at least for now.

People are worn out. Some are sniffling, a few are crying. They are terrified and they don't even know the whole of it yet.

O'Malley finishes his count.

"Twenty-two," he says. "Everyone except for Bello. Em, what happened to her?"

I start to talk, but my throat stings too much to speak. I draw in a couple of breaths, try to steady myself.

"They took her," I say.

"*Who* took her?"

I look at the group. Aramovsky is close by, breathing as hard as I am. He looks at me with that arrogant face of his—I'm convinced he knows what I am about to say before I say it.

Maybe he deserves to be arrogant: because he was right.

"Monsters," I say. "In the trees . . . monsters attacked us."

Aramovsky's eyes widen at the sound of that word. He nods, slowly and solemnly, as if he always knew this moment would come.

All down the hall, faces stare at me in shock. *Monsters . . .* their leader just told them that monsters are real.

O'Malley shakes his head. "That's ridiculous. There's no such thing."

Bishop shoves O'Malley's shoulder, almost knocking him down.

"Shut *up,*" Bishop says. "You don't know, O'Malley, you didn't see them. I did. I saved Savage."

O'Malley's fingers flex on the knife handle. He snarls at the bigger boy, starts to step forward, but I put myself between them.

"It's true," I say. "There *were* monsters. Bishop killed one, I saw it. Another one of them took Bello."

O'Malley looks at me in disbelief. "Wait . . . the monsters *took* Bello? You mean she isn't dead?"

The way he says that, the astonishment in his voice, it makes things hit home—I left Bello alone. I abandoned her.

"I . . . I don't know," I say. "Maybe she is."

The moment those words leave my lips, shame hammers home. A piece of me—a nasty, small, horrible piece—actually *wants* Bello to be dead, because if she is, we don't have to go back for her, we don't have to return to the Garden and face the monsters.

O'Malley is shocked. He looks from me to Bishop, back again. "They took Bello, and you told us to *run*? We *left* her?"

The words sting. I want to argue with him, but I can't because that's exactly what we did.

Bishop's hand slams into O'Malley's chest: this time O'Malley hits the wall and falls to the floor. Bishop steps forward, points a finger down at O'Malley's face.

"You weren't *there*," Bishop says. "You didn't *see,* so you shut your mouth. We all know you heard Em's scream for help—everyone did—but you stayed where you were because you were afraid!"

O'Malley springs to his feet far faster than I expected. Faster than Bishop expected, too, because before he can react, the tip of O'Malley's knife is pressed against the base of Bishop's throat.

I feel my hands move the spear, move it as if they aren't a part of me, as if they act on their own. I see the bloody blade hovering a finger's width from O'Malley's belly.

"Put the knife away," I say. "Right now."

He stares at me, astonished, maybe even a little betrayed. I know how this looks—like I am willing to hurt him to protect Bishop.

O'Malley lowers the knife. He stomps off to the rear, shoving people out of his way.

I hear Spingate's voice: "No . . . no, it's not possible."

She is farther forward, standing by the bones and the footprints. Tears stream down her face. Her lower lip quivers.

"Not possible," she says again.

I rush to her side. "It *is* possible, Spin. They were monsters, I saw them."

She looks at me with those big, watery green eyes. She shakes her head.

"I'm not talking about monsters."

She points down at the dusty bones.

"It's impossible for *those* to be here, Em. Don't you see? These can't be here because *we walked in a straight line*."

One of the bones is mostly free of dust, as if it was picked up, brushed off, and set back down. It is a skull with a jagged, triangular hole smashed through the top.

Six sets of footprints lead away from the bones, down the long, white hallway. The footprints seem to begin at an archway on my left.

An *open* archway.

I know what that door leads to. Inside are coffins. Six empty, six with little corpses inside. And one of those empty coffins is where I first woke up, screaming in agony, trapped in the dark.

We are right back where we started.

TWENTY-EIGHT

This doesn't make any sense.

I walk to the coffin room. I know exactly what I'm going to see, but I must be missing something. I have this wrong, somehow, and so does Spingate.

I enter—two rows of six coffins, a well-trampled aisle of dust between them. At the end of the right-hand row, I see the broken lid of my coffin, sticking straight up into the air.

This is impossible. . . . We worked so hard. . . .

I walk to Brewer's coffin. The little corpse dressed in big clothes is still inside, the dried flesh flaked away from the skull right where Spingate touched it.

A boy at my side: O'Malley.

"We walked in a straight line," he says. He doesn't sound mad anymore. He sounds stunned, like it's hit him as hard as it's hit me. "We walked straight so we wouldn't get lost."

Doing so was my decision. Mine. I don't understand what happened.

The hope we felt in the Garden, it's gone. I feel numb again.

"I did something wrong," I say. "I . . . I don't know what happened. I tried to get us out."

I tried. And all I did was bring us back to the same spot. Yong is dead. So is Latu. I lost Bello. No, I *left* Bello. I ran away so we could wind up right back where we started?

We're never going to get out of this place.

We will all die here.

O'Malley puts his hand on my shoulder. I know he's trying to be nice, but it feels awkward. He senses it, too, takes his hand away.

"Em, Bello wasn't your fault."

I look at him. Those blue eyes, the shape of his face . . . how did he know I was thinking about Bello? I wish O'Malley and I were somewhere else, together, the two of us, some place without the fear and the confusion.

"Not your fault," he says again. "I'm sorry I yelled at you. I wasn't in the woods, I didn't see what you saw. If you say we had to run, I know you had a good reason."

The *good reason*? I was afraid, that was the *good reason*.

O'Malley is sincere, but his sincerity doesn't change anything. Reality is what it is. I was voted the leader. Everyone did what I told them to do, and we wound up here. O'Malley is wrong—this *is* my fault.

I don't want this stupid spear. I rest the butt in the dust. The blade—the blood on it tacky and half-dried—points to the carved ceiling. I could let go of it, just let it fall. Someone else should carry it for a while.

Gentle fingertips caress my temple. It stings, but not because of O'Malley's touch.

"You're hurt," he says.

I reach up and feel the spot. A lump, from when the monster slammed me against the tree. It's sticky there, and also down my cheek, my neck. I crane my head to look at my shoulder—spots of blood dot the white fabric.

I am clean no longer.

O'Malley touches my arm. The contact makes my skin break out in goose bumps.

"Your arm is hurt, too," he says. "Did the monster grab you?"

Four parallel red lines mark the skin there—obviously the shape of fingers gripping far too hard.

"Yes," I lie. "The monster grabbed me."

It was Bishop, his crushing strength, but he didn't do it on purpose. I don't want to give O'Malley a reason to hate Bishop even more than he already does.

O'Malley's fingertips reach out again, trace a warm line down my cheek. This time, his touch doesn't seem awkward. It seems *right*. Everything fades away, everything but O'Malley's eyes, the feel of his skin on mine.

"We'll figure out what's going on," he says softly. "You can't know everything. What's happening here is crazy, I know, but you're the best leader for us. The people follow you, Em."

I answer him in a whisper. "But *why*? Why do they follow me? I have no idea what I'm doing."

He shrugs. "Because there's something about you. And no matter what's happened so far, it's better to have you as the leader than Bishop. You saw how he knocked me down? You saw Gaston's eye, Latu's cheek?"

I nod. I'm glad I didn't say it was Bishop who bruised my arm. O'Malley is right, though—Bishop has a history of hurting people.

But then I remember what Bishop said in the hallway: when I yelled for help, he plunged headfirst toward unknown danger.

O'Malley did not. O'Malley stayed with the others, he didn't come after me.

My opinion of the two boys seems to waver based on which one I'm talking to. That's not how things should work.

"Maybe you're wrong," I say. "Maybe Bishop could be a good leader."

O'Malley huffs. "He's a bully. He throws his weight around, he intimidates. If he winds up in charge, it's dangerous for all of us. You're a good leader, Em. Bishop *acts*. You *think*."

I gesture to the room. "I'm a good leader because I *think*? Look around, O'Malley. Look where my thinking got us."

I want to trust in what O'Malley says. He's helped me make hard decisions. If it wasn't for him, I wouldn't have won the vote. But the fact that we are back where we started makes it clear: when it comes to his confidence in my leadership, O'Malley is plain wrong.

Another boy pops into my thoughts. Yong this time—the look on his face when I stabbed him, and what he said right before he attacked me.

You tried, Em, but you failed.

Maybe he was right.

I open my hand and let the spear fall away. It drops like a cut tree, slowly at first, then picking up speed before smacking into the aisle and kicking up a long puff of dust.

"I had my turn," I say. "Let someone else have theirs."

O'Malley shakes his head. "You can't quit now. We need you. I'll help. When you're in doubt about something, anything, you pull me aside and we'll figure it out together."

He should hate me right now. I'm sure the others do. I somehow led us in a circle, yet he says that's not my fault. Maybe there is a good reason he didn't come to help me in the woods.

Maybe he thought someone had to stay with the group, keep them together, keep them safe. The things he's saying right now, the intensity of his quiet voice . . . O'Malley *believes* in me.

Maybe he's the only one who does.

He's so close I can smell him. I shut my eyes, feel heat pouring off his body.

I have never felt like this before. I can't remember much, but I know that I have never been kissed.

I want O'Malley to kiss me.

Someone rushes into the coffin room. It's Spingate. I quickly lean away from O'Malley, like I've been caught doing something wrong.

"Em, I know what happened!" Tears still gleam on her cheeks, yet she is wild-eyed with excitement. "I know how we wound up back here! Raise the spear, Em. Bring everyone in and I'll explain."

She finds an area with undisturbed dust, kneels and starts drawing lines with her finger.

What is she doing? What is she going to say to everyone?

I look at O'Malley.

He picks up the spear. He brushes dust off of it, then offers the spear to me.

"We don't just need a *leader,* Em," he says. "We need *you.*"

I have no faith in myself, but for now, maybe I can rely on his faith in me.

My fingers curl around the spear. I lift it slightly. It feels heavier than it did before.

I walk into the hall. All heads turn my way. Some people glare with open anger. Some look at me with hope, with expectation . . . they still think I can guide them out of this place.

I raise the spear.

"Come into the coffin room," I say. "We'll figure out what to do next. El-Saffani, stay out in the hall, yell if anyone comes."

El-Saffani nods. People filter into the room, but Bishop lags behind. He walks to a skeleton. He reaches down and picks up a thick thighbone. He grips it in both hands, gives it an experimental swing.

Then he raises it above his head and he whips it down. It smashes against the skull with the triangular hole, shattering it, sending shards of bone skittering across the hall.

A piece of what used to be a person is now a weapon.

Bishop shows the thighbone to El-Saffani, gives a single, firm nod. The twins nod in return. They grab thighbones of their own. Without a word, they take up positions on either side of our coffin-room door.

Bishop has changed. Killing the monster affected him. He looks so solemn, so serious. That little-boy smile is nowhere to be seen.

And on his face, for the first time, I see a faint hint of stubble.

Bishop isn't a kid anymore.

I enter the coffin room.

TWENTY-NINE

Spingate draws pictures in the dust.

She uses her fingertip to make a line or a curve, then stops to think. When she does, she touches her face, leaving smudges and broken lines on her skin.

We all stand and watch. No one knows what to say about the magic that brought us back to where we started.

We went straight. We didn't turn left, we didn't turn right. There were no bends in either direction, not even subtle ones. We would have seen them when we looked far down the hall-way. Even when we were walking in the dark, it was still *straight*.

Minutes pass. There are twenty people in this room, sitting on the floor, leaning on coffins. Everyone waits. Spingate stares into space. She doesn't seem to realize that we're there.

Bishop leans toward her, over her, but he's not looking at the drawings—he's looking at her face.

A blast of anger wrinkles my nose and narrows my eyes. Does Bishop think Spingate is pretty? Her red hair, her long legs, her shirt tight against her woman's body . . . there's no way I'm as pretty as she is.

I rub at my eyes. Why would I worry about that now? My thoughts keep running away from me. Bello is gone and there are monsters—I don't care who Bishop looks at.

He spits on his index and middle fingers. He kneels, dips them into the dust. He drags his fingertips first down one side of his face, then the other.

Bishop stands. He has two lines of wet, dark-gray dust running down each cheek. His eyes are cold and hard.

He walks to the archway, bone clutched in his hand like a club. He leans out and quietly says something to El-Saffani. I know Bishop saved me from the monsters, but right now he's making me nervous. The look on his face, the sharpness of his movements . . .

He is *scary*.

Spingate draws another line. She had me call everyone in here because she said she knew how we wound up at the same pile of bones. Her silence makes the room heavy and awkward.

A few heads turn my way. Then a few more. People are waiting for me to speak.

But it is Aramovsky who finally breaks the silence.

"Tell us what happened, Em," he says. "Tell us what happened to Bello. Tell us about the monsters."

Now everyone is looking at me. Everyone except Spingate, who seems to have forgotten that any of us exist.

I take a breath. I didn't tell them before because I didn't want them to panic. They did what I asked them to do. Now these people—*my* people—deserve to know what happened.

I start talking. I tell as much of it as I can recall. The whole thing was a blur of movement and noise, of shapes and emotions. I tell them how Bello and I walked into the woods. I tell them why we went, no longer caring that I'm supposed to be embarrassed at how my body works. I tell them how she was taken, dragged through the underbrush. I tell them how I went after her.

Then I describe the monsters. Two of them, one tall, one about my height. Wrinkled and black. Not dark brown, not white or tan or pink or any of the skin colors in this room, but black like my hair.

As black as *rot*.

Spindly arms and legs. Hands like skinny spiders. Red things that might be eyes. Hissing voices, voices that made my nerves shudder—but I don't tell everyone how the woman's voice sounded strangely familiar. That part I keep to myself. I'm not sure why.

I tell them about the bracelet that might have been a weapon, and when I do, my stomach flops: dammit, whatever that thing was, we should have taken it off the corpse. Now it's too late.

As I tell the people what I saw, I see their fear swell. Our bodies are grown, but our hearts and minds are still those of twelve-year-old kids. I'm telling them that not only is the bogeyman real, he took one of our own.

But . . . those bogeymen can die. I tell them how Bishop killed one. Brave Bishop drove the spear into a monster's heart. The intensity of my words hides neither my admiration for Bishop nor my hatred for the creatures.

Gaston raises a hand—he has a question.

I almost laugh. I'm standing here lecturing while wide-eyed children wearing adult masks listen to me like I am their teacher.

I nod to him.

"You said the monsters *talked*," he says. "Tell us what they said."

I try to remember. So much happened all at once. I was furious and terrified.

"The little one said, *Take her.* I remember that part, but the rest . . . I'm sorry, I'm not sure."

Gaston scratches at his ear, thinking.

"I don't doubt what you tell us," he says. "I don't know that they were *monsters,* but whatever they are, they're down here with us. If we can learn something about them, it could be important. So try and remember, did they say anything else? Anything at all?"

He wants me to remember more, but I don't want to remember any of it. It was such a blur. That cold hand on my wrist, pulling me. They got Bello. They almost got me. My body starts to shiver. I don't want to think about that anymore, I don't, and yet . . . I do recall something else.

"The one Bishop killed. After Bishop stabbed it, it said, *I gave up everything.*"

A murmur rolls through the crowd.

Gaston waits for me to say more. When I don't, he holds up his hands, annoyed.

"That's it? What does that mean, Em?"

I shake my head. How would I know what that thing meant? Wait . . . the tall one said something else . . . what was it?

My shivering stops. My breathing stops. Maybe my heart stops.

I know what it said.

You always were a bitch, Savage.

It knew my name.

If it thought I was a bitch, it knew more than just my name—it knew *me.* That monster knew the person I was before the coffin stripped away my memories, before it erased my life.

And now that monster is dead.

But there are more of them. The little one, at least, and I didn't see how many actually took Bello. The monsters might know who I am. If I can find them, I can make them tell me.

This is important information. I should share it but I stay silent, like I did about the familiarity of the little monster's voice. There is something lurking in the muddy parts of my brain, something beyond a simple memory or two. When I think of discovering my past, an emotion overwhelms me.

Horror.

Who am I, really? What have I done? And do I actually want to find out?

Spingate finally stands. Her face is so smudged she looks ridiculous.

"A circle," she says, satisfied and proud. "We walked in a circle."

Her comment is random and jarring. A circle? What is she talking about? We walked straight.

Aramovsky steps toward Spingate. He smooths his hands down his white shirt before he speaks, as if wrinkles might get in the way of words.

"We didn't *turn*," he says. "To walk in a circle, we would have to turn right or left. Don't you know that?"

Spingate points to the ceiling. "Remember how it felt like we were constantly walking uphill?"

She scans the floor, looking for an untouched patch of dust among the hundreds of footprints. She finds a spot next to a coffin that holds the dried-up corpse of someone who was once named *N. Okadigbo*. Spingate kneels, draws a new circle. Inside that circle, on the bottom, she draws something I recognize instantly—a stick figure of a person.

Spingate puts her finger to the left of that figure, then slowly slides it through the dust, following the circle's inner curve.

"We *did* walk in a circle," she says. "That circle was *beneath our feet*. The floor kept curving up, but the circle is big—*really* big. We didn't understand what was going on."

She makes a new drawing: an oval. From the top and bottom of the oval, she draws two straight, parallel lines leading off to the right. She then connects the ends of those lines with a curve that itself runs parallel to the oval.

It's a *cylinder*.

Inside the cylinder, she draws another tiny stick figure, this one standing on the bottom line.

I realize what she's saying. I hear people murmuring to each other as they realize it, too—Spingate thinks we walked *up* that curve, gradually looping around until we returned to where we began.

We did walk straight, and we are here, so the picture makes sense. Kind of. But if we walked up the cylinder wall, why didn't we fall back down? I start to ask her, then stop myself: I've made enough mistakes already. If I ask a stupid question, everyone might think I'm too dumb to lead.

Spingate wipes her sleeve across her face, removing some of the dust and smearing the rest into long, gray streaks.

"The scale is wrong, though," she says. "The stick figure is way too big for what I drew. I think I could figure out how big the cylinder is. I need to do the math, do some . . . ah, what's it called? Oh! I remember now—I need to do some *geometry*."

This word pleases her, or perhaps she's just thrilled that she remembers something. Maybe our past isn't erased. Maybe it's just hidden away from us.

Gaston steps forward, pushing people out of the way more than sliding around them as he usually does. Stunned, he stares down at the image in the dust. He then looks up at Spingate.

"Amazing," he says. "You are amazing."

Spingate's proud smile blazes.

O'Malley shakes his head, trying to understand. "But how come when we got to the top we didn't fall on our heads?"

I smile a little. I kept that question to myself, yet he has no problem asking it out loud.

Spingate stares at the cylinder. She seems frustrated, as if she knows all the parts of the answer but can't quite put them together.

Aramovsky fills the silence.

"It's obvious," he says. "The gods don't want us to fall down, so they make our feet stick."

My smile fades. He's going to talk about this nonsense again? Now?

I'm surprised to see many heads nodding, agreeing with him. To them, it isn't nonsense at all. The word *gods* made eyes widen, made people stand up straight.

But why should I dismiss what he says without considering it? We didn't think monsters existed: Then I saw one. I didn't think gods existed, either—how can I say they don't?

Gaston starts to laugh.

Everyone stares at him. He looks around, surprised no one else finds it funny. His laugh dies.

"There are no gods," he says. He doesn't sound very convinced.

Aramovsky points to the dust-drawing. "No gods? Look at that. What else could keep us from falling, Gaston? I can't jump up and stand on the ceiling, can I? No, I would fall back down. It *has* to be magic, it has to be the work of the gods."

Gaston shakes his head. "You're wrong. It's got something to do with the size of the cylinder." He looks down at the drawing. "I . . . I can't quite remember, but I think the reason you don't fall is that you're not actually standing *on the ceiling*."

Aramovsky shrugs. "According to Spingate's drawing, standing on the ceiling is exactly what we did. Are you saying Spingate is a liar?"

Gaston's head snaps up like someone slapped him. "No, of course not."

"So we *did* walk on the ceiling," Aramovsky says. "If it wasn't the gods that kept us from falling, how could such a thing be possible?"

Gaston glares. He doesn't like Bishop, he doesn't like O'Malley, but he despises Aramovsky.

The taller boy crosses his arms. "Well, Gaston? We're waiting."

Gaston glances at the drawing, then back again.

"Just because I can't answer your question doesn't mean gods are real," he says.

Aramovsky's smug smile shows he doesn't feel the same.

"You should watch your mouth, Gaston," he says. "You shouldn't say the gods aren't real."

Gaston's eyes narrow in anger. "And why is that?"

Aramovsky looks around the room as he answers, making sure that everyone sees his face, feels his confidence.

"Because saying the gods aren't real makes them angry. And when the gods are angry, the gods punish us. They send pigs to kill Latu. They send monsters to take Bello."

Fury wells up within me. I told him not to talk about that, I warned him.

"Aramovsky," I say, "you need to shut—"

A booming voice cuts me off.

"The gods aren't *angry*, they are *testing* us."

Everyone looks to the door. Bishop stands there, his face completely covered with wet, dark-gray dust. He doesn't look like a person anymore, he looks . . . he looks like a monster himself. The whites of his wide eyes blaze brightly.

"Maybe we did something wrong," he says. "Maybe the gods are testing us to see if we're worthy. We will show them that we are by going to the Garden and taking Bello *back*."

That stops Aramovsky cold. When he speaks again, his voice is calm, soft. He's being careful of what he says to the hulking man with a face covered in dust and spit, and I can't blame him.

"The gods wanted Bello, the gods took Bello," Aramovsky says. "It is not our place to try and get her back. Do you want more of us to be taken?"

Bishop's upper lip twists into a fluttering snarl.

"I killed one of them," he says. "Maybe the gods sent the monsters, but the gods don't *protect* them. We are stronger than the monsters. We're faster. If they try to take more of us, then we will kill more of them. We need to go after Bello right now."

Farrar bangs a fist against his solid chest. Bawden lets out a bark of support for Bishop's words. The circle-stars adore Bishop, are ready to follow him to the Garden.

I thought the circle-stars accepted me as the leader, but maybe that was only because Bishop did.

O'Malley stands on a closed coffin. He holds the knife at his side.

"Strength and speed don't matter," he says, loud enough to be heard over the circle-stars' grunts of excitement.

Bishop sneers. "What do you know, coward? You haven't even seen one."

The insult hits home. O'Malley's jaw clenches tight. He points the knife at Bishop.

"You think I'm a coward? Come and find out if you're right."

Bishop doesn't hesitate. He raises his thighbone and strides toward O'Malley.

I slam my spear shaft against a coffin lid. The sound echoes sharply off the stone walls, makes everyone jump, makes Bishop stop. These boys are going to tear each other apart if I don't do something.

"That's *enough*! *You*"—I point the spear at Gaston—"will stop insulting everyone, and *you*"—I point it at Bishop—"will stop puffing up your chest every time someone says something you don't like, and *you*"—I point the spear at O'Malley—"will *stop* pulling that knife, or I will take it away, and *you*"—I point it at Aramovsky—"will stop talking about gods and magic and other such *foolishness*."

When the echo of my words dies down, there is no noise. No one speaks.

O'Malley stays quiet. My rant doesn't seem to have bothered him. He lowers the knife. Bishop looks down at the floor. So does Gaston.

Aramovsky stares straight at me, his nostrils flaring.

"We are in a magic prison," he says quietly. "Monsters have taken Bello. I will keep quiet for now, but if you think that what we have seen is *foolishness*, then you do not believe what your own eyes show you."

Spingate and the others watch the five of us, waiting to see what happens next.

Bishop is all emotion. He wants to rush off without thinking, without making a plan. His passion is contagious, but I can't let it sway me. We have lost three people—I can't bear to lose any more.

O'Malley is the opposite of Bishop. He always seems to think things through. I need his opinion.

"I saw Bishop kill the monster," I say. "He's right, O'Malley— our circle-stars are faster and stronger. So why do you say strength and speed don't matter?"

"Because of the bracelet," he says. "If the monster was going to shoot you with it, that means they can hit us from a distance. Now that we've killed one of theirs, I doubt if they'll let us get close again. Strength and speed don't matter if the monsters can shoot us before we get near them."

That didn't occur to me. We don't know what the bracelets do, but we have to assume whatever they "shoot" can hurt us, maybe kill us. O'Malley is right.

Bishop doesn't give up.

"Then we stay quiet and hidden," he says. "We slip into the Garden, sneak into the woods, and we find Bello."

He's desperate to go after her. He's ashamed he left her behind. So am I, but I can see it's worse for him. It's tearing him apart. I want to save her, too, or at least find out if she's dead, but if those bracelets really are weapons, we . . .

Wait a second—Gaston's story about the haunted room, with the three unbroken pillars.

"Bishop, the spear," I say. "You found it stuck in a body. Gaston said that body had something on its arm. Gaston, what did you call it?"

"A shackle," Gaston says. His eyebrows rise, he looks at Bishop. "The monster's bracelet, was it the same thing we saw on that body?"

Bishop thinks, then nods. "Yes. I should have thought of that, but when I saw that thing attacking Em, I . . . well, I should have thought of that."

My thoughts race, but this time, it isn't about boys or who wants to lead, it isn't about who is the prettiest.

It's about staying alive.

We walked in a circle. It doesn't matter if that was because of magic, or gods, or by some means Spingate can't quite explain.

What matters is we wound up back where we started. As far as we know, there is no way out. We could be here for a long time. If we are to survive, we need food and water, and there's only one place we know of that has those things.

The Garden, where the monsters are.

Monsters who have weapons that we don't.

"We're going to the haunted room," I say. "We need to find that bracelet. I'll go. Bishop, you come with me, and we'll bring—"

"*No.*" His word is a roar. His gray face clouds over. "We go after Bello, and we go *now.*"

The room is silent. Bishop stares at me. I stare back at him.

"The bracelet in that room could be a weapon," I say. "It's important."

I see the pain and conflict in his eyes. I ordered us to run away, yes, but doing so was his idea before it was mine and he knows it. He feels responsible.

"Bello is *more* important," he says. "They could be killing her right now. We can't wait. We'll beat the monsters, Em. Lead us to the Garden."

To everyone else, I know he sounds strong and confident. But his face, his eyes . . . he is pleading with me. He wants to fight.

I'm suddenly so grateful O'Malley talked me out of quitting. We don't understand how we wound up back here, but that doesn't mean walking straight was the wrong choice. I did the right thing. I did the smart thing. I kept us together.

O'Malley said it best: Bishop *acts,* I *think.*

And as badly as Bishop wants to redeem himself, I can't let him, not yet.

"This isn't only about Bello anymore," I say. "It's about all of us. We need to survive. I am going to the haunted room, Bishop, and you will take me there. We need to go with strength, but we also need to protect the people who will stay here. So, you decide who goes with us, and who guards this room."

Our stare-down continues. We are on the edge of coming apart, of the group splitting in two. That smile Bishop gave me back in the Garden, I doubt I will ever see it again—right now, he hates me.

He can hate all he wants, as long as he does what I need him to do.

Finally, the stare breaks. Bishop looks around the room.

"El-Saffani comes with Em and me," he says. "And Visca. And Bawden."

The tension in the room eases slightly, but it's not gone. The others are glancing my way. They think we should go after Bello. They are angry we left her behind. I led these people in a circle, so I can't fault them for doubting my decisions.

Bishop points his club in turn at two circle-stars. "Farrar, Coyotl, you guard this room." To my surprise, he then points at two more people. "Okereke, Smith, you help Farrar and Coyotl."

Okereke and Smith are surprised to be chosen for this duty, honored to be recognized by the biggest of us all. They aren't circle-stars, but I understand Bishop's choice. Okereke is strong and has an air about him that makes him lean toward danger rather than shy away from it. Tall, skinny Smith moves with grace and speed. She never stumbles or falters. Maybe she's a fighter as well as a healer.

Bishop then points the club at Gaston.

"And you," Bishop says. "The door to the haunted room only opened for you, so you've got to come."

Gaston puts his hands to his face. "Crap. I forgot about that."

Spingate shakes her head. "Gaston shouldn't go. He's too little, there are monsters now, and—"

"I'm not *too little*," Gaston snaps. "They can't get in if I don't go."

She shakes her head again, harder this time. She holds up the scepter. "They can take this, I don't care. I'll show them how it works."

"It didn't open with a scepter," Gaston says, his voice kinder now. "It opened for *me*. If I don't go with the group, there's no point in them going at all."

Spingate looks like she's fighting back tears. I can tell she has a hundred questions about how the door works, why someone else can't open it, but Gaston's face is set—he's going.

"Spin, we need him," I say. "Bishop will make sure he stays safe."

She looks at the gray-faced boy. "You better."

Bishop nods once.

"I'll go as well," O'Malley says.

His tone is hopeful, but not as firm as Gaston's. I think O'Malley already knows what he's going to hear.

"I need you to stay," I say. "You'll be in charge while we're gone."

Aramovsky huffs. "Really? Yet another terrible idea. O'Malley, do you believe in the gods?"

O'Malley shakes his head. "There's no such thing."

Aramovsky looks around the room, spreads his hands as if to say: *There, you see?*

"Em wants someone who thinks the gods don't exist to be in charge," he says, playing to the crowd. "Do you think the gods are going to like that? I don't. I should be in charge while she's gone, wouldn't you all agree?"

Some heads shake, but most nod.

A wave of fury wells up in my chest. He wants to take leadership away from me? I wonder what it would feel like to shove the spearpoint into Aramovsky's throat. If he contradicts me again, I could kill him just like I killed Yong.

No . . . Yong was an *accident*. I didn't kill him, he ran into the knife. That's what happened.

Isn't it?

I give my head a hard shake, clear my thoughts. Yes, Yong was an accident. I'm not going to kill Aramovsky for speaking his mind—that's crazy.

I think back to the Garden, to Aramovsky standing tall. People sat around him, watched him reverently, listened to his words. What was he saying to them? And, more importantly, what will he say while I'm gone? Bishop is in danger of splitting the group, but I don't think he means it or even knows he's doing it. Aramovsky, on the other hand, knows exactly what he's doing.

So it's best not to let him do it.

"You can't be in charge here, Aramovsky, because you're coming with me."

He's surprised. He wasn't expecting that.

"But I would be no help in a fight," he says. "It doesn't make any sense for me to go."

"You seem to know religion better than the rest of us," I say. "What if we run into something we don't understand, and we do the wrong thing? We might accidentally anger the gods if you're not there to give us guidance."

When he first spoke of gods and magic, many heads nodded. Those same heads nod again—they believe in him, think it makes sense for him to come along on this important mission.

Aramovsky's eyes harden. He knows I've used his own words

against him. If he doesn't go now, he's basically telling everyone he doesn't give a damn about his gods.

"Fine," he says, and forces a smile. "I'll do my part."

"Then let's not waste another second," I say, and walk to the door.

We move out, the eight of us—Bishop, El-Saffani, Bawden, Visca, Aramovsky, Gaston and me. I'm trying to do the smart thing, but the truth is I'm acting on a hunch. The bracelet *might* be a weapon, *might* let us take the Garden and hold it against monsters or any other threat.

Hunch or no hunch, I've made my decision.

And if I'm wrong, I know it will be the last decision I get to make.

PART IV

SELF AND OTHERS

THIRTY

We run uphill.

There are many footprints in the dust. The biggest ones are Aramovsky's, the medium-sized ones are from O'Malley and Yong and Spingate.

The smallest ones are from me and Bello.

I see the same bones, the same burn marks on the walls, the same open archway doors. Through those open doors, I see coffins. I know corpses lie inside them.

There are new footprints as well, along the corridor's edges. Those are from El-Saffani. The twins are once again out in front of us, ready to be the first to face any danger.

El-Saffani is shirtless, as is Bishop. All the circle-stars—Bawden included—wear only pants. They have covered their faces, chests, arms and hands with caked gray dust. The twins had beautiful, caramel-colored skin. Bawden's was a light brown. Visca's had that pinkish hue.

Now all five of them are the same color.

Bishop is at my right side, the thighbone clutched in his hand.

Aramovsky and Gaston are behind us. Bawden and Visca bring up the rear.

We move in silence for a long time. We move fast, or at least as fast as we can with Aramovsky and Gaston. They were slow to begin with and are already tiring. They will have to keep up. We have a long way to go to reach the place where we met Bishop and his marchers.

When we first made this trip, we were walking, we didn't know where we were going, and we moved cautiously because we didn't know what would come next. Now the distance goes by so much faster, although there's still plenty of time to think.

Latu told me her coffin was already open when she awoke. I haven't had a chance to ask the others about their experience—did anyone else have to fight for their life?

"Bishop, tell me about when you woke up."

He explains as he runs.

"We were in a cradle room. El-Saffani, me and Coyotl. The door to our room was shut."

"How did you get out of your coffins? I mean your *cradles*."

He shrugs. "They were open."

Same as with Latu. "There was no pain? What woke you up?"

His brow furrows. It's strange to carry on a conversation with him now: his eyes look so white in contrast with the gray paste caked on his skin.

"I think there was a little tingling sensation," he says. "I woke up kind of slow. A little bit at a time, you know? The cradle was open, so I got out."

Sounds like the same mild electrical shock that woke Spingate.

"And the door to your room? How did you get that open?"

"After we were awake for a little while, it opened by itself," he says. "We walked out and started running into other groups. That's when I got everyone organized."

No snake-tube attacking him, or Latu or Spingate or anyone else. No needle. No pain.

So why *me*?

We run on in silence. It isn't long before we leave the archways behind and see nothing but blank white walls on either side—we will be at the place where our two groups met much sooner than I anticipated.

I hear Aramovsky breathing hard behind us, hear Bawden hissing at him to pick up the pace, and I can't help but smile.

We keep moving. I figure we're more than halfway there when Bishop glances at me.

"Savage, you know what's funny?"

"I think you can call me *Em* now, Bishop."

He considers this, then shakes his head. "I can't remember much, but I know what the word *savage* means. It fits you."

I blush. He doesn't mean it as an insult. Coming from him, from a circle-star, I think it's a compliment.

Maybe it is, but not to me. I think of how I lost my temper back in the coffin room, how I pointed the spear when I yelled at Bishop and the others. Was I doing that to make things clear, or was I implying a threat against anyone who would not do what I said?

Bishop grins. His teeth seem so bright compared to his darkened skin. "Savage, you kind of lose track of things a lot, you know that?"

I nod. "Sorry."

"So, do you want to know what's funny or don't you?"

"Sure," I say. "What's funny?"

"If we took a vote now, with the people in *this* group, I wonder who would win."

I don't break stride, but his comment chills me. What does he mean by it? He came with me to get the bracelet, but it was a close thing. The next time he disagrees with me, will he go his own way, and will he take the circle-stars with him?

I look over my shoulder at the people following us. How long have we been awake? Gaston and Aramovsky look the same, but in the short time since we came out of our coffins the circle-stars have transformed into something else. It's not their gray color alone—it's in the way they walk, in their hard eyes. They carry bones as weapons, and look ready to use them.

If we voted now, Bawden, Visca and El-Saffani would choose Bishop.

I face forward and keep walking. My grip tightens on the spear.

The thought of Bishop trying to take over . . . it makes me *angry*. Just like it made me angry when Yong wanted to be the leader. Just like it makes me angry when Aramovsky plays his word games in front of everyone. I was ready to stab Aramovsky when he suggested he should be in charge. I was ready to *kill* him.

Bishop was the leader once. Does he feel the same anger toward me that I feel toward Aramovsky? That I felt toward Yong?

Out of all of us, only Bishop and I have taken life.

I realize why his comment affected me so: if he really wanted to lead, he wouldn't need a vote. We're far from O'Malley and the others. The circle-stars seem to follow Bishop, not me. If he kills me here, he can make up any story he likes when he gets back, then simply declare himself the leader. Maybe someone would call for a vote, and maybe Bishop would make them back down. He used force to take over his group of marchers—what's to stop him from doing it again?

I shake my head. I'm being crazy. Bishop wouldn't hurt me. He likes me. He said so. And it's not as if he tricked me to come out here, away from O'Malley and the others. I asked him to come, basically *made* him come. Still, I hope we finish this search soon so we can rejoin the group.

My crazy thoughts, how I lose track of things . . . since I woke up, it's been so hard to control my emotions. I'm happy and laughing one second, sad the next, paranoid and ready to kill someone the moment after that. I wasn't like this before, I'm sure of it. I don't need to remember the faces of my parents to know I was a good girl. The way my mind seems to change directions . . . that frightens me even more than Bishop does.

After a time, I see the intersection where Yong died. A wide splotch of mostly dried blood-slush is all that remains. Our footprints lead away from that spot.

Bishop glances my way. I told him how I killed Yong. He must realize that this is where it happened.

El-Saffani looks back at me, asking if we need to stop here. I point the spear straight down the hall: *Keep going*. They do.

When I pass by the intersection, I'm careful not to step on the dried blood-slush. Down that hallway to our right is an archway door, and through it, a coffin that holds Yong's body.

We leave the intersection behind.

From then on, no one says a word for a long time, until we reach the second intersection, the one where our two groups met. Instead of going straight like we did before, we turn right, toward where Bishop came from.

My legs recognize the difference instantly. Just like in the Garden, we're now walking level. We must be going down the length of the cylinder instead of up the curve.

We walk for a long ways, following two neat, dense rows of footprints. When Bishop was the leader, he made his people march in orderly lines. Those footprints make it easy to retrace his path.

It's dimmer here. The ceiling doesn't glow as bright. In some places, round patches of it are completely dark.

I think of rot. I think of the monsters.

Hallways start to branch off. There are so many directions we could explore, but we came here for a specific reason. We follow the footsteps. Sometimes we go straight, sometimes we turn.

It isn't long before we see bones.

The carnage begins with a few skeletons. At first I think Bishop and the others overreacted when they told us how bad it was in their area.

Then it gets worse.

The archways gape open, the stone doors neatly out of the way in their wall slots. We can see into the poorly lit rooms that we pass by, see the horrors left by the Grownups.

We had bones outside our coffin room, evidence of an intense battle, but it was nothing like this. Here, room after room is littered with death. Some of the dead are skeletons, some are withered corpses of dried flesh. Everywhere we look, it seems, skulls grin back at us.

Many of the bodies wear the clothes they had on when they died. These Grownups did not dress like us. They all wear a one-piece outfit that is both pants and shirt together. The outfits are in different colors: orange, yellow, blue, red, some greens, and, once in a while, purple. Dark stains dot the fabric. Judging from the fact that those stains are darkest where an arm or a leg is missing, I realize most are from long-dried blood.

Some rooms have tangled bodies stacked so deep I can't even

guess how many lives the twisted limbs once represented. Other rooms don't have full skeletons at all, only teetering piles of bones—arms and legs, severed before or after death, thrown together haphazardly like children's toys.

One room makes me stop and stare, because there is nothing but skulls. They are neatly stacked into a shape I recognize—the same squat, stepped pyramids that were carved into my coffin.

The Grownups turned death into art.

I look at Aramovsky, wondering what he thinks of his angry gods now. The skulls frighten him, but also *excite* him. He finds all of this fascinating.

As we walk, as we look through open doors, things get worse: skeletons hanging from the ceiling by metal rings around their wrists and ankles; a room with nothing but the bones of a hundred left arms arranged in pinwheels of overlapped hands; a room where skeletons sit in chairs, facing each other, held in permanent poses by stiff, curling wires.

El-Saffani continues to walk ahead of us, but the twins don't seem as brave anymore. They're scared, just like me, just like Bishop, just like the rest of our group. I think we're all waiting for the skeletons to move, to laugh, to rise up and come after us.

After a while, I try to stop myself from looking into the rooms full of mangled people, but every time I fail. I notice a pattern: a few of the shriveled dead still have dried skin on their faces. On those corpses, I can sometimes make out forehead symbols.

And every symbol I see, every last one, is an empty circle.

My symbol.

I stand closer to Bishop, close enough that I keep bumping against him as we walk. So many dead. So many bones—broken, blackened, shattered, sawed and chopped.

Why did the Grownups do this to each other?

Up ahead, the twins hesitate at an intersection. We catch up to them and I see why they stopped. My stomach flutters at the sight: two neat rows of footprints going both left *and* right.

"Bishop," I say, pointing to the tracks, "did you cross over your own path on the way here?"

He scratches his cheek. A little of the dried gray dust flakes away. I shiver as I realize the dust covering the circle-stars is basically the same stuff as the dead bodies we've passed by.

"Yeah, I guess," he says. "We turned around a few times. Maybe we walked the same halls more than once."

Is he lost? Did we waste precious time coming here?

"Bishop, focus," I say. "We need to find the haunted room. You said it had three pedestals and a ladder, remember?"

I'm hoping those details will jog his memory, but as he again scans the footprints and the hall, I don't see a flicker of recognition.

He leans into an archway, looks around, leans back out. He seems confused.

"It's close to here," he says. "I'm pretty sure."

Gaston steps forward.

"I know where the room is."

He speaks quietly, as if he's afraid that simple statement will somehow anger Bishop. Gaston's eyes keep flicking toward Bishop's bone-club. Maybe Gaston realizes—like I did—that we're far away from the others, that Bishop and the circle-stars could find a way to make him vanish and no one would ever know.

Bishop stares down at the smaller boy. I brace myself for yet another argument.

This time, however, there isn't one. Bishop sighs and nods.

"I really don't remember," he says. "Gaston should take over."

Gaston lets out a held breath, sags as the tension leaves him.

"You got us most of the way, Bishop," he says. For once, he's not poking fun. I could be wrong, but I think he's trying to make Bishop feel better about getting lost.

Gaston examines the footprints, thinking. He points down the dim hall that leads right.

"At the corner up there, we turn left. At the end of that hall we turn right." He looks at me, speaks quietly. "On the way there, you'll see four archways. I wouldn't look in the third one if I were you." He shifts his gaze to Aramovsky. "Both of you . . . just don't look."

I see Bishop shudder. The twins stare at the ground. Visca and Bawden drift close to each other, so close their shoulders touch, as if the memory of what they saw drives them to seek comfort.

Whatever waits in that room, it must be beyond anything we have seen so far. How it could be worse, I can't imagine.

Bishop nods. "Gaston is right. I remember what's in there. You don't want to see it. El-Saffani, lead the way."

The twins head down the hall. We follow. We turn left.

Bishop is giving orders now? Maybe he does want to take over. I'll need to be careful and pay attention to everything he does.

We pass four archway doors. At the third one, I think of following Gaston's advice and keeping my eyes straight ahead. No, I don't have the luxury of ignoring things. I am the leader: I need to know everything that we face.

I look in.

There are shriveled-up bodies, but they are much smaller than those of the Grownups.

Smaller than us.

Smaller than the ones we saw in the coffins with the torn lids.

So tiny, I easily could hold them with one arm.

Babies.

Hundreds of little corpses dangle from the ceiling, so thick I almost can't see the ceiling itself. They hang from chains that end in metal hooks slid through their rib cages. Cracked, dry skin has peeled away from their bodies, showing the bones beneath. Clumps of fallen flesh cover the floor like some horrid scattering of snow.

Seeing this makes my body rebel, makes me want to vomit. My stomach churns. I put a hand on my knee, try to catch my breath. This is wrong, so *wrong*.

How could people do something so evil?

"Told you," Gaston says. "Next time I tell you something, Em, maybe you should listen."

I nod slowly. Maybe I should.

He takes my hand and pulls me away. There is something about this boy that makes me know I can rely on him, no matter what. In that way, he reminds me of Latu.

We make the final right-hand turn. Not far ahead, the hallway ends in a white wall with a small plaque: a palm print embedded in a rectangle of dark glassy material. On the floor below it is a square of smooth, black metal.

Bishop points at the square.

"That's the door," he says.

I had assumed it would be stone, like every other door in this place. Unless that melted metal we saw earlier was a door, but we have no way of knowing for sure.

The handprint in the plaque, there is a golden symbol in it: the jagged circle. The same symbol that is on the foreheads of Gaston, Spingate and Beckett.

Gaston walks to the plaque. *Strides* to it, more accurately. He presses his palm to the handprint. The black door in the floor hums, then rises up on a hidden hinge, revealing a narrow tube leading down. A ladder runs its length, vanishing into deep shadow.

He crosses his arms. His smile is so smug it could make Aramovsky's look humble by comparison. The time for being quiet and modest is apparently over: Gaston is back to normal.

"That's how it goes," he says. "It opens for me. Some people are more important than others, it seems."

El-Saffani talks, the boy first this time, then the girl.

"Bishop tried it—"

"—then we tried—"

"—but it didn't work for us."

Bishop is glowering, waiting for us to finish. He doesn't like the fact that Gaston can do something he can't.

"What about Beckett?" I ask. "Did he try?"

Gaston nods. "It didn't work for him, either."

I thought perhaps the door recognized symbols, somehow, but if Beckett can't open it, it's not about the symbols alone. Is it something particular to Gaston? Or, maybe, particular to only certain people?

"I want to try," I say.

Gaston again puts his hand to the print. The door closes. He gives a deep, comical bow and steps aside.

I press my hand into the depression, feel the cool material against my skin. Nothing happens.

Gaston holds the back of his hand to his forehead, pretends to be faint.

"Oh dear, our fearless leader is denied! Whatever will become of us now?"

He is so strange. We just saw butchered babies, hundreds of dead people—maybe *thousands*—and he's making jokes? I want to shake some sense into him. But perhaps jokes are his way of dealing with this. It's certainly better than how I reacted, which was to almost throw up.

Aramovsky walks to the plaque. He presses his hand to the glass.

The door hums: it opens.

Bishop laughs and shakes his bone-club. "Ha! I guess Gaston isn't so special after all!"

Gaston's face shifts from happy smile to glaring scowl. When he smiles, he is cute; when he looks like this, so hateful and furious, he is ugly both inside and out.

Aramovsky breathes out a sigh of delight. "The door opens for me because I am chosen. I *knew* it." He looks at Gaston with an expression of deep respect, of acceptance. "As are you, Gaston. You are also chosen. I apologize if I offended you earlier, my brother."

Gaston snarls. I would have never guessed something like this was so important to him.

I brought Aramovsky so he wouldn't talk to the others while I was gone, so his words wouldn't create more problems—now he has gained some kind of stature. I wonder if I will ever make the right choices.

The ladder waits for us. I want to get the bracelet and get away from this slaughterhouse, but I don't want to rush things and make even more mistakes.

"Bishop, you said this room is haunted?"

He nods. His jaw muscles twitch. He will go down there with me, but he doesn't try to pretend he's not scared.

"You didn't see ghosts or something," I say. "Right?"

Bishop shrugs. I turn to Gaston.

"Well, Gaston? Ghosts?"

The small boy swallows. He's no longer in a joking mood.

"The room is . . . *weird*," he says. "It's small and dark. You feel heavier, like an invisible hand is squeezing you, trying to make you sit. Our legs got tired fast. And we both felt like . . . like something was watching us. I wanted to get out of there. To be honest, Em, I don't want to go back down."

He's asking without asking if he can stay up here. I would love to let him do that, but he's the smartest of us.

"I need that big brain of yours," I say. I tousle his black hair, trying to make light of the situation. "What if there are things down there that won't work for anyone but you? Maybe there's something you and Bishop didn't see, something like the hidden panels in the archways."

"Those things would work for me as well," Aramovsky says. "Or perhaps we'll find things that *only* work for me."

He's right. Besides, if I leave him up here with the circle-stars, who knows what he'll tell them. I'm afraid of Bishop because he is big and strong. He could hurt me. I'm afraid of Aramovsky, too, but I'm not sure why.

"I'll go first," I say. "Then Bishop, then Gaston, then Aramovsky, then El-Saffani."

The twins step forward in unison and start down the ladder before I can even say a word to the contrary. Maybe they're just as afraid as I am, but if so they hide it well. Or maybe they are actually brave, like Latu was.

I look at Bawden and Visca.

"You two guard the door, okay?"

The two gray-faced people nod.

I start down the ladder.

THIRTY-ONE

I hold the spear in one hand, use my other to grip the ladder rungs as I descend.

It's easy at first, but it quickly gets harder the farther I go down. I understand what Gaston was saying about something pushing him: I feel *heavier*, like I'm progressively carrying more and more weight.

It hits me how clean this tube is. Other than some footprints on the uppermost rungs, probably from when Gaston and Bishop first came down, there is no dust at all. Has the door above me always been closed?

I reach the bottom. The circular floor is strange. Like the black door, it's metal, a grate of some kind. I can see through it to a black, curving surface below. The curve seems to slope up equally in all directions, becoming curved walls that join together to make a curved ceiling.

Before, we were inside a cylinder. Now, we are inside a ball.

My eyes adjust to the darkness.

I see the body Gaston told us about, a long bit of light gray that stands out from the shadows. It is chest-down on the metal-grate floor, arms spread wide. The skin-taut skull is facing us, greeting us with an eternal smile. A once-white body suit drapes thin ribs, hides arm and leg bones. Splotches of different colors—faded red, yellow, grayish black—stain the fabric. The biggest stain is in the middle of the back, where the spear must have dug deep, ending that person's life.

I see the "shackle" Gaston described. Yes, it is *exactly* like the one the scarred monster aimed at my face. It is on the corpse's right wrist. The rod connected to the bracelet points out, parallel to the metal-grate floor.

A few steps past the corpse, I see the three pedestals Gaston described. Unlike the other pedestals we've seen so far, these are unbroken. In full light, they would be white; right now they are a pale shade of gray. Gold symbols line the round stems. Their flat, square tops sit empty. If we could figure out what is supposed to be on top of those pedestals, I think that would connect a few more dots of the puzzle that is this place.

I take a few steps: my feet feel like they are weighed down by thick stones.

"Gaston, why are we heavier?"

He starts to talk, then stops. That frustrated look comes over his face again.

"I think it's similar to how we didn't fall from the ceiling, but"—he looks at Aramovsky—"I really don't want to argue with you about that right now."

Aramovsky actually bows. "Of course not, my chosen brother. Please, continue."

Gaston sighs and shakes his head. Maybe he liked the confrontational Aramovsky better than the friendly version.

"Anyway, it's like my brain is trying to tell me why we feel heavier, but it doesn't know where that information is kept. So many things are still . . . blanked out."

That phrase, *blanked out*—it's his version of the sludge-brain sensation I defined as *muddy*. Gaston's word feels more accurate.

I look at the body. So gross. My stomach feels queasy again. I've seen worse things, far worse, but knowing this person was speared in the back makes me wonder if the same thing could happen to me.

I need to focus: what we came for is lying right there.

"I'll get the bracelet," I say.

Gaston kneels next to the body. "No, let me. The look on your face makes me think you might throw up. And if there's one thing nastier than a corpse, it's a corpse covered in puke."

I'm more than happy to let him do it. I don't want to even look at another dead body, let alone touch one.

Gaston tries to move the bracelet. The stained fabric has dried to it—he has to give it a little bit of a tug before the fabric pulls free with a crackling sound.

"Eww, gross," he says. He gently slides the bracelet off the skeletal arm. He stands, starts to offer the prize to me, then stops and holds it close to his face.

"Uh-oh," he says. "This can't be a good thing."

He points at the base of the long rod. The white jewel there is cracked in several places. A few small pieces of it are missing.

I reach out a fingertip, feel the broken lines.

"When the monster pointed his bracelet at me, the jewel glowed," I say.

Everyone looks at the device in Gaston's hand. We don't know how it works, but it is obvious to all of us that this jewel is never going to glow again.

Aramovsky sighs.

"Brilliant work, Savage," he says. "You dragged us all this way and what do we get for it? *Nothing*. Instead of going after Bello, we did this. She's probably dead by now. Maybe we could have saved her if we'd acted quicker, but now it's likely too late."

He didn't want to go after her in the first place. He wanted to abandon her to the monsters to please his "gods." Why is he changing his story? Is he trying to make me look bad again?

Bishop is staring at me. His eyes narrow. He wanted to try to rescue Bello, but I wouldn't let him. Now I understand— Aramovsky's words weren't meant to make me look bad, they were meant to remind Bishop that coming here was my choice.

Aramovsky is trying to turn Bishop against me. Not that doing so will take much effort, I suppose: Bishop was right, and I was wrong.

I wasted precious time. I split up the group for nothing. If I don't fix this, they'll replace me as leader. I can't let that happen. I have to admit it to myself; I *want* to be the leader. I am the one who makes decisions. I know I've made mistakes, but I don't trust anyone else to do a better job than I can. If we're going to stay alive, if we're going to make it out of this awful place, if we're going to survive the monsters, I know our best chance is if I stay in charge.

Aramovsky sighs again, louder this time. The sound makes me want to knock him down. It must be so easy to judge the decisions of someone else when you sit back and do nothing.

He strides to the middle pedestal, runs his finger along the flat top. He looks at his fingertip like he's checking for dust. He turns his back to the pedestal and smiles at me.

"We don't have the Grownups' weapon," he says. "If it is a weapon at all, which we don't know, because we've learned nothing. Bello is gone. Yong and Latu are dead. Perhaps Bishop isn't the only one who wonders who would win a new vote."

The middle pedestal begins to glow.

I take a reactive step back. The others do the same. Aramovsky realizes something is behind him, turns sharply, sees the glow and lunges away from it.

The glow increases, a buzzing cloud that hovers in midair. The light doesn't come from the pedestal itself, but rather from the empty space above it. Dozens of black spots appear within that glow, spots that shift and change.

I point my spear at it.

Bishop and El-Saffani hold their bone-clubs toward it. Gaston scurries behind Bishop. Aramovsky hides behind me.

I want to run, but I stand my ground—by *choice* this time, not because my feet won't obey. The glow is mesmerizing, almost hypnotizing.

The floating black spots swell and bloat. They meld together, merge even as the glow itself begins to fade. The shifting black shape forms a circle . . . no, an oval.

Inside that black form, two red dots take shape.

And then the image above the pedestal becomes clear.

I am looking at a monster.

And that monster is looking back at me.

THIRTY-TWO

The monster is so real I step back and bump into Aramovsky. Only the head and shoulders are visible. Its black isn't a color as much as it is an absence of light. Wrinkled, gnarled, leathery . . . *vile*. The thing is repulsive. Simply looking at it makes me want to destroy it, the same kind of instinctive reaction I'd feel if I saw a hairy spider crawling across my arm.

Bishop creeps closer to the pedestal. He pokes his thighbone at the face, tentatively, as if he knows the monster isn't really there but he has to be sure. The bone goes right through, distorting the face in a little puff of multicolored sparkles. Bishop pulls the bone back; sparkles cling to his club for a moment, then dissipate into wisps of nothingness.

If Bishop can be brave, so can I. I step forward to stand at his left side.

The monster's eyes swirl with many shades of red, from a rich almost-black to a bright flash that burns yellow. When it speaks, I see the jaw moving, but can't make out a mouth behind those disgusting folds.

"Bishop, look at you," the monster says. "Already with a weapon in your hand. Why am I not surprised? And what did you smear all over your body? You're so frightening."

A man's condescending voice delivered in a whispering hiss, the sound of dust sliding across stone. It makes my skin crawl. Whatever this monster is, every ounce of my body screams that it should not exist.

Bishop glances at me. I see the fear and doubt in his eyes. If there was something to attack, he would attack it. Since there is not, he tilts his head toward the pedestal.

He thinks I should do the talking.

I stand up straight and try to look like a leader.

"How did you know Bishop's name?"

The black thing's head bobs a little. It makes a new sound, a sound like two bones scraping together. Is that . . . *laughter*?

"Even though I can't see as well as I used to, there's no mistaking his muscular body," it says. "And the Bishop I know is seldom without a weapon. Some things never change. Never-never-never."

A hand on my shoulder. Not one of support or threat, but to gently guide me aside, just enough for someone to lean in. It's Aramovsky.

"Are you a god?" he asks the monster.

The monster stares for a moment. "I do not recognize you. What is your name?"

"I am Aramovsky."

Wrinkled, withered shoulders shake, and again I hear that sound of scraping bone—the monster is laughing.

"Aramov*skeee,* way up in a *tree,*" it says. "I'm surprised you made it. Of course a double-ring would assume I am a god a god I am. I suppose I do have the power over life and death. By definition, therefore and wherefore, the answer is *yes.*"

I don't know what a god is, exactly, but if gods do exist, they don't look like this thing.

Aramovsky's eyes are wet and shining. He is afraid, but also enthralled—he doesn't see the threat that Bishop and I see.

I shake the tall boy's hand off my shoulder, then step forward.

"You know Bishop," I say to the monster. "And you know Aramovsky. Who are *you*?"

"Who am I? A god with a cod."

He is playing with us.

"I don't think so," I say. "You are no more a god than I am."

The red eyes flicker and swirl. "I do not recognize you, girl. What is your name?"

"Yours first."

The wrinkled thing laughs. I want to drive my spear right through its face.

"I am Brewer," he says.

Brewer. Like the boy in our coffin room. Could they be related?

"I told you my name, girl," it says. "Now, what is yours?"

I stand a little straighter. "My name is Em."

The red eyes swirl faster. "Em? There is no *Em* in the command caste."

"I am the leader," I say. "We voted on it."

"A *vote*? How interesting."

The red eyes seem to look me up and down, then lock in on my forehead.

"You're a *circle*?" He speaks that word with utter disbelief.

I say nothing. The monster stares at me for a long moment. I stare back, not knowing what else to do.

It makes a noise that might be a cough: a dry, rattling thing that pulls the narrow shoulders closer together. When that passes, the monster makes grunting sounds, like it's trying to clear a throat that we can't see.

Finally, it seems to recover. Its red eyes slowly swirl.

"I don't know anyone named Em," it says. "That doesn't seem possible, unless . . ."

He looks off to his right. His attention is elsewhere for a moment, then the eyes snap back to me.

"Em? As in the *letter* M?"

How do I respond? Do I lie, like O'Malley would? I don't know that a lie helps us any more than the truth, so I nod.

The monster leans closer.

"Are you . . . *Savage*?" His voice, full of both awe and horror.

Like the monster in the Garden, this one seems to know me. It is all I can do to contain my hope and excitement.

I nod again. "You know who I am?"

The monster leans away.

"I can't *believe* it," it says. "Yes, I know who you are, little circle. I know all too well. You are the person who murdered me."

THIRTY-THREE

This creature doesn't know what's real. He's alive, he's talking to me, but he thinks I killed him?

"Little Savage," the monster says. "You seem so strong, so healthy." His tone has changed—loathing drips from every word. "Do you feel hot, Em? A fever cleaver in your head, perhaps?"

Even if I was sick, I wouldn't tell him, I wouldn't show him any weakness.

"I feel fine."

The monster sighs. "It's been so long since the husks were serviced, I shouldn't be surprised. The needly wheedly must be jammed, much like I am."

Needly wheedly? Does he mean *needle*? The one that stabbed me? How could he know about that, unless . . .

"That tube in my coffin. *You* made it attack me?"

"So many malfunctions," he says. "Other husks far worse than yours, some far better. Broken valves, frozen hinges, corrupt controllers . . . the centuries have not been kind to the Cherished. I hope the newer ones are in better condition. We'll see soon enough."

"Answer my question." My voice doesn't sound like my own: it is cold and hard, the edge of the spear blade turned into sound. "Did *you* make that needle stab me?"

"Of course I did," he says. "You murdered me."

Again with that gibberish. I'm the only one that woke up like that. And he . . . wait, his words earlier . . .

"You mumbled that the needle *jammed*," I say. "What would have happened if it hadn't?"

His red eyes bore into mine. "Pain in the brain, little circle girl. A slow demise was your prize. I wanted your death to last, as did mine."

He tried to kill me. Me, no one else. A *malfunction* is the reason I am alive.

"Where are we, Brewer?" I ask. "What is this prison?"

He laughs again.

"Prison? For a *leader* you are wrong-wrong-wrong quite a lot, are you not?"

"What else was I wrong about?"

"You said I am no god. And yet I am your eternal protector. You and yours are alive because of me."

I shake my head. I will not play games with this creature.

"Protector? You just admitted that you tried to kill me. And your kind attacked us, took one of us away."

The black face leans forward. The red eyes swirl faster, narrow to slits. "Which one? And where was he abducted?"

He pretends he doesn't know? More games.

"*She*, not *he*," I say to the monster. "Bello. Taken by your kind. In the Garden."

A wicked hiss slides out of its hidden mouth. "*Bello?* That's not fair, it's *not fair*! I will fix that, oh yes I will. You said *the*

Garden? You must mean the orchard. The only way there is through the empty section, but I sealed that off." He looks off, thinking. "The scepter in your coffin room. I never did get it out of there, not that I wanted to touch my own murder weapon. Theresa must have used it."

The tool we've been using to open doors . . . that's what someone used to smash in little Brewer's skull.

The monster's eyes again settle on me. "Is anyone in the orchard now?"

I shake my head. "Everyone is out. I won't tell you where."

"I'm not the one you need to hide from," Brewer says. "They know you are awake. It had to be Aramovsky, that insightful man. That's not fair, that's *not fair!*"

I turn to the tall boy standing behind me. Aramovsky's mouth hangs open. His tongue is moving, as if he's trying to say something but can't quite remember how to speak.

I again look at the monster. "There is another Aramovsky?"

The monster nods slowly. "Oh, yes. I know that bastard only too well."

"And we know another Brewer," I say. "There was a boy in a coffin . . . in the room where you tried to murder me."

My words drip with venom, with raw fury. All the pain I felt, it's because of this creature.

"*Coffin?*" The red eyes narrow, the thick folds of jet-black skin at the edges deepen. "Why do you call it that?"

"Because that's what they are. Many of us died in those boxes."

The monster pauses. He seems to calm down a bit. He nods again.

"Perhaps *coffins* is a fitting name after all. At least for the boy named Brewer. I waited for him for so long, but you killed him." He starts to bob back and forth, slowly picking up speed. "They cracked open his husk—what you call his *coffin*—and they slaughtered him. He was helpless. They didn't care. After that I tricked them, gas fools the lass, and I locked them out. They couldn't get me they didn't *dare* because I would kill them like they killed me and I wanted them to suffer wanted *you* to suffer damn them to hell they are the demons and I will get them oh *yes I will get them* and make them *hurt* in the worst way, they—"

"Shut *up*," I snap. I don't want to hear any more of his deranged rambling. I have the spear: he *must* listen. "Tell us where you took Bello. And where are we? What is this building? Are we buried underground?"

The bone scraping comes again, louder than before. He laughs so hard that some of his black wrinkles flop around like rolls of fat.

I am tired of being laughed at. I glance at Bishop, see him snarling—he's tired of it, too.

The monster's laugh abruptly changes to another cough, this one far worse than the first, a grating sound that reminds me of when I awoke with all that dust in my throat and lungs. The way Brewer shakes, it looks painful. It takes him a few moments to recover.

His eyes are now more black than red.

"You haven't figured it out yet," he says. "You're not a very good leader, *Em*. You're *just a circle*, wasn't that their words? How they belittled your acumen. How foolish they were, remember?"

I shake my head. "No, I don't remember anything."

"Ah, of course not," Brewer says. "Then again, you were always smart enough to use people smarter than you. Where is Okadigbo? Is she still alive, or did you kill her again?"

"I haven't killed anyone, Brewer."

Yong's gasping face flashes through my thoughts. The wide

eyes, the shock, the terror-filled knowledge that he was as good as dead.

It was an accident. . . .

I focus on Brewer's words. *Okadigbo,* he said. That's a name on one of the coffins in my room. A shriveled skeleton in a big, white shirt. She's dead, yes, but I didn't kill her. I couldn't have. Unless I did it before someone put me in the coffin, and I can't remember that just like I can't remember school, or the face of my father.

I shake my head, sharp and fast. Brewer is trying to confuse me.

"Stop lying to us," I say. "And tell me where we are!"

"No Okadigbo? Oh, well, I should have checked the husks, but there wasn't enough time and time was all that was enough. How about your nemesis, Theresa?"

I don't know what a *nemesis* is. I don't know who Theresa is, either.

"Oh, you don't recognize that name?" Brewer says. "Of course you wouldn't, not at your age. But if she lived, you might know her last name—is Theresa *Spingate* still alive?"

I shouldn't be surprised that he knows more of us, but I am. Surprised and furious. I won't let anything happen to her. I've lost Latu and Bello. There is nothing I won't do to protect Spingate.

"I wager that Theresa still lives," Brewer says. "I'm surprised she didn't tell you where you are. Perhaps she hasn't figured it out yet—side effects of the husk are so bad-bad-bad I am not glad. Or maybe she *has* figured it out and chooses not to tell you. So many secrets locked away in that pretty red head."

I can't take it anymore. I step forward. I lean in close to the strange, floating presence that is Brewer's disgusting face. My words come out as a brutal scream.

"*Tell me where we are!* Tell me or I will find you and I will cut you open. I'll watch you die, Brewer. I will make you *hurt*. Do you hear me? *Do you?*"

The red eyes gaze back at me, so close, so real.

"You already did that," he says quietly. "You hurt me more than you could ever know. Now you threaten me again? Some things never change, never ever never. You always were a bitch, Savage."

I lean away so fast I stumble. Bishop's hand on my back keeps me from falling.

The scarred monster in the Garden said the same words.

These things . . . they know who I am.

Brewer sighs as if he's disappointed in me.

"Little circle girl, you are not in a building," he says. "You are not underground. You are not underwater. You're not *under* anything. And you're not in a prison—not for you, anyway, although that's exactly what this place is for me. Me-me-me a sad cat in a sadder tree."

Madness bubbles from his every word. He's insane. Insane enough to have made pyramids of human skulls? Or to have arranged severed left arms in a big pinwheel?

Enough to have impaled babies on hooks?

I try to keep my own murderous anger in check. I try so hard, but I can't hold it all back. My words are a growl, a low, grating promise of revenge.

"Tell me what this place is, Brewer."

"Oh, little circle girl, don't you know it is better to *show*, rather than *tell*?"

Below, above and around us, the curved, black walls flicker and swirl, a million colors suddenly twisting and spinning. As quickly as they came, the colors fade away. Somehow, I am now looking *beyond* the curved walls, into a different kind of blackness: a blackness that seems to go on forever. In that blackness, I see tiny points of bright light.

Points of light, moving slowly—almost imperceptibly—*upward*.

I feel a fuzziness in my head; my brain is reaching, grasping, trying to beat past the *blanked-out* parts. And when it does, when it connects the images to words, I realize what I am looking at.

Stars.

Those points of light, those are *stars*.

"Little leader learns the truth," the monster says. "Take a look behind you."

All of us turn away from the pedestals.

I see the backs of Gaston and Aramovsky, of El Saffani. I see the ladder that brought us down, and past it, the clear, curved wall. But beyond that is something so big I can't even comprehend it. Out in the star-speckled blackness, I see a vast, slowly rotating disc of brown and green and blue.

Another word connects, clicks into place.

I am looking at a *planet*.

"Space," I say. "We're in a spaceship."

THIRTY-FOUR

You are wrong-wrong-wrong quite a lot, are you not?

That's what Brewer said to me. He's right.

We all stare at the spinning sphere out in the blackness. Below us and on our sides, the moving stars seem to spin in time with the planet, as if they are pinned to it by infinitely long invisible sticks.

Stars and planet, all spinning in the same direction.

The twins stand close together, their clubs now aimed past the ladder, perhaps at the planet, perhaps at space, perhaps at the stars.

"We should be falling," Boy El-Saffani says. "Why aren't we falling?"

Girl El-Saffani stamps her foot, testing the firmness of the metal grid below us. The metal rings, vibrates.

"Solid," she says. "Does the floor keep us from falling down?"

Boy El-Saffani shakes his head. "It's in front of our faces." He points his bone-club at the planet. "We wouldn't fall *down,* we should tumble *forward.*" He turns and looks at me. "Shouldn't we, Em?"

He thinks I have any idea what's going on?

Gaston pushes past them, slides around the ladder. He reaches out with both hands. I start after him, scared he is going to fall off the edge, but stop when his hands press against the barely visible curved wall. He leans forward, fearless.

"The stars aren't spinning, *we* are," he says. He turns, his smile wide, his face alive with joyous amazement. "Hey, Aramovsky, remember how Spingate said we were walking on the ceiling and you argued with her?"

Gaston points a finger straight up.

I look. The ladder is still visible, but the tube around it is not. The ladder rises up into another impossibility: Spingate's *cylinder*. It is smaller than the planet, I think, but still so big my brain can't make sense of it. A coppery color, huge, sprawling, sides curving up and away, the length of it stretching out and out and out for I don't know how far. The surface is dented, scratched and pitted, like the hallways where the battles occurred. The cylinder doesn't spin at all: it is fixed in place above us.

Only now do I truly understand what Spingate meant. We walked along the inside of that cylinder, as small as insects. We walked straight, but in a circle at the same time, until we looped up and around to wind up where we started.

This ball-shaped room we're in is *outside* that cylinder, connected by the tube that contains the ladder. The metal-grate floor of this ball is parallel to the cylinder's surface.

At the top of the ladder, I see two confused, gray faces peering down: Bawden and Visca, probably wondering why they can suddenly see us. To them, it must look like we're standing in space.

Gaston snaps his fingers and laughs.

"It's because the cylinder *rotates*," he says. "That's what makes us stick to the inside. I can't quite remember how it works, but if it spun faster, we would feel heavier, and if it spun slower, we

would feel lighter. That's why it's heavier here, in the ball, because
we're actually spinning faster than the cylinder below us. The farther out we are, the heavier we feel. I bet at the center of the cylinder, we wouldn't weigh anything at all. We would *float*."

Float? Gaston sounds even more insane than Brewer. What he
says is *impossible*. But the room of dead babies taught me that
when he talks, I should listen. I need to listen to him now.

Aramovsky raises his hands, tilts his head back.

"Miracles," he says. "We float above a planet, we float in
space, but we do not die. The gods protect us. *Brewer* protects
us—he truly is one of the gods."

I turn back to the hideous head hovering above the pedestal.

The stars spin behind him, too, but in the opposite direction.
On my left, the stars seem to move from up to down; on my
right, from down to up.

"We're in a ship," I say to Brewer. I know it's obvious. The
words just come out. "A ship, all this time?"

"It's called the *Xolotl,*" he says. "I find it hard to believe Theresa didn't figure it out. Perhaps she is not as smart as she thinks
she is. A shame to blame the game, but a tame dame never came
to fame."

He's babbling again, talking to himself more than to us.

I point behind me, toward the spinning brown, blue and green
planet. "What is that?"

"That was supposed to be our home, our new beginning.
Well, for me and Bishop and Aramovsky, anyway. For you, my
little Savage bird, I doubt it would have been paradise, at any
price, with or without sparkly ice."

Gnarled, black fingers come up to scratch his head. Fingertips
dig between the wrinkles. He stops, puts his hands down and
stares at my symbol.

"*Em,*" he says, speaking the word like it is the answer to all questions. "I can't believe I missed it, but of course. Of course *you* survived. Of course *you* are the leader. Would you like to know your first name?"

My heart bangs so hard I feel it in my throat, in my ears.

I need to know who I am.

I nod.

"Very well," Brewer says. "Your name is Matilda."

Matilda . . . Matilda . . . Matilda. The word echoes through my head, discovers itself hidden deep in the blanked-out areas. I know he speaks the truth.

My name is Matilda Savage.

The feeling of relief overwhelms me. Despite the horrors we've been through, the problems we still face, I can't help but smile.

Bishop slaps his chest. "What about me? What's my first name?"

The monster's spidery hand gives a dismissive wave. "It hardly matters. Everyone knows you as Bishop, and Bishop you are."

Brewer's voice lowers, softens, becomes sad and wistful.

"All of you can have what I can never possess. You could go to that planet."

Gaston slides between me and Bishop. He moves close to the monster's face, even closer than when I lost control and screamed horrible threats. Seeing little Gaston standing right in front of Brewer makes me wince, as if the monster might reach out, bite down and drag Gaston into nothingness.

"Is it safe?" Gaston asks Brewer. "The planet?"

Brewer laughs so hard his furrowed head tilts back and he starts to shake. As before, the bone-scraping sound grinds into a coughing fit. This one racks his body, makes his limp hands flop about like boneless birds. Fluid bubbles up from leathery folds covering where his mouth should be—grayish red glistens on black.

It takes a few minutes for the coughs to ease. We wait.

He finally gets it under control. "Who are you, little tooth-boy? I don't recognize you."

"My name is Gaston. Gaston, X."

The monster rubs a skeletal black hand across his face, across the leathery folds of his mouth. He looks at his palm, seems sad to see wetness there.

"Not fair," he says quietly. "Not fair-a-dair."

He focuses on Gaston.

"Without the burns and scars, you aren't nearly as dashing, Xander. Yes, the planet is safe. Well, the air won't kill you, any-way. Hopefully you can break the mold. If you can't, that was one very long trip for nothing."

I wonder what it's like down on that planet. I try to imagine a place with no walls. Sky instead of ceiling, sky that goes on forever and ever. A place where the dust of the dead doesn't cover everything, doesn't coat our tongues and invade our lungs.

Something about that planet calls to me.

I don't even care if it's safe: I would rather die down there than live up here.

A very long trip . . . the centuries have not been kind . . .

Brewer's words push and pull at my muddy mind. A sliver of memory sneaks out: a planet, but not *this* planet. Something brown, ugly. The thought slithers around like a snake, feeding, growing, becomes almost clear. Another planet . . . a *dying* planet. A desperate need to flee.

And then, I understand.

The planet we're looking at doesn't just call to me, it calls to *us*.

It calls to the sleepers.

It calls to the birthday children.

"That's what this ship was made for," I say. "To bring us here."

The monster nods. "Very good, Miss Matilda Savage. And the journey took a mere ten centuries."

Bishop huffs. "No one lives that long."

"Some do," Brewer says. "Many more should have, but revolts can get in the way."

A thousand years. If Brewer has been alive that long, maybe he is some kind of god.

I think of all the bodies we've seen. So many corpses on this ship. A trip of a thousand years. More things click into place.

"The Garden," I say. "All that fruit . . . food for the trip. And the pigs. Were they meant to be food as well?"

"Filthy beasts," Brewer says. "Did you know swine are smart enough to learn how to open basic husks? Simple buttons were a design flaw, I fear. Live and learn. Swine are always after that calcium. I warned against bringing them. The smarter a creature, the less likely it is to behave. Once they got out of their section, there was no getting them back in. You don't see cows and chickens and sheep turning against their masters, do you?"

Gaston gives a doubtful look. "Livestock? You'd need a lot of space for cows, and we haven't seen any cows at all. Or chickens. Or sheep."

The image above the pedestal blurs and shifts. Brewer's head disappears. In its place, a grassy field with dozens of animals. They have black fur, like the pigs, but are much bigger. Are those cows? In the distance, I think I can make out thicket walls.

So the Garden isn't the only room with food after all.

The image shifts again. A tall metal rack filled with small cages, and in each cage, a black bird. These I recognize: chickens.

The image blinks, and we're again looking at Brewer's horrid head.

"Don't base reality on what you have seen when you have seen very little," the monster says. "The *Xolotl* is vast. Far larger than your young minds can comprehend. You might say that the journey of a thousand years begins with more than a single flightless bird."

This ship came from another planet, a trip that seems desperate and impossibly long. People must have worked together to make that happen. And it seems like they had plenty of food. How many people were on this ship before the killing began?

"Brewer, what happened here?" I ask. "What made you do these things to each other?"

He raises a long, bony black finger and wags it side to side.

"Oh no-no-no, Miss Savage. You won't get me to laugh again, no matter how funny you are. What happened? Some people do not approve of being sacrificed."

I look at Bishop; he shrugs. Brewer is talking in riddles and I'm getting tired of listening to him.

I feel Aramovsky's hand on my shoulder again, gently pushing me aside so he has room to speak.

"The bodies," he says. "The adults, the children . . . they were *sacrifices*?"

I don't like the way Aramovsky speaks that word, so breathy and excited.

"Not all," Brewer says. "Many, yes. Many more chose to not go gentle into that good night. For twenty years, this ship shuddered from war. A war to liberate those that did not need to be liberated. And in the end, they're all dead anyway."

War. Revolt. Sacrifice. The Grownups did this to themselves. It has nothing to do with us. If we stay here, we'll wind up like them—butchered and burned, our flesh turned to powdery dust.

"Brewer, how do we get down to that planet?"

"You fly," the monster says. "Fly-fly-fly, a rocket in the sky. Down there you can start over and never-ever-never worry your pretty perfect little heads about the *real* cost of your trip, about the sins of those who came before you. To get down there, you need a special ship, a *shuttle*. And oh, irony of ironies, as big as the *Xolotl* is, only one shuttle remains."

A shuttle. The word calls up a flash of memory—a long ship with wings. It will take us away from here. We can go where we were meant to go, and, maybe, leave these monsters behind forever.

"One shuttle," I say. "Does that mean if we take it, your kind can't follow us down there?"

Two gnarled hands rise up, slowly clap together.

"You understand what the word *one* means," he says. "And people said that Matilda Savage was stupid. Correct, my kind can't follow you, but you can also never come back."

I fight to stay calm. If he's telling the truth—and I have no way of knowing that he is or isn't—we can leave this nightmare behind.

"Tell me where the shuttle is."

Brewer sighs, a chest-puffing thing that rattles the black folds hiding his mouth.

"Long, long ago, during the revolt, I sealed your chambers off from the Mutineers. I had machines destroy corridors, cut away floors, even melt doors to your area."

I think about the first intersection we found, back when our long walk began. The black wall that looked like frozen ice. Brewer did that? To keep us *safe*?

"Why did you protect us? You say I killed you, yet you keep talking about how you kept us alive. Why would you do that?"

Brewer doesn't answer immediately. We wait, long enough

that I'm not sure he heard me. I'm about to repeat the question when he finally speaks.

"I've asked myself that a million times," he says. His eyes have calmed down to a pale red. "Sometimes it is because I hope that I can change the way things work, even though I know that is impossible. Sometimes it is for revenge. Sometimes it is because if all of you die, who will I have to keep me company? These reasons and more, but looking at you now . . . maybe it is none of them. Perhaps the real reason is because I've known all along that you were made for the planet below. A millennium's worth of lies leads to a single truth—the future belongs to the young, if the old would kindly die and get the hell out of the way."

I'm not entirely sure what all of that means. I latch onto one part of it.

"We were made to be down there," I say. "You're right. I can feel it. Let us do that, Brewer. Let us go where we belong. Tell us where the shuttle is."

"Ah, yes, the shuttle," he says. "Fly fly fly, like a rocket in the sky. For centuries they have tried to get to you, and for centuries I have stopped them. Sadly, Miss Savage, when I sealed you *in,* the shuttle was sealed *out.* You will have to go to the Mutineers' section and take it. And while you're there, see if you can find your Bello, because that is where she'll be."

Bishop takes in a sharp breath of surprise. "You think she's still alive?"

"Perhaps," Brewer says. "Although I suppose that depends on your definition of the word."

More riddles. I wish this thing would give us straight answers.

According to Brewer, our way off the *Xolotl* is to go where these "Mutineer" monsters are. We will have to face the things that attacked us, that took Bello.

Bello . . . could we get her back *and* get out of here?

I glance at Bishop, wondering if he's thinking the same thing. His chin is at his chest. He's staring at Brewer's image from beneath furrowed brows. If there is any chance to get Bello back, Bishop is ready to take it.

Knowing he is with me gives me strength. I stand tall once again.

"Brewer, tell me how to get to the shuttle."

The monster shakes his head. "If they found you, then you found them. As the cleaning flea said to the dirty elephant, *Perhaps I missed a spot.* Surely I can't let you sully a pristine, perfect planet if you're not smart enough to figure things out for yourself."

I whip the spear down, a short arc that rips through Brewer's head in a spastic cloud of sparkles. The blade *clonks* against the pedestal top, taking a chunk out of the white stone.

"Stop playing games with us! We've already lost three people. The longer we stay, the more that will die. *Let us go!*"

He gazes at me for a long time.

"Maybe I kept you all in your husks because I didn't think you would survive outside of them," he says. "But you have. I tried to kill you, little Savage, and yet here you are. Maybe I was wrong . . . maybe you can make it off this ship. If you do, you deserve to create a world in your own image, not ours. Those that don't know history aren't poisoned by it. I will wipe the records clean. And when you go, don't forget to take your little friends. I'll start waking them up now."

Little friends? Does he mean there are more of us?

"Brewer, you—"

A sparkle-wave ripples his face. His image bloats into a black cloud, then vanishes.

Brewer is gone.

Bishop nudges my arm. "Em, what did he mean?"

The air above the right-side pedestal flickers, glows.

A black face with red eyes appears, but it is smaller and slimmer than Brewer's. Rage billows within me when I recognize it—it's the female monster from the Garden.

She stares at me like I am the only one here.

"You found your way to the Crystal Ball," she says. "It used to be my favorite place. In a way, I suppose I should be proud."

That voice, the voice of death. So similar to Brewer's—old and hissy and ancient and *wrong*—but different, *so* different, in a way that makes me start to shake.

I realize why the voice is familiar: I *know* this creature.

My teeth grind as I fight to get my body under control. I can't show weakness, not now. I squeeze the spear shaft so tight it makes my fingers hurt.

"I am the leader of our group," I say. "Who are you?"

The new monster shakes her head. "You haven't figured it out yet? That's too bad. You are the leader of nothing. You *are* nothing. You aren't even a person."

Why does her voice terrify me so? I know her, I know this thing. I know she hasn't always looked like this, I feel it in my chest, but I can't put the pieces together.

"I *am* a person," I say. "We all are, including Bello. Give her back to us."

"You are *property*," the creature says. Her eyes narrow, the swirling red eyes squeezing into thin slits. "You are an empty shell waiting to be filled, an egg with no yolk. You will lay down your weapons and stop fighting us, and you will do it at once."

That voice . . . *that voice* . . .

My breaths are ragged gasps ripping in and out. My head hurts. A realization is bubbling up through my mind, pushing away the muddy thoughts, and now that I almost have it I suddenly, desperately don't want to know. I want my brain to *stop*, to leave it alone, but it's too late for that. Cold stiffness spreads through me, swirls in my belly and turns my heart into a frozen lump.

Bishop's hand on my arm, reassuring, supporting—whatever we face next, he will face it with me.

I shake my head. "We will not lay down our weapons."

"You should," the monster says. "It's a big ship, but there is nowhere to run."

"If we run, you will hunt us. If we kill you, then—"

"Then you are forever free," the monster finishes.

She knew what I was going to say, yet I've never spoken those words out loud. I've only *thought* them. A new strain of anxiety swirls inside me, a sense of foreboding and despair. The mud is sinking, retreating, a hard knowledge is solidifying . . . it's almost here, almost here and I don't want to know I *don't want to know.*

I scream at her, a three-word roar so loud it could shake the stars themselves.

"Who . . . are . . . you?"

"You still don't know? Amazing."

The truth erupts, stabs through me like a thousand spears shredding my flesh. I finally understand my fear, and I know why this thing is death.

I recognize her voice, because it is *mine*.

"My name," she says, "is Matilda Savage."

THIRTY-FIVE

The monster is me.

I am the monster.

I want to shout out that this thing is a liar, but there is no point. At the core of all that I am, I *know* she is telling the truth.

How can this be? How can I be in two places at once? How could I look like *that*?

Everything goes black. Falling. I feel Bishop's hands around my waist, lifting me. I must weigh nothing at all, it seems so easy for him. My feet find the floor. I stand on my own, woozy, head swimming.

I look for my spear.

Aramovsky is holding it. He's smiling. None of this bothers him. In his mind, the way things are is the way his precious gods want things to be.

"Go back up the ladder, Em," he says. "It's all right. I'll handle things from here."

Bishop reaches out fast, tears the spear from Aramovsky's hands. Bishop hands the spear to me.

Aramovsky doesn't stop smiling. *Perhaps Bishop isn't the only one who wonders who would win a new vote.* That's what Aramovsky said. At the time, I thought he was saying Bishop would win.

But maybe he wasn't thinking about Bishop at all.

Matilda speaks; her voice drowns out all thoughts of Aramovsky.

"We don't need everyone," she says, now calm and loving. "If you and the ones we *do* need put down your weapons, fulfill your obligations, then the ones we don't need will be allowed to live."

She wants me to agree to this?

"The ones you *don't* need get to live," I echo. "Which means the ones you do need . . . die?"

"None of you will die," she says. "Not that any of you are alive to begin with. At least this way, some of you get to carry on with your excuse of an existence."

Bishop snarls, shakes his head. He won't give up any of our people, and neither will I. Not to this vile *thing,* not to anyone.

"We refuse," I say. I will fight her, fight for my own life, fight for all of our lives, but I'm reeling, in danger of going as insane as Brewer. My voice is harsh and defiant one second, softly begging the next. "How can I be you? I don't understand."

"Of course you don't," Matilda says. "You're not old enough to understand."

"Just tell me!"

It's hard to know what her facial expressions mean when she doesn't have a human face, but she seems to be getting annoyed.

"Brewer woke you," she says. "He did it to hurt me, to hurt all of us. That *bastard.* Every moment you are awake, girl, it puts my life at risk. Every piece of information you learn, it puts my life at risk."

How can that be? How can my learning something be a danger to her?

We stare at each other, two Matilda Savages locked in a battle of wills, the *same* will, separated by whatever magic made this happen. She needs me, yet I want nothing to do with her. No, that's not true—I need to know what this is all about, and she can tell me.

"If you want me to consider your offer," I say, "then explain how it's possible you and I are the same person."

She sighs, a sound like ripping paper. "I accept, but we aren't really the same person. *I* am a person—*you* are property. This ship traveled from a place to which we can never return. We left there to find a new home, a new world. We knew the journey would take centuries. To survive the trip, our bodies were permanently modified. They cannot be changed back. We were remade as you see us now."

"Ugly," I say before I can stop the word.

Matilda nods. "Yes, the process made us ugly. It also brought constant pain, pain we have endured for longer than your unfinished mind can comprehend. When we started the trip, the Cherished began cultivating copies of their bodies, making what we call *receptacles*. These receptacles were modified to survive on Omeyocan, the planet below."

Omeyocan.

Brewer didn't tell us the name of the planet. *Omeyocan* . . . the word is a song that makes my brain tingle and my throat tighten. It is where we belong.

She also used a word that Brewer said earlier: the *Cherished.* Is she part of that group? Are we? I don't think it matters. If we can get to Omeyocan, we can leave this all behind.

"Receptacles grow very, *very* slowly," Matilda says. She's talking to me like I am a child, or stupid, or both. "When we arrived here, we were to transfer our thoughts and memories to the receptacles so that we could live on the surface without disease, immune from Omeyocan's subtle poisons that would have slowly killed us."

I look at the planet hanging in the starry blackness.

"So why didn't you do the transfer?"

"On the way here, there was a . . . let's call it a *disagreement*," she says. "Some people had to be taught a lesson. Brewer was one of those people. The bastard tricked us, found a way to lock you away from me. You were supposed to come out of the husk two centuries ago, when your body was twelve years old—just as the scripture requires. But you didn't come out, because of Brewer. Your body kept growing, becoming older and bigger than it was supposed to."

My reality is crumbling. I was in that coffin for two hundred years? No, that's the *extra* time I was in there. That's why our clothes are too small—they would have fit the twelve-year-old me. And it's why they are so big on the people who died as little children. Had those kids stayed alive, they would have grown into their uniforms. But many, like the other Brewer, didn't get that chance.

You are the person who murdered me, he said.

Now I understand. My skin crawls anew at the sight of this evil thing before me.

"You killed the Brewer boy in our coffin room. He was just a child."

Matilda scoffs, a sound like gravel scattered across a hard floor.

"Don't be so dramatic," she says. "Not a *child*, a *receptacle*. Nothing more than a shell waiting to be filled. You, little leader, are *my* receptacle. Understand now? You're not a person at all. Brewer has held you hostage for centuries. He said that if we came after him, he would destroy my receptacle the way I destroyed his. He must be dying. He woke you up out of spite, so that I could know my chance to be born again was fading away forever. He did it to *hurt* me, to make me suffer. But he made a mistake. Now that you are out, he can't simply press a button and kill you in your husk."

It's all so much, *too* much.

"Brewer said he protected us."

Matilda laughs. "Did he? No, it was his threat to kill you that kept me away all these years. But now his leverage is gone. I can finally have the reward I was promised."

What she says is impossible. Yet, once again, I know she is telling the truth. I am her *reward,* like some animal to be given away as a prize. But she said I wouldn't die. Would this process fill in my missing memories? Would it end the madness of not knowing who I am? My parents . . . I might finally remember my parents.

"If you transfer your thoughts, what happens to me? Would I know what you know?"

Matilda pauses. "In a manner of speaking, yes. We are the same person. The transfer would make us whole."

She's not lying, but she's also not telling me all the truth.

"It would make *you* whole," I say. "I asked what happens to *me*. If you do your transfer, what happens to the person I am?"

"You are not a person! You are—"

I shake the spear at her. "Then make another copy! You can't have me! You can't have *any* of us!"

The red eyes fade to a reddish pink. She visibly calms herself. The loving voice comes back—does she think she can soothe me the way a parent soothes a little child?

"We can't make more receptacles," she says. "The process takes *centuries*. Mental maps, synaptic connections, baseline

memories that form neural pathways—if these things aren't a
match, if the foundation isn't identical, then the transfer can't
overwrite."

Overwrite. The word instantly terrifies me. The word is worse
than *death,* worse than *murder.* If Matilda gets me, my body
will live on, but who I am—*what* I am—that will be erased.

I was created to be destroyed.

"So if I'm you, why can't I remember? I know how to speak
and read, but my past is all muddy, all blanked out. Why?"

"Because you don't really *have* memories," Matilda says.
"Language, math, science, skills . . . those things are the frame-
work of a mind. It is our experiences that make us what we are.
Individual identity forms in the way we perceive things, the way
we react, the way we feel. The knowledge your brain received
while you were in the husk provided the biological scaffolding
needed to support who *I* am. You're a *shell,* little leader. I am the
yolk. You were made so that I can live. You're my only hope.
Come and merge with me now so we can be as we were meant
to be."

I thought she was a monster because of the way she looks, but
her evil goes far beyond appearances. She wants to make me
vanish. She wants it to be like I never existed at all, and she's
trying to make that sound like it is a beautiful thing.

I shake my head. "I refuse."

The colors in her eyes darken, spin faster.

"You don't understand," she says. "You're not old enough to
understand. I am your progenitor and you are my receptacle—
you can't make your own decisions!"

Maybe she knows more than I do, more than I could ever
learn, but she doesn't know *me.*

"You're wrong, Matilda. I've been making decisions since the
moment I woke up. And I'll keep making them. I think I get it

now—the longer I live, the better the chance that you'll die. And you should have died a long time ago."

She is so angry she shakes. I see a bit of fluid leak down the left side of her face, a thin rivulet that gathers in one wrinkle before overflowing it, oozing down to the next.

"What about the ones we don't need?" she asks, obviously fighting to control her rage. "Don't you want them to survive, little leader? Their progenitors are already dead, so they can't be overwritten. Come to me willingly, and they will live. If I have to hunt you down, I will kill them all, each and every one. I will torture them first, tell them that their agony is because of your selfishness. I will—"

"You will *never* get me." The words come out like grinding glass. Matilda had her life, and she can keep it—my life is *mine*. "You won't get me. You won't get *any* of us."

She leans forward until her furious red eyes fill the air above the pedestal.

"I'll find you. Brewer held you hostage, but that is over. Come to the orchards, girl. You will come or I swear by Tlaloc that all of your friends will suffer."

That name again . . .

"Tlaloc," I say. "I remember that name. Who is it?"

Matilda leans back. "You're lying. You don't remember that name. You *can't* remember things like that, it's not part of the process." She's more agitated than angry now. She seems worried. "Do you remember anything else?"

I do. I remember the smell of pork chops. I remember how it felt to be mocked and ridiculed. I remember that Tchaikovsky was a musician. I remember the trip to the farm. But if Matilda is this upset about that name, *Tlaloc,* telling her more could make her panic. She wants me to come to her: that gives us a little bit of time, time we probably won't have if she comes after us instead.

"Not really," I say. "Hints of things, vague emotions, but . . . I don't remember anything."

Matilda's sigh of relief makes her face-folds flutter.

"That's good," she says. "Brewer obviously made mistakes in the process, but it is not too late. The longer you are away from me, the more memories of your own you form, the more likely the overwrite will fail and we will *both* die. Come now and I promise you that I will be humane to your friends."

Humane . . . the same word I used when Bishop and I killed the pig. More wisps of memory filter in from that trip to the farm. The farmer told us that when they slaughtered the pigs, they tried to do it as quickly and painlessly as possible. He called that "being humane."

Kill them fast or kill them slow, the pigs all wound up dead. That's all we are to Matilda . . . livestock.

She is a monster, a thousand-year-old abomination. She wants me to fulfill my "destiny," a destiny defined by her.

"We are not your property," I say. "Our lives are our own."

The ugly thing shakes its head.

"Sooner than you think, hunger and thirst will drive you to me anyway," she says. "Throw down your weapons, come to me now, and at least your friends will live. If we have to hunt you, they will all die. Last chance, girl—what is your answer?"

In that moment, I know that if I ever come face-to-face with Matilda, I will kill her.

We are the Birthday Children, and we will find a way to survive.

"My answer is *never*," I say. "And one more thing—you always were a bitch, Savage."

I look over to El-Saffani, point at the three pedestals.

"Break those, then follow me."

I turn my back on Matilda and walk to the ladder. I hear her screaming at me, saying something about how I *must* listen, how I *must* obey, how I'm not old enough to really understand.

I start up the rungs, leaving behind the sounds of destruction.

PART V

UP AND DOWN

THIRTY-SIX

We run downhill.

We run past the severed arms, the mangled bodies, the piles of skulls.

The more I know, the more all of this makes sense.

Brewer is one of the monsters, one of the Grownups, one of the "Cherished." Maybe those are all the same things. His copy, his *receptacle,* died—murdered by the woman that is me—leaving him stranded in an ancient, twisted body. A journey of over a thousand years, and at the end he will simply wither and die. He has no hope.

I might go crazy, too.

We reach the intersection where our two tribes met. We turn left. We are again tiny insects crawling in the long, straight hallway that runs along the inside of a giant cylinder. We are heading back to our people.

What happened on this ship? *Some people do not approve of being sacrificed,* Brewer had said. There was a revolt, a war.

Many died. Did everyone on this ship have a copy? Was everyone promised a new life on Omeyocan?

The answers don't really matter. Choices have consequences. The Grownups made choices that destroyed their lives. Our choices are yet to be made, our lives are yet to be lived—*if* we can get away from here.

We run and run and run. Matilda's monsters will start hunting us soon, if they aren't already. We have to get to our friends before her kind gets to them first.

Brewer didn't tell us where the shuttle was. He didn't have time. Matilda pushed him out somehow, or maybe broke his pillar, I don't know. He was toying with us, though, and in his toying was a hint—I know how to find the shuttle, and, hopefully, we will also find Bello.

Before, I wasn't sure if I should be the leader. I'm sure now. Among all of us, I am unique. I think, I don't simply react. I make decisions when doing so is hard. I know what it means to kill. I will make sure we do what must be done, even if I have to force those who disagree with me into cooperating. I'm going to get my people out of here and get them out alive—if they want to vote for someone else when we're all safe, that's fine with me.

The Grownups divided their tribe and fought each other. I will keep our tribe unified, and we will fight as one.

I make so much noise when I run. Gaston does, too, and also Aramovsky, the three of us huffing and puffing, our feet slapping on the floor. I wouldn't have noticed except for the silence of the circle-stars. I can barely hear Bishop even though he is twice my size and is right next to me.

Before long, I see the dark spot on the floor where Yong's life leaked out into the dust.

But something is different.

The hallway on the left, the dark one where O'Malley and

Aramovsky took Yong's body . . . it is brighter. And we were careful to move around the bloody slush—now it is trampled as if a dozen people ran through it.

I hear voices coming from the intersection. No one should be here. Everyone should be in our coffin room, protected by Coyotl and Farrar.

"Bishop, someone is up there."

He nods. He heard it long before I did.

"Get ready to fight," he says.

Are Matilda's monsters already here?

El-Saffani slows, waiting for us to catch up.

Voices filter from out of the once-dark hall, but they aren't the hissing obscenities of the Grownups. These voices sound normal, like ours, but strange. Higher pitched. Excited. *Loud.*

We move closer to the intersection, just a few steps away now. My clumsiness and the noisy feet of Gaston and Aramovsky must alert them: a person turns the corner and stares at us, wide-eyed.

A young girl with dark brown skin.

She's wearing a clean white shirt, a red tie, a red and black plaid skirt.

The clothes fit her perfectly.

I slow to a stop. So do Bishop, El-Saffani and the others.

The girl's mouth hangs open. A skinny boy turns the corner and joins her. Then another. And another little girl. Uniformed children quickly fill the intersection, gawking at the gray-skinned adults carrying bones as weapons.

Gaston moves to my side.

"Em," he says, "who are they?"

I have no idea.

But I think on Brewer's words, and I remember what he said.

Don't forget to take your little friends.

Little friends. This is what he meant.

Another body turns the corner, one we see clearly because he is head and shoulders taller than the others.

It's O'Malley.

A smile breaks across his face, wider than I have ever seen. He is alive. He is beautiful.

He awkwardly slips past the children, careful not to bump them. They grab at him for comfort, slide in behind him to hide, their eyes never straying from the frightening images of Bishop and El-Saffani.

O'Malley walks to me.

Bishop steps aside.

O'Malley opens his arms and pulls me in.

"Em, we didn't know if you'd make it back."

He squeezes me tight, lifts me off my feet. For a perfect moment everything goes away. He smells of sweat. His body is warm and firm. I will protect this body, protect *him*—I will not let Matilda take O'Malley.

I glance at Bishop, wondering how he might react to the hug, but he is making a point of looking the other way.

I hear more people approaching.

O'Malley sets me down as Spingate, Beckett and Smith come rushing around the corner. They slide past the kids. Spingate runs to Gaston and almost knocks him over with her flying embrace.

She squeezes him far harder than O'Malley squeezed me.

"I didn't know," she says. Her voice cracks, her words sound wet. "You were gone, and . . . I didn't know . . . if you . . ."

Gaston hugs her back, pets her thick red hair.

"We're fine," he says. "Everyone made it."

Beckett stands there, smiling and awkward, unsure if he should hug someone, shake hands or just stay quiet. The lanky

Smith greets Aramovsky first. She laces her fingers together, presses her palms against her sternum, and she bows her head. The gesture is disturbingly formal, almost . . . subservient.

If there was another vote, she would choose Aramovsky. Those others that seem to hang on his every word, they would as well. With Spingate, Gaston, O'Malley and Bishop behind me, though, it doesn't really matter. Whatever Aramovsky's plans might be, they will have to wait until I have us all down on Omeyocan.

Spingate lets go of Gaston and launches herself at me, crushes me in a tight hug.

"Em! I'm so happy to see you. Did you find anything?"

I hug her back, almost as hard. She smells nice. She smells like home.

"We did." I gently push her away. "What are you all doing here? You were supposed to stay in the coffin room."

Spingate throws up her hands, gestures to the children. There must be twenty of them in the hall now, maybe more.

"They just started showing up," she says. "Those closed archway doors by our coffin room? They opened, all up and down the hall. Kids walked out. We gathered up as many as we could and put them in our room, but we could see more in both directions. We came this way. O'Malley sent Coyotl, Farrar, Opkick and Borjigin the other way."

She points down the hall where we left Yong.

"When we got here, it was all lit up, like someone had turned on the lights. There were kids wandering around. We went down the hall until it ended at another melted door, so we think we've found all the kids we can. We were about to head back to our coffin room when we heard you coming."

The first girl we saw walks up to me. Her legs are skinny. She has the bony knees I thought I had when I woke up.

She reaches out and takes my free hand in hers. She stares up.

There is a jagged circle on her forehead. The black symbol complements her dark brown skin and eyes. There are a few dust smudges on her shirt, but no blood, no grease, no sweat stains and no dirt. She hasn't fought. She hasn't feared. She hasn't killed. She is clean, unblemished in any way.

She is what we were all supposed to be.

I squat slightly so I can look her in the eye.

"What's your name?" I ask.

She smiles. "Zubiri. I think. That's what it said on my bed."

To her, it wasn't a coffin, it wasn't a cradle, it was just a bed.

"That's a nice name," I say.

My friends and I woke up before her. We're larger, *physically* older, but after what Matilda told me I think I know how this works.

"Zubiri, how old are you?"

"I'm twelve," she says, perking up instantly. "Today is my birthday."

I can't help but smile.

"Happy birthday." I look at the other clean faces staring my way. "Happy birthday to you all."

Once again, everything has changed. My friends and I thought we were twelve years old. We're not, not after what we've been through. But these kids *are,* at least as far as they know. Twelve-year-old minds in twelve-year-old bodies.

Brewer entrusted these kids to us. He felt we could get them to the planet below. I still don't know his story. I don't know why he fought Matilda. I don't know who was in the right and who was in the wrong. I will probably never know. But Brewer seems to understand me—I think he knew I wouldn't be able to leave these children behind.

They were made to walk on Omeyocan.

They are coming with us.

If anyone gets in our way, they will learn that the Birthday Children—together, as one people—are extremely dangerous.

The kids are already wandering around the hall. My stomach churns when I see that two of the boys are giggling while they throw chunks of dried blood-slush at each other.

I turn to Bishop. His dust-caked face seems calm, as if he's waiting for orders.

"Bishop, can you get these kids organized? We have to move fast."

He glances at O'Malley with cold eyes. Is he jealous of the way O'Malley hugged me, the way I was jealous when I thought Bishop was looking at Spingate? Part of me hopes he's not, and another part hopes he is. Both parts, though, can wait—we all have important work ahead of us.

Bishop nods. "I can," he says. "Do you want me to do it my way?"

"I wouldn't have asked you if I didn't."

The gray-caked mouth twitches with the slightest of smiles. He draws himself up to his full height and starts yelling.

"New kids! Form two lines, right arm straight, right hand on the right shoulder of the person in front of you. Don't make me ask twice!"

The wide-eyed children practically fall all over themselves scrambling to comply. In seconds, the mob forms two neat lines. Without a word, Bawden and Visca take up positions behind them. The twins take their usual place out front.

Bishop smiles at me. "What now, Em?"

"Back to the coffin room," I say. "As fast as we can go."

His chest swells as he draws in a huge breath.

"You will all follow El-Saffani! Match the pace of the person in front of you, and if you fall behind, you'll have to answer to me. Understand?"

Twenty-odd heads nod rapidly. I wouldn't want to answer to Bishop, either.

"Good," Bishop says. "El-Saffani, move out!"

The kids and the circle-stars take off, moving as a single unit. I'll say one thing for Bishop: he's great at getting people to march.

Gaston and Aramovsky run along behind them, as do Smith and Beckett.

That leaves me standing alone with O'Malley.

"The kids are a problem," he says quietly. "We have maybe fifty in the coffin room. If Coyotl found as many in his direction as we found here, there might be a hundred, total. Maybe more. If the monsters come, how are we going to defend that many people?"

A memory bubbles up through the mud, a memory of a man's face. Pieces of it, anyway, vague images. A black mustache. Soft, loving eyes, eyes that could also be hard, separated by deep furrows and a flaring nose.

That voice in my head . . . it belongs to him.

He is my father.

And yet he is not. Those vague memories are a lie. That was Matilda's father, not mine. I don't have parents, because I wasn't born—I was created.

I was *hatched*.

The man is not my father, yet his words bounce around inside my brain. His words are the only real connection to my past.

And his words feel right.

"We're not going to *defend* anything," I say. "We attack,

O'Malley. When in doubt, attack, always attack, never let your enemy recover."

O'Malley gives me a curious look.

"What does that mean?"

"It means we're going to the Garden. Every last one of us. We're going to find Bello. We're going to find the way off this ship, and if the monsters get in our way, we are going to kill them and be forever free."

I meet his deep-blue eyes. He's observing me, measuring me.

"Em, sometimes you're kind of scary."

I nod. "Thank you."

"And what do you mean, *off this ship*? We're in a building."

"Come on, let's move. I'll tell you everything when we're all together. I have a plan."

We run downhill.

THIRTY-SEVEN

I stand on Okadigbo's coffin.

The room is so full of people I can't see the floor. They sit cross-legged in the aisle of dust, they sit on coffins, they stand with their backs to the walls. Faces stare up at me, both familiar and new. I tell them what I know. I describe what must be done.

O'Malley counted. The numbers are hard to accept. I was a leader of twenty-two people; now I lead a hundred and thirty.

How will we take care of these kids? I don't know. Neither does O'Malley. We have to figure it out. We will not leave a single person behind to have their newly hatched minds wiped out by the evil that runs this ship.

I understood Brewer's riddle. *If they found you, you found them.* There is much more to this "building" than we first knew. Beyond the doors that Brewer melted shut to keep our older selves away, beyond the Garden's walls, there lie seemingly endless sections of this ship.

If they found you, you found them.

When we opened the door to the empty section, as Brewer

called it, we broke his seal. Did Matilda know that someday kids might escape the coffins, and if they did, they would eventually wind up in the Garden? Maybe. Maybe she waited centuries for someone in a white shirt and a red tie to go there, so she would know there was finally a way through Brewer's defenses.

Matilda got Bello in the Garden. We will find the path the monsters used to attack us there, and we will use that same path to attack them.

We will capture a Grownup. We will make that monster tell us what we need to know: the location of Bello, the location of the shuttle and how to use it.

The faces look up at me. I tell them about Matilda, Brewer, the husks and the receptacles. I tell them about the *Xolotl* and the Crystal Ball. I tell them about Omeyocan, and the shuttle that will take us there if we can find it.

I tell them we are being hunted.

I tell them what the Grownups will do to us if they catch us.

And then I tell them my plan.

As I expected, Aramovsky doesn't like it.

"That's ridiculous," he says. "You're going to get us all killed. Even if we do survive, the gods will be furious at our insolence."

He's using bigger words now. All the older kids are, including me. It happened gradually, I think, but now I'm noticing it—especially when Aramovsky talks. He doesn't like my plan? Something tells me he wouldn't have liked *any* plan I put forth. He wants to contradict me no matter what I say, so that the people who think he is "chosen" will pay more attention to him.

He objects, but as I figured, his objection doesn't really matter right now—because my friends believe in me.

"It will work," Bishop says. "We can beat them, I know we can."

The circle-stars grunt. They thump their chests. Bishop has

their backing, and I have his. As long as that holds, there's nothing Aramovsky can do. The five circle-stars in this room are itching for a fight, and that's what I aim to give them. Only El-Saffani isn't here: the twins are in the hall, preparing.

Bishop, Coyotl, Visca, Farrar and Boy El-Saffani used O'Malley's knife to cut the legs off their tattered pants, which are now roughly the same length as the short skirts of Bawden and Girl El-Saffani. I think the circle-stars also cut themselves to make fresh dust-paste: they are coated head to toe in a red-gray that is almost the same color as the scarred monster's blood.

Shirtless, bare-legged, with paste caked on their exposed skin, on their faces, even mashed in their hair, the circle-stars all look the same. We can barely tell the boys and girls apart.

O'Malley has his knife back. He fiddles with it, absently moving it from hand to hand. He has that look on his face again, like he wants to tell me something but doesn't want to say it in front of the others.

"Out with it, O'Malley." I say. "What are you thinking?"

He glances around the room, sees that everyone is waiting for him to talk.

"The bracelets," he says. "We didn't go after Bello before because the monsters can hit us from a distance. That's still the case, so why attack them now?"

Heads nod, arms fold across chests. I understand why he wanted to ask that question in private, but I have an answer.

"The Grownups want us alive," I say. "Their lives depend on it. They don't recognize us, at least not right away. I think that will give us time to use our speed, to reach them before they figure out who they need."

"You *think*?" Spingate says. Her arms are crossed, too. "What if you're wrong? What if they just shoot us?"

Bawden thumps her fist against her chest.

"Then we *die*," she barks. "We die attacking, not hiding in this room like cowards."

The circle-stars roar their approval. Bawden's beautiful brown skin is invisible—she is reddish-gray, she is painted for war.

I continue.

"Our best chance to survive is to never be alone. Older kids will stay in groups of four. Don't get separated, even if there is fighting. Beckett and Smith will protect the younger kids."

Over a hundred small heads turn to look at those two. Strawberry-blond Beckett smiles uncomfortably. Skinny Smith tries to look fierce. She can't fully hide her fear.

We are almost ready, but Aramovsky won't give up.

"They are *monsters*." He turns as he talks, looking to his supporters. "The gods sent them. We need to talk to them, beg them for mercy. I have seen what they can do. Unless you want to wind up as a pile of chopped-up arms and legs and severed heads, listen to me. And what good does it do us to stay in groups of four? If you want a fight, Em, the circle-stars have their clubs, so send *them*."

I hop off the coffin and walk to the open archway. I wave El-Saffani in.

They enter. Boy El-Saffani carries a double armful of thigh-bones. Girl El-Saffani passes them out to each of the older kids, starting with Beckett and Smith.

I take one, then hop back up on the coffin: bone in one hand, spear in the other.

"Now we *all* have clubs," I say.

I toss the bone at Aramovsky. He catches it on reflex, stares at it.

"We *all* go, Aramovsky. We *all* fight."

On top of Okadigbo's coffin, I am taller than anyone else in the room.

Maybe I am not as good a speaker as Aramovsky, but I've been paying attention. I've watched how people react to different things. I've recognized that certain words have power, that they dictate how people feel, how they respond—I will use those words now.

"Aramovsky is right about one thing," I say. "There are *monsters* here. If they weren't sent by the *gods,* then we have a right to defend ourselves. If the gods did send them, then we will prove ourselves worthy. No one is coming to *rescue* us. No one is coming to save us. We will not cower in this room waiting for someone else to decide if we live or die."

So many faces gaze up at me, eyes big and wide, bodies leaning slightly my way. These people are terrified. They desperately need a sense of hope.

There is a final word of power I want to use, one related to *rescue* but also different, stronger. If I use it correctly, I know everyone will follow me no matter where I lead them.

"We will not be hunted," I say. "We will not be erased. I know this is a lot to handle, especially for the new kids, but we are going to the Garden. We will save Bello if we can. We will attack. We will either win our freedom, or we will die."

I raise the spear high, and I use that final word.

"If we can't be rescued, then we . . . will . . . *escape.*"

THIRTY-EIGHT

Together, we march on the Garden.

I have the spear.

O'Malley has the knife.

Everyone else carries a bone-club. Everyone except for the kids. *Kids* . . . is that what we should call them? That's what *we* were, that's how we thought of ourselves, but we're not. We are not kids, we are not teenagers, we are not adults. We are a mixture of all those things.

We move as one, thanks to Bishop's ability to organize. My friends are both out in front and bringing up the rear. Between them, over a hundred white-shirted kids marching in three long, neat rows.

Are we still afraid? Very. All around me, young faces etched with fear, but now other emotions as well. There is *rage* that they would use us up and cast us away, take over our bodies and make us just like them. There is a sense of *belonging,* in that we all fight for each other as well as for ourselves. And there is the newest feeling of all—*hope*—given to us by the promise of our own planet.

We belong down there. It's what we were made for.

We are trapped on a ship where monsters want to kill us. The monsters have been here a thousand years: now that they know we are awake, they will find us. We are hungry, and in the one place we know of that has food, the monsters are waiting.

They won't be waiting long.

We will not be used. We will not let them change us. They think we are *property*?

They are mistaken.

We march. Tracks in the dust lead us to the archway Gaston and Spingate discovered. It remains closed, stone halves pressed tightly together.

I raise the spear. Everyone stops. I turn to face my people.

"Okereke, Johnson, Gaston, prepare the torches."

Gaston and my fellow circles run forward. Johnson has a dozen long bones cradled in her arms. Okereke carries a bundle of black rags, the discarded pants legs from the circle-star boys. We won't have grease like we had when we first entered the dark section. These new torches won't last long—we'll have to move fast and hope we make it to the thicket tunnel before they burn out.

We prepare ten torches, tying the fabric tight to the bone. Three for Bishop, three for Farrar, two for O'Malley—who will be up front with me—and two for Smith and Beckett, who will bring up the rear.

I talk to a hallway full of faces.

"We don't have long before our light runs out. Stay close to the person in front of you. Ignore any side rooms. The circle-stars will run ahead and make sure those are empty."

I hope they are. If we have to fight before we reach the Garden, we'll be in the dark for sure.

The dark. If that happens, I know I won't be able to handle it. I will fall apart. For a moment I am in my coffin again, the terror rolling over me along with that feeling of being trapped . . . then I force it away. We'll make it in time. I won't be in the dark, I *won't*—I'll get these people where we need to go.

I turn to Spingate. "Open it up."

She goes to work with the scepter.

I stand in front of the door. Bishop and El-Saffani press in on my right, Farrar, Visca and Bawden on my left.

"Got it," Spingate says. The door grinds open.

Inside, darkness.

We will make it in time, we will . . .

"Light the torches," I say.

The scepter's flame flares. Each group of circle-stars lights a torch, then rushes forward. I see them darting into dark rooms, darting back out, advancing down the hall. They will make sure Matilda's creatures aren't lurking inside, ready to reach out and grab us as we pass by.

O'Malley is on my right, his knife in one hand, two unlit bone torches in the other.

I wait until the circle-stars are so far down the hall I can barely see them.

"This is it," I call out. "Move fast, stay together. Spingate, do it."

The end of her scepter sparks brightly. O'Malley touches his torch to the flame. Black fabric *whuffs* to life.

We run.

So many of us. Our footsteps thunder off the stone walls.

Behind me, I can hear kids crying. They're terrified, and I

can't blame them. We're marching them through torchlit darkness, making them run fast so that monsters they have never seen can't get them. These kids have been awake for only a few hours. They barely know us, yet are forced to take what we say on faith alone. So far, at least, none of them have had the courage to stand up to us. I'm sure that will come. I *hope* it comes, because if it does it will mean we've reached a safe place where we have the luxury of letting them argue. Are we bullying these kids into doing what we say? Yes, we probably are, but it is for their own good.

O'Malley's first torch sputters. He lights the second. I know that in the rear of our group, Smith is doing the same. Up front, Bishop and Farrar are already on their second torch, probably close to starting their last.

We are almost out of light.

I wish Latu was here. She would have gladly fought at our side. She would have protected the kids. She would have done whatever needed to be done.

Latu, Yong, Bello . . .

When this is over, who else will be gone?

Torchlight plays off the walls and the dead ceiling. We know where we are going, and it doesn't take long to get there.

Finally, we see that the circle-stars have stopped up ahead. We've reached the room with the thicket tunnel.

Bishop faces me, as if checking to see if I've changed my mind. I haven't. We will stick to the plan. Torchlight flickers against the red-gray that coats him, glistens off the wetness of his white eyes.

There is anger and determination about him, but also an air of sadness. He is leading us into battle not because he wants to fight, but because he knows this must be done and that he is the best one to do it. He has taken life: even though that life belonged to a monster, the act haunts him.

The circle-stars gather around me. All of them this time, seven warriors with red-gray faces ready to lead us in.

"We're almost out of torches," I say. "Get into the Garden and make sure it's safe for the rest of us to follow. If you see monsters, capture them if you can, but if you have to kill them to stay alive—kill them."

Seven heads nod. They really all do look the same. If my people are a spear, the circle-stars are the blade.

Bishop shoves his bone-club through the hole, then crams his way in. The twins follow him, then Farrar, Coyotl, Visca and finally Bawden.

The strongest of us have gone forward, but that doesn't mean the rest of us are weak.

O'Malley's torch starts to flutter.

I'll be in the dark again. . . . I'll be trapped. . . .

A hand on my shoulder, squeezing tight. O'Malley leans in close and whispers.

"Hang on, Em. We're almost there. Don't be afraid."

I breathe in deep, hold it, let it out slow. We're not in the dark yet. I take my mind off it by talking, going over the last few elements of my plan.

"Smith, Beckett," I call out. "Get up here."

The two slide through the lines of kids. They both hold bone-clubs. Smith's thin face is set and stern. She's ready. Beckett looks like he might throw up.

"Keep the kids quiet and be ready to come when we call," I say. "If the monsters attack, it's up to you to hold them off long enough for the kids to get through the thicket tunnel."

Smith nods. Beckett is sweating.

I know it's risky leaving only two people to protect the kids. Matilda could attack at any time, but we need everyone else up front looking for the hole she used to enter the Garden.

I hear Bawden's voice from the other side of the door.

"Em, the way is clear."

Thank goodness, I'll be in the light. . . .

I take a final moment to address my friends.

"Remember to stay in your teams of four. Be as silent as you can, because the monsters might not know we're here. If you find the entrance, shout it out. If any of you hear that shout, it means we're done being quiet—get to that spot right away. If you see a monster with a bracelet, you must attack that one first. Do not hesitate. Does everyone understand?"

They all nod. They know this is their one chance to survive. They are as ready as they can be.

I push my spear through the hole, then follow it. I crawl into the pigs' thicket tunnel. My friends are right behind me.

The curved roof's light beams down. The fist in my chest eases, then fades. At least I'm out of the darkness.

I crawl out and stand under a fruit tree. It takes me a moment to spot the circle-stars, even though they are quite close. Their red-gray bodies blend in with the trees and shadows, making them nearly invisible.

I move left. My group moves with me: Spingate, Aramovsky and Gaston. I kept Spingate with me because I feel a need to protect her, make sure nothing happens to her. Gaston won't leave her side, so I put him in my group rather than risking an argument in front of the others. As for Aramovsky, I can't trust him—I'm not letting him out of my sight.

Bishop slides out from behind a tree. Without a word, he points to groups, then points where he wants those groups to go. He points at me, then to his chest, then to his right. As we planned, both of our groups will explore the area where Bello was taken. That is the most likely spot for Matilda's hidden entrance.

Bishop's group includes El-Saffani—of course—and also D'souza, the circle girl. She holds her bone like she's afraid it will come to life and attack her. The four of them move quickly through the knee-high grass. My group follows.

The light above and grass below gives way to tree shade and creeping vines, then we slide into the thicker underbrush. Our feet crunch through brittle leaves, rotting fruit and dried twigs, making it hard to move quietly. Up ahead, I can barely see D'souza, and can't see Bishop or the twins at all.

We reach the Garden's thicket-covered wall. This is where it happened, where the monsters took Bello away.

The eight of us spread out, reaching hands through the thicket. The winding stems are so deep I have to turn my head to the side, press my cheek into them for my fingertips to reach the wall. Somewhere nearby, perhaps, one of us will feel empty space instead of stone.

"Em."

A soft whisper, but it scares me so bad I yank my arm out, tearing the skin on thick vine-stalks. It's Bishop. He moved up behind me and I never heard him coming.

My arm is scratched deep. A few drops of blood drip to the ground.

He points at my spear. "Use that instead," he says, then walks a few feet away and starts poking his bone-club through the thicket.

I look at my spear as if I didn't even know I had it. I push the spearpoint through the stems until it taps the stone wall. I try it again; it sticks in a vine somewhere I can't see.

This is much better than reaching my arm in there.

I look over at Bishop and smile. He smiles back, his white eyes and white teeth bright against the red-gray of his caked-on dust.

A girl's scream, from the right.

Bishop turns and sprints toward it, plowing through the underbrush. El-Saffani is right behind him. White-shirted D'souza has a moment of indecision, unsure whether to go or stay, then she chases after her group.

This is it . . . we're going to fight. The thought of one of those things grabbing me, wrinkled black spider-hands holding me down . . . it's almost enough to freeze me in place. Almost. This time, I won't let the fear stop me.

I lock eyes with Spingate, Gaston and Aramovsky. Spingate has the scepter. Gaston and Aramovsky hold thigh-bones. The weapons look clumsy and awkward in their hands.

"Stay together," I say. "When we see a monster, hit it as hard as you can."

They nod, wide-eyed. In times of safety, Aramovsky might argue with me, but not now.

Another scream. A boy this time, from far to our left.

And another behind us, from somewhere out in the grass.

We're under attack.

Spingate turns in place, her hands clutching the jeweled scepter. She doesn't know which way to go. Neither do I.

I hear Bishop roar, hear the El-Saffani twins let out a simultaneous boy/girl scream of rage. From all over the Garden, the ash-faced warriors shout in challenge and anger, their noises joining howls of pain and fear.

Doubt explodes inside me: I have chosen wrong. My plan was bad, I shouldn't have split us into groups—we need to be together, to fight *together*. Fear sinks talons into me, paralyzes me yet again. . . .

No.

Matilda must not win, must not take even one more person.

I am the leader. My people need me.

I raise my spear high: my voice booms out louder than I could have imagined possible.

"Everyone, fight your way to me!"

Spingate, Gaston and Aramovsky stare at me, shocked. From across the Garden, from all over the woods, the war cries of my people echo back. They heard me and are urging each other on.

The thicket behind me rustles. Before I can turn, an arm snakes around my stomach and a cold, bony black hand clamps down over my mouth. In that moment, I smell what is right below my nose—gnarled flesh that stinks of rot and decay and something artificial.

I'm yanked backward into the thicket. Woody stems scrape at my skin and pull my hair. I kick my legs hard, clutch at anything my fingers touch. Hands grab my feet, but these hands are *warm,* trying to pull me back into the light.

There is a moment where I am motionless, a living rope in a game of tug-of-war, then the warm hands slip off my feet. Vines and leaves fall away: I am through the other side. I am being dragged along a hard surface. Dark here, barely enough light to see.

My spear is gone.

(Attack, attack, when in doubt, attack.)

I grab the hand that covers my face and shove a rancid finger into my mouth. I bite down as hard as I can.

Something brittle cracks between my teeth; the taste of death squirts across my tongue.

I hear a scream that isn't human. The hand on my face lets go, but the one around my middle holds firm and now there are two more arms clutching at me, one wrapped tight to my chest and the other over my left shoulder.

My fingers claw, my feet kick. "Let me go! *I'll kill you!"*

I hear something burst through the thicket. I see the flash of my spear. The cold hands drop away. I scramble to my feet, ready to fight.

I find myself standing face-to-face with Aramovsky.

He holds the spear. The blade drips red-gray. At first I think he will also stab me, but he is wide-eyed and terrified. His chest heaves. The weapon trembles in his hands.

I turn and look at my attackers.

There are two of them, creatures barely visible in this dark place beyond the thicket. Swirling red eyes stare out. The bigger of the two is bent over, clutching its leg. Red-gray squirts through skeletal black fingers, drips down to a metal floor. There is something familiar about that monster, but I can't place what.

The other one presses its gnarled left hand hard against its wrinkled right shoulder. Red-gray oozes down its chest and arm.

This monster is only a tiny bit shorter than me.

Just one look, and I know who it is.

I am staring at Matilda Savage.

THIRTY-NINE

t's so dim in here I wonder if their red eyes can see what I can't. Why would creatures of the shadows need light? The one holding its leg, it seems to stare at us. Black hands slide free of the still-bleeding wound, and it stands.

So *tall*.

No, it isn't staring at *us*—it stares at Aramovsky.

The swirling red eyes change somehow, they soften.

The creature reaches a gnarled, blood-coated hand toward him, not in aggression this time, not to grab, but with fingers outstretched.

It reaches out like it wants to touch.

"Finally," it says in a dry voice that sounds much like cracking thicket branches. "I have waited for so long."

Aramovsky lowers the spear tip.

His jaw hangs slack. He blinks slowly. His shirt is no longer neat and clean—it is torn, the white stained by spreading lines of red. He must have forced himself through the thicket, ignoring the pain.

He fought his way in to save me.

And now he has eyes only for the monster, the first living thing we've seen in this place that is taller than he is.

"You," Aramovsky says. "I am . . . am I *you?*"

In that whispering question is the same tone of shocked recognition I heard in my own voice when I spoke with Matilda. Aramovsky is asking, but he already knows the answer.

The mouthless nightmare nods. "Come with me. The gods say it must be so."

Aramovsky drops the spear. It clatters against the hard floor.

"My creator," he says, and steps forward.

Is he crazy? Are they doing something to him to make him act like this? I grab Aramovsky's wrist and try to pull him back.

The tall monster waves his fingers inward—a kind, inviting gesture.

"Come," it says. "It is right for you to join me."

Aramovsky acts like he doesn't even know I'm pulling on his arm. He steps toward the creature, dragging me along.

Off to my right, I see a flash of movement . . . Matilda, reaching for my fallen spear.

I let go of Aramovsky and launch myself at her, punching and kicking. My fist hits something soft, something that squishes from the blow. I hear my creator's cry of pain and she falls away. I snatch up my spear: its familiar solidity instantly comforts me.

I point the tip at Matilda, hold it so close to her chest that we both know the message—if she moves, I strike. Her hands press to her right eye. Darkness and gnarled fingers don't completely hide the damage. Her eye used to bulge out; now it sags like broken fruit. A thick, yellowish-gray fluid seeps down her face, glistens in the dim light, gathering on the disgusting vertical folds that cover her mouth.

I look back to Aramovsky. He stands in front of the tall monster. They embrace: bloody, white-shirted arms wrap around wrinkled coal-black skin, wrinkled coal-black arms wrap around the bloody white shirt.

Aramovsky rests his cheek on the monster's black chest.

The thicket behind me suddenly rattles and shakes like it was hit by a storm. Something big and strong and heavy tears through it. A flash of gray and red, of muscle and scattering leaves. A thighbone cuts through the air, a blur of white that passes right over Aramovsky's head and smashes into the monster's face.

The thighbone cracks in two, one piece spinning into the darkness, the other still held in Bishop's hands.

The tall monster's legs go slack. It sags back, sliding out of Aramovsky's arms. It turns as it falls, landing facedown.

Bishop steps forward. He holds the broken bone in one hand. The jagged tip points down like the blade of a misshapen knife.

Aramovsky looks dazed. He sees his creator flat on the floor, trying to crawl away.

Bishop raises his bone-dagger high.

Aramovsky's hands shoot out to block the blow, but he is too late.

The broken thighbone punches deep into the black monster's back.

Everything stops.

Bishop's panting breath is the only sound.

He is bleeding from the shoulder, from the forehead. His red blood runs thick trails through the dark dust that covers his skin.

He stands there, staring down, chest heaving, then grabs the bone and yanks it free.

The tall monster trembles. With painful effort, it slowly rolls to its back. It ignores Bishop, stretches a shaking hand toward Aramovsky.

"So . . . close," it says.

The hand drops to the floor, limp.

Aramovsky's monster is dead. I turn to face mine.

Matilda hasn't moved. Neither has my spear.

If she dies, I am forever free.

I press the spear tip forward. Hands still covering her eye, she backs up until she bumps into a metal wall and can retreat no more. Her face isn't human, but I recognize her fear.

Matilda is terrified. Like with Aramovsky standing at Latu's grave, her fear excites me, it *feeds* me. I feel it tingling across my skin and fluttering in my belly.

This vile thing created me just so she could destroy me, but I will destroy her.

My hands tighten on the spear. All it will take is one strong thrust. . . .

She shudders. She is so afraid. She *bleeds*.

My joy at her fear, it fades, it drains.

She is me.

No . . . she is *not* me. I am not *her*.

A hand on my shoulder. I glance and see O'Malley. His knife, knife hand and sleeve are soaked in red-gray. Red blood—*his* blood—spills down from a gash on his cheek to stain the collar of his white shirt.

"Em, don't," he says quietly. "We need her."

It takes me another second to realize he's really there, not a product of my imagination. I keep the spear tip pressed against Matilda's chest. My eyes have adjusted; I can see more now. My people are in here with us. Bishop and his dust-faced warriors, El-Saffani, Spingate and Gaston, Coyotl and Okereke, Cabral and Borjigin, *all* of them. Farther back, Smith and Beckett, and all around them a countless cluster of terrified children.

I'm almost afraid to believe what I see. "We made it?"

O'Malley nods. "The monsters attacked. They didn't have bracelet weapons. I don't know why. They tried to grab us. Because we were in groups of four, everyone was able to fight them off. We killed some of them—it was bad, Em." He closes his eyes for a moment. "*We* were bad."

When he opens his eyes, I see something in his face, an expression I haven't seen before. Whatever he experienced out there in the Garden, whatever he did, he's trying to push it away.

"The monsters ran," he says. "We went back and got the kids. Your plan, Em . . . your plan worked."

My people are alive.

"Did we lose anyone?"

He nods. "Harris, a circle. He's dead."

Harris. All I knew of that boy was that he didn't seem to trust me. I don't think I even had a chance to talk to him. And now he's gone.

I notice Bishop watching me. He's still panting. Is that from exertion, or the emotions of killing yet again?

I face Matilda.

"You've lost," I tell her. "You will take us to Bello, then to the shuttle."

Her one eye glares out. She's trembling, clearly in great pain, but she stands up straight like a leader should. She refuses to back down.

"I will not take you anywhere. And your friend Bello is dead. You are too late."

She says it mockingly, accusingly, as if it's my fault Bello is gone. Bello didn't hurt anyone, didn't even argue with anyone. A boulder of anger tumbles through me, rolling and unstoppable . . . this can't be, it *can't*.

I lean in so close I smell Matilda's rotten stink. I move the spear tip up to where her throat should be. I press the point into the disgusting folds of skin.

"*Liar*," I whisper. "You tell me where Bello is, then you take us to the shuttle, or I will end you."

My creator slowly shakes her head.

"You are me, and I am you," she says. "You know I am telling the truth."

Tears well up in my eyes even as my fury grows. I'm almost sure Matilda is telling the truth . . . *almost*. I could keep asking her, I could torture her, but if Bello really is dead, then every minute I spend here is a minute the rest of my people are in danger. The *Xolotl* is massive; we know nothing about it, while our enemy knows every inch. My people will not be safe until they are on Omeyocan.

I know I will hate myself for this decision, but there is no choice. For the second time, I choose the safety of the group over the life of just one person.

"The shuttle," I say. "Take us to it."

Bishop runs to my side. "Em, no, we have to find Bello first. This thing is lying. Bello can't be dead, she can't—"

"*Be quiet*," I say in a voice not so different from Matilda's.

Bishop's face grows hard, icy. He stands too close, this angry man, painted dark red-gray and streaked with blood. His fists clench. I see his pulse dancing in his temples.

I am aware that the others are watching. O'Malley, Spingate, Gaston and Aramovsky, Bawden and Coyotl and all the rest. I'm aware of that, I sense it, but my world has narrowed to a single point of focus: Bishop.

I stare straight into his dark yellow eyes.

"Step *back*," I say. "The decision is made."

Maybe he will hate me. Maybe the others will, too, but the

group's safety matters more than Bello's life. And, our survival is infinitely more important than what the group thinks of me.

Bishop's nose flares. His lip curls.

He steps back.

I focus my attention where it belongs: on my creator.

Matilda's one good eye sparkles.

"Very good, little one," she says. "You project such authority, as I did when I was your—"

I push the spear tip a tiny bit farther. The point pokes into her diseased flesh, cutting off her worthless words.

"The shuttle," I say again. "Take us there, or die."

Matilda stays so very still.

"No, little one," she says. "I know who I was at your age. I know you better than you could ever know yourself. You *can't* murder me."

I told myself that when I saw her, I would kill her. I want to push the blade into her throat, I want to feel her terror again, maybe hear her *beg*—but my arms refuse to obey.

She's right: I can't do it.

But I have to get my people to safety. The monsters could be regrouping. They will come at us again, and this time, they might use those bracelets.

"If you don't show me where the shuttle is, then you pay for what you have done to us," I say. "Maybe you're right. Maybe I can't kill you. Good thing for me that I don't have to. Bishop, take care of this."

In the dim light, Bishop smiles. He is angry and frustrated. The chance to unleash his rage on a target—any target—seems to satisfy him in a deeply wicked way.

Bloody bone-dagger clutched in his right hand, he steps closer.

Matilda looks at Bishop, then at me, then at him again.

He raises the bone.

Matilda lifts both hands up, palms out, as if that will stop the blow. The ruin of her eye gleams wetly.

"I'll take you! I'll take you to the shuttle!"

I put a hand on Bishop's chest. His skin is hot to the touch.

He looks at me. His face slowly returns to normal. He lowers the weapon.

Matilda trembles uncontrollably. She is alone and at our mercy.

"Bishop," I say, "give this *thing* one chance. If she doesn't take us to the shuttle, or if you think she's tricking us, kill her."

He nods.

I face my creator. "You will *never* have my body, so either take us to the shuttle, or die in the body you have."

Her shoulders droop and her head hangs down. I do not know *how* I know, but this monster's will has finally broken.

We have won.

FORTY

Bishop carries Matilda cradled in his arms, as if she weighs nothing at all.

She's led us into unknown areas. We run across a flat surface, which means we're moving down the length of the cylinder instead of up or down the curve. Everything is dark. Thin lines of glowing colors stretch across the floor—it's enough light to keep me from panicking, but barely.

El-Saffani is once again out in front. Bishop, O'Malley and I are a few steps behind them. The rest follow, including the three lines of kids. Some of them are crying, whining for mothers and fathers that don't exist, but they stay in their ranks and they keep pace. That's all we can ask for. Bawden and Visca bring up the rear, my ash-covered warriors making sure no one attacks us from behind.

All of this is catching up with me. The march to the Garden, the fighting, the fact that I have been going for so long, making all the hard decisions . . . I am so tired. Every muscle screams at me to lie down, to give up, but we can't stop now: we must escape before it's too late.

"Keep moving," I call to the others. "Keep moving."

We are all close to quitting. The fighting in the Garden must have been bad. We leave a trail of blood behind us. There isn't time to fix our wounds. I should have had us grab fruit to eat as we run, but I didn't think of it and now it is too late to go back.

Matilda has us following a blue line. The ceiling is somewhere high above, the walls are hidden by shadows. The echoes of our footsteps tell me this area is big . . . bigger than the Garden, bigger than anything we have ever known. We don't have time to explore, and even if we did I wouldn't want to know what the darkness holds.

"Monster," I say to my creator, "how much farther?"

"We are the same person," she says. "You should call me by our name."

"How much farther?"

She sighs, seems to wince at the same time. The fight was bad for her, too. She'd been waiting at the hidden opening she used to attack Bello and me. She knew we would come: she is me, after all, and attacking the Garden is exactly what she would have done in the same situation. She laid a trap for us, but she hadn't planned on our ability to organize and work together, or on our ferocity. Maybe in her mind, we are still kids—it should have been easy for her kind to overwhelm us.

Things did not go how she expected.

When I poked my spear through the thicket wall, the blade pierced her shoulder. An accident, but at least we finally had some luck go our way. Matilda has lost a lot of blood. And then there is her ruined eye. She's in great pain, doing her best to not show it.

"The shuttle is close," she says. "Can't you see your people are exhausted, little leader? We have time to stop and rest."

I sense she's lying about time, but telling the truth that the shuttle is near. I think she's trying to stall. It doesn't take the brilliance of Gaston or Spingate to know why—her friends are preparing to come after us . . . or are already on the way.

Up ahead, the dim blue line on the floor splits in two. Part of it keeps going straight, part of it angles off to the left. El-Saffani stops there, looks back at us.

A dried-up black hand reaches out, points a thin finger to the left.

"That way," Matilda says.

In the darkness, El-Saffani's cracking red-gray paste makes the twins look identical, neither boy nor girl but some combination of both. I point down the path to the left, and they go rushing on ahead.

We all follow them.

It's still too dim to see, but the echoes of our footsteps change: we have entered a smaller room.

Lights come on.

Too bright, so bright it burns. I shield my eyes, blink as something starts to take shape.

Something . . . *long.*

Unlike everything else on board the *Xolotl,* there are no runes or carvings.

It is not made of stone.

It is smooth, sleek, gleaming metal. It is big enough to hold all of us a dozen times over.

The shuttle.

If we can figure out how it works, Omeyocan is ours.

FORTY-ONE

Memories roil in my head. My brain searches for words to describe the things I see. The shuttle's tail is off to our left. The tapered nose points to the right. A long, thick tube—thicker than four or five of us standing on each other's shoulders—connects them. At the tube's middle is a wide metal platform. A ramp—running perpendicular to the shuttle—leads from the floor to that platform.

We are perhaps a hundred steps away from the shuttle.

The gleaming hull is smooth as glass, even where the platform is: I don't see a way in.

I look around. We've passed through an archway of heavy, rust-free metal. Like all the archways before, this one is dense with images, but these are images I have not yet seen: planets, groups of stars, long cylinders and some things I don't recognize.

This room isn't much taller than the shuttle's tail. Above it, a curved ceiling of crisscrossing white bars. A short distance from the shuttle's nose stands a second archway—the biggest I have seen yet, big enough for the entire shuttle to pass through. The doors within it are metal, not stone.

I wonder if the blackness of space is beyond them.

"Bishop, bring the monster. Everyone else, stay here."

We run to the ramp. The ramp's surface is sharp, maybe to keep people from slipping. Small, hard points dig into the soles of my feet, reminding me how sore and swollen they are.

We stand on the platform.

"Matilda, tell us how to get in."

Her head lolls over Bishop's thick arm. I don't know if she's faking or dying. Her half-limp hand points to a spot on the shuttle's hull. There, I can make out a thin-lined square about the size and height of my face.

"Do we press it?" I ask. "Tell us how it works."

Shriveled shoulders shrug. "I don't know. I'm just an empty."

An *empty*? What is she talking about? Is she lying about not knowing how it works? Is she stalling again? No, I sense that she's telling the truth. We came all this way and now we can't get in. We're running out of time. We have to do something, and fast.

I need someone smarter than me to figure this out.

I look back to our group. A hundred steps isn't that far away, but beneath this room's sprawling ceiling my people look so small. The children stand packed together with my friends surrounding them, protecting them.

"Spingate, Gaston, get up here!"

The two sprint to join me. I turn back to the gleaming shuttle, to examine that square—and for the very first time in my life, I see *myself*.

A beat-up girl's reflection stares back at me in wide-eyed disbelief.

Those eyes . . . they are brown.

Strands of heavy black hair hang down my face, drape across my shoulders. The braid that Bello lovingly made is now a tattered mess. Red-gray ooze has dried on my cheek and chin. My upper lip is split and bleeding. One of my eyes is swollen, the skin there discolored and blacker than Gaston's was when I first met him. I see a growing, shiny lump on my forehead. I am covered in cuts, scrapes and bruises. Ripped shirt, scratched skin, bloody and beaten . . .

. . . I am *beautiful*.

Not "beautiful" as in what I could be when all of this goes away, but rather what I am right now, with these badges of bravery spotting my skin. Someday these wounds will heal, and I will see myself as Matilda intended me to be, but for now this face—the battered face of a fighter, a warrior—is mine and mine alone.

Spingate and Gaston thump up the ramp.

I have to tear my attention away from my reflection. It is a hard thing to do. I point at the hull's gleaming surface without looking at it.

"That square is the way in," I say. "Matilda claims she doesn't know how to open it."

Spingate caresses the metal, slides her hands across the lines almost like she's smoothing out invisible wrinkles. Her fatigue and fear vanish. Here is a puzzle: her whole being responds instantly.

She puts her hand on the square, pushes it in, then turns it. The square slides away inside the shuttle, revealing the same kind of plaque we saw in the door that led down to the haunted room—black glass with the imprint of a hand, and in the center of that hand, a jagged circle.

No, wait . . . I finally recognize that symbol—it's a *gear*.

I cup Spingate's elbow.

"Spin, put your hand on it."

She licks her lips, takes a breath, then presses her palm to the imprint.

Nothing happens.

Gaston nudges me, grins.

"Well, I guess it's time for me to be the *real* hero, huh, Em? Should I give it a try?"

He's got a splatter of red-gray across his chest, and his right ear is a sheet of blood that stains his shirt collar. Fighting monsters and running through an unknown ship haven't dulled his arrogance, not in the least.

I nod at him.

He rubs his hands together like he's trying to warm them, flicks his fingers outward once, twice, three times, then presses his hand to the black imprint.

The shuttle vibrates.

More lines appear in the metal, emerging out of nowhere as if the hull is splitting. The lines form a rectangle, taller than Bishop and wider than it is tall. Like the small panel Spingate pressed, it recedes slightly back into the ship.

A vertical line forms down the middle of this rectangle, cutting it in half. Without a sound, the halves slide away.

The shuttle has opened.

It is dark inside.

"El-Saffani," I say, my voice a bark that echoes through this cavernous room. They both sprint to the ramp. In seconds, they are at my sides. Oddly, neither of them are bloody; the battle must have missed them. I point my spear into the shuttle's darkness.

"Find out what's in there."

They adjust their grips on their bone-clubs, then step inside.

The moment they enter, lights snap on. It is a corridor that runs left and right, a corridor of red cloth walls and a black metal floor. I can't see anything other than the red corridor wall opposite me.

The twins step inside and dart right, disappearing for a moment. Seconds later, they pass in front of me, silently heading the other way.

O'Malley walks up the ramp to stand at my left. Bishop moves slightly to stand at my right, Matilda still cradled in his arms. Along with Gaston and Spingate, we wait, both hopeful and full of dread at what El-Saffani might find inside.

This has to be it. It *has* to: we have nowhere else to go.

El-Saffani returns to the opening.

"No one here—" Boy El-Saffani says.

"—it looks safe," Girl El-Saffani says.

Boy El-Saffani points to his left, my right, toward the shuttle's nose.

"A door that way, locked tight," he says.

Girl El-Saffani points to her right, my left. I've never seen her so excited.

"That way is a big room," she says. "With *hundreds* of coffins."

Coffins? No, that can't be. Hundreds of us, hundreds of coffins . . . I'm so tired, and this is starting to confuse me. I won't lie in a coffin again, no matter what . . . I *will not*.

But if there are hundreds of coffins, that means the room is big—big enough for all of us. It doesn't make any sense to leave our people outside the shuttle, exposed if the monsters come.

"O'Malley, get everyone up here," I say. "Let's get them inside."

Bishop leans close to me. "Post guards at the bottom of the ramp, Em. In case we're attacked."

I nod, annoyed at myself. "Yes, of course. O'Malley, tell Coyotl and Farrar to stand guard at the base of the ramp. El-Saffani, join them."

The twins rush out of the shuttle and take up their positions.

O'Malley runs to the others, waving and calling them all to him.

Spingate and Gaston step into the shuttle. They go left, toward the room with all the coffins. I don't stop them.

Bishop, Matilda and I remain on the platform.

He holds her out to me like she is some kind of offering.

"We don't need this anymore," he says. "Do you want me to kill it?"

I do. I want that very much. I want him to smash her, stomp her head in so I can see her brains spill across the platform. Her one eye looks at me.

"Go ahead," she says, her voice croaking, spent.

Images flash in front of me, conflicting visions: Bishop strangling the life out of this thing, and Yong, terrified . . . dying.

(Kill your enemies . . .)

"Go ahead," Matilda says again. "If it was anyone other than me, you'd have already told your Bishop to cut my throat."

It would be so easy. I don't even have to touch her, I can just tell Bishop to do it.

Yong, gasping for breath, his eyes asking me *Why?* over and over again.

(If you run . . .)

We've made it. No one needs to die.

I shake my head. "You're wrong, Matilda. You are a prisoner, I won't kill a prisoner."

Her eye narrows—she doesn't have a mouth, but I know she's smiling.

"I'm not wrong," she says. "You won, little leader. I wasn't that much older than you when I handed out my first death sentence. I *know* you would kill your enemies, because that's what I would do." The eye closes. Her voice becomes a regretful whisper. "It's what I *did*."

(Be forever free . . .)

She ordered people's deaths? I think of all the bodies in the *Xolotl,* all the sacrifices and the mutilation. A shudder ripples across my skin. All those bodies . . . were they because of *her*?

My knife sliding into Yong's belly. The rage I felt, the hatred. He thought he could hit *me*? He thought he could take away my leadership?

Finally, that confused, desperate moment with Yong becomes clear. My memories crystalize, come into sharp focus.

I know what I did.

And I am horrified by it.

When Yong attacked me . . . I *stabbed* him. I remember pointing the knife, I remember the small step forward as he came in.

I remember jamming the blade into his belly.

And, I remember sneering when I did it.

Stabbing him felt . . . it felt *good*.

Yong's death was no accident: I killed him.

Guilt pours over me like an icy waterfall. *I killed Yong.* My brain played some kind of trick on me, hid the truth away, but now that I've seen it for what it is, I will never be able to *un*-see it. I don't know if it was right or wrong. *He* attacked *me*. I don't know what would have happened if I hadn't stabbed him, I will never know, but there is no denying the fact that when he came at me, I cut him down.

It's all too much to handle. I need someone to help me understand. Perhaps the only one who can is the creature who made me.

"Matilda, did you ever kill anyone?"

She coughs. "I told you I did. So many people."

I shake my head. "No, not *order* someone to die . . . did you ever kill anyone yourself?"

Her one eye stares at me like I've asked her a question in another language. The silence is its own answer. She's responsible for the deaths of hundreds of people, maybe thousands, but she commanded other people to do the dirty work.

She's never taken a life.

Her hands have always stayed clean.

Yong died right in front of me, staring at me with accusing eyes. He died crying for a mother who never existed. Maybe it was just a playground fight to him. Maybe he was just being a bully. Maybe he didn't understand who he was attacking, and that ignorance cost him his life.

I killed him. His blood was on my hands. It was on my shirt. It was all over me.

Unlike Matilda, I know what it feels like to take a life, to see the look of intelligence wiped away, to know that I have forever ended a person.

Bishop glares at me, shakes his head in disapproval. "Em, don't listen to this thing. Give me the order."

It would be so easy to do that. Matilda is my enemy, and I want her dead, want it so badly. . . .

No. That's what she would do, this creature that I could become, that in some ways I already *have* become. If I make the wrong choices, I could follow her path.

I know what it means to kill.

Even though she is far older, she does not.

And that knowledge, I hope, is the thing that will let me be different.

I shake my head.

"We still need her," I say.

Bishop's eyes narrow. I'm not sure he believes me. Maybe he's judging me because I can't do what needs to be done. If so, he has every right—the leader has to make the hard decisions.

I take a deep breath, try to calm myself. I enter the shuttle.

As the twins said, to my right is a closed metal door. It has rounded edges and a wheel in the middle. I haven't seen a door like this before. I walk to it. There is no handle. I try the wheel: it won't budge.

At the wheel's hub is a circular plaque. In the middle of it, a golden gear.

I quickly go back the other way. The short corridor leads me to a low-ceilinged room.

When I enter, I see that El-Saffani was right.

Gaston and Spingate stand in a wide central aisle. On either side of them, long rows of plain white coffins, the same kind the pigs opened to eat the skeletons inside.

Aisles also line the outside of the room. There is so much space in here, space for people to sit, or walk, or lie down, or *play*, or whatever anyone wants to do. We don't need to actually use the coffins; there is enough room for all of us without getting in them.

I return to the platform. At the base of the ramp, my people are waiting: the circle-stars, the kids, O'Malley and the others. They have been through so much, even the children who have only been awake for a handful of hours.

I wave them in, point toward the coffin room.

"Get in here, fast. Find space and sit down while we get the shuttle going."

They filter past me. *Can* we get the shuttle going? I don't know. It isn't from a lack of memory or a muddy mind—I have no idea how this thing works, and I know Matilda has no idea, either.

The kids are dirtier now, grease and grass stains on their

clothes. As for those who are my age, their shirts are torn, streaked with dust and blood. They carry clubs of bone. They have fought to get here, faced down nightmares to earn this moment.

Then I see that girl, Zubiri, the tooth-girl with the dark skin. She walks to me. Her eyes are round, terrified discs.

"Em, are we going to die?"

"No, honey," I say. "It will be all right. I have to show you something scary, but I'll be right by your side, so don't be afraid."

I take her by the hand. I push down my revulsion at the thought of all those coffins, and I lead her to the room.

My people spread out. They wander around. They collapse in the aisles. To my horror and amazement, most of the children crawl into coffins and lie down. People are everywhere—the circles, circle-stars, circle-crosses, the tooths and the double-rings. Every last one of them is exhausted. They have given everything they have to give, and now, hopefully, their efforts are at an end.

Aramovsky is sitting on the floor of an outer aisle, his back against the red-carpeted wall. He isn't looking at anything. He's just staring. His shirt is bloody, torn and—finally—wrinkled. At last he looks like one of us, but is he? He stabbed his progenitor, drove the spear into the ancient Aramovsky's leg. If our Aramovsky hadn't done that, would the two of them have already been gone by the time Bishop ripped through the thicket? Our Aramovsky does not look well. Once we make it to Omeyocan, I'll have to keep an eye on him. If he needs help, I will help him.

Zubiri tugs on my hand. "What's scary, Em?"

I point to the coffins.

She laughs. "Oh, those? Those are beds."

Zubiri stands on her tiptoes, pulls on my hand. I bend toward her—she kisses my cheek, then runs into the room.

This little girl isn't afraid of the coffins, but I can barely even look at them? Some leader I've turned out to be.

Zubiri sits cross-legged in the aisle. She takes a deep breath. She's already relaxed and resting.

Very soon I can rest, too, but not yet: the other door awaits.

"Gaston, Spingate, come with me."

Bishop is still in the corridor, still holding the thing called Matilda. O'Malley stands with him. As I move past them, they follow me, falling in with Spingate and Gaston.

I stand in front of the strange door.

"Gaston," I say, "get up here."

He does. He looks at the wheel's hub, then at me. The sly, self-confident smile again lights up his face.

"Open it," I say.

Gaston puts his hands on the wheel. Left hand presses down, right hand presses up: the wheel turns.

"It's good to be me," he says.

There is a heavy click, and then this final door opens.

FORTY-TWO

I don't know what I expected to see, but I did not expect a blank room.

There is nothing in here, nothing but a black, sparkly floor and four black, sparkly walls. This can't be right.

What have I done?

I walk in. There has to be something here. There *has* to be.

There is not.

I turn to the others. Spingate and Gaston are standing in the doorway, looking around. Bishop still holds the monster that is myself.

"There's nothing here," I say. "What do we do now?"

I feel lost. I led everyone here. I have made a horrible mistake. This shuttle must be where the monsters wanted us to go. Matilda tricked me. The monsters will catch us, take us away. We will all die, we will all be *overwritten*. Our brief, fear-filled lives will cease to exist.

Gaston smiles. Not his arrogant smile, not the joking grin he has when he tries to annoy Bishop. This smile is genuine. It is sweet. It is a smile of pure wonder, the smile of a twelve-year-old boy who remembers something truly astounding.

He walks forward. The room comes alive.

Lights flash everywhere, not just on the walls and floor and ceiling, but in the air itself. Streams and streaks of color swell and move, turn and twist. Red and blue and green and yellow, lines and dashes, glowing dots. It overwhelms my senses.

A new voice speaks from nowhere and everywhere all at once, a voice that is neither male nor female.

"Welcome, Captain Xander."

Gaston walks up to me. He has never been this handsome. Joy radiates from him, makes me want to hug him, kiss his cheeks. Lights play across his face. Glowing dots dance on his eyebrows, his lips, moving when he moves as if they are a part of him.

He takes my hand and squeezes it tight.

"Em . . . you did it," he says. His eyes gleam. He looks at me like I am his hero. "You saved us. Spingate and I will take it from here."

What does he mean? "I . . . Gaston . . . I don't—"

"Xander," he says. "My name is *Xander*."

He raises his right hand above his head. Yellow and green lines bathe his fingers and palm, as if he's wearing a glove woven from light.

He again flashes that stunning smile at me, gestures to the room that has come alive.

"Em, you got us here," he says. "No one knew what to do, but *you did*."

The madness of this room makes no sense to me. Shouldn't I understand some of this?

O'Malley sees my dismay, and speaks for me.

"You're right, Gaston, Em got us here. Do you know what to do next?"

The glowing boy shrugs. "Not yet, but I have some ideas. I think I know how to fly. I just have to remember."

Spingate stands next to him. She, too, is painted in light.

"I'll help Xander," she says.

I look at my hands and see that they're normal. There are no lights on me. There are none on O'Malley, either, or on Bishop.

Spingate looks tired and drained, but elated as well. She glows like a living torch. She is so happy it's impossible not to fall in love with her all over again from simply looking at her face.

"Go talk to the others, Em," she says. "Tell them everything will be okay. Tell them . . . tell them that we're going *home*."

Home. She's right. The *Xolotl,* with its Garden and its coffin rooms, its pigs and Grownups and butchery, this place is not ours. Neither is the dead planet the monsters left behind so long ago. Those places were never our homes.

We were *created* to live on the planet below.

We were made to walk on Omeyocan.

An arm around my shoulders. O'Malley, guiding me out of the strange room. I walk with him. I stop at the wheel door and look back.

Spingate and Gaston shine like a pair of angels. The black walls and black ceiling have vanished. In their place, I see many pictures floating free, so realistic you could reach into them, touch whatever was there. One picture shows the chamber outside this shuttle. Another, the dark hallways we just walked through. Another, the brown and blue and green planet below. And yet another shows a long, spinning copper cylinder . . . the massive ship we are still inside of.

O'Malley pulls gently, gets me moving again. He guides me to the shuttle's entryway, where Bishop is waiting, Matilda still cradled in his arms. The platform is empty. At the bottom of the ramp, El-Saffani, Coyotl and Farrar stand guard.

Bishop leans in close. "O'Malley and I talked," he says. "Do we do it in the new coffin room, where everyone can see, or outside the shuttle?"

Matilda has given up the fight. She lies limp, awaiting her fate. She looks at me, her one good eye a swirling red jewel.

My legs won't hold me up much longer. They shake from fatigue. I need to find some space in the aisle between the coffins. I need to lie down, I need to sleep.

Wait . . . Bishop asked a question. *Do we do it in the new coffin room?*

"Do we do what, exactly?"

He lifts Matilda slightly, answering my question by showing her to me anew.

"Gaston can fly the shuttle," he says. "So we don't need her anymore."

Matilda's body shivers; I hear the sound of bone scraping on bone.

"Bishop is asking if you want to kill me quietly, or execute me in front of the others," she says. "Do it in front of the others, little leader—it is important you show people what happens if they cross you."

The way she's speaking now . . . she thinks she's helping me. She thinks she's dying. I am her legacy, the part of her that will live on, and she wants that part to succeed, to have power. Matilda is telling me what she would do if our positions were reversed.

Some people do not approve of being sacrificed.

That's what she wants: she wants me to sacrifice her, make an example out of her so that everyone will fear me. Fear, and obey.

All the bodies, all the death, the massacre of the *Xolotl*. How much of that was by her command? Matilda doesn't really think she murdered anyone at all; she thinks her butchery served a greater purpose.

If this woman is me, how did she become like this? Did something happen to her after her twelfth birthday that turned her into an obscenity? She is an appalling creature that shouldn't be allowed to exist.

If anyone deserves to die, it is Matilda.

But if I give that order, will it end with her? Who might be next, and for what crimes? Matilda today for mass murder, and because she is a threat to us. If Aramovsky challenges my leadership again, does that make him a threat?

The question isn't if I have the power to order death, because I obviously do. The question is: if I use that power now, will I use it again?

The answer terrifies me worse than anything I've seen or experienced so far, because I can't deny the hard truth: the answer is yes.

I shake my head. I am not her. I am not Matilda. I am *Em*, and Em has a choice to become something better.

I point down the ramp. "Leave her there. She led us to the shuttle. She did what we asked, so we let her live."

O'Malley and Bishop stare at me like I'm crazy.

"She is our *enemy*," Bishop says. "She wants to erase you."

O'Malley nods vigorously. "Bishop's right. Matilda has to die."

They *agree*? The two boys don't agree about anything, yet they find common ground when it comes to murdering a prisoner? Bishop I get, he sees things in simple terms, kill-or-be-killed terms, but I thought O'Malley was more . . . complex. Disappointment wriggles uncomfortably in my chest.

"I said *no*. We're getting away. No one else dies. Once we're down on the surface, she can't follow us. She won't be able to hurt us anymore. My decision is final."

Matilda nods, understanding. "I'd forgotten," she says. "Sacred Cinteotl bless me, I'd forgotten how idealistic I once was."

I'm sparing her life, and she's mocking me?

A scream—a battle cry—makes me jump.

El-Saffani, racing away from the base of the ramp, leaving Farrar and Coyotl to stare. The red-gray-caked twins, screaming, waving bone-clubs over their heads, sprinting toward the archway. There, a pair of wrinkled, coal-black monsters walking in, each step a twitching, jittering, painful effort. One monster carries an axe. The other a jeweled scepter.

They have found us.

"El-Saffani, *come back!*" My shout echoes through the room, but if the twins can hear me over their own violent howls, they don't respond.

I start down the ramp, make it two steps before a boy's hand locks down on my arm. O'Malley, holding me, but I yank my arm free and hear my shirtsleeve rip. The ramp's hard points dig into my running feet. Bishop thunders along behind me.

I'm halfway down when Spingate's shout stops me. She leans out of the shuttle entrance.

"Em, get everyone inside! We can see the hallway, more of them are coming! Gaston thinks the shuttle will protect us!"

Down the ramp. My feet slap against the metal floor. El-Saffani halfway to their target. I look to the archway: my heart turns to ice.

The two monsters weren't alone.

Hundreds of them pour through, their movements stilted and halting, as if each step brings a bolt of agony. An army of ancient darkness, of diseased bodies that should have died centuries ago.

And on some of their arms—silver bracelets with a long point that ends at their wrist.

I stop. Bishop stops next to me, Matilda still in his arms.

"It's about damn time," she says, her voice full of appreciation and—possibly—*hope* that she might live through this after all. "Captain Xander finally broke out the guns."

Bishop's roar makes my best sound like a whisper.

"El-Saffani, *stop!*"

His voice echoes off the floor, the ceiling, the walls. Again, the twins don't hear. They charge, bellowing, brandishing their clubs.

The pieces click together with a nearly audible *snap*. We beat the Grownups in the Garden because they didn't bring the weapons, because they wanted to take us alive. But now we've got the shuttle, their only way to reach Omeyocan. How could I have been so stupid? They would rather kill most of us than let us strand them here forever.

The monsters raise their arms. Bracelets glow with a white heat.

The twins almost make it.

A crackling sound I've never heard before, like a living animal boiled in oil, then narrow cones of shimmering energy blaze from the bracelet tips. A white flash silhouettes El-Saffani: their backs are black shadows against a blinding light. I see this for a split second, then I can see *through* their backs.

The El-Saffani battle cry ends forever—a hundred bloody pieces scatter across the floor, rolling and flopping to a wet stop at the monsters' feet.

A howl rips from my lungs, launched so hard and so instantly that my throat shreds and burns.

Those butchers murdered my friends.

Tears well up. Despair crushes me, compresses me, but I clench my teeth and force it away. There is no time.

I grab Matilda's wrist, yank her out of Bishop's arms. The ancient creature falls hard to the floor.

"Everyone, back inside!" I sprint up the ramp. The circle-stars are so fast they pass me by. O'Malley and I rush in. As soon as I'm through the door, I scream to my right. "Gaston! Get us out of here!"

Coyotl and Farrar run to the coffin room. Bishop and O'Malley stay with me in the corridor.

The floor vibrates: shuttle doors closing. Through them, at the base of the ramp, I see Matilda Savage. She's lying on one hip, looking at me with her single swirling red eye.

My creator's stumbling, shambling people close in. They point their arms at me, the white glow of their bracelets building to a blinding shimmer.

The shuttle doors hiss shut. One second I am at the edge of death, the next there are red metal walls a hand's width from my face. I hear something hit the shuttle with a sizzling sound, but nothing comes through.

Gaston's voice booms from everywhere and nowhere at once, comes from the shuttle itself.

"Get in those coffins! Get in and lie still!"

I'm being pulled—Bishop drags me toward the big room.

I won't go into the darkness again, I *can't*.

My hand is a fist: my punch drives square into Bishop's eye. I think of Latu in the fraction of a second before Bishop grabs my forearms so hard I feel bones bend.

Gaston's voice, roaring: *"Hang on, we're going home! Get in the coffins or you'll die!"*

I try to yank my hands free, but Bishop's grip might as well be the metal bars that once held me in my coffin.

"Bishop *let me go* I can't go in there *I can't!*"

I am lifted, thrown over his wide shoulder. He carries me into the coffin room.

I punch at him, try to kick him. I rake his back with my fingernails.

"Don't you *dare*, Bishop! Don't you leave me in the dark!"

I rake him again, feel his blood on my fingers. I'm in the aisle now, coffins on my left and my right. People who aren't already in coffins are scrambling to find empty ones.

Hands grab my wrists—it's O'Malley.

"Em, stop it! It will be all right!"

I lift my head, see deep-blue eyes drowning in helpless fear. I feel my face twist into a wicked snarl. I hurl my hate at him.

"O'Malley, *kill Bishop!* He's trying to trap me in the dark and I'll die *I can't go back there!*"

I fight and kick and twist, but the two boys are far stronger than me. Why don't they understand? Things *bite* in the darkness; the shadows want to hold me down and suffocate me. I'll be trapped again, trapped *forever*.

This is a trick of Brewer's. He's working with Matilda to capture us all, to capture *me* and erase my mind. They will overwrite me, but that's not enough for them: they are going to put me in the *dark* first, to punish me, and—

The world spins. It takes me a second to realize what's happening, to understand what the padding under my back means.

My friends put me in a coffin.

Hands hold me in place. I'm thrown to the left, smashed up against the padded wall—that wasn't the boys, it was the shuttle itself, moving. An instant of realization cuts through my blinding terror, lets me think straight for a brief moment—Gaston and Spingate . . . the shuttle is leaving the *Xolotl* . . . they are getting us out of here.

Bishop and O'Malley pin me down, using only enough strength to stop me from sitting up or lashing out at them. I'm in a coffin, I am going into the darkness, my friends have betrayed me, I have to fight, I have to *kill*.

A face close to mine, peering in at me. A small face. A girl. She's wearing a clean shirt. She has dark skin, jet-black hair, dark eyes. There is a jagged circle on her forehead.

It's Zubiri.

"Em, it's going to be okay," she says. "Don't be afraid."

She smiles.

The girl is so calm. None of this frightens her? I am older than she is . . . shouldn't I be the one comforting her?

"I can't be in here," I say to Zubiri, as if the tiny girl can overpower Bishop or give orders to O'Malley. "I can't be in a coffin again. *Tell them.*"

I want my voice to sound angry, dangerous and threatening, but what comes out is a pathetic whine. I'm not commanding anybody: I'm begging.

Zubiri shakes her head. "It's not a coffin, Em. It's a bed. You have to be in it right now. Do you know what *g-forces* are?"

I don't. I've never heard those words. I shake my head.

"It means that if you're not safely protected, you'll be thrown all over this cabin." Zubiri's voice is soothing. She isn't worried at all, not even a little bit. "When this shuttle flies, Em, if you're not inside you'll probably die."

She wants to help me. But to let her help me, I have to stay in this nightmare box.

I look at Bishop.

"Be still, Em," he says. "It will be all right."

I look at O'Malley.

"You're safe," he says. "You got us out. Now lie back so we

can leave. I don't want to die up here when we're so close to Omeyocan."

Omeyocan.

We're going down to the planet. That's what we were made for.

The world lurches again, so violently that O'Malley, Bishop and Zubiri tumble away, fall over and slide into other coffins. For a moment, no one is holding me down. I could run . . . but I do not.

If I don't stay here, in this coffin, they will try to catch me. If Zubiri is right, the boys could die trying to keep me safe.

Better I go mad in the darkness than see any harm come to Bishop and O'Malley.

I close my eyes and force myself to stay still.

The coffin's padded sides press in on me. My neck tingles, waiting for the needle sting that I know is moments away. This time it won't be clogged, the poison will give me a fever cleaver and I will die, burning and screaming—but I remain still.

Gaston's voice rips the air.

"Last warning, people. We're leaving!"

I hear O'Malley scramble into the coffin on my right. Bishop lunges into the one on my left.

On either side of me, a boy's hand reaches over the coffin's edge.

My fingers seek out theirs. They intertwine.

O'Malley holds my right hand. His skin is warm and soft.

Bishop holds my left. His hands are rough and blistered. He squeezes so tight it hurts, but I don't mind—it makes me feel protected.

I hear something, lift my head to see. A lid is sliding up from the foot of the coffin, slowly sealing me in. It moves past my knees, my thighs, my hips. . . .

I let go of both boys.

I rest my hands on my chest, left over right.

The lid slides past my face.

All is dark.

There is a click, then a hiss. The coffin presses into my sides, my back, my chest and my face. A scream builds up inside me, unstoppable, the product of my body's instant and futile need to *move,* to fight my way free.

Then I smell something odd. Almost instantly, my body starts to relax.

The world shifts again. No, not the world, the shuttle. I feel a hard pull to the right, then left, then up . . . if the coffin wasn't pressed tight against me, I would sail through the room, smash so hard against a wall or a door or the ceiling that my bones would shatter.

Zubiri was right.

The coffins once promised death: now they are life itself.

The pulling sensation eases . . . then it's gone.

We are floating.

My eyes droop. That smell . . . it's nice. I'm not stressed anymore. I'm tired . . . so very tired.

I blink, or try to, but once I close my eyes they won't open again.

There is a moment before sleep takes me, a moment where the events of my impossibly short life play back in my head. We saw so many horrors. I killed Yong. We lost Latu. We lost Bello. We lost El-Saffani.

Tears flow for my dead friends. There is nothing I can do now, no reason to battle against the waves of despair coursing through me. They are dead, and I will never see them again.

But despite our losses, our tragic and *stupid* losses at the hands of creatures who should not exist, I know my friends didn't die for nothing. I am proud of them all, and the survivors as well, because together, we *won*.

We woke up in a prison. We were made to be erased. The Grownups said we were property. They said we weren't people.

We showed them they were wrong.

The Grownups, or monsters, or Cherished or whatever they are, don't care about us. They don't care what we believe in, what we stand for, they don't care what we like or who we love or what we think—they just want copies of themselves. They would kill the children so they could live forever.

We were made to be like them, but we've earned a different path. They can't follow us. We can be whoever we want to be. We can make a new future now. If we make mistakes, at least those mistakes will be ours.

As the darkness within my head swells to match the darkness without, one last thought fills me with peace before I drift away.

We are the Birthday Children.

We are on our way to Omeyocan.

We *fly*.

AN OH-SO-POLITE REQUEST FROM THE AUTHOR

Dear Reader:

Thank you for spending your time with my novel. I hope you enjoyed it thoroughly.

Not to be presumptuous, but I have a favor to ask—consider the people after you who want to experience the story's twists and turns for themselves.

In other words, my request is this: *no spoilers.*

Pretty please.

In this world of blogging, Goodreads, Amazon reviews, Twitter, Facebook and whatever social media powerhouse comes next, it is disconcertingly easy to amplify your affection or distaste for a piece of work like this one. If your broadcast to the world includes key plot points or reveals, other people lose their chance at the moments of discovery that can make fiction so special.

A reader only gets one chance to be surprised.

So if you tweet and blog, if you review and share (and I hope that you do!), please avoid giving away the good stuff. You had a chance to enjoy this story spoiler-free—I'd appreciate it if you'd preserve that same chance for others.

Thanks,

Scott

ACKNOWLEDGMENTS

Scott would like to thank the following people for their research expertise:

Dr. Joseph A. Albietz III, M.D.
Dr. Nicole Gugliucci, Ph.D
Dr. Phil Plait, Ph.D
Sydney Sigler
Maria Walters

And these peeps for story feedback:

Julianna Baggott
Byrd Leavell
Rebecca E. Rae
Holly Root
Jody Sigler

Special thanks to Justin Manask, who put me on the path for this book, and to A Kovacs, my business partner, without whom none of my stuff would ever get finished.

ABOUT THE AUTHOR

New York Times bestselling author SCOTT SIGLER is the author of fifteen novels, six novellas, and dozens of short stories. He is also the co-founder of Empty Set Entertainment, which publishes his YA Galactic Football League series. He lives in San Diego.

scottsigler.com
Facebook.com/scottsigler
Twitter.com/scottsigler
Instagram.com/scottsigler
scottsigler.tumblr.com

ABOUT THE TYPE

This book was set in Sabon, a typeface designed by the well-known German typographer Jan Tschichold (1902–74). Sabon's design is based upon the original letter forms of sixteenth-century French type designer Claude Garamond and was created specifically to be used for three sources: foundry type for hand composition, Linotype, and Monotype. Tschichold named his typeface for the famous Frankfurt typefounder Jacques Sabon (c. 1520–80).